For You

A NOVEL

JODI ELLEN MALPAS

WWW.JODIELLENMALPAS.CO.UK

For You was first published in 2023 by Jodi Ellen Malpas

ISBN eBook - 978-1-957597-40-9
ISBN Paperback - 978-1-957597-41-6
ISBN Hardback - 978-1-957597-42-3

Editing by - Marion Archer

Proofing by - Karen Lawson

Cover design by – Hang Le

Praise for Jodi Ellen Malpas

"Malpas's sexy love scenes scorch the page, and her sensitive, multilayered hero and heroine will easily capture readers' hearts. A taut plot and a first-rate lineup of supporting characters make this a keeper." —*Publishers Weekly* on *Gentleman Sinner*

"This book is JEM at her best, the secrets, lies, enemies... and tongue it cheek humour. It's all there on every single page! I had no idea where this book was going or how the book would end. The journey was as captivating as it was enigmatic." - *Kindle and Koffee Book Blog on Wicked Truths*

"It's just twist after dark and delicious twist; a completely, unquestionably unpredictable ride from start to finish. This is the kind of book where every page is important, because there is just SO MUCH going on, and it's an intricate dance from loathe to love for this couple." - *Jeeves Reads Romance on The Brit*

"So it's safe to say, Jodi has once again completely smashed it with another sensation making it the best read of 2021! Hold on tight your about to be enthralled." - *Booksobsessive on The Enigma*

"A magnetic mutual attraction, a superalpha, and long-buried scars that are healed by love. Theo is irresistible." —*Booklist* on *Gentleman Sinner*

"Filled with raw emotions that ranged from the deepest rage to utter elation, Jodi Ellen Malpas wove together an incredible must-read tale that fans will certainly embrace." —Harlequin Junkie on *Gentleman Sinner*

"The characters are realistic and relatable and the tension ratchets up to an explosive conclusion. For anyone who enjoys *Sleeping with the Enemy*-style stories, this is a perfect choice."——Library Journal on *Leave Me Breathless*

"*The Controversial Princess*, told from Adeline's POV, is thick on plot, rich in character development with Kindle-melting sex and the perfect blend of twists and turns, shockers and villains!" —SueBee, Goodreads Reviewer

"*The Controversial Princess* is an all-consuming, scorching hot, modern royal romance with twists, turns and a jaw-dropping cliff-hanger that will leave you begging for more." —Mary Dube, *USA Today HEA*

"*The Controversial Princess* provided us with the romance our hearts needed, the passion our hearts craved, with jaw dropping twists and turns that kept us guessing and eagerly flipping the pages." —TotallyBooked Blog

"A brave, cutting-edge romance...This is a worthwhile read." —*Library Journal* on *The Forbidden*

"Unpredictable and addictive."—*Booklist* on The *Forbidden*

"*The Forbidden* proves that Jodi Ellen Malpas is not only one of the romance genre's most talented authors, but also one of the bravest. In this raw and honest portrayal of forbidden love, Jodi delivers a sexy and passionate love story with characters to root for. *The Forbidden* is easily my favorite read of 2017!"—Shelly Bell, author of At His Mercy, on *The Forbidden*

"*The Forbidden* is a gut-wrenching tale full of passion, angst, and heart! Not to be missed!"

For my mum & dad.

JODI ELLEN MALPAS

W hen I met Billy Harper, I wasn't certain of much in my life. My mother had committed suicide a few years before after a lifelong battle with depression, my father had met another woman and was moving to Canada, and my career had hit a brick wall. Actually, my career hadn't even gotten off the ground. I was twenty-three and lost, struggling to discover who I was exactly. Life just felt like an uphill struggle. Everything seemed impossible.

Then I suddenly wasn't struggling anymore. Instead, I was tumbling down life's hill and falling deeply, madly, and passionately in love. Love is the cure for all things.

It cured *me*.

Billy Harper and his love and encouragement helped me realize who I was. It gave me purpose and life—a life I wanted to share with him. He was the beginning of me. His flare, his ambition, his drive, his boyish handsomeness, and his infectious laugh were all just bonuses. Because Billy's best quality was how much he loved *me*. With everything he was, he loved me. He encouraged me. He pushed me to realize my dream of all things vintage and helped me set up my cute store on Carnaby Street. He said he loved my kookiness. He said he loved me every single day, more than once, or even twice. I loved him with equal fierceness.

Our love was the purest kind. The kind that people envied. The kind that made people smile when they simply saw us together. We were perfect. I knew it. He knew it. Everyone who knew us knew it.

We would be together forever.

It was undisputed.

I didn't think there was anything in the world with the power to break us.

Until there was.

Part One

Lo & Billy

Chapter One

L ondon – 2015

Reclined on the couch with my cocker spaniel, Boris, curled into my side, I pout at the pages, my heartbeats beginning to race as Heathcliff begs Catherine's spirit not to leave him. I know he's begging in vain, yet each time I read my favorite novel, I wish for a different outcome. How would the story have played out had Catherine lived? Would Heathcliff have shed his need for vengeance?

My shoulders dropping in disappointment, I rest the book to my thighs and look at the ceiling. Such a toxic, damaging thing is love. And so enriching and nourishing too. I blindly reach for Boris's ears and give them a little scratch, smiling when he groans his pleasure.

"Is it working?" Billy's voice drifts into my sub-conscience, and I drop my eyes to the doorway. He's leaning on the doorframe, his overnight bag by his feet.

I hold back my smirk as I tilt my head in admiration, taking in the fine form of a man who will tomorrow be my husband. "Is what working?"

"Your attempts to kill time." He wanders over on his bare feet, his hair damp from his recent shower. Looking down at the open hardback on my thighs, he smiles fondly at the dog-eared pages.

"No," I admit. Every second feels like an hour. Every minute like a day.

Boris, aware of what is about to happen, drags himself up and jumps off the couch, yawning and stretching. I reach for the waistband of Billy's jeans and tug him down to me. The book gets knocked aside in favor of Billy's body, and the moment his lips are close enough, I cover them with mine, humming my happiness. I know these lips like I know how much I love the bones of this wonderful man. "I want it to be tomorrow already," I say, locking my arms around his wide shoulders and my thighs around his waist.

He pulls back, the smile that has sent me dizzy since the moment I set eyes on him working its usual magic. His dark gaze glimmers, his freshly shaved jaw smooth and kissable. I try to tug him back so I can do exactly that. Kiss him. But he foils me, his strength far greater than mine. The playful half-grin I know all too well makes an appearance, and I grin right back.

"Let me kiss you," I order.

He shakes his head, his gaze jumping across my face. "Let me look at you for a minute," he whispers. "I'm not going to see you until tomorrow." He rubs his nose with mine. "I'm going to miss you like crazy."

"But then you'll never have to miss me ever again."

"I can't fucking wait." He nibbles at my cheek on an over-the-top groan, making me giggle and writhe under his hard body.

"Stop it." I laugh, not really wanting him to stop at all. If Billy Harper stuck himself to me, that would suit me fine. He eventually does stop, burying his face into my neck and breathing in deeply.

"I'm going to make you the happiest woman alive, Lo Evans."

"You already do," I reply, meaning it with every ounce of truth in me. "You have since you told me we were going on a date after meeting me only two minutes before." I feel him smile against my neck, and I find myself smiling too. It's just the way of things with us. He smiles, I smile. I smile, he smiles. We bounce off each other in the best ways.

"Any woman who wears dungarees to a cocktail bar deserves an opportunity to explain why."

"They were comfortable."

"And three sizes too big." He pulls back and brushes my blonde hair from my face. And just gazes at me with so much love in his eyes. The way he's looked at me like this every day since we met three years ago has defined the woman I have become. Bottom line, his. Completely and utterly his. "I can't wait until they're no longer too big." His eyebrow hitches cheekily, and my lips twist in return.

"And when might that be?"

"The moment I put a baby inside you." He dips and makes a meal of my neck. I laugh hard, so very hard, but I don't argue with him. Because I want that too. It's the natural progression. Our plan is so well-thought-out, and it has been since we decided to rent this place together. We will rent for a year or two until we've replenished the savings we used to pay for the wedding, and then we'll buy. I'll get my little vintage store to a stage where it's profitable, and then hire a manager to join my team. Then we'll have babies. Two, and we're not fussy about whether they're boys or girls. Or one of each. I'll stay at home for a while, Billy will continue expanding his surveying firm, and we'll live happily ever after. It's so ideal, it's almost sickly. I like sickly. Especially with Billy.

"Here." He pushes himself up and retrieves my book from the floor, sitting back on the couch. Helping me to turn, I settle my head on his lap. He flicks the pages until he finds the one he wants, and then slides his hand up my oversized shirt until it's resting on my tummy. *"'Be with me always – take any form – drive me mad,'"* he reads, and I smile. Always this part. *"'Only do not leave me in this abyss, where I cannot find you! Oh, God. It's unutterable! I cannot live without my life. I cannot live without my soul.'"* He sighs deeply.

"I love it when you read to me." Billy doesn't like reading. Unless it's sports related. He doesn't particularly like English Literature, and he definitely doesn't like Heathcliff. He wasn't all that into vintage stuff, either, until he met me.

Lowering the book, he gives me a half-smile as he strokes my tummy softly. "Every time I read it, I kinda hope the story has somehow changed and Heathcliff has miraculously grown some balls."

I smile like a crazy woman. "Me too."

"You're such a romantic."

I give him an incredulous look that he totally ignores, smiling as he leans down and brings our mouths together again. I may be a romantic, but I have nothing on my man. "Why'd you have to go?" I whine.

"Because I'm marrying you tomorrow morning and it's bad luck to see your bride on the morning of your wedding."

"Do you believe all that nonsense?"

My lip is bitten and dragged lightly through his teeth before he gets us both up off the couch. Squeezing my cheeks in his palms, he lays his lips on my forehead. "I don't know, but if it is true, I don't want any bad luck interfering with our heaven."

I sigh, taking his wrists and holding them as he spends some time breathing me into him, my eyes closed, my skin warm under his mouth.

Our moment is interrupted when we hear knocking at the front door. Actually, it's not knocking. It's banging. I try my hardest not to shrink so much that Billy notices, but I fear I've lost my battle when he looks at me with a knowing smirk. He recognizes that bang too. "My mum." He indicates for me to hop on.

"No, your back was aching yesterday."

"It wasn't. Shut up and get on."

I scowl and get raised, expectant eyebrows in return. I saw the discomfort on his face last night. He's lying. Yet I know when I'm going to win, and this isn't one of those times. I get up and gingerly climb onto his back, and he starts pacing to the door. "Please don't leave me alone with your mother," I beg, making him laugh loudly. "I'll do anything." It's safe to say that I love every inch of Billy . . . except his mother.

"It's just for a few hours so she feels part of the celebrations."

"She'll feel part of it tomorrow when we're actually getting married." Tonight was all about wine and chatter with Penny and Helen. Since Billy is staying at Penny's place with her husband, Gareth, and Helen's husband, Lewis, it made sense for the girls to stay here with me. "She doesn't think I can look after you like she can," I grumble moodily. I've long given up trying to prove my worth to my soon-to-be mother-in-law.

"My mother has never looked after me, Lo," Billy reminds me, still laughing. "She can barely look after herself or Dad."

My nose wrinkles in annoyance as Billy yanks the door open, but I just manage to wipe my disdain from my face in the nick of time before Linda's eyes land on me. "Hi," I chirp, clinging to Billy's shoulder more tightly, nuzzling my face to his. I don't think Linda dislikes me. I think she more dislikes the fact that Billy and I are so in love. So tactile. So into each other. Being rather cold and hard-hearted herself, she doesn't understand why Billy and I feel the need to smother each other every waking second. And sleeping second, for that matter. I've never understood her. Not in the three years Billy and I have been together. You'd think a mother would be thrilled to see their only child so besotted and in love.

"Oh, put her down," she immediately chastises, passing us at the door and disappearing into the kitchen. I can't see her now, but I know she'll be finding something to do in there, something that I have failed to do. Like take a teaspoon from the sink and put it in the dishwasher. Or fold the tea towel. Or wipe the worktop down. Anything to make a point, whatever that may be.

I remain exactly where I am on Billy's back as he shuts the door and takes us to the kitchen to join his mother. "If she starts harping on about the seating plan again, I may cancel the wedding altogether."

"No, you won't." Billy chuckles, quite rightly. Nothing will make me cancel tomorrow, only death itself. "Humor her."

"I always do," I mumble. But only for Billy. Linda definitely wouldn't win any Mother of the Year awards, yet she seems to be on a mission whenever I'm around to prove that she should. She's a selfish soul, all *me, me, me*. I've long learned never to ask how she is, because there is always some ailment plaguing either her or Billy's father. Headaches. IBS. Arthritis. Stress. She's not happy unless she's ill or has something to moan about.

Billy turns at the worktop and lowers me onto the surface, my watchful eyes on Linda as she faffs around my kitchen looking for something to do. She'll find nothing. I blitzed the kitchen this morning as part of my killing-time mission. "Your hair looks nice, Linda," I say, reaching for the Pringles and popping the lid.

Her hand lifts to her freshly dyed strawberry-blonde hair and feels. "Three bloody hours in the salon, and one hundred quid," she practically shrieks, looking at Billy. "Your father will go spare."

"It's a special occasion." Billy approaches her and kisses her cheek, while I munch through my crisps. Linda doesn't embrace her son's affection. In fact, she goes somewhat stiff. I've often wondered whether her lack of tenderness and warmth towards Billy when he grew up is the reason he craves non-stop attention from me. I shrug to myself. Maybe I should thank her, because her loss is certainly my gain.

Billy makes it back to me, and I spread my legs for him to lean back against the worktop. Dangling my arms over his shoulders, I hold a Pringle in front of his mouth. He takes it all in one go.

"Why are you still here, anyway?" Linda asks, opening the fridge. There are no faults to be found in there, either. I emptied and cleaned it this morning, ready to restock once we get back from our honeymoon.

"He can't bear to leave me," I tell her offhandedly, circling my legs around Billy's waist. "Can you, baby?" I push my face into the side of his head, and he laughs, while Linda simply rolls her eyes, giving her attention to Boris who's circling at her feet. She shows our dog far more affection than she does me, Billy, *or* her husband. "He's probably hungry," I tell her, aware that I've just made her privy to the one thing that I haven't done this evening. I know she'll run with it.

"Oh, Boris. Is she neglecting you?" She fusses over him, playing up to his act of starvation as he follows her to his bowl and waits for her to fill it with biscuits. As no one can see me, I roll my eyes, stuffing another Pringle into my mouth. Billy turns towards me, his smile epic. Because he knows what I'm thinking.

"Take her with you," I whisper-beg in complete vain, pulling another crisp from the tube.

On a smirk, Billy leans in and swipes it from between my fingertips with his teeth, proceeding to crunch his way through it. "No." He lands me with a hard kiss, blitzing my mind of all things my mother-in-law. I vaguely hear the doorbell ring.

"That'll be the girls," I mumble into his mouth. "I hope they've brought lots of wine." Linda is far more tolerable when I have alcohol inside me.

"I'd better go." Billy pulls me down from the worktop and confiscates my Pringles. "You want to get into your dress, don't you?" He ducks when I swing at him, then wrestles me into his hold, my back to his front, my arms crossed over my waist. He starts walking us to the door, biting at my neck as I wriggle and laugh, trapped against him. "Stop."

"Never," he growls, securing my wrists in one hand and using his free one to pull open the door. Penny and Helen wave bottles of wine at us, their bags piled behind them. "Are those bottles open already?" Billy asks.

They both answer by taking swigs, and I laugh, loving the direction of this evening.

"Make sure she's at the church on time," he warns, releasing me and fetching the girls' bags, dumping them in the hallway.

"Yeah, yeah." Penny pushes past us. "What are you still doing here, anyway?"

I smile when Billy shakes his head to himself, collecting his overnight bag. "I'm just leaving." He slips his trainers on by the door and unhooks his suit bag off the picture rail. When he reaches me, he stops and dips, getting his dark eyes level with mine. "See you tomorrow, gorgeous."

"If you're lucky." I grin, pressing my lips to his and keeping them there as he backs out of the house, me following, our mouths attached.

"Oh, you two," Helen sighs. "You make me want to throw up."

We smile against each other as I take the side of the door. "Tomorrow."

"Tomorrow," he confirms, breaking away and laughing when the girls claim me and haul me back.

"We'll look after her," Penny calls, slamming the door. "Now" —she swings around and holds up her bottle— "I have no kids for the night so I'm about to get blind drunk." Swigging back a good few inches of the bottle, I watch on with wide eyes.

"You're supposed to be looking after me," I point out. These women, the wives of Billy's two best friends, are, technically, friends of mine by default, for that reason alone. Really, it's a good job we get on like a house on fire.

Helen links arms with me and we start walking through to the kitchen. "She has a toddler and Gareth is trying to get her knocked up again. She's taking each and every opportunity very seriously."

I laugh as I look back, finding Penny toasting the air in agreement. "Are you ready to sign yourself over for life?" she asks.

"Just try and stop me."

Chapter Two

W ith the absence of my own father, who couldn't make it over from Canada, and the lack of willingness from Billy's father to say a few words, only Billy and his best man, Gareth, gave speeches. It didn't matter. Gareth took the time that should have been allocated to fathers and ran with it. In typical best man style, he had everyone laughing their socks off, including me, telling tales of their college days and young adulthood. I squeezed Billy's knee as he cringed all over the top table, constantly apologizing on his best mate's behalf.

"And I feel it only right to warn the new Mrs. Harper of my mate's alter ego." Gareth sweeps his hand out in gesture to the projector screen at the back of the room, looking as smug as smug could be. "Ladies and gentlemen, I give you Bolly Harpton."

My eyes swing up toward the screen, along with everyone else's in the room, and my mouth falls open. "Oh my God." Rapturous laughter erupts, and Billy's forehead meets the table, mortified. My husband is gracing the screen, looking uncannily similar to Dolly Parton, from his white-blond wig, to the two giant balloons stuffed down his pink jumper. My eyes bug when I make it past his mini skirt, my hand slapping over my mouth. "Your penis is hanging out," I yell, much louder than I should. Because maybe nobody would notice. Or maybe I'm a total fool.

"That isn't me," Billy whispers in my ear as I stare at the part of Billy's body, one of my most favorite parts, along with pretty much every living soul I know. And some that I don't.

"You sure?" I ask. "Because I'd recognize that part of you anywhere." I break out in laughter along with our guests, sliding down my chair and holding my tummy.

"The thong I had on wasn't very accommodating," he grumbles, his nose wrinkling at the screen. "It kept slipping out."

"Oh God," I howl, falling forward onto the table, my head on my arms. "Make him take it down before your mother has a fit."

"Too late."

My head shoots up, and I find Linda quickly, the only person in the room who isn't amused. "Oh dear."

Billy shakes his head in despair, tossing Gareth a dark look, which goes straight over his head. "You bastard," he mouths.

"Sorry, pal." Gareth shrugs.

"You said that photo was lost in history."

"Turns out it was lost in the special box I've been keeping for this very moment." Gareth wanders over and opens his arms to Billy. "Give your mate a hug."

Billy can't conceal his secret smile, getting up from the table and throwing his arms around his best friend. "I cannot believe you did this to me."

"Believe it." Gareth flashes me a cheeky smile as I wipe at my eyes with a napkin, the remnants of my laughter making my body jerk erratically every now and then.

"Good job, Gareth." I chuckle as they break apart, Billy taking his seat and Gareth returning to his. "When was that?" I ask, taking Billy's empty glass and passing him a fresh drink. He looks like he needs one.

"We'd won the cup final. Mid-season, we didn't stand a fucking chance. Clever clogs here said that *if* we won, I'd dress up as a woman on our customary night out on the last day of the season. Gareth started scoring goals like a machine from the second I uttered the words." He takes a long glug of his champagne. "And we won the league."

I snort, quite unattractively for a bride, patting at Billy's knee reassuringly. "I still love you."

"Of course you do." He flips me a wink, pulling me onto his lap as his best man wraps up on his mission to kill Billy with embarrassment.

"But in all seriousness"—Gareth takes his glass and drops his speech to the table, turning towards us— "today has been just about perfect, guys. Not just because the wedding was beautiful, but because if there are two people in this world who should be together, it's you two." He raises his glass. "I love you, and I wish you every ounce of happiness. You both deserve it and more. To Billy and Lo."

Everyone stands, holding up their glasses too. "To Billy and Lo."

I drop my face into Billy's chest, hiding from all of the eyes as they clap and cheer. "I'm up, baby," Billy says quietly, encouraging me out of his chest. As I press my lips together in nervous anticipation, he places me back on my chair and drops the gentlest of kisses on my lips. He doesn't look in the least bit nervous. Not even when the room falls silent.

He doesn't call upon any notes. He doesn't face the room. His dark eyes are set squarely and unmoving on me. He swallows. I swallow. I think I hear everyone in the room swallow.

"I can't say that I ever believed in love at first sight." He smiles a little, holding his hand out to me. I take it, and he squeezes. "I never saw myself meeting that one woman who would turn my world upside down. A woman who would dazzle me so much with her brilliance and gentle soul, that I would change my plans right there and then to make room for her in my life. Would make *her* my life." Dipping, he rests his lips on the back of my hand. "Lo

Evans was that woman. They say that behind every good man is a good woman. They're right. I know I'm a better man with Lo behind me, and with every day she blesses me with her love, I become an even better man." He briefly casts his eyes around the room, while I try and fail to hold on to my emotions. A tear rolls down my cheek. I don't bother wiping it away. There will be many more. "This woman is the most selfless, loyal person I've ever encountered. The kindest, the most passionate. She loves with everything she has, and I'm fucking thrilled, lucky, and blessed that she is mine." Turning back to me, he lowers to his knees and takes my neck in his palms, pulling me forward. "I'm going to do you so proud as your husband, Lo." He kisses me gently, muffling my little sob. "And I'm going to be the best father to our children." He smiles, wiping under my eyes with the pads of his thumbs. "My life is dedicated to you—to keeping you safe, making you happy, and fulfilling all of your dreams."

"My dream is you." I throw my arms around his shoulders and hug him to death, aware of the sniffles penetrating the room. Sniffles that aren't mine.

"We're going to be so happy together." Billy sinks his face into my hair, clinging to me. "I will worship the ground you walk on until the day I die, Mrs. Harper."

I smile through my happy tears. "And I will worship you."

Part of me doesn't want the day to end, but the biggest part of me just cannot wait to get away from all of these people and start our married life together. I swirl my drink in the glass, catching my first moment of the day alone at the top table, watching as Billy tries to make it back to me. Everyone is stopping him, either cuddling him, shaking his hand, or trying to talk to him. He's gracious, but I can see it on his face. He wants to get us out of here too. I look down at my wedding ring, thumbing it around my finger, lost in my thoughts. Thoughts of him. Thoughts of the next two weeks on a tropical beach in the middle of the Pacific with only each other for company. I smile, though it falls when I hear the beginning of a familiar track. A track that Billy blasts in the house every Sunday morning to stir me before he crawls all over me and wakes me up in his own adorable way. His favorite track. I look up and find him, as he finds me. With every beat, one more person in the room disappears until it is only us. Us and the music.

He jerks his head for me to go to him as he walks into the middle of the dance floor. Goodness, my throat is clogging up as I stand and pick up the bottom of my dress and Steven Tyler breaks the music with the first line of *"I don't want to miss a thing."*

Billy must get impatient waiting for me, because once I step onto the edge of the floor, he comes to me, taking my hand and yanking me into his chest. I look up into his eyes. "Very smooth," I whisper.

"Very beautiful," he counters, starting to sway us so very slowly. And he kisses me. And he doesn't stop until the track is over. I wish it would never be over.

Two thrilling weeks are ahead of us. Two weeks of sun, sea, indulgence, and no one but each other to focus on. Neither of us have had a holiday for nearly two years, our time and money being spent on our special day. I can't wait to be lazy. To wallow on the beach. To listen to Billy reading to me as I draw the words across his chest. To let him feed me cocktails. To have his lips on one part of my body or another constantly, because I know he won't let go of me at any point. To swim in the clear ocean on his back. Shower together, sleep together, eat together. Everything, together.

I sigh as we pull up to the airport, my head resting on Billy's shoulder as he plays with my wedding ring. "You can sleep on the plane," he says, kissing my head before getting out of the cab.

"Shall I get a trolley?" I ask, not waiting for him to open the door for me. I get out and scan the drop-off zone for one.

"Don't worry, the cases are on wheels."

"But your ba—"

"Is fine," he finishes, giving me that warning look he does when I fuss. Waiting for the cabbie to pop the boot, he grabs the handle, breaking out in a smile. "But it means I can't carry you. Do you think you'll make it to the departure gate?"

I roll my eyes as I watch his body engaging, preparing to haul my mega-huge case from the cab. Of course, sarcastic comments were made on my obscene overpacking, since, apparently, I'm not going to need any clothes.

Billy feigns straining as I make my way over, going through my bag for my phone. But then, very suddenly, his expression changes, something blasting from his eyes that I don't recognize.

His body jolts.

I stop in my tracks.

The suitcase hits the floor with a thud.

It takes me a moment to decipher the look on Billy's face, but I soon realize it's a look of pain. No, not pain. Agony. "Billy?" I say, my stomach bottoming out.

He stills, frozen in his bent position. "I'm all right," he breathes, though his words are cut with pain. "Just give me a second."

I hurry over to help him, but he moves before I get there. It's just a fraction of a movement, hardly even a move at all. But it's enough. His entire body seems to fly into spasm, and his head cracks violently back on his neck. And he screams, the sound piercing and soaked in agony. My blood runs cold. "Billy!"

"Fuck!" As quickly as his body tenses, it loosens, sending him crashing to the concrete with a bang. His screams come on louder, constant and raw, the air drenched with the sound of his pain.

"Oh my God." I fall to my knees next to him, scared to touch him as water leaks from his closed eyes. "Billy, what is it?"

"My back," he chokes, rolling over to his side. He throws up. I yell my shock, my worried eyes scanning every inch of his jerking body as he cries like no man should cry.

"Call an ambulance," I yell, searching for the cabbie. I find him behind me, looking on in shock. "Please, call an ambulance." I return my attention to Billy, his body lurching as he heaves, only worsening the pain that's slicing him. "I'm getting help," I tell him, pushing his hair from his sweaty head. "Just hold on."

He shakes his head and looks at me. That look will haunt me for the rest of my days. *Fear*. I've never seen it on him before. He's never been scared. He's always been the strong one. Protecting me from everything. Now he needs me, and I don't know what to do. My helplessness accelerates my emotions, and I burst into uncontrollable tears, feeling at his cheeks. His eyes start to roll. His face is a roadmap of painful lines.

And then he's unconscious.

He remains that way for two solid days. They induced his coma in the hope that his lack of movement, even just breathing, would give them time to figure out what was wrong without him experiencing anymore pain. X-Rays. Tests. MRI scans. It has been one thing after another, a process of elimination. I've had a constant sickly feeling. A gnawing ache inside my tummy. The last scan they did revealed a mass at the base of Billy's spine. Tests revealed it to be cancerous. I could only stare at Dr. Smith as he explained the position, the size, and the next steps. Nothing was sinking in. All I heard was *surgery*. He was taken down almost immediately, giving me not nearly enough time to wrap my mind around what was happening. I tried to be positive, but the urgency of the doctors, their constant looks of empathy, didn't make it easy. I received no words of reassurance. Was offered no signs of hope.

He was in surgery for five hours. The longest, most fraught five hours of my life. Billy had no idea what was happening to him. He would wake up and find he'd been cut open and then learn why.

He'll be out of action for weeks. Maybe months. But at least the lump would be gone.

When he came out of surgery, it was all I could do not to collapse at the sight of him. My strong, gorgeous husband looked so fragile and frail. Tubes stemming from everywhere, needles in both arms, his lower body held in position by straps. I've sat by his bed in the ICU unit, slipping out only to update our friends on what's happening, struggling through my words. Struggling with the looks of anger from Linda each time she visited, as if it was somehow my fault.

A few days ago, Billy and I were ready to embark on our life together. I was filled with nothing but happiness and excitement.

Today, I'm full of trepidation and fear.

A few hours after surgery, Dr. Smith is confident that he has Billy's pain under control with morphine, but there's no telling until he comes to. So I hold my breath and pray as they slowly bring him out of his sleep.

The relief I feel when Billy opens his eyes is profound, but I'm breathless, waiting for that shrill sound of his pain to kick in. It doesn't come. He blinks a few times, trying to register his surroundings. I inch forward in my chair, taking his hand and getting as close as possible. Confusion takes over his expression as he flexes his grip around mine. "You're in hospital," I tell him, looking to Dr. Smith for his reaction. He's quiet, making notes. I return my attention to Billy, finding him swallowing repeatedly. He's thirsty. "Can he have some water?" I ask, taking the cup from the cabinet before I get my answer.

"A little," the doctor confirms, going to the machinery and checking a few things. I don't know what. The unknown is terrifying.

I guide the straw to Billy's mouth and fight back my emotion as I watch him struggling to lift his head from the pillow. "Just a little," I affirm as he draws water greedily. On an exhausted sigh, he relaxes back into the pillow.

"What's going on?" he asks groggily, looking to me instead of the doctor.

It kills me that now, when he's not at full strength, he'll be told what's happened since he collapsed at the airport. Where do I begin? How do I explain that his life has become a question mark as we wait to see how his body responds now that the cancerous tumor has been removed? I place the water back on the side table and take both of his hands in mine, swallowing, trying to find the words.

"How are you feeling, Billy?" the doctor asks, probably seeing my struggle. He rounds the bed to the other side, looking down at him. "Any pain?"

Billy simply shakes his head, closing his eyes. "What's wrong with me?"

"Let's get you comfortable, maybe something to eat, and then we'll talk."

Billy opens his eyes. "I'm comfortable. I'd like to know now." His heavy eyes fall onto me. "What's happening?"

My lips press together, his suffering killing me. I want to be the one to tell him, but no matter how deeply I search, I can't find the will to break the news that I know will crush him. He's going to be immobile for weeks. He's going to be laid-up, relying on me to look after him, and I know he will hate that. It's his job to look after me. He tells me every day. It's a job he loves, one he cherishes.

Pulling a chair up to the bed, Dr. Smith takes a seat. "We found a malignant tumor on your spine, Billy. Lo tells us you've suffered in recent months with back pain."

I close my eyes, so wishing I had enforced my demand for him to see his GP.

"Nothing major," Billy says, his voice terribly sleepy. "The odd twinge here or there, but it wasn't affecting my lifestyle."

No, because the stubborn ox refused to let it. He carted me around like my weight was nothing, and he chastised me every time I protested. In the end, I didn't see his winces because he hid them from me, knowing I'd be on his case, and perhaps because I would have stopped him doing what he loves doing: carrying me. Figuratively *and* literally.

The doctor nods, thoughtful, and inhales before going on. "The tumor is larger than we anticipated."

I still, staring at the doctor. "But you removed it, right?" I ask, not liking the stoic expression on Dr. Smith's face. That isn't the expression of a man who has good news. News that'll relieve us of worry. News of the cancerous lump being removed successfully.

He clears his throat and crosses one leg over the other. "When I operated to remove the mass, I found that it was wrapped around the base of your spinal cord. I'm afraid it was too risky for me to continue."

"What?" I breathe. It's the only word I can muster. I don't mean to tighten my grip of Billy's hand, but it seems my body isn't my own. They sewed him up with a deadly lump still inside him?

Keeping his attention on Billy, Dr. Smith goes on. "The type of cancer is called Chordoma. It's very rare and can go without symptoms for some time before it's discovered. It's very unlikely had you visited your GP regarding the back pain that he would have referred you."

Billy remains silent, just looking at the doctor. I feel numb. A rare cancer. I didn't hear *cancer* so much as I heard the word *rare*. I'm taking that one word, *rare*, and concluding one thing. My new husband has less chance of survival than someone with a common cancer. A cancer that had been researched more. A cancer that probably has a ton of treatments. Rare to me means less chance of survival. Limited treatment options. Bleak outlook. *Fatal*.

"What's the prognosis?" I blurt, my voice shaky, my palms sweaty. I didn't want to ask that. I didn't mean to ask that. I would grab those words and stuff them back in my mouth if I could. But I can't.

"Each case is unique," Dr. Smith says. "I have limited experience in this area, and at this point, since even removing part of the tumor wasn't possible, I'm inclined to get Billy on a course of radiotherapy to see if we can at least shrink it. We can revise our treatment plan from there."

Billy releases my hand, and I drag my gaze from the doctor to my husband. His eyes are closed. He's hiding from our stark, agonizing reality. "You won't even *try* to remove the tumor?" I ask, fighting to keep myself together. I can't fall apart. Not in front of Billy.

"No, Mrs. Harper. I'm not confident anything will be gained, but much will be lost."

"Like what?"

"The sacral nerves, which will likely result in motor, sensory, sphincter, or sexual dysfunction. The extent of dysfunction depends on which sacral nerves must be sacrificed. In general, the higher the tumor extends in the sacrum, the more sacral nerves must be sacrificed, and the more dysfunction will be experienced. Not to mention the risk of paralysis."

I can only stare in shock, the onslaught of shitty information too much to hear. To bear. *Why didn't he tell me before Billy woke up?* But God, would I have wanted him to?

"From what I saw in the operating theater," Dr. Smith says with way too much regret in his tone, "those dysfunctions are guaranteed should I operate. I'm not confident I can remove even part of the tumor without damaging the spinal cord or nerves. It's not a risk I will knowingly take."

My eyes fall to the sheets of Billy's bed. The silence is excruciating. A heavy silence, laced with grief and hurt. So he can live with this tumor until it kills him, or he can lose some of his functions for the rest of his life. I know my husband. I know the latter isn't an option for him.

Peeking up at Billy, I see he's still holding his eyes closed, his hands now safely from my reach, clasped together on his lap. He's shutting down. No. He can't.

"There's a doctor in The States," Dr. Smith goes on. "He's a specialist in Chordoma. He may be able to help."

"The States?"

"He's a private doctor. I can pass Billy's records over to him to assess."

"You mentioned radiotherapy, too," I say, my jaw and throat tight with the strength it's taking me to keep my voice steady and my lip from wobbling. "When?"

Dr. Smith stands, putting the chair back in its place. "I'm drawing up a treatment plan." He smiles sadly, flicking his eyes to Billy. "I'm sorry it's not better news." He turns and leaves, and if the silence was excruciating before, now it's screaming, horrifically unbearable.

I reach for Billy's hand and grab it before he can try to withdraw. "We'll get through this," I tell him, with one hundred percent confidence. He's young. He's strong. Radiotherapy will shrink the tumor and then the doctor can remove it. "We'll reach out to the specialist in America. Everything will be fine, just wait and see." His lack of response hurts me more than imaginable. He's just lying there, eyes closed, silent. I need him to tell me it'll be okay too. "Billy," I beg, losing all control of my emotions. "Tell me it'll be okay." I burst into tears, my body shaking hysterically as panic of the cruelest kind overwhelms me. He has to believe everything will be okay. He has to! "Please," I sob.

His eyes slowly open, and he looks at my terrible state with a tired gaze. And he swallows, opening his arms to me. "Come here," he says quietly, helping me crawl carefully into his side. He hugs me weakly, kissing the back of my head as my tears continue to roll. "Of course we'll be okay."

But for the first time since I've known Billy, I don't believe him.

Part Two

Lo

Chapter Three

L ondon 2017 – Two Years Later

"Are you coming for a drink, Lo?"

I turn at the revolving door as I wrap my scarf around my neck, finding Scarlett sitting on one of the couches in our reception area, slipping on some strappy shoes. The woman, my boss, makes me feel dowdy every day of my working life. She's just about as perfect as a female could be—tall, leggy, well-dressed, successful, and the life and soul of any party. And brave. Because those heels in this biting cold? If I didn't admire her so much, I'd hate her. "Thanks for the offer, Scarlett, but I really need to get home."

She pouts, but I don't miss the wave of sympathy that glides across her flawless face as she stands and throws her cashmere shawl across her shoulders and collects her Mulberry. "Okay. See you bright and early tomorrow morning."

"Bright and early," I confirm, as if she needs any confirmation.

In the two years I've been Scarlett's PA at her media firm, I've never once been late. Promptness and reliability are two of my best-known qualities. I wish they weren't. I wish a whole host of other traits could be what I'm best known for. Beauty. Success. Ambition. But, alas, I am simply the girl in the office who everyone can depend on. My days humming the time away in my lovely little vintage shop are long gone. It didn't provide enough income. It was another huge loss when I gave it up, on top of so many other huge losses.

Pushing my way into the dark evening air, I shiver and pull the collar of my old faux fur coat up around my ears. I watch as many of the staff from my building hustle toward the Tube station, envying them, as they will soon be down in the warm bowels of London. I, however, will brave the chill and walk home.

I start toward the crossing that'll take me onto Shaftsbury Avenue.

"Hey, Lo." Matthew falls into stride beside me, his shoulders brushing his earlobes in a hunched-up attempt to protect himself from the freezing air. "Jumping on the bus?"

I smile tightly at him, noticing his old-fashioned glasses are askew. With his floppy hair, that's well overdue for a cut, and his freckled face, he looks so completely like the geek he is. In his fifties, single, and the brainbox tech guy at Scarlett's firm Red Well. If there's anything he doesn't know about IT, then it isn't worth knowing. "I feel like a walk," I say, pushing the button at the pedestrian crossing.

"Are you insane?" He stops with me, his face bunching in horror. "You'll be an icicle by the time you get home. It must be four miles, at least." Pointing to the bus stop, he links arms with me. "Come on."

"No, Matthew, honestly." I gently but firmly wriggle my way from his hold. "I want to walk." What can I say? That I'm broke? That my bank won't allow me to go anymore overdrawn than I already am? That I really can't afford the measly few pounds for a bus fare? It's payday tomorrow, something that usually puts a smile on people's faces. Not mine. My wages will barely cover my overdraft, and that's before I pay the rent and the bills. "I have a terrible headache. A brisk walk and fresh air will clear it."

"You mean artic air, right?" He shakes his head and backs away. "Have fun." His quip makes me smile slightly.

"See you tomorrow." I hurry across the road, trying not to feel too deflated by the fact that my day's work is finished, but my night shift has only just begun.

My bloody toes are like ice cubes by the time I make it to my front door. Looking up at the old townhouse, I wonder how long it'll be before I can no longer keep up with the rent and upkeep. I'm literally hanging on by my teeth. On a sigh weighed down with hopelessness, I worry the key into the lock and let myself inside. Placing my bag on the table in the entrance hall, I wriggle out of my coat, listening for the pitter-patter of paws to hit the wooden floor. When they eventually come, I smile, taking some comfort from the familiar sound that always welcomes me home.

"Hey, boy." I crouch to let Boris trample all over my lap. His excited panting and the whipping of his tail back and forth turns my smile into a light chuckle. I rough up his ears and give him all the fuss he's used to. "You hungry?" I ask him, dipping and kissing his furry head before pushing him down from my lap and standing.

"I've fed him."

I look up and find Magda standing at the entrance to the kitchen, a cup of tea in her hand. "Evening," I greet, approaching and eyeing that lovely hot cuppa. "What are you still doing here?"

She smiles and hands the mug to me, and I wrap both hands around it, relishing the warmth seeping into my numb fingertips. "I thought I'd hang back for you to get home."

"You didn't need to do that." I take a sip of tea, humming as I feel the hot liquid trickle down my throat and warm my insides. "It's so cold outside."

Magda shakes her head, her thoughts no doubt centered around the fact that I've walked home again instead of taking the bus or the Tube. But I won't be getting into that conversation, so I pass her static form and make my way into the kitchen, being hit by the delicious smell of . . . something.

"I hope you don't mind," Magda says, as I settle on a stool and she pulls on an oven glove. "But I had some spare sausages at home so I made you a casserole." She opens the oven and pulls out a pot, sliding it onto the stove. Boris catches a whiff and makes a beeline for her ankles. "Should be about perfect by now." Looking down at my dog, she chuckles. "It's not for you."

She just happened to have some spare sausages? Of course she did. "Magda, you really shouldn't—"

"Let's not make a huge fuss over it." After ridding her hand of the oven glove, she smooths back a few gray wisps of hair into her tightly secured bun. For a woman in her sixties, she looks remarkably well. She insists that her clear complexion and healthily plump frame are down to a lifelong Mediterranean diet. She's been threatening to get me on that diet for months.

"You're not here to cook for me."

Rolling her eyes, she collects her huge duffle coat from a nearby chair and slips it on. "You will eat," she orders sternly, looking me up and down. "You're no good to anyone if you have no energy, Lo." Collecting her bag, she makes her way to the door, stopping on her way when she reaches me. Offering a small smile, bursting at the seams with that dreaded sympathy, she reaches up and smooths down the cold skin of my cheek. "Try to get some sleep, Lo. You look tired."

I nod and take her hand, squeezing my understanding. Sleep is rare. "As soon as I've scoffed your sausage casserole."

Magda smiles mildly. "Good night." A breeze of cold wind

whips around my legs a few seconds after I hear the door shut, and I shudder before quietly taking in the kitchen. Silence. The silence of my home is beginning to drive me mad. But it's quickly broken when my stomach rumbles, and I reach down and circle my flat tummy with my palm. I'm suddenly starving, but before I allow myself to tuck into Magda's casserole, I make my way up to the bedroom.

With every step I take, I breathe in more air, trying to keep a hold of the inevitable emotions. It's a silly effort. As soon as I'm on the threshold of the bedroom, I see him, lying as still as can be, tucked in neatly. The sight of Billy looking this way will never fail to break my heart that little bit more each time. Today is a bad day. A day when he doesn't get out of bed. A day when I wonder if this is the beginning of the end. He's virtually skin and bones, his skin practically transparent, his eye sockets dark. Even his thick hair looks as if it's lost weight. I reach up to the door frame to steady myself, my eyes filling with the usual, hopeless tears. The man before me is a shadow of the strong, handsome man I married. That was twenty-five months ago. Month after month of hurt, pain, grief. *Anger.* So much anger. Life is so cruel. I close my eyes and hear his squeals of agony, shuddering where I stand, the sound haunting me once again. And the look on his face before he passed out. I swallow and open my eyes. He knew. That look on his face before he closed his eyes, he knew something was horribly wrong.

The aggressive course of radiotherapy Dr. Smith put him on didn't shrink the tumor. The limited medicines on offer had no effect. Our only other option was the specialist in America who was prepared to operate to remove as much of the tumor as possible. It was hope in our turmoil, but that hope was quickly dashed. The cost of the treatment would buy a small flat. The banks wouldn't lend us the money. Our parents aren't wealthy people. We don't own our home. Short of begging the specialist in America to waiver the medical bills, something Billy has refused to let me do, I've explored every avenue. And found a dead end each time. My husband's life is in the hands of God, and I've prayed to Him every single damn night for help. But He's not hearing my prayers. Billy's getting weaker by the day, his body thinner, and his resolve is dying along with it.

He's giving up.

But I won't.

A small twitch in his arm prompts me to quickly wipe away the tears streaming down my face, knowing he'll get agitated if he catches me crying again. I sniff and make my way over, sitting in the chair beside his bed. I can see how much effort it takes him to open his eyes. And the effort it takes him to smile a fraction when his dull brown eyes find me. Today really is a bad day. They're coming more often now. "You're home," he croaks, letting his heavy head flop to the side on the pillow so he's facing me.

"I'm home," I confirm. "How are you feeling?"

"Amazing," he sighs, his frustration evident—he's so tired of me asking that question. And not because he feels like shit. He always feels like shit. He's just tired of telling me so. "How was work?"

"Busy."

He nods, struggling to hold my eyes. "A man called today."

I shrink in my chair, not wanting to ask the question that would naturally come next.

"A debt collector." Billy wheezes the words, and I look away.

"I have everything under control," I assure him, not wanting him to worry about our finances. As a self-employed surveyor, Billy's income stopped as soon as he stopped working. All of our savings went on the wedding. He hadn't taken the initiative to get private medical insurance, not that it would have been much use to us. They wouldn't have funded the surgery in America, or the cost of getting him there.

Billy lifts a hand and reaches for me, and I shuffle forward to take it, relieving him of the strain. "Lo." He closes his eyes and struggles to reopen them. "Just put me in a hospice. Let them take—"

"No." I drop his hand and shoot back in my chair. "I'm not listening to this again." He's talking this nonsense more and more often. I can't stand it.

"Lo, just—"

"I said stop," I yell, unable to hold back *my* frustration. My voice is hoarse as a result. I fight to level my tone and calm myself. "Today is just a bad day. Tomorrow will be better." I plead with my eyes, begging him not to continue with his unspeakable pleas. "Something will come up. We'll find a way."

"There is no damn way," he grates, and it takes everything out of him, his chest starting to heave from the strain. "Stop burying your head in the sand and hoping for a miracle, Lo, because it isn't going to happen."

My bottom lip trembles as I mentally damn him to hell for being so negative. "There's a way." America is the way. I just need to scrape the money together somehow.

He sighs. "I'm a burden on you."

"You're my husband."

"I'm a dying man, Lo. And I'm stopping you from getting on with your life."

I jump up from the chair, devastated as I always am when he does this. "I am your wife. For better, for worse. In sickness and in health."

"You're young, beautiful, and healthy. I'm wearing you down to nothing. I can't see you looking so exhausted, trying to make ends meet, having no social life, being forced into caring for me. It's killing me quicker than this fucked-up disease."

"I'm not listening to this." I stomp toward the bedroom door, furiously thrashing my palms over my wet cheeks. I slam it as hard as I mean to, wanting him to know just how mad I am. How can he say those things? How can he tell me to do that, to walk away as if he never existed? Get on with my life without him? Never.

I land in the lounge and scan the floor. My book is open and face down on the carpet. My laptop is open, my browsing of local vintage stores from last night probably still on the page. Why do I keep torturing myself like that? Turning through webpage after webpage, reminding myself of my dream that's lost? I move my mouse across the screen, set on closing my laptop down. The GoFundMe page that I set up appears. One thousand pounds. Billy would go spare if he knew I'd done this.

Snapping the lid down, I go to the hallway and snatch Boris's lead off the coat stand, hook him up, and then I tug on my coat and wrap my scarf around my neck, all heavy-handed. I would rather face the bitter cold than face my husband's bitterness.

But once I hit the street, I don't feel the cold at all. Billy's words, playing on repeat in my mind, are distracting me too well. I absentmindedly cross the road and head down the path into the park, the streetlamps illuminating my aimless way. As soon as I breach the entrance of the grassy expanse of land, I free Boris and let him scamper off, dragging my feet slowly behind him with only my thoughts to keep me company. Thoughts I'd rather not have. Thoughts that torture me daily. Thoughts that I wish I could rip out of my head and throw down a drain. But they'll never leave me. I'll never be free from this torment. Our lives have been in turmoil for so long, I've forgotten what it's like to be normal. To do the simple things. To go out for dinner together. Or even to go to the supermarket together. To sleep in the same bed together. To cuddle, to kiss, to make love. On a good day, I can almost manage to get him around the park for a walk with Boris. Sometimes I might get him to the couch to watch TV with me. Although even those simple things, simple things I have come to appreciate more than they should be appreciated, are becoming few and far between. But at least he can still walk. That's what I have to tell myself. And at least he's still alive.

I don't bother to wipe the tears from my eyes as I wander through the park. Not only because it's dark and the chance of anyone seeing my grief is slim, but because I can't be bothered anymore. I work so hard at the office to keep it together during the day, that by the time I get home I've lost any strength to hold my emotions in check. My husband is dying, and there's nothing I can do about it. And worse of all, he's asking me to do the unthinkable. To leave him alone in his suffering. How could he ask me to do that?

I drop down onto a bench and let my tears turn into a full-blown crying session. I need to get it out of my system before I make my way home. Out of my system for tonight, anyway. Tomorrow will be a repeat. And the next day. And the next. It's just one vicious circle of grief and misery. And I have no idea when it will end. When he will cease to be here.

When he will stop fighting.

The ring of my mobile phone sounds from my pocket, and I pull it out to find Billy's mother calling. I uncharitably consider letting it ring off, the thought of talking to her not appealing in the slightest, but she'll want to know how her son is, and she won't stop trying until I answer. So I take the call, using my scarf to wipe at my eyes as I get up and start wandering toward where Boris in sniffing around a tree. "Hi, Linda."

"How is he?" she asks immediately, avoiding a customary hello as always.

"Resting."

"And where are you? You sound like you're outside."

"I'm walking Boris." I shoo him away from the tree and get him back onto the pathway.

"Then who's watching Billy?" she asks, obviously not happy that her son is alone. I gather my patience and bite my tongue to stop myself from spewing a barrage of expletives down the line. *She's his mother*, I tell myself. She's worried.

"Magda's stopped by as usual while I was at work." I know it would be silly to mention the row Billy and I just had. Of course, it'll be my fault in some way, shape, or form. "I've been gone ten minutes and will be home in another ten."

"Magda," she mutters, and I brace myself for what I know is coming. "You're his wife, Lo. *You* should be taking care of him, not some strange Spanish woman."

My willpower to hold back buckles. "She's a trained nurse," I point out. "And our lives might be falling apart, but I have to work to pay the bills, Linda."

"We've had this discussion. If we had the money, we would lend it to you. But with Billy's father's dodgy heart, he can't work anymore, and we barely survive on my wages."

I grate my teeth. "I wasn't asking for your money, Linda. I was asking for your understanding." The woman is infuriating. My relationship with her hasn't strengthened in the face of tragedy. It's weakened.

"You should be taking care of him." She sniffs, completely ignoring my appeal to her compassionate side. But, of course, Billy's mother doesn't have a compassionate side. She must realize that what she's suggesting is out of the question, unless she wants her son being cared for on the damn street. I'm already being stretched to my limit to make sure that doesn't happen. Without my salary, we'd be in even more financial shit.

I spot Boris up ahead sniffing in the direction of the road. It gives me the perfect excuse to end my call with my difficult mother-in-law. "I have to go, Linda. Boris is heading for the road." I hang up before she can accept, or maybe not accept, and go darting off to catch my dog. "Boris!" I call, unraveling his lead from around my neck. "Boris!" Thankfully, he pays attention and looks up at me, coming to a stop just inside the gate that leads out onto the main road. "Good boy," I say, attaching his lead and giving him a rewarding scratch of his ears. "Come on, let's go home."

We make our way out of the park, and I try so hard to push back the unpleasant conversation I just had with Linda, but, of course, that just leaves oodles of space for the conversation I had with Billy to fill my mind again. Fresh tears pinch the backs of my eyes as a result. The glare from the streetlamps and traffic lights become blurry as the water works its way to the front on my eyes and collects, ready to stain my cheeks again. What did we do to deserve this kind of punishment? What happened to our happily ever after? My mind drifts, seeking comfort, calling on happier times.

"It smells fusty," Billy says on a wrinkled nose, taking the military jacket away from his face and dumping it on the counter. "I can't believe people buy this stuff."

I smile and kick a few black sacks out of my way, heading for my new pay desk. "They'll be washed," I assure him, putting myself in front of my new cash register. Well, new to me. It may have been new to someone else sixty years ago. "Isn't it cool?" I say, pressing down on a few buttons, delighting in the old clicking sounds.

"Very cool." Billy moves in behind me and crowds my back. "Since I've slaved away all day in your very cool new shop, do you think I might be rewarded?"

"Maybe." I smirk to myself as I press the button that releases the money drawer on a ding.

"Ding indeed." He lifts me from my feet and walks us across the shop floor. "These changing rooms look comfortable."

"Your incorrigible." I laugh, taking in the space, so happy with my theme of animal print and industrial woods and metal. It's cozy but chic, cool but classic. He sits me on the cowhide stool in the corner and looks around at the mirrors on all three walls. He grins, gazing down at me. Then he reaches back and grabs the cowhide curtain, yanking it across, closing us in.

"Get those dungarees off."

"Lady," someone shouts, yanking me back from my memories. My head whips around to find out who's yelling and to who. "Lady, get out of the road." A man on the curb waves his arms frantically at me, and it's then I realize that he's bellowing at me. I frown, noticing I've absentmindedly wandered into the road. And then I hear the sound of screeching tires. I swing around and come face to face with a set of headlights racing toward me, and my entire body locks up, my exhausted mind shutting down, failing to deliver the command to move to my legs. "Lady, move!" The distant shout is drowned out by the increasing noise of the tires coming closer and closer to me.

Move! Get out of the way! Damn it, Lo, snap out of it!

A blaring car horn is added to the screeching tires, yet it doesn't prompt me to dive from the car's path, leaving me a sitting duck in the middle of the road. Crazily, as it tears toward me, I start to think so very clearly.

Maybe this is the best way.

Maybe my time is up before Billy's.

Maybe this is supposed to happen and we'll meet up very soon in God's green garden, happy and healthy and ready to have our happily ever after.

I won't want to be here when Billy's gone. I won't survive on my own, won't know how to live again. I've pretty much been dead for the past two years anyway. A shell of a woman, staggering aimlessly through this shitty life, my identity lost. I don't want to do it anymore. I don't want to wake up every morning and dread the day ahead. I don't want to look at my dying husband and know that I can't make him better or ease his pain. I'm tired. I have nothing left to live for. Nothing left to give. No fight.

Closing my eyes, I breathe in my last breath and wait, trying to cast my mind back to find our happy times again. How we met in that cocktail bar. How quickly we fell in love. Our trip of a lifetime to Australia. Our beautiful wedding day. I smile to myself, seeing a vivid image of my husband, strong and healthy. My memories narrow into a tunnel and the noise around me distorts into a calming buzz of nothing. A sense of peace washes over me, something I haven't felt for such a long time, and the weight of my world slowly lifts from my shoulders. I feel light. Free.

Only death would ease me this much.

"Jesus Christ!" I'm jerked from my trance by the alarmed voice, a pair of hands grabbing me. I look down and find the headlights of the shiny BMW mere inches from my kneecaps. "Are you okay? Fucking hell, I thought I was going to hit you."

Looking up blankly, I come face to face with wide, panicked eyes. They hold mine while his hands hold me in place, ensuring I won't crumple to the ground. So worried. "I'm sorry," I mumble mindlessly, moving back, out of his hold. "I . . . I wasn't paying attention." A soft whimper at my feet pulls my stare away from the stranger's eyes, down to the road where Boris is looking up at me, appearing shocked himself. I'm brought back down to earth with an almighty bang. Oh my goodness, what was I thinking? Suddenly embarrassed and ashamed of myself, despite no one possibly knowing my bleak thoughts or intentions, I turn and hurry away, more damn tears welling in my eyes. How could I? How could I think to do such a thing?

"Hey." The stranger calling after me only makes me pick up speed. "Hey, wait a minute."

I dash onto the pavement, tugging Boris along, not prepared to be yelled at by the rankled driver. "I said I'm sorry," I sob, as I rush away. My path is suddenly blocked by the tall frame of a man, my feet skidding to a stop before I crash into his chest.

"Don't run away," he says, his strong London accent soft but firm. "I just want to make sure you're okay."

"I'm fine," I insist, refusing to look up at him, instead focusing on his expensive-looking gray-suited chest.

"Well, I'm pretty shaken up, even if you're pretending not to be." He laughs lightly, nervously, a low, smooth laugh that lifts my eyes to his. "And you're not pretending very well, just for the record." He reaches forward and wraps his hand around my upper arm, squeezing gently. "You're shaking." He hunkers down, concern drenching his face, which I inappropriately register is very handsome. Classically so, with a strong jaw full of scruff and big green eyes.

I remove myself from his hold. "I'm sorry," I repeat, struggling to find any other words.

"I heard you the first time."

I glance back up at him, noting his expression is a mixture of curiosity and concern. Then I feel the tears that have been building in my eyes roll free and tumble down my cheeks. I quickly scrub them away as he rakes a hand through his neatly cut dark hair. "Well, this is new." He almost laughs. "Women usually smile suggestively at me, not cry in my face."

"Sorry," I whisper once more, totally bypassing what I'm thinking is his attempt to lighten the situation.

"Will you please stop apologizing?" Now he sounds slightly mad. "Tell me you didn't purposely step into the road."

"No," I blurt, unashamedly outraged by his question.

"No, you won't tell me, or no, you didn't intentionally step into the road?"

"I didn't intentionally step into the road." It's the truth. I didn't. I did, however, intentionally stay there waiting for him to run me over and take me away from this godforsaken life. But he doesn't need to know that. "I was shocked. Couldn't move."

"Then it's a good job I'm a great driver, isn't it?" He stuffs his hands into his pockets. "Or you and your furry little friend here would be toast."

I'd laugh at his continued attempt to make light of this, but his reference to Boris brings on another wave of guilt. And yet more tears. Tears I don't want him to see. So I skirt past his tall body and hurry away, refusing to look back, and refusing to acknowledge that I very nearly let myself smile at the stranger's quick wit. I have nothing to smile about.

I only make it a few wobbly paces when my arm is yanked back, and annoyed that he is yet again hampering my escape, I swing around, ready to let out the building emotion and yell at him. But my rant is sucked back as I realize what's actually pulled me to a stop. It isn't the man who very nearly flattened me. It's Boris. His body is sprawled across the pavement on his side, his eyes closed. "Oh my God." I drop his lead and drop to the ground, my hands reaching and retracting constantly, unsure whether I should touch him. "Boris?" His little chest is pulsing wildly, up and down at a rapid rate. "Boris." Looking up, I see the stranger slowly approaching, his face a picture of concern. "Help, please," I beg.

He crouches down next to me, looking Boris over. "Has he been unwell?"

"No." I stroke his head, frantically trying to figure out what I need to do. I'm drawing a blank. "He's getting on a little."

"I don't think this is a case of old bones, darling." He looks across at me, his lips straight as he searches my distraught face. "Do you know where the nearest vet is?"

"It's out of hours. Our regular vet is closed."

"I'll google it." He pulls an iPhone out and quickly types in something. "A mile." Slipping his mobile back into his inside pocket, he reaches forward and scoops Boris into his arms.

I quickly stand. "What are you doing?"

He strides toward his car, looking back at me. "Helping you."

"There's no need. I can get there myself." I don't know why I'm being difficult about this, especially since my beloved Boris's life is at stake. Just let him take us. Let him help.

"It's a twenty-minute walk, and that's without carrying a dog.

It's a five-minute drive." He stops at his car, which is still abandoned in the road, nodding at the passenger door. "Get in."

My feet are taking me to his car without any more hesitation, my focus set on Boris. I open the door and slide in, and then he slips Boris onto my lap. The negotiation of my dog's body in his arms brings his face very close to mine, and I get a waft of his aftershave. It's nice. Fresh and crisp. Alive. "Got him?" he asks.

I nod and he pulls the seatbelt across my body, leaning over to clip it into place. He smiles, and it's a friendly smile of reassurance. I don't think he'll ever know how much it means to me. Someone trying to ease my worry, no matter what that worry is, is a feeling I have forgotten. Shutting the door, he rounds the car quickly and falls into the seat beside me. I focus my attention on Boris, smoothing the hair of his head and keeping a close eye on his pumping chest. "It's okay, boy," I soothe quietly. "It's okay."

The stranger pulls off quickly and seems to navigate his way easily to the nearest out-of-hours veterinary surgery, pulling up outside on double yellows. "Here, let me take him," he says gently once he's opened my door. Leaning in, he scoops Boris up and steps back, allowing me to get out of his posh car. Stupidly, I place a bet that Mr. Smart here has never had a dog in his swanky car before. Boris doesn't stink, not by any means, but I guarantee he'll be finding dog hairs in his posh motor for months to come. "Thank you." I reach to take my dog, but he backs up with Boris.

"Do you have anyone I can call to come and be with you?"

I falter for far too long, stupidly thinking about his question. No. I have no one, and I tell him so on a shake of my head. We haven't seen our friends for months, not since Billy became more bedbound. My husband is a proud man. He doesn't want anyone to see him like he is, not even me.

"I'll carry him inside."

"You don't have to," I say out of pride more than anything else. Truth be told, I want him to. I don't want to be alone in my worry.

"But I want to." He smiles, jerking his head toward the doors, prompting me to rush forward and open them for him. I don't care that he feels sorry for me. It's the story of my fucking life. I'm now used to it. "I'm sure you have better things to do," I say as he passes me with Boris.

"Not particularly."

The lady on the desk looks up and clocks Boris laid across the arms of the man who I still don't know what to call. "Oh dear," she says, rushing out from beyond her desk towards Boris.

"I don't know what's wrong with him." I watch as she strokes his head and looks him over. "We were walking and he collapsed." As I utter the words, Boris starts convulsing, his little body jerking wildly before going very still. I gasp, and Mr. Smart looks down with worry, evidently firming up his hold.

"Pass him over," the receptionist says, claiming Boris.

"What is it?" I ask, my eyes bouncing from her to my dog. "What's wrong with him?"

She rushes off with my beloved Boris, heading for the double white doors. "Please, take a seat."

I stare at the swinging doors once she's disappeared, lost and full of worry, and my hand comes up to my mouth to stop my distraught sob from breaking free.

"Are you okay?" His voice, soft and full of concern, washes over me.

"Yes," I squeak the lie, not turning to face him. "No." My head starts to shake, my eyes dropping to my feet. "I don't know." A handkerchief appears in my downcast, blurry vision, and I accept it, sniffling into the cotton. "Thank you." He must wish he'd driven off after nearly mowing me down. He didn't ask for any of this.

"Would you like me to get you anything? A tea? Water?"

"No, I'm fine, honestly." I turn and scan the waiting area. "I'll just wait. You really don't have to stay." He's already gone above and beyond. He must have a life to be getting on with—a life that's not weighed down with misery and hopelessness.

He shrugs. "My grandfather always taught me never to leave a woman in distress."

Distress? My life is one big, fucked-up mountain of distress. This man here knows only a fraction of my anguish. I clear my throat, hoping my next words are steady and strong. "I'm not distressed."

My claim makes him laugh lightly, his hand coming up to his smooth cheek and stroking down his skin. "Darling, I don't know who you are, or anything about you, but I know one thing beyond doubt." He looks at me, shaking his head in dismay.

"What?" I ask, confused.

"You're a very bad liar." He looks at me expectantly, and I hate that I have to look away from him, annoyed that he's got me all figured out. "Besides," he goes on. "I'd like to know that your furry friend is going to be okay. He's quite cute. For a dog."

The mention of Boris kicks my emotions back in, and for all the will in the world, I can't stop myself from blubbering again. This is my fault. I cover my face with my palms and sob into them, wondering when some good luck might come my way. It's just one thing after another, constant challenges and tragedy.

"Oh, heck," the man mutters, and before I know what's happening, I'm engulfed in his body, my arms bunched between his chest and mine. "Everything will be okay."

He's wrong, but his gesture is kind. I can't remember the last time someone threw their arms around me and told me that everything was going to be okay. It doesn't matter that he's so mistaken. It doesn't matter that he knows nothing of my sadness and grief. And it doesn't matter that once he releases me, all my problems will be back.

But for now, I allow myself to absorb his comfort, because despite him being a stranger, and despite it just being a hug, it's what I need.

So when he gently breaks away, I can't help but feel slightly resentful that he's stolen away my tiny piece of respite. He has accomplished what nothing has for two long years. He made me think of something besides my sadness. And quick on the heels of that respite comes guilt. So much guilt, my chest starts to ache. What am I doing? What am I thinking, taking solace in the arms of a complete stranger? I'm despicable. I'm an awful person, an awful wife. My husband is at home waiting to die, and here I am relishing in the amazing feeling of another man's arms.

I quickly turn on my heel and pace to the hard, plastic seats lining the far wall, sitting myself down and keeping my eyes on my lap. "Thank you for your help."

"Stop thanking me."

"I'm married," I blurt, stunning myself, the guilt now doing the talking for me. A hug. It was just a hug.

He nods down to my left hand. "I noticed," he says simply, lowering to a chair a few seats away from me. My gaze follows him the whole way until I'm staring at his profile. "But if it's all the same to you, I'd like to stay." He pulls his phone out and starts tapping at the screen, and my mind instantly wonders if he's messaging someone. His girlfriend? His wife? My eyes fall to his left hand. No ring. I look up and find his perfect white teeth sunk into his bottom lip as he taps away, and I start to wonder about everything there is to wonder about this man. His name. His job. His personal circumstances. He's smart, drives a nice car, and I bet he's super successful. Happy. Fulfilled. I bet his life is the complete opposite of mine. It's late evening, and he looks pristine, whereas I must look like a bedraggled state. My image hasn't mattered for a long time. I never wear makeup, rarely blow-dry my hair, and I dress for comfort rather than style. *Because who the fuck cares anyway?*

Looking back to the man next to me, I find that he's no longer on his phone, but looking at me. "These chairs aren't very comfortable, are they?" he asks, wriggling his tall body on a grimace. "If we sit here too long, we may get piles."

I laugh, and the sound shocks me. It's so unfamiliar. "Maybe you should stand."

"Nah." He points to his feet. "New shoes. My feet are shredded."

I wince on his behalf, quickly diverting my eyes to the double doors when the receptionist appears. I stand and make my way over. "How is he?" I ask, nervous for her answer.

"At the moment we suspect that your little man had a heart attack, but we'll need to do tests to determine that."

"A heart attack?" I gasp. Oh my God, this is all my fault. I stood in that road waiting for a car to take me out. Poor Boris must have been terrified.

"I need a few details from you." She motions toward the desk, and I follow. "His name, for a start."

"Boris. It's Boris."

"And how old is Boris?"

"He's nine."

She notes it all down. "His registered vet?"

"Goddard on King's Road," I answer swiftly, and she proceeds to ask more questions that I reel off answers to easily.

"And who is he insured with?" She looks up at me, and I freeze.

"He's uninsured," I murmur, hating myself for being so stupid. Boris's pet insurance was one of the first things I culled when things got too tight after Billy was diagnosed. I had to make cutbacks, and since I'd never once claimed on his policy in the whole time I'd had him, it was common sense to cancel it.

"Oh." The receptionist pulls a face that can only be interpreted as disappointed. She thinks I'm an irresponsible owner. She thinks I don't care about Boris's wellbeing. "So you'll be settling the bill today." She doesn't ask it as a question, because there's only one right answer.

I nod and reach into my pocket, pulling out my wallet. I find my card and slide it onto the counter. "Yes." I breathe in, closing my eyes.

"I'll just get an itemization for Boris's treatment," she says, disappearing again. I use the time while she's gone to pray. Pray that my bank doesn't reject the transaction. The receptionist is back moments later, presenting me with a sheet of paper. Then she proceeds to go down the long list that consists of scans, drips, medications, an overnight stay—and that's just for now. "We'll re-assess in the morning, but for now this is what's due." She circles the figure at the bottom of the sheet, and I break out into a cold sweat. Seven hundred and sixty-five pounds? I'm already over my overdraft. I know that my bank won't approve this transaction. But I still insert my card into the machine, begging for a miracle as I punch in my PIN number.

DECLINED

"Oh," the receptionist says, frowning down at the machine. "I'm afraid that didn't go through. Should we try again?" She looks up at me in question.

"Here." A hand passes over my shoulder, a card held between his fingers. "You can charge it to this one."

I watch as the lady takes the card, which I note to be an American Express. "No," I blurt, swinging around to face him. "No, I can't accept that."

"Do you have a choice?" he asks gently, which no umbrage tinging his question. It's just a simple question.

But still, it makes me tearful, and I look away, embarrassed. "No," I admit, my lip quivering.

He moves forward and sees to the payment of my extortionate bill, with not another question asked or word said. I thought I couldn't feel any more useless. Turns out I was wrong.

"We will call you tomorrow with an update," the lady tells me, pulling a receipt from the printer and handing it to the stranger. "But for now, he's stable and comfortable, so please try not to worry."

"Thank you," he says, taking my arm and gently guiding me out of the building.

Only when the cold air hits me do I snap out of my trance. "Why did you do that?" I ask.

He drops my arm. "Why wouldn't I?"

"Because I'm a stranger to you." I almost laugh, but my self-pity prevents it.

Nodding, as if agreeing, his green eyes harbor a million questions I just know I won't want to answer. "I don't think I've ever seen anyone with so much sadness in their eyes," he says quietly.

His words hit me like a brick in the face. It's just like I thought, and resentment bubbles as a result. I don't want him to feel sorry for me. Everyone feels sorry for me. "I'll pay you back, of course."

"Do you have the money to pay me back?"

I shoot him an indignant look, one that I have no right to flash him. "Yes," I lie, holding out my hand. "So, your details?"

He pulls out his wallet, and then a silver card. "Here."

I take it and stuff it in my coat pocket. "Thank you for . . ." I drift off, feeling small and worthless. How did it come to this? How did it come to me resorting to strangers for help?

"Keeping you company? You're welcome," he finishes for me, and I look at him in question as he gestures toward his shiny silver BMW. "Let me take you home."

"Thank you, but I've already taken up too much of your time."

"It's nothing, really." He holds his hand out to me. "I'm Luke."

"Luke," I mimic.

With his hand still suspended between us, he asks, "And you are?"

"Lo. My name is Lo."

"Pleasure to meet you, Lo." He smiles, and I find my lips lifting at the corners too, slowly forming a smile.

"This is the part where you take my hand and shake it," he

says, still smiling. I look at his offering, stalling. "I've already given you quite the hug in there, Lo. It's just a handshake."

My smile widens as I accept his hand. "Nice to meet you, Luke."

He flexes his fingers around mine, getting a better grip. "Now, about that lift home."

Home. My home. Where I should be, not here with this stranger. Smiling. Thinking of something other than my heartache. "Home," I say, gently pulling my hand from his. "You know, I think I'll find my own way home." I start to back away, and he doesn't try to stop me.

Instead, he nods his acceptance, slipping his hands into the pockets of his trousers while he studies me as the distance between us grows. "Thank you for everything." I smile again, finding it all too easy.

He nods sharply. "Goodbye, Lo."

"Goodbye, Luke." I turn and hurry on my way, peeking over my shoulder when I reach the end of the street. He's just getting into his car, and he lifts a hand in a small wave. I wave back and round the corner, wrapping my arms around my body and picking up my pace to keep warm.

The house is drenched in the usual silence when I get home, and the first thing I do is go to the downstairs bathroom. I don't need the toilet. I need a mirror. I wasn't even halfway home when the tears found me again. Tears for Billy. Tears for Boris.

Tears for me.

What confronts me when I stare into the oval glass hanging above the sink is unrecognizable. I endure the dismal sight as I wipe away the evidence of my sadness, not wanting Billy to see it. It's silly of me. A perfect stranger saw my plight. I have dark rims under my eyes, a gray complexion. Hair that hasn't been cut and colored for months, leaving me with my natural dark blonde at the roots and bright blonde highlight through the ends. I reach up and flick my locks from one side to the other, counting at least three inches of roots. And I pout, trying to recall the last time I painted my lips. My fingernails catch my eye. Short, neat but bare. Long gone are the days when they were immaculate, never chipped, or without a color—usually a shade of bright pink. Bright and alive. *"I don't think I've ever seen anyone with so much sadness in their eyes."*

I sigh, bracing my hands on the edge of the sink and dropping my head. Is that what he sees? So much sadness? Sadness I could never mask, even if I had the means. Attention to my appearance is a luxury I can't afford anymore, both in time and money. And energy.

Pushing off the sink, I make my way up the stairs. The smile I found earlier felt lovely, the laugh even more so, but everything real about my life slowly returns to where it should be with each step I climb. On my shoulders. The momentary light feeling vanishes into thin air, and the heavy feeling returns, except now it's heavier.

Peeking my head around the bedroom door, I see Billy's asleep, looking peaceful, and the glow of the silent television is illuminating the room. I can only hope for a peaceful night. Not that I'd sleep if it was.

"That was along walk," Billy says as I'm backing out, closing the door.

I still, holding the door open a little. "I had to take Boris to the vet."

"What happened?"

I let myself into the room and make my way to his bed, keen to put his mind at rest, even though Boris's condition is up in the air. "He collapsed. They think he had a heart attack."

Billy tries to sit up, but I hurry forward to stop him. "Why didn't you call?"

I pull up for a few moments, wondering what he thinks he could have done. He can barely walk today, for goodness sake.

"Someone stopped and helped me," I tell him. "Took us to the nearest emergency vet."

"Oh good. Did you take her number? You should send some flowers or something."

"It was a man. A businessman. I don't think he'd appreciate flowers." I smile awkwardly and set about tucking him in better and making sure he has plenty of water. I shouldn't have told him that. He'll hate that another man was forced into helping me because he couldn't be there. "The vet will call me tomorrow to update me. Have you had all your pills?"

"Yes," he says quickly. "Thank God for pet insurance. This won't be cheap."

I swallow and reach for the remote control, flicking the television off. "Can I get you anything before I go to bed?"

He shakes his head and closes his eyes. "I'm sorry for upsetting you earlier."

"Stop it," I say. "I understand." I don't understand; how could I? To me, the thought of being without Billy is . . . well, unthinkable. How he could tell me to walk away is beyond my comprehension. But he'll do it again on another bad day. And he'll apologize again.

"Goodnight, Lo."

"Goodnight," I whisper, dipping and placing a kiss on his gaunt cheek. "I love you."

Billy doesn't respond, just nods. And my heart shatters one more time for the day. I don't think he realizes how much I need to hear him say it. He used to say it so often. Every day. With every kiss. With every hug. With every touch. Now? He never tells me he loves me. He never kisses me. He never hugs me.

So each day, I long for the most important three words that could provide a glimpse of hope. *Of joy.* Anything to tell me he will fight. For him. For me. For us.

But in order to distance himself, he denies me those words. He's out of fight.

My heart aching, I leave him and make my way to the spare bedroom, the place Billy told me to move to two years ago, because he couldn't sleep with me anymore.

After I've stripped down to my knickers, I climb under the sheets, missing the warmth of Boris, who normally snuggles up to me most nights. Making sure I never sleep alone.

But tonight, I'm alone.

Alone and empty.

Chapter Four

With my hands wrapped around my mug, I stare out of the kitchen window, my mind on Boris. It's a momentary respite from my mind being on Billy.

As I hear the front door open, I empty the last inch of my coffee into the sink, looking back when Magda wanders into the kitchen. Her eyes are not on me. They're on the dish sitting on the hob. The dish that is still full of sausage casserole.

I wince, placing my mug on the drainer. "I got a good night's sleep." Such a lie. Between my words with Billy and my walk with Boris, I didn't sleep a wink.

"Where's Boris?" Magda asks, looking down at her feet where he would usually be circling her thick calves.

"He had a heart attack." I say it so matter-of-factly, like shitty news is all I have to tell these days.

"Oh, that's terrible, Lo. I'm so sorry."

"Me too," I breathe, heading for the hallway to get my coat. "The vet said they'll call with an update this morning. I'd better get going."

"Walking again?"

I turn back toward the kitchen, shrugging on my coat. "Yes."

Magda nods, lips straight. "Lo," she says, taking a deep breath. "I didn't want to bring it up, but, well, it's been two weeks now. I have bills to pay myself."

"I get paid today. I'll make sure it's transferred before the end of the day." I scoop up my bag. "I'm sorry, Magda. Things are—"

"I know," she says, looking at me, full of sympathy that I just cannot bear. "And I wouldn't ask, but—"

"Magda, you don't have to explain yourself."

"Lo, far be it from me to interfere with that part of your life, but am I an expense that you could do without? I mean, I just pop in twice a day and make a nuisance of myself. Billy has made it clear that he doesn't want me here."

"I feel better knowing someone is checking up on him while I'm at work. Making sure he eats."

"Very well," she concedes, slipping off her gloves. "I'll get to making his breakfast."

"Thank you." I turn on my heels and brace myself for the cold, pulling the door open and shivering when it hits me. "Jesus," I mutter, taking the steps down to the street. My hands go to my pockets to find my gloves, but I find something else instead. Something cardboard. Stopping in my tracks, I pull out what I've found and stare down at the silver card.

Luke B Williamson
Managing Director
LBW Security
M: 07951 902877
E: lbw@lbwsecurity.co.uk

My heart slows, my nerves getting the better of me. I don't have the money to pay him back, even though it's payday. I'll call him. Ask if I can have more time. It's not a call I'm relishing making. I'm asking a perfect stranger for a favor. Or maybe I don't have to call at all. I scan the card for the email, thinking that would be the perfect solution. Yes, I'll email him. Just as soon as I get to work. At least then I won't stutter over my embarrassment.

I swear, I feel like a snowman by the time I make it to the office. This winter is brutally cold. I let myself through the security barrier by swiping my card and join a crowd of people at the bank of elevators. While I wait, I wriggle my toes to life, looking up to the ceiling to flex my neck, which I'm pretty sure is stiff from frost-bite. Something catches my eye in the corner where the ceiling meets the wall, a small black dome. I frown as I squint, trying to decipher the type on the glass.

"LBW Security," I say to myself, looking across to the other corner and finding another dome.

"Well, yeah." Matthew laughs from beside me, and I slowly drop my stare to his. He pushes his glasses up his nose and points to another dozen cameras dotted around, and then to the security room on the other side of reception, which I know to be kitted out with the most intelligent security system, monitors, and control panels. A private bank operates from the third floor, and I know there's a bank of safety deposit boxes somewhere beneath this building. "If you're serious about security, only LBW will do," Matthew goes on. "They keep ninety percent of commercial build-ings in the city safe and sound." The doors to an elevator open and he gestures me to go ahead, which I do, spotting yet more cameras in the lift. I've never paid much attention to the security in our building, but now, everywhere I look there's a camera. A camera with his initials on it. Luke B Williamson. He owns the company? I let out a puff of disbelieving breath and let my back fall to the wall behind me. No wonder he cast off that vet bill as if it was nothing, because to him it actually *was* nothing. But I'm still paying him back.

I nod to myself and hop out of the elevator when it stops at my floor, mentally running through the list of things Scarlett has to do this morning. My desk phone is ringing when I get there. "Hello?".

"Mrs. Harper, it's Prim from the vet. I'm calling about Boris."

I lower to my chair, my heart skipping a dozen beats. "How is he?" I ask, tentative but hopeful.

"It seems your little friend has epilepsy."

"Epilepsy?" I question, utterly stunned. "I thought he had a heart attack."

"It was suspected, but tests have shown conclusively that Boris had a seizure."

I don't know if that's good or not. "Will he be okay?"

"He'll be just fine with the right medication."

I sag in my chair, so relieved. "Thank you."

"He's ready to go home when you can collect him."

"I have somewhere I need to be this afternoon," I explain, not particularly looking forward to Billy's hospital appointment. "I'll be there as soon as I'm done. Probably around four?"

"See you then, Mrs. Harper." She hangs up, and I let a small smile free. He's okay. Thank God, he's okay.

Once I've emailed Scarlett, filled her water jug, and made sure her lunch reservation is confirmed, I settle down to start the email to Luke.

A whole hour later, I'm still typing—and deleting—words. I start with a formal "Dear Mr. Williamson" and then delete it and replace it with a not so formal "Good morning." And after pondering my new greeting for a good ten minutes, I delete that too, and type a very informal "Hey." Slumping back in my chair, I huff to myself. It's just an email. He seems like a nice enough, stand-up guy. I'm sure he'll understand. It only occurs to me now that Luke B Williamson has no line of contact to me at all. He doesn't know how to find me. He gave me *his* card. If I don't contact him, then I won't have to spill my excuses for delaying paying him back. Speaking of excuses, what will I tell him? That my husband hasn't worked for two years because he's dying? That I'm living on the breadline? That I have debt collectors chasing me? If I chose to share my plights, it will be one more person in this world to feel sorry for me.

I sigh and reach for the delete button, hitting it four times, leaving me with a blank screen once again. *He already feels sorry for you, Lo. Without your tragic story.*

The phone ringing on my desk gives me a perfect excuse to stall some more. "Lo Harper," I say, glancing up at the clock.

"Lo, there's someone in reception to see you," Teresa, the lady from the building's reception desk, tells me.

I frown. No one ever comes to see me at work. "Who is it, Teresa?"

"Mr. Williamson?"

I go stiff in my chair, my hand gripping the receiver of my phone so tight I might crumple the plastic. "Mr. Williamson?" I breathe, staring at his email address on the monitor of my computer.

"Yes, shall I tell him to take a seat?"

"Yes." I drop the phone and take a few moments to think. Oh no, has he come for his money? Maybe he's concluded that I might not contact him like I promised. And, more importantly, how the hell does he know where I work? "Oh, God," I whisper, slowly rising to my feet. I hold the edge of the desk to try and steady myself, super nervous, my legs jelly-like. How am I going to explain that I'm broke? How am I going to explain that I have no clue when or if I can ever pay him back? *He knows where I work. He's in security. He could have me fired.*

"Lo, are you okay?" Scarlett asks as she approaches me from the boardroom, a coffee in her hand, a frown on her face.

I look at her blankly for a few moments, trying to remember what she's asked me.

"Lo?" She comes to a stop before me, her frown morphing into concern. "Lo, is it Billy? Do you need to go home?"

"No." I swallow and look at the button that will call the lift. "I have a visitor in reception. Do you mind?" I want her to tell me that she has something for me to do, something that can't wait, therefore my visitor will have to. Hopefully he'll get bored and leave, and my need to explain my circumstances will be gone. My humiliation will be avoided.

"No, of course not," she says. "But are you sure you're okay? You look a little pale."

I strain a smile and press the button. "I'm fine."

"Oh good, for a moment there, I thought . . ." Her perfectly painted lips straighten. "Well, never mind." Scarlett gets on her way, stopping at her office door and smiling back at me. *Sympathy.* There it is.

As I ride down, I puff out air and drag it back in again, filling my lungs with confidence. And perhaps the strength I need to be honest with Luke Williamson and tell him I'm not a flake, that I do intend to pay him, but . . . well, what *can* I say? God, how I hate this additional layer of humiliation.

The doors part, and I quickly straighten my shirt and step out of the elevator, my shoulders pushed back. And like my eyes sense exactly where to find him, they home in on one of the eight couches lining the reception area.

He looks up, smiles, lifting a hand in hello. I smile back, and he stands, taking measured, long strides, until he comes to a stop a good few meters away. "This is as far as I can come," he says.

For a moment, I wonder what he means by that, but then I follow his outstretched arm to the barriers that separate the elevators from the rest of the reception area.

"Oh." I reach to the belt hoop on my trousers, pulling my access card to full length on the retractable cord. Presenting it to the scanner, I wait for the waist-high glass screen to slide across.

"Hi," I say, passing through and slowing to a standstill a couple of paces away from him. "What are you doing here?"

"Oh." He reaches into his inside pocket and pulls something out. "You left these in my car."

"My gloves." So that's where they went. I roll my eyes and take them. "Thank you. How do you know where I work, Luke?"

"You remembered my name?"

I point to a camera above my head. "You're suddenly everywhere."

He looks up, smiling. "Oh, so I am." Dropping his eyes, but keeping his head tilted back, he grins, and just the mere sight of it pulls a grin from me too. It has a cheeky, mischievous edge. "I own a small security firm."

"Small?" I laugh. "How modest of you."

"I don't like boasters." He winks, making me laugh once again.

"You didn't answer my question."

His eyebrows pinch. I ignore the fact that he looks quite adorable when he does that, his manliness turning boyish. For the first time, I wonder how old he is. Late thirties, maybe? Early forties? "What was your question?" he asks.

"How did you know where I work?"

"Ah, that's easy. You gave your work details to the lady at the vet. How's Boris, by the way?"

Of course. And there was me thinking he couldn't find me. "He's good. They think it's epilepsy but with the right medication he should be fine. I'm picking him up later this evening."

"I'm glad to hear it."

"Me too," I say, smiling. "Listen, I was actually just emailing you."

"What for?"

I feel my cheeks fill with blood, but I'm also frowning. "Well, about the money I owe you."

He huffs, waving his hand flippantly. "Don't worry about it."

Is he serious? "No, Luke, I want to pay you back," I insist, standing my ground. He must be mad. He hadn't known me for five minutes before he was pulling out his black AMEX. "Every penny. You didn't ask for any of what happened last night."

"Oh, yes, I did."

I slowly shake my head as he starts to slowly nod his, a tiny smirk forming on his face. "How?" I ask.

"Well, by day I run a security firm. By night I skulk around London in my mask and cape rescuing women. Just call me the caped crusader." He grins, and I laugh lightly, now shaking my head in bewilderment.

"I'll email you for your bank details so I can transfer the money I owe you. It might be a few weeks or so, but I'll make sure you get every penny."

"If it makes you happy."

"It does."

"I'll have my lawyer draw up a payment plan," he says, his perfect white teeth sinking into his bottom lip, and I shoot him a startled look. He's doing that to stop himself from smiling.

"You're messing with me." I roll my eyes. He's quite the comedian.

"Of course I'm messing with you." He smiles brightly, nearly blinding me. "I didn't come here to talk about the money. I just wanted to return your gloves and make sure Boris was okay."

"Well, you've done both of those things." I wave my gloves at him. "And again, thank you for being a knight in shining armor. I really appreciate your help."

"No problem."

Luke doesn't realize the half of it. He will never know how much he really saved me. Because in that moment in time, when his car was coasting toward me, death seemed like the easiest way out of my hell-hole of a life. Thank God for his driving skills. "I'd better get back to work."

"Of course." He looks down at his expensive watch. "Shit, I'd better be running too." He turns on his heel and darts off across the lobby, looking over his shoulder. "See ya, Lo."

I see it, the impending disaster. A woman places her bags down, right in Luke's path. Not that Luke would know, since he's still facing me while he rushes blindly across the lobby. "Luke," I yell.

My warning comes too late.

"Shit!" His feet get all caught up in the bags, sending him sailing through the air. I slap my hands over my eyes, cringing, waiting for the sound of his body to hit the marble floor.

Thud!

"Motherfucker," he curses, and I peek through my spread fingers, seeing him sprawled all over the floor, lost amid a heap of bags. His curse, as well as the crash he went down with, silences the entire foyer. I press my lips together, starting toward him, but his hand held up stops me. "I've got it," he says, scrambling to his feet as the woman, whose bags he's kicked all over the foyer, watches on with wide eyes. Luke makes quick work of gathering up all of her things and passing them to her on an awkward smile.

She accepts, silent, staring at Luke, and I smile as he fixes his suit. Straightens his tie. Takes a quick peek around at the peanut gallery of people. Then he takes an over-the-top bow.

I burst into laughter as Luke shakes his head, giving me a mortified look. "I'll be going now," he says, taking a more unhurried walk to the revolving doors, shaking his head to himself.

With the clown now having left the building, everyone returns to their business, including me, and I wander back to the elevator. But I'm still laughing. And then I realize I've laughed twice in the last twenty-four hours because of Luke Williamson. And it feels good.

Chapter Five

I leave work at lunchtime, having taken half a day holiday, and I know the moment I lay my eyes on Billy when I get home that I'm going to have a challenge on my hands. His appointments at the hospital are never anything to celebrate, and they always leave us both silent for the rest of the day, sometimes even the whole week. Because there's never good news. We never get told anything that gives us hope. There's no miracle cure, and Dr. Smith hasn't changed his mind about operating. Billy's had two rounds of radiotherapy to shrink the tumor, but each one has failed to do anything other than make him feel even more poorly than he does already. And even more grumpy. And even more negative. And whatever Billy feels, I feel too.

"I'm not going," he states with utter finality before I can even ask him if he plans on showering before we go. He's lying on the bed in his dressing gown, watching golf, the curtains drawn, blocking out what there is of daylight outside.

I swallow and walk across the bedroom, pulling the curtains back. "We must go," I say, sounding positive and trying to feel it too. Despite the negative news at each appointment, there's still a part of me that hopes. That prays. "Dr. Smith said at your last appointment that he would consider another round of radio-therapy."

"Two tries haven't worked, Lo. I'm not going through that shit to be told it was for nothing again." He looks across at me, the frustration I'm feeling myself written all over his pale face. "Shut the curtains."

I sigh, leaving the curtains open. "So that's it? I've just got to sit back and wait for you to die?"

He looks away from me, focusing back on the damn television. "I'm not up for living like a cripple for the rest of my life. We both know the only thing that can save me is out of reach. So get used to it, Lo."

"It's not out of reach," I whisper. I know I sound unconvincing, but hope is all we have. Hope that by some miracle, the money we need to get Billy to the specialist in America will magic its way into our lives and save him. Save *us*.

Billy laughs coldly. "Why? You playing the lotto every day?"

For a stupid moment, I tell myself that tonight I will play the lotto, because some good luck has *got* to come our way soon. Then I remember how broke we are. I don't have my bus fare to work, let alone spare money to gamble away. "How can you give up so easily? You hardly ever leave this room anymore. It's always dark, the television is always on. You haven't joined me for dinner in weeks, and I can't remember the last time you walked Boris with me, even just to get some fresh air. We wouldn't have to go far. Just a slow stroll. Please, Billy. Just—"

"Shut up!" He slams his fist down on the bed, and I stagger back in shock at his outburst. "Just shut up, Lo. I'm dying. So forgive me if I don't fucking want to go for a fucking walk in the fucking park. Forgive me if I haven't got a fucking appetite. Forgive me if I want to drown in my fucking sorrows—" He starts coughing violently, choking on nothing, but when I'd usually rush to help him, this time I stay where I am, stunned into still-ness and quiet. "Just leave me alone. Go. And shut the damn curtains." He slumps back on his pillow and closes his eyes, breathing heavily.

Quickly yanking the curtains across, I hurry from the room, feeling the lump in my throat growing. And as soon as I'm out of earshot, I let my emotions pour out of me in loud, body-jerking sobs, hearing his angry words playing on repeat in my head. I make it to the bottom of the stairs before I collapse to my arse on the last step and cradle my head in my lap to stifle the noise. My heart aches with hopelessness, and my head's pounding with a stress I can't take for much longer. I feel like I could break at any moment.

I somehow muster the energy to dial Dr. Smith's office. But I don't have energy beyond that to talk to him, so I leave a message with his secretary telling her we won't be there for Billy's appointment. Then I grab my bag and Boris's lead, and head out. I need a time-out. Space to clear my head and try to find the determination that Billy just so easily knocked out of me. So I head off to pick up my dog, hoping he's well enough to take a slow stroll home.

His tail is spinning like a propeller when they bring him into the reception area, his paws slipping across the tiles as he fights to get to me. "Boris," I shriek, so happy to see him.

"He's been a terrible guest," the vet says, laughing. "Whining, scratching, and barking."

"He was missing me." I drop to my knees and let him trample all over my lap, giving him a day's worth of love that he's missed. And that I have missed too, for that matter. "Will he be okay?" I ask, looking up at her. "You said epilepsy."

"Yes, but medication will keep his seizures under control." She reaches for a paper bag and hands it over. "One tablet every day with his dinner."

"For the rest of his life?" I take the bag and slip it into my handbag.

"Afraid so. Now, we only usually prescribe a month at a time, but I've bagged three-months' worth until he needs to be assessed again, just to make sure all is as it should be. We'll forward all the details of his treatment to his regular vet." She hands me a sheet of paper on a smile. "Here's the final bill. For the medication and the extra tests that we had to undertake."

My eyes drop to the bill as my heart drops into my stomach. Oh, God, more tests, and now medication too. I swallow and take the paper, glancing down at the bottom line. It's all I can do not to burst into tears when the figure greets me. "Four hundred and fifty," I say to myself, reaching for my purse out of habit. Will they seize Boris because I can't pay? Will I have to do a runner and hope they don't find me before I have the money to settle my bill? Boris will die if I can't pay for the medication he needs. Like my husband. I blink. Swallow. I can't breathe through the blockage in my throat.

The lady spots my card in my hand and shakes her head. "The final bill's been settled, Mrs. Harper. That's just your copy of the invoice."

"Excuse me?"

"A gentleman came by earlier."

"A gentleman?"

"Yes, the man who you came in with last night. He paid the bill, but said he couldn't take Boris as he had a meeting in a hotel that had a strict no pets policy. He said you'd be stopping by to get him." She reaches for Boris's head and scratches. "So we had to listen to a few more hours of your howls, didn't we?"

I slowly rise, taking the lead from the vet. I should be smiling, overjoyed that Boris is okay and that I don't have an enormous, unpayable bill to settle. But I'm a bit shell-shocked. "Thank you," I whisper, hoping she hears gratitude past my obvious shock.

Why would he?

"You're very welcome. Please call if you have any concerns."

I nod on a weak smile and wander away, coming to a stop outside. He paid another bill? That's over one thousand pounds he's parted with. I look down at Boris, who's sitting at my feet patiently, waiting for me to kick myself into gear and take him home. But I'm standing there for a good ten minutes in the cold, running over the same question.

I find his card and text him to ask.

> Why?

His answer comes quickly.

> Call it compensation for nearly killing you.
> Luke x

I shake my head on a disbelieving smile. The man is mad. I reply with a thank you and an assurance that he'll get all the money back. Then I attempt to put one foot in front of the other.

Call it compensation for nearly killing you.

Who are you, Luke Williamson?

Pushing my way through the front door, I come to a startled stop when I find Billy sitting on the stairs. My natural instinct is to panic. I drop Boris's lead and rush toward him. He must see my worry, because he's quick to ease it. "I'm fine," he says, taking the rail and heaving himself up with too much effort. I wince and hiss with him, all the way until he's standing, though I don't help, knowing he won't want me to.

"You're up," I say like a fool.

Hitting me with dull but sorry eyes, he swallows. "Takeout and a movie?"

My throat is instantly swollen, tears stinging the backs of my eyes. *Don't cry on him, Lo.* "I would love that." I force my words past my happiness and go to him when he opens his arms. I could tell myself not to cry until I'm blue in the face. I'd still fail. My cheek meeting his chest, he takes me in a cuddle as I silently sob into his bathrobe, feeling his mouth on the back of my head. I hate that he feels remorse. I hate that he feels he has to say sorry. But I love this. I miss this. So much. This cuddle, this closeness, the fact that he's suggested eating and he wants to snuggle on the couch. Such simple things, but things that fill me with untold joy.

"Come on." He wraps his arm around my shoulders and leads us to the lounge. *He* leads us. Not me leading him. I'm not holding him up or encouraging his steps. I know he's making a point, but it's hope I need to cling to with all my might. I can't remember the last time we did this. *Months?* "Boris seems sprightly." Billy motions for me to sit, which I do, Boris jumping up too. He collects the remote controls and walks, albeit slowly, back across to me.

"He has epilepsy." I give Boris's ears a scratch. "But he'll be fine. They've given him pills. One a day."

Billy lowers to the couch and lifts his arm, and I eagerly crawl in under it, closing my eyes in complete contentment. We don't need to eat. We don't need to watch a film. We could just be here, together, cuddling. "I bet the bill was something to wince at."

"It's taken care of," I murmur, pushing back all thoughts except for those of this moment. Because it's magic.

Chapter Six

T he next two days pass by quickly, thanks to the madness of Scarlett's meeting schedule and the need for coffee and cakes on loop. I've been feeling quietly guilty for more or less forcing Billy into feeling bad and giving me what I needed the other night. After getting himself down the stairs and to the couch, eating, talking, and watching a movie, he paid for his overexertion. Dr. Smith called yesterday morning to talk about Billy's missed appointment. What could I say other than the truth? He refused to go. He asked how he was. "Terrible" was the only word I could find. He sent Billy's GP for a home visit. It was point-less, Billy's general practitioner simply assessing him in order to report back to Dr. Smith. On leaving, he told me that if Billy's condition deteriorates, I should let them know so they can act. And do what exactly? The only way they'll get Billy into hospital is if he's unable to protest. How poorly will he have to be for that to happen?

Friday lunchtime, as I'm finalizing the diary for next week, the ping of my phone has me grabbing it blindly while I scroll through Scarlett's calendar. It's Magda.

A quiet day here so far. I'm off now as my niece
is visiting from Spain. I'll see you on Monday.
Have a lovely weekend.

I send a quick reply to thank her, blinking my eyes clear. I've been staring at the computer screen all morning and it's taking its toll. My stomach rumbles loudly, reminding me that I haven't eaten since yesterday lunchtime. It's no wonder I'm tired. I pull my top drawer open in search of the biscuits I keep for emergencies when I need a quick sugar hit. An empty wrapper greets me, and I pull it out, pouting at it. And my tummy rumbles again.

Food. I throw my phone in my bag, swap my heels for my trainers, snatch my coat from the hook, and rush out of the office to grab myself some lunch. The freezing cold air does a good job of waking up my brain as I hustle down the street to the nearest Nero's. I burst through the door, grimacing at the long lines of people on their lunchbreaks. Being poor isn't the only reason I avoid this place.

I head for the fridges and settle on a tuna baguette, my mouth watering just looking at it.

"Lo?"

I turn, seeing a man at the front of the line waving at me. "Luke?"

"Quick." He ushers me to him with a frantic hand, and as soon as I make it, he swipes my lunch from my hand. "What are you drinking?"

I look back and see many people in the queue scowling at me.

"I'm holding them up, Lo," Luke says, motioning to the menu.

"Oh," I scuttle closer, maybe hoping for protection from the angry glares. "A latte, please. Extra shot."

His green eyes widen somewhat. "That kind of day?"

"You mean long? Yes."

"Mine too," he confirms, tapping his American Express on the

71

card reader. He hands me my drink as soon as the server slides it onto the counter and I accept with a smile, going to my bag.

"Don't offer me any money," he warns, collecting his own drink and my lunch.

"More compensation?" I ask dryly, taking a sip of my lovely warm coffee with extra caffeine.

He nudges me in the shoulder as we wander away. "No, I'm just buying you a sandwich."

"And a coffee." I raise my cup, smiling. "Thank you."

"No sweat. You're providing me with my daily good deeds. I can live in harmony with myself." He motions to a table as I laugh. "Got time for a chat?"

My laughter dries a little, my head cocking. "About what?"

"I don't know. What do friends chat about?" He sits, taking my sandwich from my hand and placing it on the table. *Friends.* Why does that sound so lovely?

"So we're friends?" I ask, as if I need confirmation. And perhaps to confirm that we could be nothing more if that is where his mind might be wandering. Although, and I hate to admit it, why a handsome, successful man like Luke could be interested in me is quite laughable.

"I saved your life. That makes us friends for life." He reaches for my arm and guides me to the chair. "Sit."

"You also nearly *took* my life," I point out, wriggling out of my coat and letting it pool on the seat around me. I realize my error in an instant when Luke doesn't come back with some wisecrack, instead looking at me with way too much curiosity. I divert my gaze to my sandwich and start unwrapping it, avoiding his look. If he asks, I'll just leave, and I really don't want to leave. He makes me laugh. He's someone nice to talk to without me worrying that he's going to drown me in those awful looks of sympathy.

"Want to share?" he asks, pulling my worried eyes up quickly. "The sandwich." He points to my hand, and I look down, relieved.

"I can hardly say no, since you paid for it." I break the baguette in half and pass it over, smiling when he winks and takes a huge bite from the end. I remove the cucumber from my half and join him, though my bite is far more ladylike.

"So what do you do in that posh office of yours?" he asks, his mouth still half full.

"I'm an assistant." I shrug, a little unimpressed with myself. "It's not exactly the dream, but it pays the bills."

"What's the dream?"

What's the dream? I had it. Then it was cruelly snatched away from me. I push my depressing thoughts to the back of my mind and engage in the normal conversation Luke is offering. "I used to own a vintage store." I miss that store so much. I miss sorting through endless bags of people's castoffs and discovering little treasures while Boris slept in his basket under the cash register. I miss Billy meeting me from work at six o'clock. I miss him walking me there in the mornings and getting coffee with him before he headed to his office. I miss sitting at the iron tables and chairs outside the café, even in the dead of winter, talking about what our days had in store.

"Used to?" Luke asks, before taking another bite of his baguette. Two bites and it's nearly gone.

"It didn't exactly provide a good income." I avoid the wretched truth. The real truth. I didn't need a good income at the time because Billy provided that, and he was just so happy for me to lose myself in my shop. Eventually, I would have started making a profit, my plans for my business vast and exciting. But, of course, I didn't get to realize that dream. No dream, in fact. "So I had to get a proper job and wear boring office clothes." I shrug and work my way through my sandwich. "What about you?"

"What about me?"

"What's your dream?"

He pouts, looking past me for a beat. "Well, it *was* to start my own security firm."

"You can tick that one off," I say, smiling when he nods to himself. "What else?"

"I don't know." He frowns. "Early retirement would be nice. Travel the world, buy a nice country retreat."

I notice he hasn't once referred to a wife or girlfriend. "Are you married?"

He snorts, placing the last inch of his lunch on the wrapper before me. "No, but I *do* have a daughter."

I don't know why this surprises me. "So you're divorced?"

He shakes his head. "I never married Tia's mother, thank God."

"How old is she?"

"Tia, or her mother?" He smirks when I give him a tired look. "Twenty-three."

"Twenty-three?" I blurt, shocked as shit. He doesn't look old enough.

"Yes, twenty-three."

"How old are *you*?"

"Forty-two."

"Fuck."

He laughs, reaching for his nape and rubbing at it. "Tell me about it. I ask myself *what the fuck?* at least ten times a day."

"If it's any consolation, you don't look a day over forty."

He wrinkles his nose at me, making me smirk. "What about you? Kids?" He reaches for his coffee cup, and I unwittingly freeze in place, my baguette halfway to my mouth. He notices before I can rectify my reaction to his simple question.

"No kids," is all I say. "I'm not ready." Total lie. I've been ready for years. We were so sure of our future.

Any woman who wears dungarees to a cocktail bar deserves an opportunity to explain why.

They were comfortable.

And three sizes too big. I can't wait until they're no longer too big.

And when might that be?
The moment I put a baby inside you.

I find myself swallowing hard, my appetite gone. Dropping the rest of my lunch to the table, I brush crumbs off my hands and force a smile. Luke sees my struggle, though he doesn't question it.

"Now," he goes on, "since we're getting personal, how old are *you*, Lo?"

"Twenty-eight."

He nods, and I guess it's because he estimated around that mark, but then he pauses, and I know he's wondering what could have happened to a twenty-eight-year-old to make them so sad. But, again, he doesn't ask. Whether that's a sixth sense in him or not isn't something I'm about to question. I'm simply thankful. "Well, I have a mental age of twenty," Luke says casually. "So we should get on just fine."

I smile, resting back in my seat and sipping some coffee. "Did you do much damage?"

He frowns across the table. "To what?"

"Yourself." I laugh. "When you went arse over tit in the foyer of my building."

"Shit, yeah." He grimaces, a mixture of embarrassment and probably a reminder of the pain. "I have a tidy bruise on my shin. I swear, that woman must have had rocks in her bags." Reaching down, he hisses, rubbing at the bruise. "In my forty-two years, the only time I've ever fallen over is when I've been steaming drunk." He pouts. "I thought I styled it out well."

I reach over and pat his hand. "No. Not even a little bit. What hurt more, the pain or the embarrassment?"

"I'm not sure," he admits, and I laugh, sitting back again. "I think my street-cred plummeted drastically."

"The bow helped, but only—" I'm cut short when a woman appears at the side of our table, and I look up. I find the most preened, perfect example of a woman I could imagine. Nails, hair, lashes, clothes, it's all perfect. She doesn't speak, just casts her eyes between Luke and me, until I'm forced to look at him to establish if he's going to ask if we can help, or I am. The second I clap eyes on him, it becomes very apparent that Luke knows her. He looks uncomfortable, and that in turn makes me feel uncomfortable.

"Hi," she chirps, but there's no mistaking the resentment lacing her greeting.

Luke visibly withdraws, coughing. "Hi." He forces a smile. It's nervous. I feel my brow furrow as I look back to the woman. She's younger than me, for sure. His daughter, perhaps? But then why the clear animosity? I don't know, but I'm keen to break it. I shove my hand toward her and smile. "Hi, I'm Lo."

Her eyes fall to my hand for a few seconds as it hangs awkwardly between us, and, unsure, I look to Luke. He shakes his head mildly, making me withdraw my offer.

"Nice to see you've moved on," she quips sarcastically. I flinch on Luke's behalf, now pretty sure that I'm faced with an old flame. And she thinks I'm his new flame?

"You're looking well, Jasmine." Luke motions across the table. "This is my friend Lo. Lo, meet Jasmine."

I give him wide eyes, silently asking him what I should do? He just shrugs. "Nice to meet you, Jasmine," I say lamely.

"Whatever," she sniffs, rearranging her posh bag on her shoulder. "I feel it only fair to warn you, Lo. Don't get too attached." She tosses Luke a dark, cutting look, turns, and stomps out, slamming the door behind her.

"Yikes," I quip. "Ex-girlfriend?"

"No." He rakes a hand through his hair. "I was seeing her. There's a big difference, but just you try and tell Jasmine that."

I hold on to my laughter. Just. The poor man. "How many Jasmine's are there, Luke?" I ask, sensing there are a few. My thoughts are only confirmed when he cocks a brow at me. "All mid-twenties?" I ask. And perfectly preened too, I expect. Luke has a type, and I'm quite relived that I'm not it.

"Older women want babies and marriage," he mumbles, shifting uncomfortably in his chair. "Don't judge."

"I'm not judging." I'm totally judging.

"Liar." He scowls through his smirk, and it goes completely over my head as I glance down at my phone.

"Shit!" I jump up, grabbing my bag and coat. "I'll be late back to work."

Luke stands, collecting all of our rubbish. "Same time next week?"

I falter in my movements, slightly taken aback. But I can't deny it's been fun hanging out with him, if only for half an hour. Call me selfish, but it's been a relief seeing someone else's problems, even if they're trivial. It takes my focus off my woes. It's like having a clean slate with Luke. He has no idea about my situation, and, hopefully, given his mental age of twenty—*funny man*—he won't ask. And we can stay in this easy and carefree friendship. And for that reason, I feel comfortable about accepting his offer. "Sure." I skirt round the table. "Thanks for lunch." I reach up and kiss his cheek. "See you next week," I call, jogging out of the coffee house.

Part Three

Luke

Chapter Seven

I pull the cue back and smack the white, sending it sailing up the table. Connecting with the balls on a piercing smack, it disperses them far and wide. I pocket two yellows.

"Jammy bastard," Todd mutters. His Scottish accent is mild after twenty years in London, but it's always thicker when he's pissed off. Like now. Losing. He snarls as he sups his beer. "I'm not playing anymore. You're practicing while I'm not here." He tosses his cue on the floor and stomps his way to the bar.

I laugh my way over to him, keeping hold of my cue. "You know the solution to your problem, right?" I ask, taking a stool as he hitches an eyebrow over the rim of his bottle. "Build yourself a man's room like mine." I motion around the room in my home that's been converted into the best kind of man's hangout. A pool table, a jukebox, a dart board, and a bar. "Then you can practice all you like, and *maybe* someday you'll beat me."

"My apartment has no spare space," he grumbles, slumping over the bar. "And girlie shit is appearing left and right taking up what available space there is left."

"Ohhhh." I flinch on his behalf. "Has she got a drawer yet?"

"Two," he spits. "I've been seeing her for a month." His head hits his forearms on the bar, and I smile at his exasperation. I know how he feels. "Now she wants to know when I eat, piss, and shit."

"Get out, bud. Get out now."

He physically shudders. "How long do you think it'll be before she gets the message?"

"Never. Women are good at ignoring what's staring them in the face," I tell him, slapping him on the back as I get down from my stool. I head for the jukebox and put on some music. Nelly Furtado. "Maneater." Perfect.

Todd slowly lifts his head and tosses me a dark look. "Prick."

I chuckle my way back to the pool table and pot a few more balls. "Hadn't you ought to be going home before she comes looking for you?"

"I might slum it in Luke's Bar." He points his bottle to the comfiest leather couch on the planet. It doubles as a bed for Todd at this stage in most of his relationships. If you can call them relationships. Accidental relationships.

"I like my own space," I tell him, not for the first time. He doesn't ask my permission to invade my couch. "Go see Bert. He'll give you nifty advice."

Todd smiles at the mention of my grandfather. "How is the legend?"

I cast my mind back to yesterday when I paid him my usual visit. "Well, he can still drink me under the table."

"That's not hard," Todd says, polishing off his beer. "You've always been a lightweight."

"Not a lightweight. Sensible. The last time I got so drunk I couldn't remember anything, I wound up with an ankle biter."

Todd sighs, and another smile comes, this time at the mention of my ankle-biter, who isn't much of an ankle-biter anymore. At twenty-three, she's a woman, and that's a fucking kick in the teeth for my ego. Where the hell did those years go? "Where in the world is she now, then?" Todd asks.

"Rio." I grab my phone and pull up my texts, passing it over the table to my friend. He looks at the image that Tia sent me yesterday, smiling brighter.

"Traveling does our girl good."

"And my bank balance bad." I laugh, but I have to agree with him. She looks radiant, full of energy and a zest for life. Her mother thought our girl's plans to travel the world was a hare-brained idea, just an excuse to put off getting a *real* job after she finished university. I, however, saw it as an amazing opportunity to experience life. Maybe because I missed out on that after saddling myself with a kid so young. I don't know. All I know is she's having the time of her life, even if it's costing me through the nose.

Todd hands me back my phone, and I take it, having another quick look at my girl before tucking it away in my jeans pocket. Her eyes are the exact shade of my green, her hair dark too. Her nose slim, her cheekbones cut. She's a stunner.

"Ever worried that she won't come home?" Todd asks what I have refused to ask myself.

"Of course she will. She loves her daddy too much." I dismiss his question with all the casualness it deserves.

"And his bank balance." Todd laughs lightly, leveling serious eyes on me. This worries me, if only because my best mate doesn't do serious. "Or maybe she'll find a man."

I snort my thoughts on that suggestion. I know my Tia inside out, and I know she finds the idea of lumbering herself with a relationship disgusting. I've never argued with her. I'm the only man she needs in her life. Me and my grandfather. "That isn't gonna happen."

"You hope."

God, yes, I do. I can only hope there isn't an older fucker out there like me hitting on her. *Old enough to be your father* is different in our situation. And God, I saw the irony when Lo raised her eyebrow at me at our first lunch when Jasmine stopped by. Jasmine's only a few years older than Tia.

Todd collects his cue from the floor and sets his beer on the edge of the table. "Hey, there's a champagne lunch tomorrow at the Sanderson. Coming?"

"I can't. I'm meeting a friend." It'll be the fourth week in a row that Lo and I have sat in Nero's, stuffing down a sandwich, sipping coffee, and chatting about anything and everything. Everything except her husband. I'm thinking he must be a bit of a dick, but that part of her life is none of my business. It's just refreshing spending time with a woman who I don't want to fuck and, equally, spending time with a woman who doesn't want anything from me, besides conversation. There's never a quiet moment when we're together. She seems to like my jokes, and I can't deny that hearing her laugh makes me feel good about myself. Because I can tell she doesn't laugh often. Our weekly lunch dates have simply become . . . habit. Maybe I should take her some place nicer. I'm guessing her husband doesn't. I shake myself back into the room, remembering we're playing pool. I look to Todd. His mouth is hanging open.

"A friend for lunch?"

"Yeah. Don't ask to come. She won't like you."

"She?"

He has every right to be shocked. "Yes, *she*."

"You screwing her?"

I look at him in disgust. "Lo isn't the kind of woman a man wants to screw." Lo is the kind of woman a man should want to make love to. "Besides, she's married."

His mouth falls open again, his hand blindly sweeping up his beer and taking what looks like a needed sup, his wide eyes on me. What's his problem? "Of all the beautiful, *single* women in London, you get a crush on a married one? You are unbelievable."

Huh? "Whoa." I laugh, pointing my cue at him. "No, no. You're heading in the totally wrong direction. Lo is a friend. There's nothing like that going on. Like I said, she's married." The fact I've concluded she can't be happily married is a moot point. Married is married. Though I would be lying to myself if I haven't thought about what is going on in her life. Whatever it is, it's not good. But she makes me smile, and I make her smile. She's a breath of fresh air as far as women go. I like her. A lot.

Todd's face suggests he's concerned. I don't know why. "How'd you meet a married woman? And, more to the point, how'd you get to know her well enough to have *lunch* together? You see a ring, you walk away." He shows the ceiling his palms and shrugs.

"Simple."

"Not when you nearly killed her," I say over a laugh. It's far from funny. Just one second hesitation on my part would have been the end of Lo. I shudder.

Todd leans forward, nearly halfway across the table. "Come again?"

"She walked out in front of my car. You don't walk away from a woman when you've nearly killed her." I deliberately neglect to mention that I have a horrible feeling Lo purposely stayed on the road waiting for me to take her out. He'll only stamp his assumptions all over that snippet of information and, frankly, I don't want to hear someone say she was suicidal out loud. It's hard enough to listen to my head reaching that conclusion. "Then her dog had a turn and I took her to a vet."

"So you not only nearly killed *her*, you nearly killed her dog too?" Todd falls apart, like it's amusing. It isn't. "Jesus, Luke. So, after nearly running said woman down and nearly killing her mutt, you felt some kind of need to repent your sins?"

I roll my eyes. "I was doing what any decent man would do." Not that I'd expect Todd to understand. The man has skin as thick as an elephant's.

"I agree," Todd replies sincerely. "So you dropped her off at the vet, said your goodbyes, and parted company."

I give him a tired look. I should have kept my mouth shut. I don't know why I expected my best mate to understand Lo's and my relationship. Women serve one purpose to him. Pleasant conversation isn't it. "She needed my help. We got chatting. She listens to what I have to say. I listen to her. It's a general scenario when two people get along."

Todd lets his forehead drop to the pool table and bangs it a few times. "You're doomed. Wait." His head flies up. "I'm sure I've heard your granddad telling a story of a time he nearly ran over a woman."

My jaw tightens of its own volition. "1946," I confirm. "But he was on a bicycle."

"And he fell in love with her, right?"

I scowl. I'm now royally pissed off with the conversation. It's true, though. My grandad tells the story every single time he's drunk. Milly Rose was her name. My granddad's first true love. The woman of his dreams. "Head over heels in love," I confirm. "But once again, Todd, Lo is a friend."

"Idiot," he mutters, taking a shot and missing.

I glare across the table, not bothering to put him straight. It's obvious there's little point. So I finish my beer and get another.

"Fuck it." Todd tosses his cue on the table. "Let's go out and get wasted."

"Not tonight," I say offhand, feeling his incredulous look punching into my back.

"What? Why?"

"Because, my friend, you'll get me into trouble, and I have an early start in the morning." I had to move my meetings forward if I was going to make it to lunch with Lo. Because, and this is something Todd would *not* understand, when a woman means something to you, in a friend-to-friend way, that's just what you do. *I think.* "I need a reasonably early night."

"On a Thursday night?" Todd questions with all the disgust he should. "Fucking hell, Luke. Get a pipe and slippers, why don't you."

I ignore his sarcasm. "I will bid you goodnight." I bow my head, finish my beer, and slam it on the bar with a bang. "The door's that way." I leave the room, knowing full-well that Todd will be on the couch come morning.

Chapter Eight

I exit the boardroom at 12:55 without debriefing my staff and make my escape from the office before someone can stall me. I wriggle my jacket on as I go, ignoring the look of shock from my assistant as I pass her desk. "Back in an hour," I call.

The masses of people crowding the doors of the elevators diverts me to the stairwell, and I take the steps three at a time down the five flights, landing in the lobby, too breathless for my liking. Jogging down the street, I feel around in my pocket when my phone rings. I smile. "Amanda," I answer, keeping up my pace.

"Are you okay?"

"Late for a lunch meeting," I tell her, checking the road for traffic before I jog across.

"Oh, that's a pity. I was going to see if you're free for lunch?"

I slow my jog to a walk as I near Nero's. Dropping lunch with Lo for sex with Amanda should be an easy decision. It *is* an easy decision. "Sorry, I can't cancel." I reach the door and stop, spotting Lo by the fridges looking at the selection of sandwiches. She kills me, spending at least five minutes pondering her choice each time we've met for lunch. It's tuna every time.

Lo turns a fraction, bringing her profile into my view, and I see the sadness I hate so much as plain as day on her face. "Maybe Monday?" I suggest. Amanda and I had great fun once we stumbled home after meeting in a bar last Friday night. Great fucking fun. So much fun, I saw her on Wednesday too.

"Or this weekend?" Her hopeful voice makes me wince.

"Amanda, I'd love to, but I have a date with my grandfather, a shit ton of work to get through, and an employee's fortieth birthday party."

"Oh." Disappointment. I seem to hear it a lot from women. I can't say I like it.

"Monday, yeah?" I push, keen to get into the café. These lunch hours pass by in the blink of an eye, and I'm out here wasting that time trying to pacify a woman I've slept with. Lo looks a bit down. I need to crack a few jokes and raise that smile I love.

"Call me?" Amanda says.

"Sure." I hang up and push my way into the café, heading for the fridges. I reach past Lo and snag a tuna baguette, making her jump.

"Oh." Her hand meets her chest as she turns towards me, and the sadness I saw vanishes. She smiles. "Hey."

"Hey." I dip and kiss her cheek before grabbing a bottle of water. "Usual?" I ask, heading for the counter.

"I'll grab a table." She makes off toward the window and I order our coffees, quickly paying and joining her.

"Nice blouse," I tell her, taking in the black thing with birds scattered all over it. Their wings are spread, as if every one of them are flying free. I wonder if there's a sense of irony in her choice of clothing. I've thought from the moment I met Lo that she has a certain edginess to her dress. And a need to be free.

Lo looks down, patting at the birds. "Thanks. It's old. Like 1975 or something." She looks up and smiles, pulling her plaited hair over her shoulder. "How are you?"

I open the baguette and break it in half, removing the cucumber from Lo's half before passing it to her. "Busy," I reply.

"New buildings flying up all over London, and they all need security." I sink my teeth into my lunch. "You?"

She nods, though it's a little non-committal. "So who's flavor of this week?" she asks, tucking into her own lunch on a concealed smile. This is pretty much the kick-start of all our lunches. My sex life. For some reason, Lo finds my dating shenanigans amusing.

"Amanda, and I just turned her down to keep our date," I inform her, rather smug. I'm certain she thinks I'm a serial dater. To be fair, she isn't wrong, but as if her conclusions on me need any support, the turnover of women seems to be more frequent these past four weeks. Women are getting crazier, I swear. And more boring. One date and they assume you're in a full-blown relationship. Maybe there's something in Lo's claim. Maybe I need to explore the older woman. Come to think of it . . . "Amanda's a little older, so maybe she won't be as needy or shallow."

"How much older?" she asks.

"Twenty-five."

Her mouth, which is currently wrapped around the end of her baguette, widens more. "Wow," she mumbles. "Then I'm ancient." Dropping her lunch, she gives me tired eyes. "You're forty-two, Luke."

"Don't remind me." I reach over and brush away a stray crumb from the corner of her mouth.

"Thanks." She claims her coffee and takes a sip. "I think thirty should be your bottom line." Nodding to herself, I conclude she thinks her suggestion is a good idea.

"Thirty is a bad age," I tell her. "It's the prime age for a woman to want all the things, and I'm not sure I'm ready for marriage and kids."

"Forty, then. It's still younger than you."

I shake my head, keeping my horror from my face. "Divorced. Children. Baggage. No, thanks."

She snorts, falling back in her chair. "You're priceless, Luke. So, basically, all the things you are."

I hold up my finger in protest, munching my way through my mouthful and swallowing. "I'm not divorced."

Her shoulders drop. "You may as well be."

"But I'm not." I give her a cheesy grin. "Thanks to my grandfather." Her brow furrows, prompting me to go on. "He was the only one who told me not to marry Tia's mother when everyone else was trying to wrestle me down the aisle." No one knows me like Pops. Never have, and never will. "He knew I was making a mistake."

"So he stopped you?"

"Yes. Told me I didn't have to be a husband to be a good father. I owe him. He saved me millions in a certain divorce."

She laughs, shaking her head in dismay. "You're terrible."

"Maybe, but I'm terrible *and* still wealthy." I finish my lunch and screw up my rubbish. "Though maybe not for long if my girl keeps rinsing me of cash."

"How's she getting on?" Lo asks, resting her elbows on the table. I've told Lo all about Tia's adventures around the world. I've never seen someone so keen to listen. So I feed her interest weekly with the latest update, which usually involves me transferring money to Tia's account at some point for some reason or another.

"Great. I'm missing her madly, but sometimes you just have to let go."

"Do you get on with her mother?"

"I tolerate her." I motion at her barely touched lunch. "Eat."

Looking down, she blinks a few times before doing as she's told. I don't know how I finish eating my lunch first every time when it's me doing most of the talking. I think I must have given Lo my whole life story over the past month. Told her things I've never thought to tell anyone. About my revolving-door dates, my cheeky-arse daughter. I *never* talk about Tia with the women I fuck. When I said my grandfather knows me better than anyone, I think I may have been mistaken. Lo must surely be catching up. And yet there is so much I still don't really know about her. I know she's quite quirky. I know she adores her dog. I know she works to live, rather than lives to work. Although, and I would never tell her, she hardly lives. I know she loves all things old and vintage. And I know that she isn't happy at home.

"Tell me about your week." I kick myself the second I make my request. *Damn it, Luke.* I've been having lunch with Lo for four weeks now. That question is a no-go zone. As is anything marriage related. Her face drops a little, no matter how much she tries to conceal it, and I kick my brain into action before I lose her and ruin our hour. Perhaps it should bug me that she doesn't open up about her life, especially when the women I fuck rarely stop talking about themselves. But there's something to be said for a woman who doesn't want to throw all her woes at someone. She has a hidden strength that, matched with her sadness, somehow adds to her allure. "How's Boris?" The dog. I can talk about the dog.

Her face immediately lights up, and her smile pulls its usual from me. These smiles are everything. I have to keep them on her face. "He's great. Up to mischief as usual."

"And your plans this weekend?"

Her face falls once more, and this time I drop-kick my arse across London. "Not much." She shrugs, as if it's nothing, when I just know it is everything. "You?"

I shoot her a screwed-up face. "I have a fancy dress party."

Her silver eyes light up. "What's the theme?"

"The fifties, and I haven't a fucking clue what to wear." Snagging the water, I unscrew the cap and neck half the bottle, offering it to Lo when I'm done. She drops what's left of her lunch to a napkin and accepts.

"You've not got your costume sorted?" she asks, finishing the bottle. "Leaving it a little late, aren't you?"

"I have no idea what I'm supposed to wear. Fifties?"

The bottle pauses halfway down to the table. "You have to be Danny Zuko." The sudden excitement radiating from her slight frame is tangible. "It'll be super easy to pull off too."

"Who the fuck is Danny Zuko?"

Her face is one of utter disbelief. "Grease? Only the best film ever made."

"Can't say I've watched it." I shrug. I've heard of it, of course. "What does Danny Zupo wear?"

"Zuko," she says. "Oh my God, I can't believe you've never watched it." I take offense to the shaking of her head, like I may have committed a serious crime. Apparently, I have. "All you need are some old jeans, a white T-shirt, Converse, and a leather jacket. We'll customize it with the T-Birds logo."

"Lo," I say, leaning forward across the table. "Do I look like the kind of man who has a leather jacket and a pair of Converse knocking around in his wardrobe?"

Her pout is nothing short of adorable. "Converse is a staple."

"Not in my world."

"Then they soon will be." She jumps up out of her chair and wriggles on her fur coat. "Come on." She's off out the door, while I'm still sitting at the table wondering what the hell is going on.

I turn on my seat. She's holding the door open. "What are you doing?"

"We're going to find all the ingredients to make you Danny Zuko."

I stand, dubious. "And where might we find those ingredients in"—I look at my watch— "forty minutes?"

Sighing her impatience, she comes and collects me. I'm getting way too much disapproval today. "You forget, Mr. Williamson," she says, dragging me to the door. "I specialize in vintage, and there's a store just around the corner that can help us."

I'm more or less thrust out of the café, and she's off, jogging down the street, her plait bouncing wildly across her back as she goes. "Come on," she yells, looking back at my static form.

I can only laugh as I go after her. Fuck knows what she's going to make me look like, but her enthusiasm is way too infectious to stop her. It's the most alive I've seen her since we met.

. . .

We land in the store, both of us slightly breathless, and the smell that hits me has my nose wrinkling. Jesus, it smells like old socks. Lo must catch my look because she smirks as she heads toward the nearest rail. "My store didn't smell like this," she says quietly, starting to sift through the rails. I've never seen a woman work so fast. She flicks item after item across, seeming to know exactly what she's looking for. "Aha," she sings, yanking out a leather jacket. She thrusts it up against my body and bites her lip in contemplation. "Try it on."

"Yes, miss," I quip, rolling my shoulders to remove my suit jacket. I look around for somewhere to lay it—somewhere non-smelly. There's nowhere. "Here." I thrust it at Lo and accept the leather jacket, trying not to breathe through my nose as I slip it on. "One thing is for sure," I say, taking myself to the nearby mirror.

"What's that?" She appears behind me, pulling and tugging at the material at the back, inspecting me in the reflection.

"I'm not going to score with any women smelling like old socks." I flip the collar up and get a waft of the unpleasant smell again. Lord, have mercy. "Lo, I can't wear this."

"It's perfect." She dismisses me and heads to another rail, yanking a few more pieces out. "This and this." She presents me with a pair of jeans and a T-shirt, which I'm guessing was white once-upon-a-time. Now she's going too far.

"I have a white T-shirt."

"Is it fitted?"

"Fitted? I don't know. It's a white T-shirt. A T-shirt is a T-shirt."

"Wrong." She dumps them on the counter and smiles at the man waiting to serve her. He looks as smelly as his shop. "We'll take these." Lo tosses me a satisfied look. "Oh." Hurrying over to the window, she sings delightedly as she pulls something from the display. "What size shoe are you?"

I almost don't want to tell her. "Eleven."

"And these." She holds up . . .

"What the fuck are they?" I ask, horrified. They're tatty as hell. "Converse."

I drop my head back. "I don't like Danny Lupo's style."

"Zuko." Coming to me, she helps me get the stinky jacket off. "And he was the coolest kid in town."

"I'm not a kid. I'm a forty-two-year-old man." I take my suit jacket back and give it a quick sniff before slipping it back on. Shit, it'll have to go to the dry cleaners. Me too, actually. This smell is embedding in my skin.

Lo's eyebrows form perfect arches as she gazes up at me. "Only forty-two when it suits you." Her head tilts, and I mimic it on narrowed eyes. "I'll wash it all and drop it off to you tomorrow before the party. You'll smell fresh as a daisy and you will most definitely score." She goes to the counter and asks for a total, looking back at me. "Maybe she'll even be over thirty."

I make my way over to her, and though I'm pretty clueless as to what's going on, I know one thing for certain. Lo is thriving. This is her thing. Old, smelly shit and being creative with it. I grab my wallet from my back pocket, the corner of my mouth lifting as she beams up at me. "How much?"

"One-twenty," the smelly guy states, going to his old cash register.

My fingers pause on the notes in my wallet. "Sorry, how much?" I misheard. I must have.

"One-twenty, mister."

"For a pile of old, smelly shit?" I ask incredulously.

"Luke." Lo smacks my arm, but . . . come on. "It's vintage," she argues. "Worth every penny."

I look at her like she's crazy, because she bloody is. "You told me it didn't pay," I remind her, slamming the money on the counter. "And that's why you got a real job." Jesus, one hundred and twenty quid?

"I hadn't got to the profit stage," she grumbles, taking my bag full of stinky stuff. "Stop complaining. You'll look hot."

"I better get laid too," I mutter under my breath, earning a nudge in the shoulder from her. "Ready?"

"Ready."

We wander out and walk to the end of the street, reaching the point where Lo goes her way and I go mine. "I'll call you tomorrow when I've customized your costume." She lifts the bag on a grin, and something tells me that Lo is going to have the time of her life tonight. I don't know whether to feel sad or happy for her. No, that's not true. I do know what I feel. I feel sad, because I can now appreciate exactly what she gave up. I have no idea why she had to give up her dream, like most of her life circumstances, but it's clear this is where she finds true joy. I'm also angry, because *this* was taken from her. Happiness was stolen from her.

"Okay." I dip in my usual fashion and let her kiss my cheek before she wraps her arms around me and hugs the shit out of me, much tighter than she usually does. Lord, she really is excited about her project. "Have a good night," I say.

"You too." She dances off down the street, and I remain where I am for a few moments, just watching her. I've never seen her so animated. I like it. A lot. So what if I look like a total knob? At least Lo's happy.

On an amused smile, I answer a call as I rip my eyes away from her distancing body and head in the other direction. I made that gorgeous, kooky woman happy. Extremely happy. Totally worth it.

Chapter Nine

After visiting Pops on Friday night, I decline Todd's offer to go out on the town, as well as Amanda's offer to *not* go out on the town. Work's crazy, contracts flying in like nobody's business, so Saturday morning in the office isn't avoidable. I work my way through the prepared contracts from the legal team, signing them all off. By three o'clock, I haven't heard from Lo, and I doubt very much I'll make it home before I go to this ridiculous fancy dress party tonight. I grab my phone to call her, stalling when I pull her number up. And it occurs to me . . .

I've never called Lo. She's always called me, and I hate the reason behind that. Far be it from me to judge, but she clearly doesn't want her husband to know about our friendship. I can't blame her. If I were a man, I wouldn't be pleased if my wife was meeting another man for lunch every week. And now dressing him too. It doesn't matter that there's nothing in it. I guess a husband would find that hard to believe.

I fall back in my chair, not liking the direction of my thoughts. She's unhappy. Is he cruel to her? Does he treat her right? I find myself growling at my desk at the mere thought. Lo is the gentlest soul I've ever met. The notion that someone would treat her with anything less than the softness and respect she deserves makes me mad. "Stop, Luke." It's none of my business. But she's a friend. Isn't it right to worry about a friend? And I do worry. Each time I see her and the fleeting flashes of sadness before she quickly corrects it makes me worry. What kind of day has she had? What kind of week? What would her husband do if he found out about me? Come to think of it, how did she pass off her project last night, because I'm sure as shit her husband must have been wondering what she was doing and who she was doing it for. Did he ask? Did she tell? What would he do? Although . . . maybe Lo *has* told him about me. I mean, we're just friends, and anyone who knows Lo knows she's loyal to a fault. Maybe he's so accepting of our friendship, Lo feels disappointed that it's not posing a problem. Maybe she feels undervalued. Is that why she's so sad?

My runaway thoughts are cut dead when my phone rings in my hand. I breathe out air I hadn't realized I was holding when her name flashes at me. "Lo," I answer, getting up and wandering to the window. What is that inside of me? Relief?

"Hey. Are you okay?"

I reach up to my brow and rub away some of the tension. "Yeah, I was just . . ." I pause before I get our conversation off on the wrong foot. One thing I've learned about Lo is that she's sensitive to anything remotely directed towards her home life. "I'm still at the office."

"Do you want me to come there? I have it all ready. Tell me there's a prize for the best dressed, because you, Mr. Williamson, will win it."

I laugh. She sounds so pleased with herself. "I don't know." I look out of the window across the city. It's gray out there, misty and visibly cold. I can barely see the tops of the buildings through the dense fog. "Do you mind coming here? I don't think I'm going to make it out of the office before six. I can shower here and head to the gig."

"Sure. What time do you want me?"

"Well, how long will it take you to work your magic?" I return to my desk and pull up my emails, grimacing at the amount that have landed in my inbox since I left the office yesterday.

She considers my question for a beat. "An hour, I suppose."

"Great." I give her my office address and tell her to text me when she arrives so I can let her in, then hang up and start answering my emails.

At precisely one minute to six, my phone dings just as I'm shutting down my computer. I get up and text her back while on my way to let her in. As I approach the glass doors, the first thing that strikes me is despite her beaming face, she's shaking like a damn leaf, her shoulders are hunched, her lips practically blue. The Tube station is only a few meters down the road. It must be colder than I thought.

I swing the door open, shivering myself when the cold hits me through my thin shirt, and quickly get her inside.

"Cinderella will go to the ball," she sings, holding up her bag of goodies.

With her hair in a ponytail, I can see her ears. They're red raw. "Jesus, Lo"—I place my palms at her temples, covering her ears—"you're freezing."

"It's not that cold," she argues, shrugging me away. I scowl. So does she, though hers is playful. Mine is not.

"You walked here, didn't you?" She'll catch her death, for Christ's sake.

Her eyes leave mine, confirming my suspicions. And, fuck, I feel so fucking guilty. That must have taken her at least forty-five minutes. In the dark. The freezing cold. *Shit.* Why would she walk, damn her? She lives halfway across bloody town. *You know why, Luke.* I pause my mental rant right there, thinking. Thinking thoughts I really don't want to think. Is she that hard-pressed that she can't afford public transport? Which leads me to another question . . .

Does her husband work? Is he a lazy lout who lies around? My guilt transforms into simmering anger that I need to get ahold of quickly.

I shake off the building questions—and unexpected fury—and take the bag from her hand, wrapping an arm around her shoulders in the hope that I can warm her up. "I'm ready for my makeover," I say, leading her to my office. I know I'm going to regret this. Lord knows what I'll look like when she's through with me.

"Nice office," she muses as I show her in. She makes a beeline for my desk and sits herself down. "Very swanky." Here she is in my office. She doesn't suit it. I like that she doesn't suit it. Lo Harper is a far cry from the stiff suits of the men around here, and the salon-perfect hair of the women. She has her own style. A unique style. A kooky style. I never knew, but I quite like kooky. I like that Lo is nothing like any woman I've had in my life, both personally and professionally.

"Swanky?"

"Yeah, swanky." She raises her nose and kicks her feet up onto the polished wooden surface of my desk. "Do I look important?" She takes a pen and starts tapping her cheek, pouting seriously.

I give her a dry look as I head for the attached shower room. *No, Lo, you look adorable.* "I'll be two ticks," I call back, frowning at my wayward thoughts. "Help yourself to coffee. There's a Nespresso machine on the cabinet by the window." Shutting the door behind me, I strip down and step in the stall, making quick work of washing myself down. Once I'm done, I wrap a towel around my waist, brush my teeth, and head back out. She's standing by the window, looking out across the city. Her face is blank, though I can tell her mind is whirling. What about? Whatever it is, she's deep in those thoughts. She didn't even hear me come back in the room. "Lo?"

Spinning around, her eyes fall onto my bare chest and she physically takes one step back, smacking into the window. I flinch at the sound of her body ricocheting off the glass as she quickly covers her eyes. "Ouch, fuck."

I hurry over and take her arm, scanning her up and down. "Are you okay?"

"No."

"Tell me what hurts."

"My eyes."

"What?"

"Your chest."

I look down, a little confused. *My chest?* I roll my eyes. "It's a chest, Lo. You can see them on endless billboards across the city."

"Very funny." She peeks through her split fingers. "Although those chests are harder than yours. And younger."

The cheeky sod. My chest is pretty damn prime. "Let me save you the unbearable sight," I say, snatching the bag up and finding the white T-shirt. I go to slip it on, but stall when she yells at me to stop.

She claims the T-shirt and tosses it on the nearby chair. "We need to fix your hair first. I don't want to spill gel all over it." She rummages through the bag and pulls something out. Her smile is epic. In her hand, a tub of strong hold gel.

"What's that for?"

Ignoring my stupid question, she takes my hand and leads me to my chair, pushing me down and spinning me toward her. The towel splits up my thigh and I quickly fix it before she has a meltdown over that too. Unscrewing the lid, she tosses it on my desk and scoops a huge dollop out of the tub. "How much do you need?" I question as she leans in over my legs and slaps the lot on my head. I feel the slimy goo meet my scalp, the sensation odd and cold.

"A bit," she answers, concentrating on my hair, pulling and tugging, huffing and puffing. She shifts to one side of my legs. Pulls and tugs again. Then huffs her way to the other side, trying to get a better angle.

"Here." I take her waist and place her in front of me, knocking her thighs apart so she can straddle my lap. "Better?"

She's still as she looks down at me.

"Better to split your thighs than mine," I point out, indicating to the sliver of a gap in the towel on a grin. "If you had a meltdown at my epic chest, imagine your reaction to my epic di . . . ouch!" I laugh, rubbing at my bicep where she just caught me a treat with a gel-covered palm. Lo wants to laugh. I can see she desperately wants to laugh. And I can't lie, I want her to as well. *Come on, Lo. Give in to it.*

"You're terrible," she sighs, grinning as she goes back to my hair. Okay, so it wasn't a laugh, but that grin? Magic. I watch her as she goes about doing whatever it is she's doing, tugging and pulling, smoothing and flicking. She's more comfortable now, leaning in close, her legs rubbing against mine. "Maybe a wig would be better," she says, almost to herself.

"No way, Lo," I scoff as she stands back, giving my hair the once-over. "I draw the line at wigs." I'm already way out of my comfort zone, but she's gone to too much effort. I can't refuse now.

"Perfect," she declares, reaching forward and tweaking a little bit. "Get dressed." Wandering to the window again, she keeps her back to me as I do as I'm bid. I pull the T-shirt over my head carefully so not to ruin my hair, catching a waft of the now pleasant smell. "You washed it all?"

"Of course. We can't have potential, *appropriately* aged women put off by the stench of smelly socks, can we?"

"So you agree? The clothes stank." I pull on the jeans and slip my feet into the old Converse. "The jeans are way too long."

"We'll turn them up."

When I come to the jacket, I freeze mid-swing of it over my shoulders, spotting something emblazoned on the back. *Shit.* "Did you do this?" I ask, taking in the design. She could have just painted it on with a bit of Tip-Ex, but no. Instead, she's sewn in the entire design with white cotton. It must have taken her all night.

"It was fun." Her shoulders jump up, but she doesn't face me. "Are you done?"

I quickly push my arms through the sleeves and straighten myself out, oddly wanting to impress her. Wanting to do her skills and effort justice. "Done."

She turns, her eyes clenched shut. "Glasses?"

"What?"

"There's shades in the inside pocket."

I frown at the pocket as I dip in, pulling out a pair of Ray Bans. She really does have everything covered. "Check," I declare, slipping them on. When Lo opens her eyes, I expect her to laugh at the sight of me, because I'm certain I must look like a total twat. But she doesn't. She just beams, so brightly, I'm glad I have the shades on to protect me from the glare.

"I did good." She comes over and has a little faff with my collar, and then my hair. "Seriously, you'll be fighting them off."

I snort and head for the mirror. "I'll believe it when—" I catch my reflection. Wow. "I look younger." *Much* younger. I smile to myself, making a mental note to send Tia a picture.

"But still not young enough to date early-mid-twenties women, Luke."

"Spoil my fun, why don't you." Lo hands me something. "A comb?"

"Every true T-Bird carries a comb."

I accept and run it through my hair with flair, just how I imagine a cool fifties dude to do it. I don't know if I'm on the money, but Lo falls apart laughing, and my heart soars. "Did I get it right?" I ask, strangely wanting her approval.

"It's uncanny." Walking to the table, she collects her bag. "I'd better be going."

What is that inside me? Disappointment? I have the most fun with Lo. So . . . "Hey, can't you come?" Something tells me she doesn't get out much. Or can't afford to.

"To the fancy dress party?"

"Yes. Let's get drunk and do the jitterbug." I have no clue if the move I just made resembled anything close to the jitterbug. But she laughs, so that's good enough.

"Thanks, but I really should get home."

I pout, nibbling my lip in thought. "Your husband doesn't know we're friends, does he?" My dumb question falls out without warning. But, clearly, I have to ask. And I hate the immediate falter of her smile.

"Not many women have male friends." She shrugs. "Unless they're gay."

"I'm not gay."

"Oh, I know that," she says over a laugh.

"You don't think he'd approve of me?"

Shaking her head, she wanders to the door. "I just don't think he'd understand our friendship."

What's there to understand? We're mates. There's nothing in it, other than coffee and laughs. And the odd insult. But, I suppose I get it. After all, I'm single, and even if I do say so myself, I wasn't hard done by when God gave out looks. He'd be threatened, and I don't want to make Lo's life any more difficult than I assume it already is. "So you won't come?"

"Thank you, but I don't want to cramp your style *or* your chances of scoring with a hot, *mature* lady." She flashes me a cheeky grin as she exits, leaving no room to try to convince her. I shouldn't, and I won't. Our friendship isn't about pressure. It's about an easiness we're both quite attached to. And not only that, how would she explain going out to a party with another man if she hasn't told her husband about her lunches with another man?

"I'll walk you out." I grab my keys and wallet, following on behind. "Can I drop you home?"

She shakes her head, giving me that knowing smile she always does. "I can walk."

"No." She isn't walking, not when I can drive her. If she's so worried about her husband getting huffy about me, I'll drop her at the end of her road. Taking her arm, ignoring her startled state, I lead her out of the building to my car. "In," I say, pushing her down into the seat. When I land in the driver's side, I find her grinning across the car. "What?"

"I can't take you seriously when you look like that." Her head falls back and she bursts into fits of giggles. I would scowl. If I wasn't laughing too.

Part Four

Lo

Chapter Ten

I had Luke drop me off at Sainsbury's so I could collect a few bits to make dinner, and while I was there I picked out Billy's favorite red wine, a total extravagance at fifteen pounds a bottle, but I don't let it play too hard on my conscience. I also allowed myself the pleasure of a bottle of white wine, though given the expense of Billy's bottle, I settled for the cheapest I could find. Wine is wine.

After unpacking the bags and taking Boris for a quick walk around the block, I pour a glass and take a tentative sip. Oh God, that tastes so good, cheap or not. Over the next half hour, I prepare a lasagna and set the table for two, even adding a candle. On my way home, I decided to make a special effort this evening, anything to get Billy out of the bedroom and some food in his tummy. We'll chat. Talk about . . . anything. The bad days have monopolized the good these past few weeks, so I'm risking meeting annoyance. Or, if I'm lucky, sullen acceptance. I'm not sure which I'd resent more.

Placing the lasagna in the middle of the table along with a bowl of salad, I have one last sip of wine before hurrying up the stairs to get Billy. Pushing my way through the door, I find him in his usual position, on his back, watching sports on the TV. He looks across at me, expressionless, but I still slap a huge smile on my face.

"I have a surprise for you." I walk over and offer him my hand.

"What?"

"It's a surprise. You need to come with me."

"Lo," he sighs, dashing my hopes. "I'm really not in the mood for surprises."

"Well, maybe I'm inflating it a bit. It's not really a surprise, more a treat." I jiggle my hand. "I'll help you. Humor me. Please?"

On another sigh loaded with exasperation, he starts to shift to the edge of the bed, ignoring my offered hand. I don't take it to heart too much. At least he's coming. Watching him get himself up is painful. He hisses and winces constantly, and I find myself doing the same. He shuffles like an old man, wrapped up in his dressing gown, and I hang back, only a little, to steady him if he staggers.

When he's finally negotiated the stairs, I move past him, rushing to the kitchen door, and wait for him to join me. He's out of breath by the time he makes it to me, but I try not to feel too guilty. He can sit down soon, relax, and enjoy a nice meal and a glass of his favorite red.

"Ta-dah," I sing, sweeping my arm out in the direction of the table.

Billy comes to a stop by the door, taking in the set table.

"I've made lasagna. Cheap and cheerful so I could treat you to your favorite wine." I run over to the table and grab the bottle that's been breathing for half an hour, presenting it to him on a bright smile. "I'll pour for you." I fill his glass.

Billy starts to shuffle toward the table, still taking it in. When he arrives at the edge, I point to his chair. "I put a cushion on it so it's soft for you."

"I'm not hungry, Lo," he breathes, not looking at me.

I don't let his rejection dampen my efforts. "You can have just a little." I spoon some of the lasagna from the dish onto his plate. "Wash it down with plenty of wine."

"I said, I'm not hungry."

"You must be hungry. What have you eaten today?"

"Nothing."

"There you are, then." I take his elbow and try to pull him to his chair, but he doesn't budge.

"Why aren't you listening to me? I'm not hungry." He shakes me off and looks at me, and I retract, feeling injured.

But I won't give up. We need some time together, even if it's just to look at each other. "Then just have a drink. We'll talk."

"About what?"

"I don't know. Anything."

"I'm not in the mood to talk."

"Then just—"

"No!" In the flash of an eye, he lashes out, swiping his arm across the table and sending everything crashing to the floor. The smash of dishes and glass is deafening, and I jump back on a cry of shock. "I'm not fucking hungry!" he bellows. "I'm not fucking thirsty! I don't want to fucking talk!" He waves his arms around and starts hacking violently, bracing his arm on the table to steady himself. I rush to his side to help him but get shoved back with a push into my shoulder.

"Billy," I cry, slipping on a puddle of wine. I crash to the floor, my elbow catching the table on the way. "Shit," I yelp, scrambling to sit myself up. Silence. A deafening silence. Looking up at my husband, my eyes wide, I watch as he starts to heave, coughing in between, his startled eyes darting. He looks as stunned as I feel, and I wait for him to apologize, to fall to his knees and help me up.

But he doesn't.

Instead, he clenches his eyes closed for a few painful moments, turns slowly, and walks out of the kitchen, leaving me behind with nothing to do but stare at the door after he pulls it closed.

I blink, feeling . . . numb. *Who was that man?* Swallowing, unsure how to feel, how to react, what to do, I cast my eyes across the floor. I'm surrounded by lasagna and wine. Surrounded by anger. I stare at the mess for an age, like it might clean itself up. And then, out of the blue, like my emotions are struggling to keep up with the rollercoaster of shit being served, I feel my lip wobble. I fight it with all I have, yelling at myself in my head. I deserved his anger. I pushed too hard. "You stupid, stupid woman," I croak, tears threatening as I assess through my blurry vision how far the splashes of pasta and wine have stretched and, also, sadly calculating how much of my time it will kill clearing it all up. Probably the rest of the evening. And then, out of nowhere, surprising me, something else creeps up on me.

Anger.

I try to push it back. I try so hard. But he just wiped away over twenty pounds of food and wine. Not to mention the crockery. I walked five miles to save a few quid, and he just threw it away. Like he just threw me away, without a care that I could be hurt. And that total disregard of me stings even more.

The anger only fuels my tears. Swallowing down the lump in my throat, I drag myself to my feet and fetch a cloth to get started, but a knock at the door sounds, stalling me. I momentarily consider ignoring it, but then I hear Billy's mother calling through the letterbox. I wipe my cheeks of tears as I make my way to the door. Could this night get any worse? Of all the times to just *pop in.*

Her face is a picture when she lays her eyes on me. "What on earth, Lo?" She shakes her head in disappointment, pushing her way into the hallway. "How many times have I got to tell you? Billy doesn't need to see you blubbering all over the place. Hasn't the poor man got enough on his plate?" I watch her wander into the kitchen and look around. "What happened?"

I shut the front door, searching deep for the strength to deal with Linda. Isn't it enough that I have a dying husband without his mother's constant hostility and negativity?

She drops her worn old bag to the kitchen worktop and puts her hands on her hips. The jeans she has on are ill-fitted, the jumper I'm pretty sure is Billy's father's, and her hair is scraped back in a very unflattering ponytail. I'm mentally annihilating her, because I simply do not have the energy to speak up and tell her to fuck off.

"Well?" she presses.

I stare at her as she waits for me to answer. "I can't be his emotional punch bag, Linda." I turn, walking away from her.

"No, you're his wife, and you will do what's needed to be there for him."

"I've tried, and I keep having it thrown back in my face. I can't take it any longer. He's given up. I don't know what to do anymore."

"You selfish little cow!"

Oh God. This woman.

I run up the stairs. I cannot stand there and take this right now. First my husband, then his horrible mother. No. I can't be her emotional punch bag either. My heart is beating frantically by the time I slam my bedroom door and fall against it. *You're his wife and you will do what's needed to be there for him.* I'm trying. With everything I am, I'm bloody trying.

And nothing is good enough. Nothing works. I'm not being heard anymore, not even seen. And for the first time in two years, I ask . . . what about me? Because this fucking hurts.

I can't.

I can't do this.

I. Cannot. Do. This.

I pull my phone from my pocket and dial Luke. He answers on the second ring. "'Lo?"

It's only when I hear the concern in his voice that I suddenly wonder what the hell I'm supposed to say. So I just say his name, unable to hide the emotion in my voice. "Luke."

"Where are you?"

"At home. I live—"

"I know where you live. I'll be there in twenty minutes."

He knows where I live? I know I should be asking how, but instead I find myself saying, "I'm a mess. I need a shower. I—" I stop, realizing I sound panicked.

"Just get yourself to the end of the road. I'll be there." There's concern in his voice now, and the knowledge that someone is actually worried about me, rightly or wrongly, makes me feel less worthless. Less demoralized. Less despised.

"But I'm a mess," I repeat on a whisper, looking down at my frightful state.

There's silence for a few moments, and it gives me a chance to consider what on earth I'm doing. Escaping, that's what. Running away, because now I have a friend to run to.

"I don't care what you look like. Just make sure you're wearing a smile," he finally says, soft and reassuring. "Okay?"

That alone makes me smile, even if it's through the tears still hampering my vision. "Okay," I concede, hearing the sound of a car door closing.

"I'm on my way, darling." I hear the smile in his words, and then the line goes dead.

I drop my phone to my chest and breathe in deeply. Someone's coming to rescue me from my nightmare. Because someone actually cares.

Chapter Eleven

I wander down my street, seeing the glaring headlights of a car parked up ahead. My heartbeat quickens with every step I take, and I stutter in my pace more than once, each time considering turning and running back. I shouldn't be escaping. I should be cleaning up the mess in the kitchen. It's a mental debate I'm still having when the driver's door of his car opens and he steps out. My feet don't stutter this time. They come to an abrupt halt, watching as he strides around the front of his car, visibly assessing me. In the twenty minutes I had, I only managed to wipe myself down and change into clean jeans and a T-shirt. It's an improvement, but . . . still. Then again, Luke is still dressed as a fifty's throwback, so who looks the most absurd is debatable.

"Okay?" he asks cautiously as he sinks his hands into his pockets and widens his stance.

I nod, motioning down my body. "I told you I looked a mess."

Resting his shoulder against a nearby lamppost, he swallows, and I see his Adam's apple bob. "You don't look a mess. But where's that smile I told you to wear?"

I try. I try with all I have, but I just can't seem to muster the smile he's demanded. I've never seen Billy like that. He's never spoken to me in such a way. I'm destroyed by it, and I know Billy will be too. But his frustration and anger is getting the better of him. And now it's getting the better of me.

Luke pushes off the lamp post by his shoulder and approaches slowly. "I'll ask again; where's that smile?" His eyebrows hitch in question. Then he waits patiently. "I'm standing on the street dressed like this, and you can't smile for me?"

I start to feel the corners of my mouth twitch.

"Go on," he chants under his breath, his eyes falling to my lips as he bends at the waist, bringing his face closer to mine. "Give me that smile."

My mouth stretches wide, unable to stop myself from feeding his playfulness.

"There it is." He smiles himself, satisfied, his bright green eyes shining with a delight that baffles me. "My day has been made." Straightening to his full height, he flips up the collar of his leather jacket.

I laugh under my breath. "I can't believe I'm doing this."

"Doing what?" he asks seriously. "Smiling? Laughing?"

I shrug. "Yes, actually."

"Why?"

Another shrug. "Maybe because I don't have much to smile about." I didn't mean to say that, and I fidget as a result.

He regards me closely for a few seconds, and I can tell he's trying to surmise why that might be. I look away, worried that he might discover my secrets if he looks deeply enough into my eyes. I mentally plead with him not to ask, but when he draws breath, I fear the worst. I'll run back home. I'll avoid that conversation like the plague. I'm happy to let him think whatever he might be thinking, because the alternative is spilling my woes and having him judge me . . . like I'm judging myself. Judging myself for allowing a friend in. Someone to talk to. To laugh with. Someone who doesn't know of my plight. Someone who doesn't look at me with dreaded sympathy. *Or hatred.*

I peek up at Luke and wait. And then he reaches for my face and runs the pad of his thumb under my eye, catching a stray tear. "I promise not to ask," he whispers quietly, gently. "If you promise to dry these tears." I give him a small smile. "That's my girl," he says, seizing my hand and leading me to his car.

"Not so fast." I struggle to keep up with him as I fight away the guilt and tell myself that tonight I will forget about everything. I need to forget about everything, if only to save my sanity. I have to press the reset button. I know Luke can help me do that. "Thank you," I say out of the blue, but I know he knows what I mean when he looks at me out the corner of his eye, hiding his smile.

"No sweat. You've done me a favor." He opens the door and helps me in.

"How?"

"Well, clearly this look is amazing on me. I had women falling at my feet left and right."

"More than usual?"

"More than usual," he confirms, shutting the door and rounding the car.

I turn in my seat towards him. "And you weren't tempted by any of them?"

Starting the car, he pulls off down the road. "Too old."

"Oh, boy." I laugh, returning forward. "You're no spring chicken."

"Charming. You're such a great friend."

Friends. Such a simple but needed position. "Thank you for being my friend." He'll never know how much I need him.

"We shared a near-death experience. Two actually. *And* in the space of two minutes. If that's not a sign that we should be friends, I don't know what is." He reaches across the car and squeezes my hand. "And thank you for being mine. Besides, I can tell I'm the only thing making you smile in your life right now. Who am I to take that away from you?"

"You have no idea," I say easily, but I know he won't push for more.

"Like I said, I won't ask." Luke smiles reassuringly, and once again I'm just so thankful that he nearly killed me all those weeks ago. "Now, what do you want to do?"

"I don't know." I never gave it a thought. My emergency call was made in a panic. "I'm not exactly dressed for anything special."

"Hmmm," he muses, running eyes down my seated form as he pouts. "You're not really, are you?"

"You can be quiet." I sniff, tugging on the sleeve of his leather jacket. "I look a whole lot better than you."

"True." He indicates and takes a corner.

"Where are we going?"

"To my place."

"Your place?" Luke's place. I'm suddenly riddled with thoughts of what Luke's place is like. I can guess. A total bachelor's pad, I bet.

He shrugs off my question, like what's the problem? What is the problem, I guess? I shrug too and settle, looking around his car. It's still sparkling. "Have you had this cleaned?" I ask, not noticing one of Boris's hairs in sight.

Luke shifts in his seat, looking at me out the corner of his eye. "I looked like a yeti every time I got out of my car," he mumbles, looking down at his lap and having a quick brush of his thighs as I smile like crazy. "Tell me how your little friend isn't bald, because I'm pretty sure he left his coat in my car."

I grin. "I'm sorry."

"You look it." He reaches over and nudges me in my upper arm, spiking a chuckle from me, as I admire his devilish smile. He has the loveliest smile. Pure and happy.

For a few moments, there's silence, and I quickly conclude that to be a bad thing, as it gives my mind space to fill with guilt. Meeting for lunch in my spare hour is one thing. A Saturday evening out? When Billy is in such a horrid state? When Linda is there to judge and curse me. "You have to keep talking so . . ." I bite down on my lip. "So . . ." What can I say? So I don't fall into despondency and question my integrity?

"Ever been to a fancy dress party?" he asks quickly.

I deflate in my seat. "Yes, lots. You? Before tonight, I mean."

"Nope. And I don't plan on going to another. What did you dress up as?"

My lips straighten and I look out of the window, trying not to see Billy and me together, raring to go and knocking them all dead with our amazing homemade costumes. I spent weeks on those things. We looked ace. "Wilma Flintstone."

"No way."

"Yes way." I breathe in and look across the car to Luke.

"You made that costume too, didn't you?"

"Of course."

Because Luke just knows.

I silently take it all in while we wait at the electric gates as they slowly glide open. Wow. I'm saying it over and over in my head, awestruck by the pile of bricks coming into view. Luke either doesn't notice my shock, or he chooses to ignore it. "You live here alone?" I ask, mentally calculating how many bedrooms there must me. Seven, at least. And the triple garage to the side seems to have a self-contained apartment above it.

"All alone," he muses, driving up the brick-laid road to the front of the house. "Except for Arabella when she's in town."

"Arabella?"

"My sister," he confirms, turning off the engine and jumping out, hurrying to open my door for me. "She flits between here and

Milan. She's in the fashion industry and stays with me whenever she's in town."

I nod and glance around at my surroundings. "It's quite a bachelor pad."

"It's a house. Bricks and mortar."

"It's *lots* of bricks and mortar," I point out.

"It's a house," he repeats quietly, extending his hand toward me. I read between the lines and conclude that what he's trying to tell me is that money is nothing to him. Easy to say when you have stacks. I've already decided that Luke is more than comfortable. His business, his suits, his office. His garage alone would probably fund the life-saving surgery that Billy—

I swallow and wipe my mind clear.

"I can see I need to work really hard to keep those thoughts of yours from wandering," Luke says gently, turning his hand over to prompt me to give him mine. "But I'm never one to turn my back on a challenge."

My hand lifts and retracts a few times, my mind telling me that this is all so very wrong. Everything about it. Yet my hand wants to go forward more than it wants to go back, and we're touching a second later. He applies a light pressure, and although it's only my hand in his, I feel like a magic blanket of safety has just swathed me in its warmth. I look up at him. He's studying me carefully.

"I'm your friend, Lo. Tell me," he whispers, moving in closer to me, like a silent offer of support in case I need it when I confess.

But I won't confess. Never. "You promised not to ask."

"You promised not to cry."

I blink, encouraging a drop of water to trickle down my cheek. I didn't realize I was crying, and that's sad in itself, because I'm at the point that it happens so often, I'm almost immune to sensing it. I use my spare hand to brush at my cheek.

"You don't even feel your tears anymore," Luke sighs, taking the one step closer that has me bandaged in his arms, except this time mine aren't bunched between us, so I wrap them around his back and hold him as tightly as he's holding me. I wouldn't have guessed that the cuddle he gave me at the vet could be beaten. How wrong I was, because now, here, it's on another level of comfort. My cheek is pressed against his chest, my head buried under his chin. "I want to tell you that everything will be okay," he says quietly. "But I can't because I don't know."

He breaks away and holds my cheeks in his palms. Spending a few moments wiping my eyes, his gaze flits across my face as I stand silent and still for him. The last time someone held me like this, looking into my eyes—*caring about what's there*—was on my wedding day. It's the last time I felt warm. It's the last time I felt cherished. That I matter.

"Most people avoid me," I tell him. "Most people run in the other direction, like they're scared my sorrows are contagious. But you're here."

"The only thing contagious about you, Lo, is your smile." He squeezes my cheeks. "Give me one."

It's an effort, especially with my mind constantly questioning whether I should be friends with Luke, whether it's appropriate, but I manage a small lift of my lips, albeit shyly.

"Poor attempt," he scolds, very seriously. "Try again."

I roll my eyes. "It's hard to smile when my face is being squished."

"But you look so cute with your face all squashed." He removes his hands, and this time my smile's not forced. It breaks out as if it's been waiting a century to be let loose. "More like it." Grabbing my face again, he re-squishes, crushing my smile but making me burst into laughter. "God, that sound." He slings an arm around my shoulders and leads me to the front door. "Would you like a drink?"

"I'll have what you're having."

He opens the door and I walk into an open, airy entrance hall, with a black and white tiled floor and stark white walls. It would be quite clinical, if it wasn't for the elaborate glass chandelier, the huge pieces of abstract art, and the mirrored furniture. "I'm having a whiskey." Luke walks through double doors to the right, and I follow, entering a massive . . . pub? There's a pool table, a jukebox, a dartboard, and a bar.

"Big enough television?" I ask, pointing at the wall, which is virtually covered from end to end with a massive screen.

"Welcome to Luke's Bar." He holds up a bottle. "Whiskey?"

I grimace, giving him his answer, so then he lifts a bottle of white and I nod. He gets to pouring while I look around. "This is a man's paradise."

Luke laughs as he removes his leather jacket and drapes it on a bar stool before collecting the drinks and wandering over. "I guess all that's missing is the strip pole, right?" He hands me my wine as I chuckle, and watches as I bring it to my lips. "Good?"

I'm no wine expert, the cheap stuff always doing the trick, but I can tell that this is no cheap stuff. "Very."

"Come. We'll hang out in the kitchen. You hungry?"

"I wouldn't mind just hanging out in here," I tell him, spotting a gaming machine in the corner. "Oh my God, is that PAC-MAN?" I'm on my way over to investigate quickly, excited. "I love PAC-MAN."

"Not so fast." Luke catches me around my waist with his forearm and lifts me from my feet. "It's members only in here." He carries me out, and I frown the entire way.

"Members only?" I ask when he sets me on my feet in the hall-way. "Then can I join?"

"No."

"Why?"

"Well, because I'm pretty sure you're not a bloke. It's men only." He smiles at my disgusted face.

"Who says?"

"Todd."

"Who's Todd?"

"My best friend and co-owner of the bar." He thumbs over his shoulder to his man's paradise.

"Todd's sexist," I grumble. "I want to join."

"I'll run it by Todd."

"What? Whether or not I'm permitted entry?" Is he serious?

"Yes." He shrugs. "It's a brotherhood thing." Luke walks off and looks back, jerking his head for me to follow. I kick my feet into gear and tail him to the kitchen.

"Is Todd single too?"

Luke laughs, like I haven't asked a simple question. "Not according to the woman he's been sleeping with for a month."

"Oh." I think I understand. "It's more to her than it is to him?"

"Something like that. Todd's my age and still not ready to settle down."

"Sounds like someone I know," I quip seriously, pouting when Luke looks to the sky tiredly.

"They all turned out to be needy, precious, or complete nutters. If I'm unlucky, all three."

"What about the current flavor of the . . . week? Has she been proven to be any of those things?"

"Not yet." We arrive in the kitchen and Luke goes to the fridge. "I have high hopes for this one."

I take a seat at the breakfast bar, gazing around as he rummages through the contents of his fridge, presenting a pot of salsa and some Doritos. He looks quite happy with his find as he joins me, offering the crisps. "So she's nice?" I ask, dipping and crunching my way through a Dorito.

"She ticks all the right boxes at the moment, I suppose. Who knows, but everything happens for a reason, right?"

I look up at him. I don't agree. Because if he's right, what's the reason for your husband getting cancer, and what's the reason for him dying from that cancer? Everything happens for a reason?

Luke is so far off the mark, he may as well be shooting from another country. "Maybe," I murmur, returning to my crisps.

There's not one single second of silence as we sit and snack, Luke making a conscious effort to keep the conversation flowing. I'm grateful. It's easy, so easy to be in his company, and it's so easy to laugh at his constant teasing and dry wit. "How's Tia?" I ask, as Luke refills my glass.

"She's good. Still enjoying her adventures. She's in Thailand at the moment. Island hopping."

"Lucky thing," I muse, envious of her free spiritedness, of the freedom she has to just . . . go. "Sounds amazing."

"Doesn't it?" Luke replies wistfully. "To be that carefree. To go where the feeling takes you. Of course, it helps that Daddy's there to pick up the bill."

I laugh when he gives me a sardonic smile. "I'm sure she appreciates it."

"It's my own fault. I've overcompensated in her life with material things."

"Overcompensated?"

"A lack of a stable family unit."

"Why didn't you marry her?" I never asked him the finer details.

"It just didn't feel right. She was terribly clingy. I did the right thing, though half my family didn't speak to me for months. Pops did, though."

"Because he knew."

"Yeah, he knew." Every time Luke mentions his grandfather, I can't help but notice a certain twinkle in his eyes. He loves him a lot.

"It must have been a shock to find out she was pregnant."

He laughs. "You mean the congratulations card she sent me?"

"Nice touch."

"I thought so too." He holds the salsa out for me. "Last scoop."

I accept his offer and watch as he goes about clearing up the empty crisp packet and tossing the jar in the bin. And I think . . . he's given up a night out with a guaranteed score to sit here talking nonsense and eating Doritos with me. "Thank you," I say again, just for the sake of it. I know he knows I'm grateful.

"Be quiet, Lo."

"But I ruined your night."

"No, actually, you saved me, remember?"

He's probably just being polite. "I don't want you to ever feel obligated to be friends with me."

"Obligated?" He starts to wipe his hands on a tea towel. "I don't feel obligated, Lo. Never. You're like a breath of fresh air."

I feel my forehead wrinkle. "A breath of fresh air?" He must be deluded.

"Yes," Luke confirms. He's definitely deluded. There's nothing fresh about me. I'm polluted. My life is polluted. Everything about me is polluted. Luke sighs. "Lo, trust me when I say that. All I've ever known are women who are only happy if they're showered with gifts. A broken nail is the end of the fucking world. A ladder in their tights will bring the night to a close, because God forbid anyone sees them looking anything less than perfect. A streak in their fake tan makes them suicidal. You're different." He looks at me and smiles. "I only had to hug you to feel your sorrows lift from your shoulders. And I'm hedging my bets that those sorrows aren't caused by a wardrobe malfunction or a bit of rain in your hair. So, yes, you are a breath of fresh air."

I stare at him, momentary stunned, but quickly grasp how serious he is. "You're a breath of fresh air to me too," I eventually confess.

Resting his elbows on the breakfast bar, he leans in. "Wanna have your arse whooped at pool?"

And this is why I love Luke so much. He just makes everything between us so easy. No pressure. No conditions. It's a simple, pure friendship, and I've truly never had one like it before. I've never needed it so much as I do now. "You're giving me a pass to the bar?"

"Well, you're not a piece of arse to me, more a mate, so I figure, as a mate, you're allowed a pass. Just don't tell Todd."

Brushing off my hands, I jump up off the stool. "Silly man," I sigh, wandering back to Luke's Bar. "Although you need to change out of that stupid costume first or you'll put me off my game."

"Fighting talk, darling," he calls to my back. "And I thought you said I looked hot."

"I didn't want to bruise your ego." I hear him jogging behind me on a laugh, and as I head into the bar, he heads upstairs to change. I grab a cue and a piece of chalk and coat the end generously. I have no idea what I'm doing, but this is what they do whenever I've watched it on TV. I close one eye and inspect the end. "Good enough," I say to myself, heading for the table. There are still some balls on the cloth, some in the pockets, so I set about collecting them up and putting them in the triangle that I find hanging on the wall by the dart board.

"What are you doing?" Luke asks as he enters, pulling a black T-Shirt down his chest.

"Setting up the balls."

"All wrong." He moves the red and yellows about, and when he's done it looks just like how I had them. Random. I frown at his work as he carefully lifts the triangle and hangs it back on the wall. Wandering over to me, he takes my cue and replaces it with another. "That's mine," he says.

I look at my new cue. "But I want that one."

"Tough." Pointing to the end of the table, he smiles, like he's privy to something. "You can break."

"Break what?"

"The balls." He laughs, setting the white on a little dot. "Just smack it up the table."

"I know what I'm doing," I lie, pouting as I bend over the table and get my aim right. Pulling back the cue, I strike the white with all my might, and the tip of my cue skims over the top, sending it crawling up the table slowly. "Oh."

"Good shot," he teases, laughing his way to my end of the table.

"I'll get it right this time," I tell him, collecting the white and re-setting it on the dot.

"Oh, no." Luke bumps me out of the way and levels up his cue. "You don't get another go."

"Why not?" I ask indignantly as he hits the ball with accuracy, sending the reds and yellows scattering across the green cloth.

"Because that's the rule." Two reds fall into pockets, and I balk, tossing him a disbelieving look. "Champion," he says simply, dipping and inspecting the balls' positions, considering his next shot. I stand back and proceed to watch as Luke pots every single red ball on the table one after the other with ease, leaving only yellows and the single black. "Silly woman," he muses, leveling up his last shot and sinking the black. I stare at the table in awe mixed with irritation as he unbends slowly and blows the end of his cue. "Best of three?"

Turning my eyes to his, I plan on scowling, but when I find his green eyes firing off sparks, his lips stretched in that adorable smile, my plan fails and I wind up smiling back at him. "Show-off."

"I get a lot of practice." He shrugs. "I'll let you win next time."

Snorting, I hang my cue up on the rack. "I don't like this game. Let's do something else."

"Like?"

I ponder that for a few minutes, scanning his bar. Darts? I'll lose. PAC-MAN? I'll lose. The jukebox? I'm not up for embarrassing myself with my diabolical dance moves. My shoulders slump as the colossal TV comes into my view. And I have the best idea. "We'll watch Grease," I declare.

"That TV is dedicated to sport." Obviously Luke doesn't like my idea. "It's terrible enough you're in here without approved membership from all board members. You're not putting a girlie film on my sports TV." He hangs up his cue and heads for the bar. "More wine?"

"Please." I find the remote control on the bar, turning the TV on while Luke gets our drinks. "Oh look." I find what I'm looking for on a streaming network and load. "Oops."

Looking up at the screen, he groans. "Fine. But if Todd asks, this never happened."

"It never happened," I say on a sigh, expressing how stupid I think his rules are.

"Popcorn?"

"Sure." I take my wine and park myself on the huge leather couch. "Sweet or salted?" I ask. "And we can't be friends if you say salted."

"Always sweet." Luke leaves the room as I smile, returning moments later with two big bowls of the fluffy stuff, lowering to the other end of the couch. I press play and kick my shoes off as he passes me a bowl. "Here." He collects my feet and sets them on his lap, and I recline back, starting to munch my way through my popcorn.

"It's been years since I watched this," I tell him, settling in. Luke sinks back into the couch, resting his bowl on the tops of my feet. I don't want to count my chickens, but he looks immediately engrossed as I study him watching one of my favorites. "Luke," I call quietly, tearing his attention from the TV. He looks across to me and the piece of popcorn I'm holding, dropping his mouth open. I aim, fire, and he catches, smiling as he chews.

"Thanks." Moving my feet, he mirrors me, reclining at the other end so we're facing each other. "Open."

I do as I'm told and he shoots. And scores. And that's what we do for the next hour, our attention split between Grease and the popcorn we're throwing at each other. Luke catches every piece. I do not.

"My phone," he mumbles, stretching back to reach it on the table. He frowns down at the screen.

"Who is it?"

"Todd," he says, answering my question as he answers his mobile. Luke goes stiff, throwing me wide eyes.

"What?" I mouth, pausing the movie.

Scrambling up, he casts his bowl aside. "Amanda?"

I hear the sound of a woman's voice filter down the line, and I see how uncomfortable Luke is. So I kick him in the thigh and grin when he gives me a look as if to ask what to do.

"Why are you on Todd's phone?" he asks, and I wait, curious. "You bumped into him?" He rolls his eyes. "No, not tonight. I said Monday, remember?" Luke falls back on the couch again and rubs his palm across his forehead. "I really can't."

I kick him again and tell him silently to go, but he shakes his head, so I continue to push popcorn into my mouth with a lack of Luke's mouth to chuck it at, listening as he talks with his latest woman. He eventually hangs up and looks at me. "Sorry."

Why's he sorry? "You should go meet her."

"I already told her I'm busy this weekend." He drops his phone on the couch and resumes his position, holding up a piece of popcorn. I open and catch it when he throws. "Lo, I think we have another needy nutter on our hands."

I laugh and toss him some popcorn. "Ever considered the fact that you might make them crazy?" I hold back my grin when he gives me an indignant look. "Just saying. If you had answered her calls, she wouldn't have stalked you through your mate."

"Stalked. Exactly. We've had sex a few times. Besides, I was busy."

My hand pauses midway to my mouth. Busy rescuing me. He's young, free, and single. Well, young . . . ish. He shouldn't be holed up at home on a Saturday night babysitting me. I fall silent and try to remind myself that I'm apparently a breath of fresh air to him. But deep inside, I can't help but think that he really does feel a sense of obligation. Maybe he thinks I'll try to top myself again. Maybe he does just feel sorry for me. I drop my eyes to my lap and see endless stray puffs of popcorn littering it, all bits I failed to catch when Luke chucked them at me. I've smiled more since I've met Luke than I have in two years. I shouldn't be smiling. I flinch as my thoughts run away with me. What am I doing here? This isn't my life, and I shouldn't pretend it is, not even for a fleeting second. Cleaning up shit, that's my life. Dealing with shit. Feeling like shit. Looking like shit. I wince at my thoughts again, feeling so very guilty for letting them go there. Billy's staring death in the face, and here I am grumbling about shit on every level of my life while trying to justify my decision to escape from it all for a while. There is no justification, especially where Luke's concerned. Not the sense of freedom I feel with him. Not the temporary escape from my real-life horror story. Nothing is a good enough reason. Billy can't escape. What if he tries to look for me? What if he decides he wants company now? Deep down I know he won't. He'll be exhausted after his outburst. He'll probably sleep for a week and be in more pain. For the past two years I've sat downstairs alone at night hoping my husband will come and join me. Simply sit with me. Maybe even hold my hand. Just be there. It's happening less often these days. These days, I go to bed feeling lonelier each night. Tonight wouldn't have been any different. Well, except I would have spent an hour cleaning meat, cheese, sauce, and wine off my kitchen floor, table, and cupboards. I probably would have got a few cuts from broken glass. I would have thrown away a lasagna dish we received as a wedding gift. In fact, that whole scene, that scattered, broken, and shattered mess is the closest reflection of my actual life. I would have been faced with silence and loneliness. All I need is to pretend that my existence isn't what it is for a short while. To be with someone who doesn't know the complete tatters my life is in.

No, you don't.

Yes, you do.

No, your place is at home, Lo. Dealing with shit. Taking the emotional blows, because who else will? Billy needs you. What are you doing, Lo?

I reach up and push the ball of my palm into my forehead, cursing myself.

"Are you okay?" Luke leans over again, taking my wrist and pulling my hand down.

"I'm fine." I stand and brush myself down of popcorn. "I should go, Luke."

Slowly, he stands too, but I avoid his look of concern and glance away, my head hurting with the guilt that's crept up on me. "Sure," he says softly, no question, no matter how many there are in his eyes. "I'll take you." He leaves the room swiftly, his body radiating uncertainty.

Luke drops me at the end of the street with no prompt from me, and I know he waits until I make it into my house before he leaves. Boris greets me in his usual excited style, and my guilt grows. I drop my keys on the table in the hallway and make my way to the kitchen to let him out to the garden. The poor thing must be bursting for a pee.

"The wanderer returns," Linda says dryly as I enter, pulling me to a stop. The kitchen is sparkling clean and she's at the table, a cup of tea in her hand. There's a dirty plate by the sink, a knife and fork on top. It's there to make a point. That she has fed my husband. Linda puts dirty plates in the dishwasher, and if the dishwasher was full, she'd wash it by hand and put it away. She's having a dig. Good for her. I would put my life on the fact that Billy didn't touch whatever she made him, and as if I need to prove that to myself, I walk over to the bin and step on the pedal. There's a pile of spaghetti on top of the lasagna I made. I hold my tongue and go to the back door.

"I've cleaned up your mess too," she says, clipped and curt, as if I could have missed it. "I also changed Billy's bedsheets."

My jaw tight, I close my eyes to gather my patience. I already feel like a wicked wife. I do not need my mother-in-law to help me there. I changed his sheets yesterday morning while he used the bathroom. Why is she doing this? "Thank you." I force the words out and quickly close my mouth before a barrage of bad language follows. "You can go now, Linda."

She turns on her stool and glares at me. "What kind of wife are you?"

Right now, I'm the kind that's being eaten alive with guilt. With torment. With anger. With sorrow. "Goodnight," I say on a swallow, making my way past her, keen to escape her condemnation before it brings me further down. I'm yanked to a stop when she seizes my arm.

"You are despicable," she hisses. "Where the hell have you been?"

"I needed some fresh air."

"We all need something. It doesn't mean we can have it. Billy needs health, but he can't have it. I need my son healthy, but I can't have it. What makes you think you can have what you need while the rest of us suffer?"

I swing around, my patience snapping. "I need that too, Linda," I yell. "Don't you think I pray every day for him to get better? Don't you think I want the man I married back? I would give my own damn life if it meant Billy could have his."

She scoffs, tossing my arm away as she releases me. "You're thinking of no one but yourself."

"Just get out," I order, and she stands, snatching up her bag. I've just about had enough of her. No more. I refuse to take anymore. I realize she's grieving too, but that doesn't mean she has to be so fucking mean.

"He's better off without you."

"Fuck you, Linda," I spit, shocking myself.

Slap.

I hiss, clenching my cheek when it bursts into angry flames. *She hit me?* "Enough!"

I swing around on a gasp, finding Billy in the doorway, holding himself up on the door frame. His bathrobe is loose, exposing his chest. It's getting thinner by the day. "Billy," I whisper.

His sallow face is cut with anger, and I fear the worst as he looks between us, finally settling his eyes on Linda. "You should leave, Mum," he grates.

"What?"

"I said, leave!" His attempt to shout is feeble, and he immediately starts coughing, bending at the waist. "You will not treat my wife like that, Mum. She's doing her best."

"Billy, I—"

"Just leave."

Stunned, I watch as Linda wanders out of the kitchen, her proverbial tail between her legs, stopping briefly when she passes her son. Her hand rests on his forearm for a second. No words. Then she leaves.

As soon as the front door closes, I hurry to him. "Let me help you."

For once, he doesn't argue with me, standing up straight and taking my wrists. Suddenly his eyes are so very clear. The clearest they've been in months, which undoubtedly makes the red cheek I'm sporting from his mother's slap so much clearer. And his lip wobbles. "I'm so sorry, Lo."

"Stop," I order, throwing my arms around him. "Just stop." My face in his neck, I relish the feel of my husband's arms around me, despite the weakness of his hold. "I'm sorry for leaving. I shouldn't have left." I feel his head shake into my shoulder where it's buried.

"I'm sorry I pushed you. Hurt you. It's . . . it's been a bad day," he whispers. "Forgive me."

My tears come on fast, and I sob my heart out. For Billy. For me. For us.

. . .

I worry the second I open my eyes and find Billy isn't in bed. Bolting upright, I scan the dim bedroom. No Billy. I scramble up and run to the bathroom. No Billy. Every lovely feeling of him holding me last night in bed, just the fact that he invited me into his bed, vanishes with my sleepy panic. Heading downstairs at the speed of light, I fall into the kitchen, coming to a startled stop. "Billy?"

He turns toward me, a saucepan in his hands. I'm so thrown. He's dressed. Just in a pair of joggers and one of his old football T-shirts, but it's more than he's done in weeks. "Today is going to be a good day," he says, pointing to the table with his spatula. "Sit."

Confused, I look to the table that has been set for two. Even a candle in the center. "What are you doing?"

"I'm cooking my wife breakfast." He raises his eyebrows, like a warning to do as I'm told. I ignore the obvious strain of him doing such a simple thing.

"I should be cooking for you." I pad slowly to the table and lower to the chair, keeping my eyes on him as he walks across the kitchen to me, his face cut with the effort. Why is he doing this?

"How long has it been since I cooked for you?" he asks, placing two poached eggs on my plate.

My silence is because I'm trying to remember.

"Exactly," he says, the saucepan hitting the table on a thud when he places it down, losing his grip at the very last second and sending the water splashing up the side of the pan. He grimaces.

"You don't have to do this." I reach for his hand and squeeze.

"I do, Lo." He brings my knuckles to his lips and kisses them sweetly. "Now shut up and eat your breakfast." Taking a seat beside me, he starts to pick his way through his own eggs. He has no appetite, I know that, but he's force-feeding himself to make a point. A point he really doesn't need to make. It kills me that he feels so terrible. He has no reason to. "I have an appointment with Dr. Smith on Friday." His statement comes out of the blue, and I shoot him a look, mentally flicking through the dates to find the appointment he's talking about. There isn't one. He refused to go to his last one, and another wasn't scheduled. "I called Dr. Smith this morning," he tells me, pouring us both coffee, the weight of the pot a strain on his weak arm. "He moved a few things around."

What does this mean? I want to ask but dare not. "What time?"

"One. I'd like to go alone, though, if you don't mind."

I recoil, unsure whether I should be offended. "Why?"

"It's just something I need to do." He reaches over and rests his hand over mine. "I promise I won't dismiss anything."

Hope. For the first time in a long time, I feel hope take me in its warmth and hug me tightly. I beam at him, and he smiles in return. Such a beautiful smile.

The sound of Boris crying pulls my eyes down to the kitchen floor, and I find him at my feet, something in his mouth. "What have you got?" I reach down and pull it free, frowning as I shake it out. It's a vintage Adidas T-shirt. An item of old stock from my store.

"Oh, I pulled out some of your old stock from the store," Billy informs me. "I thought you could set up an online store or something. Sell it all."

I cock my head, once again taken aback. "Why?" He can't be thinking that selling my old stock might raise enough money to get him to America. I've already calculated the money I could make, and it didn't even get past the hundreds.

"Because you should," he says simply, smiling across the table at me. "I'm not that tech savvy, but maybe a friend could help you set it all up?"

A friend? And who does he suppose that friend is? Our four best friends, Penny and Gareth, and Helen and Lewis, haven't shown their faces for months. I can't blame them. Like most people, they find being around us too much. Uncomfortable. Too real. But I can set up an online store on my own. I smile to myself, becoming excited.

"I like seeing you happy," Billy says quietly, gazing across the table at me.

I reach across and bring our lips together. "You make me happy," I tell him, ignoring the fact that his heart isn't in our kiss.

Ignoring the fact that he still can't tell me he loves me.

Part Five

Luke

Chapter Twelve

Bored. Out. Of. My. Mind.

Her mouth moves across the table as she rabbits on about . . . I don't know. The last word I actually heard was "Tiffany." Who the hell is Tiffany? I push my salmon around my plate, smiling every now and then, humming or nodding. To what, I have no idea. I'm brain-dead. I like Amanda. She seems fun, reasonably mature for her age, and she has some serious moves in the bedroom. But there's something missing.

"Luke?"

I look up, blinking. "Of course," I say, and she smiles, seeming pleased.

"Great. Pick me up at eight?" She takes her wineglass and has a sip, and the stupidest thought comes over me. Her lips are bright red. So why is there no lipstick on her glass? "It's been a lovely evening."

I hum, like in agreement, taking my glass of water. We have dessert and coffee to go yet. I don't know if I'll make it past mains. I may be asleep soon. "How's work?" In this moment, I can't for the life of me remember what Amanda does for a living. I'm hoping she fixes that pronto.

When she tilts her head in question, I tilt mine slowly too, waiting. "You've never asked me what I do for work."

"I haven't?" I rewind through our encounters, trying to locate the memory that will tell me she's wrong. I can't find it. "Are you sure?"

"Positive." She smiles suggestively over her glass, her back straightening a little, pushing her generous boobs out. "I'm in the cosmetics industry."

"And what do you do in the cosmetics industry?" I ask, fighting to keep the conversation flowing.

"I test products." She proceeds to detail her average working day. She loses me at eyelash tinting. I'm back to nodding sporadically again. The waiter collects our plates, places two dessert menus on the table, as Amanda rambles on. "Maybe we could take dessert back to your place," she suggests, browsing down the choices.

Usually, when a woman suggests such a thing, I'd call for the bill and make a hasty exit with her. Tonight, I'm just not interested. "Damn, I forgot something," I say without thought, pulling out my wallet and putting my AMEX on the table. "I said I'd see my grandfather this evening." Slapping my palm on my forehead, I shake my head to myself. "What an idiot." My phone rings, and I look down, recoiling when I see who's calling. Pops? "See?" I say, too high-pitched, swiping up my phone and flashing the screen at a startled-looking Amanda. "He's wondering where I am." I jump up and round the table, kissing her cheek. "That's your fault for constantly dazzling me." I know what I'm doing, though Amanda seems oblivious, smiling with satisfaction on a coy shrug.

"I won't apologize."

"I didn't ask you to." I look up to the waiter. "Make sure the lady gets a cab." Zooming out of the restaurant before anyone can protest, I take Pops's call. "How'd you know?" I ask, crossing the road to my car.

"Know what, Grandboy?"

"That I needed saving?"

He chuckles, the sound, as ever, causing me to grin from ear to ear. "What dating scrape have you gotten yourself into now?"

I jump in my car and wait for the Bluetooth to kick in as I drive off down the road. "You home?" I ask. It's a stupid question. He only goes wherever I take him.

"Bring whiskey." He hangs up, and I laugh.

"You got it, Pops," I say to myself. After enduring dinner with Amanda tonight, I could do with a stiff drink myself.

I collect his favorite malt on my way, pulling up at just past eight. It's late, I know I'll be chastised, but I'll work my charm. I press the buzzer and clear my throat. "Sheila," I purr, smiling at the intercom.

"Luke?"

"It's me." I hear the door unlatch without any protest, and I quickly tuck the bottle of malt under my jacket before I enter the grand entrance hall. Sheila comes hurrying through, a look on her face split between disapproval and delight. "It's late." Her lips twist, but I know she's pleased to see me.

I approach and give her a kiss on the cheek. "It won't happen again," I lie, making my way to the end of the hall. "His room?"

She waggles a finger at me. "Not too late."

I flip her a wink and pick up my stride, weaving through the corridors. It's quiet, all of the residents probably tucked up in their beds, which is a relief. My visits to Pops often cause a stir with the old dears, all of them vying for my attention.

I knock on the door and poke my head in, finding Pops in his chair with a paper and a cup of tea, the TV quiet in the background. I reach into my jacket and pull out the whiskey, holding it up. "I've brought the goods."

He looks up over his glasses, grinning. "Good. I'm all out." Lifting his mug, he drains the last of his secret stash and holds it up. "Fill it up, Grandboy."

I laugh and grab a chair, dragging it over to him and taking a seat. "How much have you had already?" I ask, unscrewing the cap and filling him up halfway.

His old nose screws up. "The cleaners found my stash," he grumbles, hitting the side of the bottle with his mug and taking a generous guzzle. "But they didn't find the miniature behind my sink." He winks, handing me my own mug that's set to the side on his table, awaiting my arrival. "Tell me about this woman."

"Lo?"

"Is that her name? Cute. Why'd you want to escape her so desperately?"

I realize quickly what I've done and rush to correct it. "No, no, Pops. Amanda is the woman I was on a date with."

"Then who's Lo?" he asks, drinking as he keeps his questioning eyes on me. "Lord, you got two on the go, Grandboy?"

I laugh. "Lo's a friend. Amanda is the woman I'm seeing." I frown. "I think."

"Jesus Christ, Luke." He reaches over and smacks my knee. "You *think* you're seeing a woman?"

"I don't know, Pops." I join him and sip back some of the good stuff, getting comfortable in my chair. "I'm not feeling it."

"Then don't waste her time. Now, tell me about Lo."

"Lo's not a woman I'm seeing."

"Why?"

I laugh. "Because she's a friend."

"Why?"

"Jesus, Pops." I toss him a *what-the-hell?* look, but it goes straight over his head.

"Why?"

"She's married," I tell him, hopefully shutting this down.

"Oh. That's unfortunate."

"Why?"

His old green eyes roll dramatically as he leans forward. "Because the second you said Lo's name, your eyes sparkled."

Oh, for God's sake. Why'd I even mention Lo? I didn't mean to, but her name just fell right out of my mouth when Pops mentioned a woman. She was the first woman who came to mind, maybe because I'm worried about her. She left hastily on Saturday night. Her carefreeness seemed to change in the blink of an eye, and it's been on my mind since. I don't like seeing her like that.

Leaning forward, too, I get our noses close, noses that are a match, and stare right into his eyes. "Believe me when I say, Pops, Lo is just a friend. A good friend."

His eyes narrow. "How'd you meet?"

There's not a cat in hell's chance of me telling him *that*. It'll only add fuel to the fire. "In a café."

He sniffs, lifting his chin and inspecting me carefully. "And why'd you run out on your date?"

"Because, Pops, like I said, I'm not feeling it." I need to tell Amanda. I'm not an arsehole. I just don't see the point of wasting a woman's time *and* mine. Don't get me wrong, I have fun, but I'm reluctant to move forward with any woman who does anything less than rock my world. They rock my bank balance. Rock my patience. They even rock my bed. But every single one of them have failed to consume my mind and steal my attention from anything but them. When you get to forty-two and you're still a single man, you begin to wonder if there's something fundamentally wrong with you. Whether you're being too picky. Whether that one person who was made for you has passed you by and you didn't realize.

"What's this, then?" he asks, waving his mug of whiskey at me. "The fifth woman you've dated in as many weeks?"

I grimace. "I'm bored after one or two dates. Besides, you said *the one* will come along one day and I'd know about it, right? Well, I'm still waiting for her, and you'll be the first to know when she does come along. Besides, I'm not ready to settle down."

He snorts, falling back in his chair. "Trust me, boy, when she comes along, you'll be ready for anything." I see his mind wander away, and I know exactly where. To the time he met Milly Rose, the woman who he claims was his one true love. Seems crazy that I feel compassion for the old fool, but I've listened to this story time and again, and each time he tells it, it's obvious he wonders what could have been. It was 1946, the summer after the war ended. Even though Gramps had only spent a year in the war, having lied about his age for conscription, he'd come home shell-shocked, and ten months later, in his words, was *still* suffering a serious case of blue balls. Step in my grandmother—a wonderful woman who Pops met through a friend. They dated for a few months, but both of them agreed they weren't exactly setting each other's world alight, so they went their separate ways. And then he met his Milly Rose. "I remember the day I nearly ran down Milly Rose on my bike as if it were yesterday," he says wistfully, smiling, and I know it's because he's picturing her face. "I kicked up so much gravel when I skidded to miss her that it took at least five minutes for me to find her in the plumes of dust." He chuckles, turning his mug in his hand. "But when that dust cleared, my God. It was like the materialization of an angel, Grandboy."

I smile and refill our cups before getting comfortable, aware that we're only at the beginning. "She asked if I was okay as she fanned her face, and in reply I blurted out an invitation to come dancing with me. An apology, I guess. She looked a little shaken. But she accepted, and I made sure I was scrubbed up well when I picked her up that night." Pops looks at me on a smile. "Could have given Fred Astaire a run for his money, I could." He chuckles and then sighs. "And Milly was most certainly my Ginger."

I rest my elbow on the arm of the chair, my chin on my palm, drinking my way through my mug of whiskey.

"I didn't know what it was like to fall in love," Pops continues. "I was walking on clouds. Thought about her all the time. Couldn't wait to see her each week. And then your grandmother, God rest her sweet soul, tracked me down at work and delivered the blow of all blows."

"Dad will be delighted to hear you say that," I quip, not for the first time.

Pops smiles. "It wasn't the news of your father's impending arrival that was the blow, Grandboy. It was the realization that I was about to lose the love of my life." He necks the rest of his drink and holds his glass out for me to refill, like he's actually drowning in his sorrows. Which, I guess, he is. "I didn't sleep for a week. Didn't go to work, and I avoided my Milly, because I knew the next time I saw her would be the last time, and I never wanted that time to come."

I've heard this story a thousand times, asked a thousand questions, but I've never asked this. "Did Grandma know about Milly?"

Pops nods thoughtfully. "She knew, but never once murmured a word about her. Back then, you just didn't. The day I met Milly to tell her I couldn't see her anymore was the worst day of my life." His palm meets his chest and rubs, an expression of hurt traveling over his old face. "A massive part of me died that day as I watched her walk away from me. I never saw her again." His old lips straighten. "Your grandmother and I had a shotgun wedding, your father arrived, and that was that. Don't get me wrong, I loved your grandma. Really, I did. She was a good woman and the mother of my boy. But not a day went by that I didn't think about Milly." He squares me with a deadly serious look, leaning forward in his chair. "What did I tell you when you went and got Janet up the duff?"

"You told me not to marry her."

"Why?"

"Because you knew she wasn't the love of my life," I answer.

"Correct." He nods to himself, happy. "Now, tell me what my great granddaughter has been up to." He changes the subject, just like that, leaving me bemused. There's usually a point to him telling me his favorite story. What was his point today? Casting my question aside before I set him off on a tangent—resulting in an encore of his tale—I fill him in on Tia's world travels and where she is right now. As always, he listens with constant gasps of shock, amazed by the concept of world travels. Before long, we've finished the bottle of whiskey, Pops is dosing off, and I'm not far behind him. I can't help but think about how much flack Lo would give me for getting steaming drunk on whiskey with my old granddad, listening to stories, dosing off with him. She'd rib me something rotten. Call me an old man. Buy me a pipe and slippers.

I sigh. "Come on." I struggle to push myself up, stumbling a few times. "Let's get you in bed, you drunken old fool." Getting him out of his chair, I expect we look like a comedy duo as I drunkenly try to get his limp body to the bed. It takes a while, and a few too many staggers, but I get him there eventually, and I get him there with no broken bones. It's an achievement, considering the state of us both. Tucking him in, I drop a kiss on his forehead, seeing double as I lower my face. "Night, old boy."

"Night, Grandboy," he murmurs, clumsily patting at my cheek. "And remember, when she comes along, don't you dare let her go."

I huff a puff of laughter. "I won't," I assure him, even though I somehow doubt I'll ever find her in the first place.

Chapter Thirteen

The sounds of an irritating, familiar whirring brings me round, and I squint my eyes open to the harsh morning light. In my half-conscious state, I roll onto my side. And freeze. "What the hell?"

Amanda's eyes peel open, and she smiles lazily. "Morning."

My brain spasms as I try to recall last night. I remember dinner. I remember abandoning Amanda at the restaurant. I remember visiting Pops. And I remember that bottle of whiskey. "Fucking hell. Pops." My throat feels like I've swallowed a pile of razors as I clumsily throw my hand out and feel for my phone on the nightstand. I also remember Amanda calling me as I left Pops's place in a cab. I collected her on the way home, because, stupid me, I left my AMEX with her.

My hand collides with numerous objects, knocking them to the floor, before I finally lay my hand on my mobile. I look at my screen, closing one eye to try and turn my double vision into single vision. Then I slowly and carefully type in a P and an O and then another P. I hit call and drop the phone to the pillow by my ear. Amanda crawls onto me, suffocating me, and I gently but firmly push her off, smiling awkwardly when she throws me a questioning look.

"Acre Residential Home," a too loud voice says. Sheila's voice, the long-serving receptionist.

"It's Luke," I say groggily, moving my ear away from my phone before the receptionist can do what I just *know* she's going to do.

"Luke," she shrieks. "Now then, what time did you leave last night?" Her tone is teasing.

"Too late," I confirm. "Is Pops up?"

"You mean after you two got steaming drunk? You know alcohol is prohibited, Luke."

"Cut the old bugger some slack."

She snorts her thoughts on that one. I know half the shenanigans that go down at the home always have a direct connection with Pops. I smile at the ceiling, hoping that I'll be as mischievous as he is when I get to his age. "He's still in bed," Sheila says.

"He is?" I pull back my phone to check the time. "But it's eight a.m. He's never out of bed later than seven. Not ever. Have you checked he's alive?" I sit up, ignoring the fact that my brain feels like it's fallen into my chest. I'm panicking.

"I'm sure he's fine, Luke."

"Check on him," I demand shortly. "Do it now while I'm on the phone." I shrug Amanda off dismissively when she takes my shoulder and tries to pull me down.

"That's not necessary."

"It is absolutely necessary." I throw the sheets back and swing my legs off the bed. "If you don't do it, I'll be there in thirty minutes to do it myself." The fact that I'm probably highly over the limit to drive isn't completely relevant in my fuzzy mind. Neither is the fact that my car is at Pops's. It's eight o'clock. Pops has never, not ever, slept in until eight o'clock. Something must be wrong with him.

"Visiting isn't until eleven onwards."

"I won't be visiting. I'll be breaking in."

She huffs her displeasure. "You're a one, Luke Williamson. Cocky like your grandfather."

"I know. Please, just go check he's breathing."

"I'm on my way," she informs me, so I wait, hearing door after door opening and shutting as I widen my stance to steady myself.

"Fucking hell," I breathe, the room starting to spin.

"What?"

"Nothing. Are you there yet?" I take slow and cautious steps across my bedroom, blinking repeatedly to try and clear my blurry vision. Fuck me, I feel like I've been pickled in a barrel of Scotch.

"Bert?" I hear Sheila say gently. "Bert, are you awake?"

There's silence, and my worry heightens. And I wait.

"Bert?" Sheila says again, but this time with more urgency in her voice, and I see her in my mind poking at my lifeless grandfather. "Bert?"

"For the love of God," Pops yells.

"Ah, you're awake," she chimes happily.

"Well I am now, you nincompoop."

I laugh hysterically, having to lunge for the doorframe to stop myself toppling. Fuck. "Put him on, Shelia."

"With pleasure."

A few seconds later, I hear snoring down the line. "Pops," I shout, wincing at the sound level of my own voice.

"What, what, what?" he yells, and I imagine him shooting up in his bed, looking around the room for me. "Where the bleeding hell are you?"

"On the phone, you old fool." There's some muffles and a few crackles, and then his voice is booming down the line at me.

"There you are."

I pull the phone away from my ear. "Don't yell."

"I'm not yelling."

"How's your head?" I ask. "Because mine is fucking pounding."

He titters down the line. "Man's drink, boy. Man's drink."

"Devil's drink," I mutter, making my way out onto the landing, leaving Amanda in my bed. "Okay, I'm going now." I need water. Desperately. "Just wanted to check you're alive."

"Okay, Grandboy. Call me when you've come to your senses."

"What senses?"

He hangs up, the ignorant git, leaving me staring at my phone on a frown. Senses? He could mean many things. All of my senses aren't as they should be at this particular moment in time, because they're hungover. I can't see, my sense of smell is being polluted by the stale stench of whiskey, my skin hurts to touch, my mouth tastes rank, and I have an irritating ringing in my ears. To put it simply, I feel like shite.

I eventually make it to the top of the stairs, and then negotiate each step in turn, holding on tightly to the balustrade. "Oh good Lord," I mumble when I catch sight of myself in the mirror on the wall in the hallway. I look ninety-two. My stubble is overgrown, my eyes look like piss holes in the snow, and the muscles of my torso are protruding more so than usual, a clear sign of my dehydration. "Liquid."

I fall into the kitchen and open the fridge, scanning the shelves for my beloved coconut water. My mouth waters when I lay my hand on the carton, and my shaking fingers can't get the cap off quickly enough.

"Hey, bro." Something hits my shoulder, and I jump a mile in the air, dropping the carton and spitting out the contents of my mouth. All over Todd. "Seriously?" he yells, grabbing a towel and wiping himself down.

"What the hell?" I gasp, my heart clattering like no tomorrow. "You scared the shit out of me."

"You look rough." Todd gives me the once-over with suspicious eyes. "You been out to play without me?"

"I was with Pops. What are you doing here?" I dip with caution to collect my carton of coconut water, grumbling because it's now half empty, the rest of my juice pooling the floor.

"I slept on the couch." Todd grabs a cloth off the side, chucks it on the puddle at my feet, and starts to swish it around with his bare foot.

"Why?"

"I told Charity I was staying with you."

"Why?"

"Because I wanted to stay out, and I didn't want her to kick me out because I stayed out. Lads' night playing cards and collapsing on your sofa to save a taxi seemed like the perfect excuse. Don't know why I didn't think of it before."

"Because it's lying." I laugh, and then wince, reaching up to soothe my head. "I don't know why you don't just go home at a reasonable hour."

"The fun only starts at midnight." Todd smiles brightly, and it pisses me right off, because I know for certain that he had a heavy night on the booze too, yet he's showing no signs of a hangover. His blond hair is too short to have bedhead, and his pretty face too pretty to look rough.

"Why don't you just end it with Charity?" I ask, not for the first time. "It's only been a couple of months."

"She had post arrive yesterday." He drops to a stool at the breakfast bar.

I sink what's left of the coconut water and gasp. "That's it, mate. You're under the thumb."

"Never."

"Hey, boys," Amanda purrs from the kitchen door, pulling Todd's and my attention her way. She's dressed. Good.

"Morning." I say, watching Todd's eyes crawl back to me, his lips stretched in an annoying grin.

"Morning, indeed," he whispers. "So you tracked him down, then?"

I throw Todd a dark look, the wanker, as Amanda struts over to me. Her lips land on my cheek and linger. "It was fun."

Was it? I can't remember. "Yeah," I say like a shitbag, straining a smile when she slinks off. "I'll call you." I'm deplorable.

The front door shuts and Todd starts laughing. "I'll call you," he mimics, his voice high and girlie.

I smile, but that smile drops like a rock from my face when I spot something on the worktop across the kitchen. "What's that?" I ask, pointing my carton of coconut water at the box on the side.

Todd looks over his shoulder. "Oh," he says, slowly turning back toward me, his lips straight.

"It is, isn't it?" I question.

"I'll get rid of it." He holds his hands up in defense. "It'll be like it's never been here."

I bristle, backing out of the kitchen. "Those things infect everything within a five-hundred-meter radius. I won't be able to touch a thing until I've disinfected the entire house."

Todd rolls his eyes dramatically, which only serves to piss me off more. He knows how I feel about those devil things. "It's a fucking kebab, Luke. Chill the fuck out."

"Loaded with fucking chilies." Todd's a nightmare for hot food, stuffing chilies down his throat until he's sweating. Hot sauce on every-fucking-thing, polluting every single perfectly fine dish he eats.

He gets up and grabs the box off the side, holding it up before slamming his foot on the pedal on the bin and dropping it inside. "There. Gone."

"Put it in the bin outside," I order shortly, heading for the shower. "And the anti-bacterial spray is under the sink."

"You know only real men can take spice, right?" he calls.

"I'm allergic, you twat."

"Seriously, dude?" He laughs. "You're not allergic, you're a pussy." Todd is standing at the bottom of the stairs when I reach the top. "Let's go out tonight."

"I'm not in the mood." I round the landing. "Fuck off home to your girlfriend."

He holds his phone up and smiles wickedly. "I can't. She's

kicked me out."

I come to a stop, my brow bunching. "Why? You had cards night here last night. She was cool with that."

"She was, until her mate called her this morning and told her that she saw me in a bar in Shoreditch last night."

"Oh? Did you happen to be with Amanda?" I narrow my eyes. "Why the fuck did you let her use your phone on Saturday night?"

"She said hers had run out of charge," he argues, defensive.

I huff. "That's shady shit." And a clear sign I should be running for the hills.

"Why?" he goes on. "Are you avoiding her?"

"Yes. No."

He grins, and I sigh.

"But it's your place. Charity can't kick you out of your own place."

"Tell *her* that."

I shake my head and brace my hands on the metal railing for some support, becoming breathless. I damn Pops to hell once again. "Just finish it, Todd. Call it quits."

"She'll go loco." He looks truly horrified by the thought. "I'll just stay here until she moves out."

"No way. You know I like my own space."

"Come on, Luke. It'll be like we're twenty-something again, with not a care in the world."

"First of all, I was never in my twenties with *not a care in the world*. I was a father, twathead," I point out. I'm still a dad. Not past tense. God, I hate being hungover. "Second of all, we're forty-something, with businesses to run and homes to pay for."

"Yeah, well, my home is currently under siege by a melodramatic female, so for the time being you're stuck with me, bro."

"Lucky me." I push myself off the railings and stretch my muscles. "I'm getting a shower and going to work."

"Great." He claps his hands and rubs them together on a devilish grin. "And tonight we're going for a drink."

"I'm not going for a drink," I assure him, my face screwing up at the thought of putting more alcohol in my body.

"Just a quiet one." Todd turns and goes back into the kitchen. "You can tell me what's crawled up your arse."

"Nothing has crawled up my arse," I mutter, hearing him laugh. "And get rid of the chilies." I head straight for the shower and let the water wash away the whiskey from my pores for half an hour.

Rubbing a towel over my head, I go to my nightstand and grab my watch, slipping it over my wrist. Something catches my eye, pausing me mid-securing of the catch. I reach forward and lift the catalogue, my frown deepening as I slowly realize what I'm looking at. A Tiffany catalogue? "What?" I ask myself, flicking through, noticing a page folded down. I drop the book the second I catch sight of the diamond ring dominating the page. "Unbelievable," I breathe. A few times under the covers and a dinner or two, that's all. Grabbing my phone, I tap out a message to Lo.

I was right. Amanda is definitely a nutter.

I spend ten minutes staring at the screen of my phone, waiting for a reply.

It doesn't come.

Playing squash on Tuesday wasn't much of a distraction. Neither were the fifty lengths I swam on Wednesday. Or the drinks I had with Todd last night while watching the Thursday evening match. By Friday morning, I still haven't had a reply from Lo. It's making me feel a little uneasy. I'm worried. I've run over last Saturday night in my mind endlessly. She was fine. Then she suddenly wasn't. Then she seemed okay when I took her home. I can't call her. I really shouldn't have texted her. It was a compulsive moment. I wanted to share my enlightenment on Amanda's nuttery with someone, and Lo was the natural person to share it with. Maybe her husband saw the message. Did he see the message? And if so, what did he do? I won't rest until I've seen her today for our usual lunch date.

My head hurts with so many questions fighting for space as I settle at my desk and fire up my desktop while listening to Pam reel off the list of things I have to do today. She goes on forever, the list endless. Good. I'll be too busy to do anything other than focus on work.

After spending all morning on a conference call to Beijing, discussing the technology behind out latest security monitoring equipment, I once again find myself fighting back my worry, telling myself I'm being unreasonable. But . . . am I being unreasonable?

At 12:45 on the dot, I'm out of the office, hurrying to Nero's to meet Lo for lunch. I get our usual and split our tuna baguette, pulling out the cucumber for Lo and setting it at the place opposite me, ready for her. I don't eat my half, leaving it on the wrapper, my fingers starting to drum the table. I look at my watch. Ten past. I look at my phone. Ten past. My eyes fall to the door, willing her to enter. She's never late. Not ever. We never confirm our lunches, either, because it goes without confirming. Has done since our second lunch. We're both just . . . here. One o'clock without fail. I look down at my watch again. Quarter past. I look at my phone. Quarter past. I hate the kick of my heartbeats with each minute that passes, my eyes constantly checking from the door, to my watch, to my phone.

Two o'clock.

I stare at our untouched lunch, the undrunk coffees, and the unopened bottle of water. And my heart sinks. She didn't come. But more than that, I start to worry. As I drag myself up, I walk slowly out of the café, pulling up her name on my phone. I shouldn't call, but, especially now, I'm so worried. She wouldn't stand me up without letting me know. I push my thumb down on the icon and bring my phone to my ear as I pace the street back to my office. My eyes close when it goes to voicemail. "Lo, it's me," I say, pushing through the glass doors when I make it to my building. "I went to meet you as usual. You didn't show up. Darling, just let me know you're okay. Please, I'm worried." I hang up and hope so much she responds.

As soon as I make it to my floor, I head to the meeting room, wrestling all thoughts of Lo to a safe place in my mind. I have a security system to sell to the Chinese government. I have to nail this. Given the advancement of the Chinese market and their enviable technology, this could be the deal of a lifetime for me and my company.

"All set?" I ask the team when I enter the room. A chorus of enthusiastic confirmations ring out as I throw my file on the table. "Good. Let's get this in the bag."

Stanley jumps up from his chair and starts tapping away on his laptop. "They'll be dialing in at two thirty."

I look at my watch, noting we have five minutes. "Still the premier's wingman?" I ask, knowing who we get to talk to matters as much as *what* we talk about.

"Yep. Remember, guys, we need to put emphasis on the sensory element of the system. It's been in use in a dozen high-security buildings across London now for a year without a hitch."

I smile, satisfied. Our newest sensor is, pardon the pun, the dogs bollocks. Pet detectors are popular in security where guard dogs are utilized, though temperamental. Not one system was failsafe in the market, with frequent false triggers and, worse, not triggering when needed. Often the sensor would fuck up, misidentifying a moving object. Until we developed the P500. It's genius, and the only sensor of its capability on the market, identifying between an animal and a human through bone structure rather than weight and height. "And the premier still has five dogs, right?" I ask.

"Yep, he does."

"Perfect. God love his love for canines. This should be a

breeze." I grin and tidy the stack of papers before me, just as the projector screen at the far end of the room comes to life, three men appearing.

I stand and smile brightly. "nǐ hǎo," I say, nodding politely.

The smiles I get in return tell me I've nailed my pitch already.

"I'm buying the drinks tonight," I call back to everyone as I make my way back to my office. "After work in The Strip."

A chorus of *whoops* and *yeahs* ring out, the office buzzing. Just how I like it. "You look like the cat that got the cream." Pam laughs as I skip past her desk.

"Oh, I am." I swoop into my office and dial Todd. "The Strip at six," I say in greeting.

"Thank fuck. I've had a bitch of a day."

"She moved out?" I land in my chair and flick through my inbox, mentally answering my new emails.

"No, she's changed the locks."

My head recoils on my neck. "Wow."

"Just tell me something," Todd says on a sigh. "Did you see any of this coming?"

"I'm not a mind reader, mate. But I'd be lying if I said I didn't find Charity . . ." I cut my sentence there, trying to think of an appropriate word. A diva? Unreasonable? A brat?

"Find her *what*?"

"Intense," I finish. "Honestly, I'm not quite sure how you let this happen."

"Me neither," he admits. "Get me a beer in if you're there before me. I need to wrap up this account before I leave."

"Done." I hang up and return to my computer, clicking my mouse repeatedly to open an email that refuses to open. "Come on," I say. Then the screen goes blank on me, the whole thing crashing. "Great." I grunt at the monitor a few times, cursing and muttering under my breath as I press every button on the damn keyboard. Nothing. "Pam," I yell. She's at the entrance to my office in a flash. "Stupid computer has crashed," I tell her, smacking the keys again to demonstrate the lack of life.

"I'll call the IT department."

"Thanks."

Of course, with nothing but a blank screen to stare at, my tools for distraction are limited and I start thinking. Thinking about Lo. Where she is. Why she didn't show up. About her circumstances. Her well-being. I let my elbows hit the desk and my arms carry the weight of my heavy head.

I grab my phone and pull up her number, pressing dial. But then I quickly disconnect and throw my phone back down, telling myself not to do anything rash. Like demand to know what the deal is with her husband, Like tell her to leave him if he makes her so unhappy, which I'm certain he does. Like beat seven days' worth of shit out of the bastard for making her so miserable. No. None of that would be good. As I've told myself endlessly, it's none of my business, and I shouldn't try to make it. So I do something else instead. I call a local florist and have some flowers sent to her office. I decline the card and message. Just the flowers. Just so she knows that I'm thinking of her. Just so she knows I'm still here. And maybe to make her smile. I miss her.

"Dereck's here," Pam says through the door.

"Oh, good." I move away from my desk and give Dereck the space he needs. "How you doing?" I ask, making small talk with him while he taps and clicks away. The computer whizz has been with me since day one, and isn't much of a talker, as proven with his grunt in reply just now. But I didn't hire him for his conversational skills.

"Done." He gets up and trots off.

"Just like that?" I ask, looking between him and my screen. What was that? Five seconds? Ten?

"I'm good with computers. Isn't that why you hired me?"

"Guess so." I sit back down and return to those emails, looking

at my watch. Four o'clock. I have precisely two hours to answer . . .
I glance at my inbox. "Seventy-five?" I flop back in my chair. One-point-six minutes per email. I click the first one open and scan the
text. It's an easy one, answered in exactly fifteen seconds, and an
hour later, I'm down to twenty and set to smash my personal best.
I want to go for a few drinks this evening with the knowledge that
my inbox in empty. It would also be good if I hear from Lo, but
I'm not banking on that.

At that very moment, my mobile rings, disturbing my flow,
and set to ignore it, I push it away with a flick of my hand. Then I
freeze and dart my eyes back to the screen. Forgoing my personal
challenge, I frantically make a grab for my phone and fumble with
the damn thing to swipe the screen. "Hello?"

"Hi." Her voice is meek and unsure. "I wanted to thank you
for the flowers."

I get up from my desk and wander over to the window, looking
out onto St. Paul's, my body shrinking with the relief pouring out
of me. "I didn't send a card. How'd you know they were
from me?"

"I don't have many potential culprits, put it that way."

"Not your husband?" The words fall right out before I can
stop them, and I cringe, giving myself a mental slap. Why would I
say that? Lo's obviously wondering the same thing, because there's
silence and it's damn well awkward. Things between us are never
awkward, and I hate myself for making it that way. "I'm sorry, that
was out of line."

"Don't worry about it. Anyway, thank you."

"You're welcome. I've been worried about you, Lo. Why didn't
you let me know you're okay?"

"I'm sorry. It's been a bit of a week."

I'm desperate to ask why but, of course, I don't. "Lunch next
week?"

"Yes, I hope so."

Silence. No reason for missing today.

"I'm glad you're all right." I know she really isn't all right, but just hearing her voice offers me reassurance. I can relax tonight, have a few drinks, and wind down my strung muscles.

"I'd better go," she almost whispers. "I'll call you next week, okay?"

"Okay," I murmur reluctantly, letting her hang up first. I bring my phone to my mouth, chewing the edge. Something's not right. Or, more accurately, something *more* isn't right. Yet my power to ease her misery is limited if she won't let me. Why won't she let me? My phone buzzes in my hand and I take it away from my mouth to look at the screen. I groan but bite the bullet. "Amanda," I breathe, taking a seat, bracing myself. I can't avoid her forever.

"You haven't been answering my calls." She sounds put out. Pissed off, even.

I inwardly laugh. Maybe because I'm terrified what she'll subtly leave by my bed next time. "Listen, Amanda, I've been thinking about us." I pause a beat, letting the start of my speech sink in to prepare her for what's to follow. Us? We fucked and ate. Not much of an us, though Amanda clearly thinks differently.

"You're breaking up with me?" she questions in disbelief.

Breaking up? I didn't realize we were together.

"It's not you, it's me." I roll my eyes at myself. Lame. *It's actually because I find you utterly boring.*

"Let's have dinner," she suggests, clutching at straws.

"I don't think that's a good idea."

"Why?"

Jesus, is she not hearing me? "I'm not in the right place at the moment for any kind of relationship. I just don't have time."

"But we're so good together."

I close my eyes, realizing that I'm not going to get off the phone anytime soon at this rate. So it's time to pull out the usual, trusty spiel. "Maybe if I'd met you at another point in my life, things would have worked out. You're a great woman, really. I just don't think I can give you what you need." *A Tiffany ring, to be precise.* "Take care, Amanda." I hang up on a cringe and silence my phone, knowing I'll be getting a few more calls. I just broke up with a woman who I wasn't even with. *Good God.*

I abandon the rest of my emails, collect my stuff, more than ready for that drink, and trudge out of my office. As I'm approaching my car, my mobile rings, and I glance at the screen, ready to reject the call. But when I see an international number, I get excited, scrambling to answer. "Hello?"

"Daddy." Tia's squeal nearly deafens me, but, God, it's so good to hear her voice.

"Hey, baby." I aim my fob at my car and unlock it. "How are you?"

"Great. I'm at the airport hopping on a plane to Cambodia."

My feet grind to a halt, and I mentally run through her itinerary, which I know off by heart. "Cambodia?" I question. Cambodia isn't on her itinerary. "You're supposed to be heading to New Zealand."

"Slight change of plan."

"Slight? Like six-thousand miles slight?"

She sighs down the line. "You're not going to have a meltdown like Mum, are you?"

I pull my car door open and fall into my seat. "No." I mean it. Janet is about as melodramatic as a mother could be. And as a female could be, for that matter. "Just curious why the plans have changed."

"Well, I met a new friend, and he's heading to New Zealand after he's done Cambodia, so I thought why not?"

I heard only one word there. "He?"

"Yes, he," she says slowly, knowingly. "Trent."

"Trent? What is he, a river?"

"Stop it, Dad." Tia laughs. "He's American."

I snarl at my steering wheel. "But he lives in London, right?"

"No, he lives in Arizona."

"Which is in London, right?" I don't like this. Not one

little bit.

"Is this the meltdown you're *not* going to have?"

"Yes." So she's changed her plans? My girl, my fiercely independent girl, has changed her plans, and not only changed them, but she's changed them for a boy?

"He's twenty-nine."

"What?" I gasp. "Did you have six birthdays and not tell me?"

She groans now, all out of sighs, totally exasperated. "Come on, Dad. You'll love him."

"What do you mean, I'll love him? I'm never going to meet him." This is getting worse by the minute. "Am I?"

"Well if I love him, you *have* to love him, right?"

I stare ahead at the brick wall through the windscreen of my car. She's done it. She's done what I told her not to do, and she's only gone and bloody done it with some twat named after a river *and* who lives in fucking America. America! "You love him," I mumble despondently. "Does your mother know?"

"God, no."

"But she knows you're heading for Cambodia?"

"Yes, with some girlfriends I met. Jesus, Dad, you're the chilled one of the two of you, and look how you're reacting."

I sag in my seat, running a hand through my hair. "Just make sure you come home, baby, yeah?" Fucking hell, this is the worst news ever.

"Of course I'll come home. Listen, Dad, I've spent my last few hundred quid on this diversion. Could you transfer some money into my account?"

Usually, my answer would be a straight yes, of course I will, but tonight I'm feeling annoyed that she's gone right ahead and done this without checking in with me, since it's wiped her clean out of cash. "Tia, what happened to managing your money?"

"But—"

"No buts. You had a flight scheduled and paid for, and changed it without even considering the costs, because good old

Dad will cough up. Money doesn't grow on trees, you know. There are people in the world scraping through, barely surviving, and you're squandering cash on unnecessary flights, spending money like it's going out of fashion."

"Jesus, what's crawled up *your* arse?"

"Nothing," I snap.

There's silence, and I picture Tia in my mind's eye gawking at the phone in shock. I never raise my voice. Not ever, especially not at her. "Okay," she squeaks. "I'm sorry, I should have checked with you."

I slam my head against the headrest, squeezing my eyes shut. "Crap," I breathe.

"Bad day, huh?"

Terrible, but I'll never be able to explain it to Tia. "Something like that."

"You need a beer."

She's right. Or maybe something stronger than beer. "I'm on my way to meet Uncle Todd."

"Oh, has he got rid of the princess yet?"

Laughing, I start the car and wait for the Bluetooth to kick in. "The princess has locked him out of his own flat, so he's staying with me until she gets the message."

Tia bursts into a fit of laughter. "So you two are back to being the eternal bachelors together again, then?"

I hum my confirmation, then images of all the women I've dated flash through my mind one by one. "Have you liked any of the women I've dated, Tia?" I ask, genuinely curious.

"No," she answers swiftly, and I recoil.

"None?"

"Not one."

"Oh."

"I mean, Mum's pretty high-maintenance, but, seriously, Dad, every single one of the women you've seen are on a whole other level of princess. And Uncle Todd too, for that matter."

"So, what are you saying?" I ask, ignoring the fact that I'm getting relationship advice from my twenty-three-year-old daughter. And the fact that she's bang on the money. I can't refute that after finding a Tiffany's catalogue by my bed the other morning.

"I'm saying you need to realize you're forty-two."

Ouch.

"Who's flavor of the month at the moment?" she asks.

Month? It's more flavor of the week these days. "Amanda. Well, she was. I just called it off, though there wasn't anything to really call off."

"Dad, you need to . . . oh, crap! It's the last call for my flight." There's a flurry of activity down the line, and I definitely hear someone call Tia's name. A man. Not a boy, but a man. "Dad, I have to go. Love you." She hangs up, and I'm left in my car, static and thoughtful for a while.

Until my phone starts ringing, scaring the ever-loving shit out of me. "Fuck," I hiss, answering as I glance at the dashboard to see who's calling. "Oh, shit." It's too late. The call connects, and Tia's mum's panicked voice fills my car.

"Cambodia, Luke! She's on her way to Cambodia. She'll be abducted. Or drown in a swamp. I can't believe I let you convince me to let her go."

I roll my eyes. "You wouldn't have been able to stop her. She's a grown woman." I won't be telling her about my own mini meltdown. "Stop worrying."

"Oh, it's all right for you, Mr. I-have-no-responsibilities. Living your single life as you please."

"Hey, I'm a good father. Just because I've not settled down and churned out another two kids like you have, doesn't mean I'm not responsible. Go give someone else an earache, Janet. Like your poor sod of a husband." I hang up and slam my car into reverse, screeching out of my parking space and then out of the underground carpark. I really do need a drink.

Chapter Fourteen

Todd gives me a *what-the-fuck* stare when I walk into The Strip but gets straight to ordering me a beer when he registers my face. "If you ask me what's crawled up my arse, I'll lump you," I warn, joining him at the bar.

His lips straighten. "What's eating you?" I glare at him, and he backs off, hands up in defense. "Okay, bro, I'll say no more."

"Tia met someone," I tell him, rejecting another call from Amanda as I do. She'll get the message soon enough, surely.

His lips twist. "I'm guessing someone means it's a dude."

"A twenty-nine-year-old dude." I grab my pint and take a huge glug. "He lives in America."

"Oh, hell no." Todd looks as horrified as I would expect him to be. "Ain't no little fucker coming along and taking our girl away to America." He's practically shrieking. "No way."

In agreement, I nod and slug more beer. "And I just had Janet on the phone screeching at me."

Todd's lip curls. "Pops did you a good turn there." He waves the barman over and proceeds to order Scotch en masse. Looks like the car is staying where it is tonight. "So, what's the plan?" he asks, passing me a tumbler.

I frown as I take the glass. "The plan?"

"Yeah, are we flying out there to claim our girl back from . . ."

"Trent."

"Trent? What is he, a fucking river?"

I chuckle as my phone chimes and pull it out to find a text from Tia. I smile as I open it but lose that smile as soon as a photo pops up on the screen. Of my girl and a bloke. He has his arm thrown around her shoulder, both of them smiling brightly and giving me the peace sign. The fucking peace sign? His dreadlocks are blanketing Tia's head, the tie-dye bandana spanning his forehead looking grubby, and his fucking beard looks like a mole could burrow in it. "Great, so Trent looks like Stig of the Dump too."

Todd snatches the phone away from me, snarling as he looks down at the photograph. "Is that a nose-ring?"

"On Tia?" I shove my face in the screen of my phone, scanning every millimeter of my girl's button nose.

"No, on The River."

My eyes divert to The River, seeing a silver hoop through his left nostril. "Perfect."

"I bet he has one in his nipple too. And his dick."

I punch Todd's bicep and knock back my Scotch.

He shrugs. "What does she mean, anyway?"

"What?"

"Here." He points at the screen. "Her message. It says, *I'm saying broaden your horizons.*" Todd looks at me, cocking his head. "What does she mean?"

"No idea." I take the phone back, hating the fact that my daughter, my fucking *daughter*, is giving me relationship advice. And, worse, she's giving *good* advice. Broaden my horizons. Women *not* like Amanda. And as if the woman has heard me, my phone chimes again. And, *again*, I reject her call.

I look up and find Todd craning his neck to see my screen. I shove my mobile away and wave the barman over. "Two more, please."

"Oh, shit. A nutter?" he asks, amused.

"Yep. I called it off. Whatever *it* was." I look at him out the corner of my eye as I pay for the drinks. "Is your apartment still under siege?"

"Yep. You still seeing the married woman?"

"I'm not seeing a married woman."

I knock back my drink again, spotting my assistant across the bar with a group of my staff. "I'm supposed to be over there celebrating a new deal." I point my drink through the crowd. "Coming?"

Todd shakes his head at me, maybe in despair, maybe in disappointment. I don't know, and I don't care. I'm not sharing anything Lo related with him. Period. "I'll catch up with you." He looks past me, his expression morphing into a big, cheesy grin, and I look over my shoulder to see a pair of lookers sitting at the bar, one blonde, one brunette, and both definitely in their twenties. "Or you could join *us*?" Todd nudges me with his shoulder as he passes, giving me wide, excited eyes.

"Maybe in a bit." I have the perfect excuse. "I need to go show my face to my staff."

"Suit yourself. I'll take them both." His cheesy grin widens, and I roll my eyes, making to turn, but stopping when I clock a woman walking into the bar.

Oh, this is gonna be fun. I find Todd and smirk. "Someone's here to see you." I point my drink at the door, where Todd's self-proclaimed *girlfriend*, Charity, is scanning the bar. Looking fucking murderous. Todd frowns, following the direction of my pointed drink. I lean on the bar, settling in for the show, and watch as Charity spots my best mate near the two hotties at the bar.

"Oh fuck," I hear Todd mutter, placing his drink on the side and widening his stance, ready for what we all know is coming.

She stomps over on her heels, throwing a filthy look at the two women that Todd's moved in on, locking and loading her arm on the way. I screw my face up, ready for the blow, and when it comes, it comes with force. The sound of her palm connecting with Todd's cheek is piercing, everyone in the vicinity flinching. "You bastard," she screams, collecting his drink off the bar and throwing the contents in his face. "At least have the fucking balls to tell me to my face."

Todd remains where he is, quiet and accepting of her outburst. "You done?" he asks, cool as can be.

She huffs and puffs a few times, before pivoting, her nose in the air, and sashaying out of the bar. I snort through my nose, the laughter I'm suppressing building to a point that I can no longer keep it contained, and Todd starts to slowly and carefully wipe himself down, turning on the spot to face me. "Do you think that means she'll get her shit out of my apartment now?" He reaches up to his cheek, which is glowing, and rubs on a painful face. "Motherfucker." Slapping a smile back on his mush, he swings back toward the two women. "Ladies!"

I laugh and make my way over to the team, chinking glasses with every drink held out to me and accepting the congratulations, as well as giving my own. Pam gives my shoulder a good rub. "Nice work today."

"Thanks." I point to her glass of . . . Coke?

"I have six babies to pack off this weekend."

"Huh?" Pam's knocking on sixty. Babies?

"Polly, my beagle, had pups. They're twelve weeks this weekend and their new owners are collecting them."

I tilt my head, surprised. "So you breed on the side?"

Pam laughs, her eyes crinkling behind her glasses. "Not really. Polly got fruity with a friend in the park. On the plus side, the fellow she got fruity with is a descendent of a Crufts champion, so I have six thoroughbred beagles earning me a grand a pop."

I balk. "Seriously?"

"Seriously." She laughs, discarding her empty glass on the side.

"Six grand, just like that? I'm in the wrong business."

"Well, five at the moment. One little man hasn't got a home yet." Pam pouts. "He's the runt of the litter, bless him. A lemon beagle. He won't make Crufts."

"I'll have him." I have not a fucking clue where those words came from, and I actually look over my shoulder, like someone behind me said them.

"What?" Pam laughs harder. "You?"

"Yes." I square my shoulders, slightly offended. "I brought up my Tia, and she turned out just fine." I ignore the fact that she's currently on her way to Cambodia with Stig of The Dump. "A puppy will be a breeze."

Pam lowers her chin, looking at me questioningly over her glasses. "You want a puppy?"

"Yes." My mind goes into overdrive. I'll meet Lo every day and we'll walk our dogs together. It's the best idea I've ever had.

"And who's going to look after the puppy while you're at work?"

"I'll take him to work with me." No problem.

"Right." Pam part frowns part laughs.

I nod decisively. "I'll pick him up on Sunday. Have him ready for six."

"Okay," Pam relents, waving to a few people by the bar. "Then I'll be off to give your new baby his bedtime feed."

"Great." I toast her declaration and polish off the rest of my drink. "See you Sunday."

Pam wanders off, and I spend the next hour drinking way more than I should, while chatting with some of my staff, most of them more pissed than I am. When Todd makes his way over to me with a huge grin on his face, I know exactly what's coming. "So"— he moves in close to my side, and my eyes fall to the two women at the bar he's spent the last hour charming— "Maxine and Cherry are up for a night at Luke's Bar."

"I love how there are no women permitted in our bar until you say so." I catch the eye of the brunette. I don't know if it's Maxine or Chelsea, but I return her smile, nevertheless.

Todd points his tumbler at them, his cheek nearly touching mine as he looks over. "Don't let me down, bro. Maxine thinks you're hot."

"How old are they?" I ask, and immediately wonder why. I don't usually.

"Who cares? We're past forty. We need to seize these opportunities when we can. We might wake up tomorrow with thinning hair or erectile dysfunction."

"What the fuck, Todd?" I cough, getting lusty eyes from Maxine.

"Hey, could be a true story."

"Not if I have anything to do with it." My hand instinctively goes to my hair and runs through the thickness.

"Then you'll come?" He looks at me hopefully.

"You have your place back now. Take Chelsea there."

"It's Cherry. And what about her friend?" Todd whines. "If you don't jump on board, they'll do that girly thing girls do when they refuse to leave each other."

"Then have a threesome." I turn toward the bar and slip my empty onto the side. "I'm not game tonight."

"What the fuck's gotten into you, Luke?" Todd gives me evil eyes. "Since when are you not game?"

I drop my head back tiredly. "Maybe I'm re-evaluating my approach to relationships."

"Oh my God. So are you telling me you're not attracted to her?" He points in the direction of Maxine.

"Of course not," I say stupidly. She's a stunner.

"Great, then you'll come." Todd slaps my shoulder and heads back to the women before I can argue with him, and I stand for a few moments, joining Todd in trying to figure out what's gotten into me. Todd has every right to be put out by my refusal to entertain the two women. It's how we roll, always has been.

When Todd looks back at me and flicks his head in gesture for me to get my arse moving, I go with it, turning and saying a few farewells before I make my way over, being greeted with a lovely smile from Maxine.

"Hi." I offer my hand. "Luke."

"Maxine," she replies, flicking an impressed look to her blonde friend. "Todd suggested a few drinks at your place."

I bet he did. I cast a glance to Todd, finding him mildly nodding. "Then shall we?" I drop her hand and motion to the door.

The girls slip down from their stools and strut out of the bar, and Todd fist-pumps the air. "We're back in the game, bro."

I laugh at the stupid twat and let him push me out of the bar.

The taxi ride to my place was pretty uneventful, Maxine and I silent, Todd and Cherry trying to control wandering hands.

As Todd pours drinks at the bar, I slip off my jacket and toss it on a chair, heading for the jukebox. I select a random playlist, and The Weeknd starts to fill the room. As I approach the bar, both of the women slip out of their coats and get comfy on bar stools, taking the wine Todd slides toward them.

It's all quite civilized for a while, the first hour spent as it usually is when we do this, everyone getting progressively drunker, Todd throwing me look after look as they start to get more touchy-feely with us. Then, as predicted, our group breaks up, and Todd leads Cherry to the other side of the room for some privacy, settling her on the couch and getting cozy.

I smile and tip my bottle of beer to my mouth, dropping my eyes to my knee when a hand is neatly placed on it. I look up at Maxine, and she smiles demurely, moving in closer. She's definitely mid-twenties. This isn't going anywhere, except to the bedroom.

"So you own a security firm?" She cocks her head, looking interested, but I've been here too many times before. I see straight through her feigned interest in what I *actually* do for a living. She's more interested in how much money I earn. I'm not in denial. I'm a mature, wealthy man. It's a fucking tragedy that early forties counts as mature these days. The fact that I have looks supporting me too, makes me a magnet for a certain kind of woman. Like this woman here. She's a gold digger through and through. Why am I only admitting this now?

"I own a security firm, yes," I confirm.

"It must be a successful security firm." She casts her eyes around my home.

"I scrape by." I have another glug of my drink but pause when my phone starts vibrating on the bar. I frown and scoop it up when I see Lo's name, feeling panicked. Shit, what if she needs me to fetch her again? I'm too pissed to drive, and I left my car in town.

> Boris says hi.

I smile at my screen, relaxing in relief.

> Hi back to Boris. What are you doing awake at this time?

It's gone midnight. And isn't it a bit risky her texting me like this? What if he catches her? What if he reads her messages? I start to worry for Lo, my worry only growing as I spend the next ten minutes waiting for a reply while Maxine drapes herself all over me, stroking my arm, whispering in my ear, trying to seduce me. Why hasn't Lo answered me? I spin my phone in my hand, totally ignoring the woman sprawled across my lap as my mind spirals. I scroll back through our exchanged messages, trying to see how they read. How suggestive they would seem to someone. Someone like a husband. What would he do?

I jolt on my stool at my straying thoughts. I have to respect that she's married, but would a friend let her go home to a monster every night? Actually, doesn't the fact that I've promised not to ask make me a terrible friend?

Why hasn't she replied?

Gently moving Maxine from my lap, ignoring her slighted face, I pour myself a Scotch and sip it while I try to figure out what to do. I honestly don't know. I can't call her in case she's with him. Fuck, this is horrible. I look up and see Todd and Cherry squirming around on the couch, going at each other like sex-starved teenagers, and Maxine has now climbed up onto the bar, attempting to grind her crotch in my face.

I turn away, and when my phone dings, I rush to open the message and breathe a sigh of relief when I read it.

> Struggling to sleep.

Why's she struggling to sleep? What's on her mind? I look up at Maxine and across to my slag of a friend, who's now starting to remove his prey's clothes. Then I feel friction in my crotch area, and I glance down to find Maxine's hand stroking me. There's not even a twitch of movement beyond my fly, and when she starts to unzip me, I take her wrist to stop her. "Not tonight." Grabbing the bottle of Scotch, I stride out of the room.

"Hey, where are you going?" Maxine calls.

"Make yourself at home." I take the stairs fast and make my way to my bedroom, kicking my shoes off, and placing my bottle on the bedside cabinet. I yank off my tie and strip down to my boxers, and then lie on the bed, propping myself up on the pillows.

> Why?

I need to know. I click send and wait, hoping she won't take too long to answer this time, because each delay increases my apprehension.

> Did you have a good night?

I stare at her reply, running the rim of my glass across my bottom lip. She's evaded my question. Why? I'm desperate to know, yet I've fast learned with Lo that I shouldn't push it. But before I answer her, another message comes through.

> Can you talk?

She wants to talk? Another *why*? She's at home. How the hell can she talk to me if she's at home with her husband?

> Is that wise? I don't want to cause any trouble.

> He's asleep.

All kinds of things are springing into my mind now. He's asleep, and Lo must be pretty confident that he's in a deep sleep if she's cool with talking. Has he drunk himself into a coma? Is that what the deal is here? Is he a raving alcoholic who gets handy with his fists when he's had too much? I shudder, wishing I could stop my mind from reeling. Lo is one of the gentlest women I've ever met. Actually, she's *the* gentlest. She's petite, so tiny and fragile. She's also timid. Did he make her like that? I try to stamp my mind clear and dial her. It rings once before her whispered *hello* comes down the line. I'm immediately more uncomfortable about this.

"You okay?" I ask, my voice close to a whisper too, like he might hear *me*.

"I'm fine. I just wanted—"

"Just wanted to what?" I place my drink on the nightstand and roll onto my side, pulling the duvet up to my waist.

"Nothing."

'Tell me," I push gently.

"I just wanted to hear your voice."

I swear, my fucking heart bursts with happiness hearing those words. "Well, here I am. And my voice." I hear her laugh under her breath, a laugh that suggests she feels silly. She shouldn't. I could listen to her forever.

"So did you have a nice night?" she asks.

"I did. I've had way too much to drink."

"I can't remember the last time I had a hangover," she muses.

"You don't drink much?" Does he drink enough for both of them?

"Not really. I don't get the chance, to be honest." She sounds almost wistful, like she's dreaming of drinking herself into oblivion.

I move my phone to my other ear so I can snuggle my head into the pillow, imagining where she is at this precise moment in time. He's asleep, so she can't be in bed. She should be in bed. It's late. "You sound like you need to."

"I do. Completely obliterated," she says decisively, like the simplicity of getting off her face would make her year. And again, my mind starts spiraling. People get plastered to drown in their sorrows. I start plotting, suddenly determined to find a way to get Lo out for a night and let her drink herself into a complete stupor. I wonder what she's like when she's drunk. I can't imagine it. Would she tell me all her secrets? Would she spill everything to me? The possibility, right or wrong, only makes me more determined to find that opportunity.

I roll onto my back and look at the ceiling. "Then we'll make sure that happens sometime soon," I say, looking at the door when I hear a few bangs from behind.

"Luke, I'm coming to find you," Maxine calls, making my eyes bug. Oh hell. I cover the bottom half of my phone and scramble out of bed, just as she comes barreling into my room. Now *this* is obliterated. She's hanging on to the door to hold herself up, her body swaying dangerously. "There you are." She staggers toward me and flops to her back on the bed. "Take me," she demands, arms and legs sprawled like a starfish.

I deflate on the spot, and I hear Lo calling my name. I step out of my bedroom, knowing I have no hope of shifting Maxine off my bed, and shut the door behind me. "Hey." I sound as sheepish as I feel.

"Everything okay?" she asks.

"Yeah. Todd's on a mission."

"Ooohhhh," she breathes. "Amanda?"

Wilting, I squeak a "Nope," not waiting for her to ask how old this one is. "Mid-twenties, I'd guess." I'm lying. She's definitely early twenties.

"Oh, Luke." Her disappointment makes me feel shitty. "I'll let you get back to your party."

"It's not really a party. I've left Todd in the bar and come to bed." I'm blabbering like an idiot.

"I should get to sleep, anyway."

I want to punch my own face in. Fuck, I don't want her to go. And I definitely don't want her to be disappointed in me. I want to tell her that Todd brought the girls back, that I had come to bed alone. There she is struggling through life, unhappy, wanting to hear *my* voice, and I'm here having a fucking party. God damn me. But what can I say? I can't go see her. I can't suggest that she has me pegged wrong, because she doesn't. All I can do is let her go and hope to God that she'll speak to me again next week. "Okay," I say quietly. "Sweet dreams, darling."

"Night, Luke," she whispers, and then she hangs up.

I stare at my mobile for a few minutes, and then sigh, letting myself back in my bedroom, ready to guide the drunk woman down to the bar. I find Maxine sprawled on my bed. She's asleep, snoring lightly. "Great," I mutter, looking over my shoulder when I hear a squeal of delight coming up the stairs. Todd is dragging Cherry up, both of them half undressed. He clocks me on the threshold of my bedroom and grins before disappearing into one of the five spare rooms.

I sag where I stand, weighing up my chances of waking Maxine. I don't fancy them. So I make my way to another room, collapse into bed, and let my brain torment me with all the endless questions I have about Lo.

Chapter Fifteen

"Holy mother of all fucking hangovers," Todd says as he falls into the kitchen the next morning. He's scratching his blond head, squinting, as I stir some sugar into my coffee.

"You look like shit," I tell him.

"How'd you look so fresh?" he mumbles, joining me at the breakfast bar and stealing my coffee.

"Maxine wasn't exactly functioning."

"Oh?" He gives me a disappointed look.

"She passed out on my bed."

"Ah, man. That sucks." He lightly punches my bicep. "Sorry for your loss, bro."

I let his joke slide over my head, avoiding telling him not to be sorry, since I'm not.

Both of us look to the door when two bedraggled women enter the kitchen, one looking satisfied, the other looking sheepish. No prizes for guessing which is which.

"Morning," I say, watching as Maxine rubs at her forehead. "Coffee?"

"Please," Cherry pipes in, eyeing Todd's torso.

"No thanks." Maxine nudges her friend in the side, giving her a look that suggests she wants to escape quickly. "We should be going, right?"

Cherry's face disagrees, but she relents, sashaying over to Todd. "Call me?"

Todd plasters on a smile that I've seen too many times. A dirty great big *fake* smile. "Sure thing, sweetheart." He kisses her cheek and slaps her arse, making her giggle as she walks out of the kitchen.

"Nice meeting you, Maxine," I call to her back as she makes a quick, embarrassed exit. I look at Todd, who I know has already forgotten about Cherry. "You're not going to call her, are you?"

"Rule number one. Always take *their* number. Never give them yours. I made that mistake once, and she moved herself into my apartment."

I laugh and get up to make myself another coffee, since Todd's kindly slurping his way through mine. "You gonna check if she's gone yet?"

"I have a locksmith meeting me there at eleven to change the locks again. Can you believe she did that?" Todd turns a pleading look onto me. "Will you come with me?"

"What, to your apartment?"

"Yeah. She might have set booby traps. I need my wingman with me."

I howl with laughter. "You're such a pussy."

"Is that a yes?"

"I'll get a shower." I head for my room and strip the bed before I dive under the hot spray.

"I can't hear anything," Todd says, his ear pressed to the wood of his door. "What's the time?"

"Eleven," I confirm, looking up as a man rounds the corner in the corridor, carrying a toolbox. "I think this is your locksmith."

"Great." Todd shakes the hand of the man and proceeds to show him ID before he gets to work on the locks.

"Bad breakup?" the locksmith asks, just as the door pops open.

"I didn't even know we were together," Todd mutters, and I laugh, watching as the locksmith pushes the door open and Todd moves back, cautious.

"Does it look safe?" I ask, craning my neck to try and see inside.

"Fucking hell," the locksmith breathes, wandering in and gazing around.

"What? What is it?" Todd rushes in after him and gasps, as I follow on behind. "The fucking bitch!" He stomps into what can only be described as carnage. It's a fucking mess. The couch has been slashed, the walls are covered in—

"Is that dog shit?" I get a waft of a god-awful smell and pinch my nose, moving back out of his apartment. Oh Jesus, it's rancid.

"What did you do to her, my friend?" The locksmith joins me on the other side of the door, covering his face with his palm.

"I can't believe she's done this." Todd grabs a scrap of material off the floor and gapes at it. "My Vivian Westwood shirt!" He covers his face with it and runs through to his bedroom, shouting when he arrives there. "She's shredded the fucking lot." He appears back in the open-plan living area, eyes wide with shock. "All my clothes. They're ruined." In a bit of a daze, he wanders through to the kitchen. I face the stench and trail him, entering the kitchen to find it looking like a bomb has gone off. Every glass, plate, and piece of dinnerware is smashed to smithereens, and red lipstick covers every cupboard door spelling out every derogatory name under the sun.

"Well, at least she's gone," I quip lightly.

"That's it," Todd barks. "I'm fucking celibate from now on. You stick your dick in a woman these days, they confuse it for a fucking proposal. I'm done." He turns into me and grabs the front of my jacket, bunching it in his fists. "Don't let me sleep with another woman ever. Do you hear me?"

"You're a fucking joke." I push his hands off, taking in more carnage. "Did she cut all the strings on your blinds?" I ask, wandering over to the wall of windows on the other side of the kitchen, where there are a million wooden slats hanging haphazardly. I turn to find Todd with his head in his hands. "This is going to cost a fortune." I motion to what's left of his apartment and belongings. "Would've been cheaper to marry her."

"Fuck off," he snaps, and I snigger, because the twat's had this coming for years. "And I don't know what you're laughing at," he mutters. "I'll be living with you until this mess is sorted out."

That soon snaps my amusement into line. "What?" I go after him as he trudges back into the lounge. "Oh no, no, no."

"Oh, yes, pal. Besides, she might come back and try to murder me in my sleep." Todd shudders on the spot and grimaces at a nearby wall, moving away from the shit-smeared mess. "The bitch must have emptied every dog-shit bin in London. Look at it!"

I glance around at the warzone, slowly coming to terms with my fate. He's right. He can't stay here, as much as I think he deserves to. Besides, I won't have to endure any more of his parties, since he's celibate now. "You have a week," I declare, making a hasty exit, my nose wrinkled as I go. I need a shower. But first, a workout.

I spend the rest of the weekend purposely keeping myself busy. I've slugged ten tons of shit out of my punch bag four times, swam ten miles, and won ten games of pool against Todd.

It's early Sunday evening, and Todd and I have picked up a crate of Bud ready to slob out in the bar for the rest of the night and watch any sport that happens to be on. We both need man time.

I bust two bottles open and hand one to my mate before I

drop down on the couch next to him in my shorts. The poor bloke still looks in shock, and to be fair, he deserves to be. Charity certainly left her mark.

"I've taken tomorrow off," he says, draining half his bottle in one swig. "Compassionate leave."

I chuckle, flicking the TV over to Sky Sports One. "Did any of the cleaning companies get back to you?"

"One out of four. Seems the mention of dog excrement is a bit of a turn off, even for industrial cleaners. A grand. A whole fucking grand, and that's just to clean the walls."

I grimace. "I'd want more than that." My phone dings from the table where both our feet are propped, and I dive forward more speedily than I mean to. I can feel Todd's alarmed eyes on my back as I check the message. "Pam?" I frown, punching in my code to unlock my phone.

"Pam?" Todd asks. "Your assistant Pam?"

"Yeah." I scan her message, my mouth falling open, our conversation of Friday night coming back to me. "Oh shit." I jump up from the couch.

"What?" Todd looks up at me, interest rampant on his face.

"I'm supposed to be somewhere." I slide my beer onto the table and grab my T-shirt, yanking it over my head while shoving my feet into my trainers.

"Where?"

I don't answer him, making a mad dash for the front door. "I'll be back soon."

Pam's face is a picture of disapproval when she opens her front door to me at 8:00 p.m. "He's been waiting patiently, watching all his brothers and sisters being taken home by their new parents. He thinks his daddy doesn't love him."

Fucking hell, talk about making me feel like shit. "Okay, so I've not got off to the best start."

She opens the door wider and ushers me inside. "Straight down the hall to the kitchen."

I follow my feet until I breach the entrance of an old country-style kitchen, spotting . . . "Is that a cage?" I ask.

"A playpen. They're perfect for keeping the little rascals contained." Pam wanders over to the white-framed cage, and I follow until a ball of white comes into view. My manly heart melts. He's sitting at the edge of the cage, all alone, looking up at me. His eyes are a little droopy, his ears huge and floppy, and his little tail starts whipping from side to side at a monumental rate when he sees me. "He's so cute," I say quietly, dipping and scooping him up with one hand. I laugh when his tongue starts lapping at my cheek, my face screwing up. "I guess we'll be off then." I turn with my new friend under my arm and head for the door.

"Um . . . Luke?" Pam calls, stopping me halfway down the corridor.

"Yeah?"

She gives me an expectant look and presents her palm to me.

"Oh, of course." I dip into my pocket and pull out my wallet. "Do you take American Express?"

Pam laughs, and I frown. "No, Luke, I do not take American Express."

"Visa?"

She rolls her eyes and heads for the kitchen worktop. "Come here, you clueless man."

I semi scowl as I wander back into her kitchen, being presented with a file full of paperwork. "What's this?" I ask.

"His papers, his vaccination record, his certificates, and his microchip details. You'll have to contact the vet to give your details."

My face must be as blank as my mind, but Pam ignores it and continues to feed me information.

"There are recommended insurance companies, his flea and worming schedule, as well as his diet details."

What the bloody hell? "For a puppy?"

"Yes, Luke, for a puppy." She's looking at me with slight amusement, and I just know she's expecting me to hand him back at any moment. "Here's a blanket with his mother's scent on it. And a bag of food to keep you going until you can get to the pet store. You can make a transfer for the thousand tomorrow. I'll remind you when you get to the office."

"Bet you will," I say sardonically, letting Pam dump yet more stuff in my arms. "Can I go now?"

She smiles. "Pleasure doing business with you, boss."

I roll my eyes and leave, hearing Pam chuckling as she shuts the door behind me. "So it's me and you, kid," I say to him, letting him continue to lick my face as I open the passenger door. "She thinks I can't take care of you." I place him on the seat and pull his seatbelt across his tiny body, clipping it into place. "There. Safe as houses." I shut the door and make my way round to the driver's side, opening the door, finding my new mate is now in my seat. "Hey, you can't drive, buster." I pick him up and place him back on the passenger seat, rearranging his belt. "Stay."

He jumps straight back onto my lap, his front paws on my chest so he can reach my face to lick it to death. "No," I say as firmly as I can, putting him back where he should be. "Stay." He looks at me, his head cocked to the side as he sits. "Good boy," I praise, starting the car. I've not even made it to the end of the street and he's back on my lap. I give up and let him stay. I'll never get home tonight. "I'm pretty sure this is illegal," I mutter as I drive home, having to take it easy and negotiate the steering wheel carefully so I don't smack him on the head every time I take a corner.

When I roll to a stop outside my house, he stands and gets his front paws on the side of the window, his inquisitive face looking up at my home. "Impressed?" I ask him, positioning him under my arm and getting out. "Honey, I'm home," I call as I shut the door behind me.

Todd appears in my hallway with a beer in his grasp. "Don't

ever say that again or—" His disgust dies and gooey eyes are born. "Oh my God, how cute is that?" He meets me halfway across the hall and forsakes his beer for my new mate, taking him from my arms and cooing all over him. "Who does it belong to?"

"Me." I dump the endless stuff Pam gave me on the table and sling my car keys next to it.

"Yours?" Todd looks at me, unsure. "You've got a dog?"

I shrug it off, like it's no big deal. Because it isn't. I head for the bar and Todd follows. Grabbing a beer, I unscrew the cap and check the score.

"You getting lonely in your old age?" Todd sits, and the puppy proceeds to get more and more excitable, jumping up on his chest, licking him everywhere. "What's his name?"

My beer stops midway to my mouth. "I don't know."

"You've not named him?" He grabs one of his back legs and lifts. "Thank God." Todd breathes. "So, what are you gonna call him?"

"Steve." The name just falls right out, and Todd looks at me like I've lost my mind. "It's a good, strong, manly name."

"Steve? You're gonna call this cute, little thing Steve?"

"Yes, Steve." I nod decisively and drop to the couch next to Todd. "All right, Steve?" I say, getting my face up close to his. I get a good long lick up my cheek. "See, he loves it."

Todd exhales on a light laugh. "Steve it is. Hey, you do realize that Steve here is like the ultimate babe magnet, right?"

My brow bunches as I look at Steve. "He is?"

"Yeah, man. Women go gooey for puppies. You'll be like the Pied Piper when you take him for a walk, women trailing you for miles." I watch as Steve settles between us on the couch, smiling when he rests his chin on his paws and looks up at me. He likes me. I can tell. This is going to be a breeze.

· · ·

"Shut that fucking dog up," Todd yells, for the millionth time. Steve is howling like I've never heard a dog howl before, constant and piercing, even from the kitchen where he's contained. I slam my head down on the pillow and grab another, covering my face. Just ignore him and he'll get bored.

"Luke, for fuck's sake!" Todd sounds like he's close to tears, and I finally relent, looking at the clock as I drag myself out of bed.

"Three fucking a.m.," I mumble, trudging downstairs in my boxers. "All right, I'm coming," I call, opening the kitchen door. "What the fuck?" I cast my shocked eyes around my designer kitchen, taking in the mess, until they fall on a white, cute, furry bundle sitting in the middle of all the duck feathers. "I give you a goose down duvet and pillow, and this is how you thank me?"

Steve whimpers, looking at me with sad eyes. The little shit melts my heart. I sigh. "Come on." I turn and make my way back upstairs, hearing his paws pitter-pattering behind me. His little body overtakes me as I make it to my room, and he charges at the bed. Jumps. And headbutts the side of the mattress. I laugh, scooping him up and setting him on the duvet. I realize I shouldn't be encouraging this, but, fucking hell, I just need to sleep. Falling into bed, I pull the covers over me and drift off to the light sound of Steve snoring.

Todd and I stand on the threshold of my kitchen, staring in silence at the mess before us. In my sleepy state last night, I didn't appreciate just how much carnage he caused. The door has been scratched down to bare wood, and the fucker has had a go on some of the cabinet doors too.

"How can such a small thing cause so much damage?" Todd asks, rubbing at his sleepy eyes. "And make so much fucking noise?"

I pad into the middle of my kitchen and gaze around. "It's not quite on the level of your apartment." Frowning, I look down, lifting my foot when I feel a wet warmth between my toes. I grit my teeth and search out the unruly puppy I've stupidly adopted. He's sitting by the fridge, his tail whacking the tiled floor. "Your behavior needs to change if you and I are gonna get along."

Steve yaps and Todd laughs, leaving the kitchen. "Have a good day, bro," he calls.

What was I thinking? "This mess better be gone by the time I get back downstairs," I snap, marching out of the kitchen, wiping my foot on a pile of duck feathers as I go.

While I get myself ready for work, Steve plays shadow, following me from the shower to the bedroom, to my closet, to the hallway and, finally, to the car. I don't bother buckling him in, letting him sit on my lap as I drive to the office, stopping off at Starbucks on the way to pick up a coffee and some breakfast for Steve.

When I get out of my car in the underground car park, I look like a frigging snowman, my grey suit covered in white dog hairs. "Great," I mutter, brushing myself down. Collecting Steve off the driver's seat, I head to my office. I get a dozen women swooning all over the pint-sized fraud on my way to my floor, and each time I grunt at their comments about his cuteness. When the elevator door opens, Pam is waiting for me, a pad and pen in her hand. She spots Steve, then my face, and she laughs.

I growl, marching past her. "Did you purposely save the devil dog for me?" I ask, pushing my way into my office and lowering Steve to the floor. He bounds over to Pam when she drops to her haunches, giving him lots of fuss. I look on in disbelief. "Don't praise him."

"Luke, he's a baby." She scoops Steve up and lets him ravage her face with his tongue. "You need to bond."

"We did plenty of that in bed last night when he wrapped himself around my head."

Pam gives me a disapproving look. "He slept in your bed? Oh, Luke, you've broken rule number one."

"What was I supposed to do? He was howling until three a.m."
I drop into my chair and run a hand down my unshaved jaw. "He's
massacred my kitchen, ripped his bed to shreds, and pissed everywhere." I throw Steve a dirty look. He looks far too pleased with
himself.

"Where's his collar?" Pam asks, looking at his neck. "And his
lead?"

"I haven't got them yet." I click my way into Outlook and scan
my emails.

"And if you're bringing him to work, you need a bed in here
for him."

"Anything else?"

"A water bowl, a food bowl. Has he eaten this morning?"

I peek up at Pam, pouting. "He had a blueberry muffin on the
way to work."

Her eyes bug. "Luke, you can't feed blueberry muffins to a
twelve-week-old puppy. What about the food I gave you?"

"We were late," I say. "Now, what's my day looking like?" Pam
places Steve on his paws and his nose goes straight to the ground,
sniffing his way around my office. I follow his scampered journey
all the way to my desk, where he squats. "What's he doing?"

Pam starts laughing as Steve's body starts to shake. "Did you
walk him this morning?"

"Oh, no, Steve!" He takes a dump right at the edge of my solid
wooden desk, and then proceeds to yap and howl around my feet,
like he's trying to get some fucking kind of congratulations.

"Steve?" Pam questions.

"Yes, Steve," I confirm dismissively. "Though I might change it
to Lucifer."

"No wonder he's being rebellious. Do you have any poop
bags?"

I look up at Pam tiredly. "Do I look like the kind of man that
carries poop bags?"

My assistant sighs in dismay and leaves my office, returning a few moments later with a plastic bag and some disinfectant spray. "Luke, I really don't think it's a good idea to bring Steve to work."

"Then I'll leave him at home."

"All day? Don't be stupid. You need a doggy day care." She makes a great job of cleaning up Steve's mess while I sift through my emails, holding my nose.

"I'll find one today," I assure her, putting that at the top of my priority list of things to do. "Now, tell me what my day's looking like."

"You have a conference call with the legal team in five minutes and a few one-to-ones this afternoon." Pam leaves the office, shutting the door behind her, and I begin dialing in on my call.

"Luke," I announce when prompted, listening to the chorus of hellos from various members of my legal department. We go through the pleasantries, everyone telling each other how great their weekend was, and as soon as they're done, I grab the tennis ball off my desk and stand, starting to wander around my office as I toss the ball up and catch it. "Where are we at on the renewal of the police interception contract?" I ask.

"Nearly there," Graham, head of legal, says. "A few i's to dot, yada yada, but all in all a smooth negotiation."

"Good. Did we get the . . . shit!" I blurt, tripping over something around my feet. I stagger a few paces, hearing a yelp, and look down to see Steve licking his front paw. "Crap, I'm sorry, mate." I drop my ball to the floor and reach down to rub his head.

"Luke, everything okay?" Lily, Graham's assistant, asks.

"Yeah, sorry." I make to retrieve my ball, but Steve swoops in and steals it, running across my office and dropping it by the window. He hunkers down on his front legs, his arse in the air, his tail wagging. Then he starts relentlessly yapping.

"Is that a dog?" Graham asks, though I can barely hear him over the noise Steve is making.

"Shhhh," I hiss, marching over to get my ball. Steve nearly takes my fingers off as I swoop to collect it, running to the other side of the office and dropping it again, before proceeding to bark his little head off. "For fuck's sake. Excuse me a minute, guys." I mute the call and stride over to my office door, swinging it open aggressively. "Pam!"

She looks up from her desk, holding back a grin. "Yes, boss?"

Steve pelts past my feet with my ball in his mouth, straight over to Pam's desk. "Watch Steve a minute," I say, quickly closing my door before she can refuse. I unmute the call and get on with the meeting.

Half an hour later, I'm done, though I don't go to save Pam. Instead, I get comfy at my desk and answer a pile of emails, before preparing for my one-to-ones this afternoon. Not once, but twice, I start drafting an email to Lo, just a friendly *Hello, how was your weekend?* kind of thing, but I delete my words both times, almost too afraid to ask. I'm desperate to tell her about Steve. But I want to see her face, see her light up with joy, as I know she will. So . . . how do I achieve that?

I ponder it for a few hours, determined to find a way to see her, and at noon, I brave venturing out of my office, knowing I'm going to get a stern reception from my assistant, but when I open my office door, I can't see Pam. Nor Steve, for that matter. Because half my company's employees are huddled around her desk making stupid baby noises. I roll my eyes and fight my way through the crowd until I find Steve in Pam's lap soaking up the attention he doesn't deserve.

"Oh, here's Daddy." Pam grins and passes Steve to me, his head a sea of hands fussing over him. "He's been a good boy, haven't you, Steve?"

I scoff and screw up my face when he attacks me with his tongue, licking and smothering me.

"He's so cute."

"Oh my God, I want one."

"I'll walk him at lunchtimes."

"Can I bring my dog into work?"

I ignore them all and make my way to the office café to get myself a coffee, hearing continued cooing in our wake. "You're a fraud," I tell Steve. "A total fraud." We enter the café to find Peter, one of my account managers, pouring a coffee.

He gleams at Steve in my arms. "So this is the new office mascot?" he says, scratching Steve's head. "I've heard lots about him."

I ignore him too, grabbing a mug from the side and pouring myself a strong coffee. "How's it going?"

"All good." He picks up a file and heads out. "I'm just off to Sharman House. The annual inspection for their equipment is underway. I want to swing by and make sure everything is set to run smoothly."

My ears prick up, and I swing around to face Peter's back. Sharman House? The firm Lo works for operates out of Sharman House. "I'll come," I blurt.

Peter looks over his shoulder, his forehead heavy. "You want to come?"

I nod, lowering and placing Steve on the floor when he starts to wriggle. "Sure. Always good for our clients to be aware of my continued interest in their business."

Peter's suspicious face is warranted. I have a whole team of people to make sure our existing clients are taken care of. "Why?"

I shrug nonchalantly. "It's a big contract. The landlords have a lot of companies operating from Sharman House. They need to keep them happy, therefore we need to keep the landlords happy."

Peter relents easily. "I'll meet you in the foyer in ten."

"See you there." I head back to my office, buzzing at the thought of potentially seeing Lo.

The crowd has dispersed from Pam's desk, and she looks at me as I pass, then looks at my feet. "Where's Steve?"

I slow to a stop, looking around my feet, too. No Steve. "Shit." Darting back to the café, I scan the space for him, my search turning up no results. Damn, where'd he go? "Steve?" I call, heading down the corridor. "Steve!"

"Looking for this?"

I turn and find Sam, one of our interns, holding Steve in her arms, her face buried in his furry head. I breathe out my relief and go to claim him but pull back when I notice Sam has her coat on and her bag over her shoulder. My conniving mine starts hatching a plan. I can't take Steve to Sharman House, and Pam might quit if I lumber her with him again. "Doing anything nice for lunch?" I ask, trying to sound as casual as possible.

She eyes me with all the confusion she should. In the six months Sam has been here, I've never asked her that question. "Meeting a friend at the café in the park."

The park? Perfect. "Want to take Steve with you?"

"You want me to walk your dog?"

I give her a pleading face. "I have a really important meeting. I need a babysitter, just for a few hours."

"But my lunch is only an hour long."

"Take the rest of the day off."

"Okay," she accepts easily and drops Steve to his paws. "Lead?"

"Oh." I look down at Steve, thinking. Fuck, I need to get that sorted. Casting my eyes around me, I search for something, anything that'll work for now.

"Your belt?" Sam says, nodding at my trousers.

She's brilliant. I unfasten the buckle and yank it out, handing it to Sam, then turn and dash back to my office. "Thanks, Sam."

Pam's looking for Steve again when I pass her desk. "He's being looked after," I assure her, grabbing my phone and jacket. "I'll be back in an hour." I head down to meet Peter.

Chapter Sixteen

As I stand in the lobby of Sharman House with the team of system engineers undertaking the maintenance inspection, I find my eyes constantly swinging to the bank of elevators every time one of the doors slides open. Each time, I breathe in, hoping one of the people who exits will be Lo going on her lunch break. She doesn't appear, and I become more disheartened each time.

Once we've been signed in and presented with visitors' passes, we're escorted to the control room where the chief engineer gives us a rundown of the equipment checked so far. The building is vast, with twelve floors and endless detectors and cameras on each floor.

"Have all the companies been informed of the maintenance underway?" I ask, scrolling down the clipboard of firms working out of Sharman House, my eyes hovering over Lo's company, Red Well.

"Yes. We've made a start in the basement." Peter looks to the chief engineer. "And we're moving up to make a start on the second floor by five?"

"One of my men will head up to the second floor to make sure they're ready for us, just as soon as he's put that detector back together."

Red Well are on the second floor. "I'll do that," I say casually, passing the clipboard to the chief engineer. "The blueprints?"

I'm passed an A3 sheet of paper detailing the camera and sensor locations on the second floor. I scan it, appearing to look interested. I'm not. What I'm actually doing is hoping I get to check up on Lo. "Thanks." I let myself out of the control room and head for the elevators, swiping my visitor's pass to get through the glass barriers. I check myself out in the mirror as I ride up to the second floor. My eyes aren't as bright as usual, and my jaw bristly. "Damn you, Steve," I mutter, exiting when the doors slide open.

"Hello, can I help you?" I'm asked by a woman wandering toward me, a tall, leggy woman, who's primped and preened perfectly. She smiles, trying to discreetly take me in.

I flash my visitor's card and a bright smile. "Luke Williamson," I say. "We're carrying out maintenance on the security of the building."

"Oh, yes." She goes into her posh leather handbag and pulls out her phone. "I recall an email."

"My team are working their way up the building. You're next."

"Oh, joy." She smiles, dragging her eyes to the screen of her phone. "I have a meeting to get to." She points to a desk set to the side. "Rachel will help you."

Rachel looks up and smiles. "Would be my pleasure." She darts a pleased look to the lady standing next to me. "How can I help?" She joins her hands on the desk and smiles up at me.

"I need to walk the floor." I flash the blueprints at her. "Just to check the locations match up with our records."

"Sure. Can I get you a drink?"

"I'm good, thanks. Shouldn't take too long." I look down at the drawing in my hand. "Oh, you could note down the departments for me." I lay the plan in front of Rachel. "I only have zones listed."

"Sure." She takes a pen and turns the paper, cocking her head as she tries to get her bearings. "Oh, right." She draws a cross. "We're here."

"Okay."

"This area here is marketing." She makes a note. "This here is sales, and here we have Scarlett's office. That's the lady who just left." *Scarlett.* Lo works for a lady called Scarlett.

"That's great, thanks." I swipe back up the blueprints and head down the corridor, taking a right at the end. Lo comes into view the second I round the corner, sitting at an L-shaped desk outside what I assume is Scarlett's office. She's tapping away at the keyboard of her computer, and the smile that slowly began to form the moment I caught sight of her dies when I see how drained she looks. Completely depleted. The vision makes my body fold slightly, and my mind races with why she looks so worn out.

Taking slow steps toward her, the paper in my hand rustles, and Lo's head lifts, but it goes back down again. Then she does a double take and shoots up from her chair. "Luke," she blurts.

"Hey." I smile, coming to a stop at the foot of her desk.

"What are you doing here?"

I hold up the blueprint. "We're carrying out maintenance work on the security system."

Her head tilts in question. "And the CEO does that, does he?"

I purse my lips, trying and failing to appear casual. "Just overseeing."

Lo's lips twist, revealing a poor attempt to keep her knowing smile contained. She has me all figured out, and I honestly couldn't give a toss. I miss her face. "Overseeing," she mimics quietly.

"Yes, and I saw the company you work for crop up. It would be rude not to swing by and say hi."

Her smile breaks, and it's the best thing I've seen all day. All week, in fact.

"Did you have a good weekend?" I kick myself when her barely there smile fades as a result of my question, her eyes suddenly evading mine. It makes my mind race further.

"Not bad, thank you." She sits back down at her desk and gathers some papers into a pile.

Shit, I'm losing her. Why'd I ask that? Especially after the weekend she thinks *I* had. She knows the truth, so I can't deny it. Although, I had no intention of sleeping with that woman. That's still slightly screwing with my head, because why didn't I? I don't know, but I need to reel Lo back in, so I perch on the edge of her desk, clearing my throat, as if I'm about to say something really important. She peeks up at me, and I give her one of my most dashing smiles. Lo rolls her eyes. I smile wider. "I have a secret," I tell her, watching as her expression drifts into curiosity.

"What?"

"I can't tell you."

She laughs. It's music to my ears. "Then why bother telling me you have a secret?"

"Well, I can't tell you *yet*."

"Then when can you tell me?"

I put my fingertip on my lips, feigning thinking. "I need help first."

She slowly leans back in her chair, twirling her pen through her fingers. "And if I can't help you?"

"Oh, you can definitely help me."

Lo's pretty forehead furrows. "How'd you know?"

"I just know." I stand up. "Are you free after work?" I hate the mental battle she's clearly having over my question. Fucking hate it, because I know for a fact that if she says no, it's not because she doesn't want to be available after work. It's because of him.

"I'm sorry," she begins, going back to her computer. "I have plans."

"Didn't I tell you once that you're a terrible liar?" I ask softly, crouching down on the other side of her desk and resting my forearms on the wood. I bring my chin to my arms and prop it there, smiling when she flicks me a cautious look. "It won't take long, I promise. And I'll drop you home. Or at the end of your street."

She's mulling it over. I can see her mind whirling, her teeth nibbling the inside of her cheek. "I can't be late."

"You won't be late," I assure her.

"Okay." She breathes out her agreement, but it's not a tired agreement, like she's exasperated by my persistence. It's an accepting agreement. She wants to help me.

"What time do you finish?"

"Five thirty."

"I'll be here." I raise and lean over the desk, planting an over-the-top smacker on her cheek. "See you then." I swagger away, pleased as punch, hearing Lo giggling quietly as I go.

I can't wipe the grin off my face all the way back down to the foyer. I spot Peter with the landlord of the building and divert toward them, handing him the blueprints as I pass. "Seems like you have everything under control," I say, getting on my way.

Chapter Seventeen

I sail through the rest of my afternoon back at the office. Steve's been curled up on the couch, sleeping soundly. Seems like that walk in the park with Sam wore him out.

Collecting my briefcase and my dog, I head out, looking forward to seeing Lo. Once again, I let Steve ride the journey on my lap, since the little shit refuses to stay put in his own seat.

When I pull up outside Sharman House at five thirty, I spot Lo waiting outside, her shoulders high, her hands burrowed deeply in the pockets of her fur coat. She sees my car and scuttles over, and I crank the heating up to make it warmer for her.

She swings the door open and drops into the seat, turning to face me. I grin from ear to ear and hold up my new friend. "Meet Steve," I announce proudly. "Steve, this is my friend Lo."

"Oh my God." Lo seizes him from my hands and cuddles him to her chest, fussing over him in a way that makes me feel slightly envious. What's a man got to do to get such genuine affection like that? Piss on her? I frown to myself. "You got a dog?" Lo looks at me, stunned. "I can't believe you got a dog."

"I've been thinking about it for a while," I lie through my teeth then pull out as Lo wrestles to get her seatbelt on.

"You don't seem like a dog man to me."

I can't hide my injured expression. "What does a dog man look like?" I ask, truly intrigued.

"I don't know," she admits, settling Steve on her lap. "This is your big secret?"

"Yep."

"So what do you need my help with?" She looks across the car at me, and I peek out the corner of my eye.

"A bit of shopping. Where's the nearest pet store?"

Lo laughs, and I savor the sound of it, admiring her from across the car—how happy she sounds. How happy she looks. And I realize that my heart is happier too. Her smile. Her laugh. Somehow, at some point, that has become so very important to me. And the past week was hard. But, I fear, nowhere near as hard as it was for Lo.

"And one of these," Lo says, dumping a squidgy toy on top of the piles of stuff in my arms. "And some of these." She collects down a box of—

"What are they?" I ask, losing sight of her when the box lands in front of my face.

"Puppy pads," she declares. "Steve will have plenty of accidents."

"You can put puppies in nappies?" I ask, astounded. Well, shit, that's all my problems solved.

Lo laughs and removes the box blocking me from view. "They're not nappies, Luke. They're like mats. Steve will pee on them instead of your floor." She heads off to another aisle, Steve tucked neatly under her arm. "You're so clueless; it's adorable."

Clueless? "That's a bit harsh," I grumble, following her. I'm the CEO of my own bloody company. That's not clueless.

"Oh, Steve, now we get to do the exciting bit." She kneels on the floor, placing Steve down with her, and rummages through—

"Are they clothes?" I gawk at the rail of full-on outfits, jumpers and . . . "Shoes?" Is she kidding?

"He needs to keep warm." She carries on rootling, not giving the panic in my voice any attention at all. "It's freezing out there."

"I've not seen Boris in clothes." A shop assistant passes me with an empty trolley, and I jump in his path, stopping him. "I'll take that, mate." I drop the piles of stuff into the cart and give my concerned attention back to Lo.

"He has a longer coat than Steve, though sometimes I have to put him in his jumper."

"Boris has a jumper?" I'm regretting this more and more. I really didn't think it through.

Lo stands and turns, holding up a camouflage print hoodie. "I think this suits his coloring perfectly."

I look down at Steve. I don't know why. Maybe hoping he'll appear as horrified by the prospect of wearing a hoodie as I am by the prospect of being seen with him in one. The traitor looks totally unfazed. "I think he likes it," I mumble absentmindedly, watching as Lo wrestles his little body into it. When she's done, she stands and joins me, and we both look down at Steve, who's looking up at us, his tail going wild.

"I think he does," Lo confirms.

I hear a low, rough snigger and look up, finding a huge dude with a Rottweiler laughing his nuts off at Steve. Or me. My dick shrivels. "Let's go." I grab the trolley and march toward the front.

"Wait." Lo grabs my arm and pulls me to a stop. "We need to get him a bed."

"I gave him a bed last night. He ripped it to shreds."

"That's what pu . . . oh no." Her attention drops to the floor. "Where's Steve?"

My heartbeat accelerates as I spin around, searching for him. "Steve?"

"Oh God, we're terrible parents." Lo runs to the end of the aisle and looks left and right. "Steve!" She disappears, and I stand like a plum for a few moments, wondering whether to follow her or head the opposite way.

"Bollocks!" I abandon the trolley and jog off in the other direction, calling him, scanning left and right down each aisle I pass. I can hear Lo across the store, calling Steve as well, sounding as frantic as I feel. When I reach the end of the row of aisles, I skid to a stop, seeing Lo down the way. "Nothing?" I call.

"Nothing." She looks stressed, and I can't deny it, I'm fast going out of my mind with worry myself.

"Go to the entrance," I yell, thinking we need to guard it in case he makes a bid for freedom. Lo shoots off toward the doors, and I retrace my steps, scouring the ground for any signs of a white blob. "Bloody hell," I curse, my panic increasing with every second that he's missing. Christ, there's a main road outside, cars whipping up and down. He'll be flattened. "Steve!" I reach up to loosen the tie around my neck, the panic wedging itself in my throat. "Steve!"

I pull to a stop when I hear a yappy bark. I haven't had my new baby long, but I'd recognize that yap anywhere. I heard it enough last night when the little shit kept me awake. "Steve?" I swing around, listening carefully. I hear it again and start following the sound, the noise getting louder and louder. My mobile rings from my pocket, and I pull it out while I take tentative steps up the dog food aisle, planning on leaving it to ring off. But it's Lo.

"Yeah?"

"Have you found him?"

"I can hear him." I listen carefully again. There's another yap, but for the life of me I can't figure out where it's coming from. "He's somewhere in the food aisle, I think."

She hangs up, and I drop to my hands and knees, the sound louder the lower I get to the ground. "Steve?" I peek under the shelving unit and come face to face with a white paw sticking out from beneath. "Steve!" Pushing my cheek to the ground, I look through the little gap. "How the hell did you get in there?" He yaps in return, sounding traumatized.

"What are you doing down there?"

I look up, being greeted by Lo's legs. My mouth momentarily falls open. I've never paid much attention to her legs. She has good ones.

"Luke?"

I get my wandering eyes under control and force my gaze to her concerned face. "He's trapped." I push myself to my knees and start pulling off the huge bags of dog food from the bottom shelf. "God knows how he got in here."

Lo joins me, looking through the gaps in the shelves. "Hey boy, we're here now."

Steve starts whining, distressed. "Fucking hell," I grunt, hoofing off a giant bag of dog biscuits. I'm fucking sweating.

"Come on, Steve." Lo reaches through the gap I've made, coaxing Steve out. "I've got him." She pulls him out and cradles him to her chest. I breathe a sigh of relief, panting like a bitch, as I move in and join her fussing over him.

"Steve, you scared the shit out of me." I drop my face onto his head and breathe in his puppy smell. "Don't do that again." It's then I realize that my head is practically on Lo's chest, and not for the first time, I notice how good she smells. It's so subtle and sweet . . . just like her. Our eyes meet, and we both smile. It's a smile of relief . . . I think.

"Collar and lead?" Lo gives Steve a kiss.

I swallow hard, my heart rate leveling out, and force myself to my feet, offering her my hand to pull her up. And once again, we're practically hugging due to the little shit in her arms, and it just feels so fucking good. This woman is good. All things good. Sweet. Kind. Pure. I've missed her. I've missed her input in my life. "Okay?" she asks.

I blink. Nod. "Yeah." I pass her, collecting the trolley from where I abandoned it and looking at Lo for instruction of where to head next. She shifts awkwardly and points past me to where a sea of leads hang. "Great." Let's get this done with. I pace toward the section I need and haphazardly select a collar and lead. Pink. They'll do. I throw them on top of all my other goods and head to the checkout.

"Pink?" Lo calls, pulling me to a stop. "And they look a bit big for him."

I scowl at thin air before me. "You choose then."

"What about these?"

I turn and find her holding up a royal-blue studded collar and lead. "Perfect." I get moving again and start off-loading my trolley as the clerk rings through all of my puppy paraphernalia. It takes forever.

"That's four hundred and two pounds, fifty, please," she eventually says.

I look at her in astonishment. "How much?"

"Did you find everything you were looking for?"

"And more." I slip my card into the machine and punch in my PIN, hearing Lo's muffled chuckle. I look out the corner of my eye and find her face buried in Steve's head, trying to conceal her amusement. That sound. Her face. I bump her with my shoulder on a roll of my eyes, collecting my purchases and instructing her to lead the way.

As I dump the ridiculous amounts of bags into the boot of my car, Lo climbs in the front with Steve, looking back. "Oh, get the doggy seatbelt."

I look inside my boot, scratching my head. "And which contraption was that?"

"The one with a seatbelt clip on the end."

I dig through the bags until I lay my hands on the only thing she could be talking about.

"And his new collar."

I grab Steve's collar and slam the boot. "There." I pass them to her. "How does that thing work?"

Lo puts Steve's new collar on with ease, and then clips the seat-belt thing through the D-ring. "And this bit goes in here." She points to the anchor for the seatbelt.

I nod my approval at the genius thing that'll stop Steve getting to my lap when I'm driving. "He'll probably chew his way through it," I grumble, starting the car and pulling away.

When we pull up at the end of Lo's street, I stop the engine and we both sit in silence for a beat, Steve looking between us. I laugh lightly at his cuteness, reaching across to stroke his head. "How nice it must be to have such a simple life," I muse, hearing Lo hum in agreement. "Shall we walk them together tonight?"

"You're going to come across town to walk Steve?"

"Thought you'd like the company."

She looks at me, smiling. "Eight?"

I mirror her smile and accept Steve when she hands him across the car to me. "Make sure you put his seatbelt on," she warns, then places her hand on my arm, pausing. I look at her and wonder what she's thinking. As always. "Thank you for this, Luke," she whispers. "I needed it. Needed . . . cluelessness." She leans across and pushes her lips to my cheek, holding them there for a few quiet seconds before pulling away slowly. As if she doesn't want to. "Meet you on the corner?"

I nod, unable to speak, and only start breathing again when she's out of the car. "Christ, Steve, what the hell is going on?" I whisper. He yaps, and I'm pretty sure it would translate to, *you're a twat*, or something equally insulting. And correct.

Chapter Eighteen

Todd's car is on my drive when I pull up. Swapping Steve's seatbelt for his lead, I collect everything from the boot and juggle it all into the house.

"Seriously?" Todd looks at me struggling into the kitchen.

"Thanks for your help." I drop it all to the floor and let Steve off his lead.

"Is that all for the dog?" He looks at the piles of goods, astounded.

"No, this is for you." I kick the side of Steve's new bed and wander over to the counter where I spot a note. I wince when I see it's from my cleaner, telling me she didn't agree to clean up dog piss. I toss the note to the side and make a mental note to leave her extra cash next week.

"And what the fuck have you put him in?" he asks, looking at Steve's hoodie.

"He looks like a cool dude," I argue as I head upstairs to get changed.

"Hey, you up for a few beers?" Todd calls after me.

"I'm going out."

"Where?" He sounds affronted, and I stall halfway up the stairs, cringing.

"Walking Steve."

"I'll come."

My cringe deepens. "I already have a dog-walking partner." I wipe my face clear and face him. "Sorry, mate."

He looks surprised, but then after a few seconds of his mind heading in the totally right direction, I see realization dawn on him. I brace myself. Todd gasps. "*She* has a dog. The married woman has a dog." He points down at Steve. "You only got this screeching little shit to get closer to her. Fucking hell, Luke. I thought you had a brain." He shakes his head in disappointment. "She's clearly leading you on, the prick tease."

I feel my blood boil over. I can't control it. "She's not a fucking prick tease." My roared words knock Todd back a bit, his mouth snapping shut. "Far fucking from it, and if I hear you utter another word to that effect about her, I'll rip your fucking head off, got it?"

Todd steps back in shock. "All right, bro. Calm down."

"And don't ever call Steve a little shit again." I dip and pick up the little shit and stomp to my bedroom, willing myself to calm down. That was way over the top of me. Way, *way* over the top. "She's just a fucking friend," I tell Steve, dropping him to his paws.

I rake a hand through my hair, sighing heavily. "Fuck it." I throw on some jeans and a heavy knitted roll-neck jumper, as well as my double-breasted navy coat and a scarf. Collecting my Timberland boots from my closet, I make tracks downstairs, set on apologizing to Todd. I didn't mean to blow my stack, and if he knew Lo, he'd understand why I did. He huffs and looks away from me when I enter the kitchen.

"I'm sorry, mate."

Todd swivels on his stool, turning his back on me. "Don't sweat it. And don't come crying to me when it all goes tits up."

"We're just friends," I say for the millionth time. "She has a dog, I have a dog. That's it."

My words prompt Todd to face me again. He looks insulted. "Put your hand on your heart and tell me you don't have feelings for her."

"I don't have feelings for her," I declare, thumping my chest. I really don't. Not those kinds, anyway. I love her as a friend. She's special.

Todd shakes his head in despair. "You're a twat."

"She's not happily married." I didn't plan on saying that, and I feel truly awful that I have. I feel like I've betrayed Lo in a fucked-up kind of way. And, really, I have no facts.

Todd looks at me with wide eyes. "But you're just friends?"

"Yes," I assure him. "I like her. A lot. She's . . . different. She makes me feel good about myself. But there was something not right from the moment I met her. She was so withdrawn, sad, and when I hugged her, she clung to me so desperately." Shaking my head, I pinch the bridge of my nose. "I don't know." I drop my arms to my side, exhausted. "The night I nearly ran her over, I think she stepped out in front of my car on purpose."

"What?" Todd recoils.

"Yeah." I roll my shoulders to rid my spine of the shiver that slivers up it. "What could push a woman to think death is the best option, Todd?"

"I don't know, but it's not your problem." He gets up and pulls the fridge open, grabbing a Bud. "Stay out of it, Luke."

I sigh, knowing deep down he wouldn't understand. He sees women in one light. I grab Steve's lead and get going. "See you later." I don't hang around to let Todd try and stop me.

A bulldozer couldn't, so Todd doesn't stand a chance. When you care for a friend, you're there for them. I'll always be there for Lo.

I've been waiting at the end of Lo's street for fifteen minutes clock-watching. It's ten-past, and I'm getting twitchy. So is Steve, throwing himself around my car, yapping and barking, dying to break free. Where is she? I spin my phone in my hand, deliberating over whether I should text her. No, that would be stupid. I'll give her ten more minutes. Those ten minutes feel like hours, and when I see someone jogging down the street, I deflate in my seat as soon as I see it's Lo. I frantically wait for her face to become clear, searching for any signs of distress. There's nothing. She raises her hand and waves, Boris trotting alongside her.

I slide out of my car, and Steve dives out behind me. "I was getting worried."

"I'm sorry." She comes to a stop and chugs in air. "I had—" She looks back at her house. "Never mind. I'm here now."

I force myself not to question her with my expression, and swallow down the interrogation. "Hey, Steve, a new friend for you." I let him pull me towards Lo and Boris, his body shaking with excitement at seeing one of his kind. Boris looks just as pleased to see Steve, and they both start sniffing each other's arses. I grimace. "Nice." Steve circles around me, and Boris circles Lo, both of them running excited rings around us, their leads getting all caught up. "Shit." I grab the side of my car, and Lo grabs me.

"My legs." She laughs, looking down at the tangle of limbs, dogs, and leather leads. "Boris, stop it."

"Whoa." I catch Lo as she falls forward, forsaking Steve's lead to save her from toppling. "I've got you," I say, wondering what on earth we must look like, causing chaos on the street corner.

I unravel my legs and dip to collect Steve's lead, holding Lo as I do. "I'm good." She chuckles, pushing back off my chest with her palms. Once we've regained control of our dogs, we start to wander down to the park, chatting easily. Always so easily. Her smile doesn't fall once. Not once. "So Todd basically uses your bar as a knocking shop?"

"Pretty much," I reply, watching Lo rub her hands together. "You cold?"

"I forgot my gloves, and this coat doesn't have pockets." She indicates down her gray, woolen knee-length coat.

I cock her my arm, encouraging her to hold on. She smiles and places her hands around my coat sleeve, and I bring my arm in close to my body so her hands are trapped between my upper arm and my torso. And it feels so . . . right. Natural. *Which is plain odd.* "Better?"

"Much, thank you. But he has his own place, right?"

I frown, trying to remember what we were talking about.

"Todd," she prompts, looking up at me with a smile.

"Oh, yes." I laugh lightly. "He does, but the girlfriend who he didn't know was his girlfriend trashed the joint."

"No," Lo gasps. "All because he split up with her?"

"He claims they were never together."

"But she was living there?"

"Apparently she snuck her stuff in bit by bit. He didn't notice until her mail started arriving."

"God, you two sure do pick them."

I laugh my agreement and something comes to me, something I haven't told Lo. "Hey, remember Amanda?"

"Whose calls you were dodging," she says sardonically, giving me high eyebrows. "You never did tell me what had you concluding she's a nutter."

"That's because you didn't reply to my text." I knock my shoulder into hers playfully.

"I'm here now," she muses, almost thoughtfully, looking forward. Yes, she's here now. *But for how long?* I swallow, getting back to the matter at hand, my mind probably diverting me away from the *other* matter at hand because I can't face the answer. "Anyway, I woke up with a Tiffany's catalogue on my bedside table."

"No way."

"Yes way. Subtle, huh?" I look down at Lo's grinning face and return her beam.

"Oh boy," she muses, and I nod my agreement. "So I assume she's been cast aside."

"I don't cast women side, Lo. I place them."

"If it makes you feel better, Luke. How's Tia getting on?"

"It does. And Tia's great. Found Stig of the Dump and decided to elope to Cambodia."

"Stig of the Dump?"

I hand Lo Steve's lead and fish through my pocket for my phone, opening Tia's text and pointing the screen at Lo. "Stig of the Dump," I confirm.

She bursts into fits of laughter, so I put my phone back in my pocket, letting her have her moment, the pleasure of listening to her too thrilling to try and rein her in. My smile is unstoppable, and so is the deep warmth in my heart. I place her hand back into the crook of my arm and take back Steve's lead as we continue down the path, Steve with his nose constantly up Boris's arse.

"You sound thrilled," Lo muses, gazing up at me. "Worried another man is going to steal her from you?"

"Very. She's a real daddy's girl. It has nothing to do with the fact that I'm a walkover or my bank balance is healthy, obviously."

"Obviously." Lo's head falls onto my shoulder, and I look down, thinking how good it looks there. Who would have thought this could be so pleasurable? Walking in the freezing cold with dogs, just chatting.

"What about *your* parents?" I ask. She's never spoken about them. About none of her family, actually. Have I overstepped the mark by asking? I don't know, but it seems to be feeling more and more unfair that I have detailed every tiny thing there is to know about me to Lo, yet she's held back so much about herself. That's not how friends work.

"My mother took her own life."

My eyes go round. "Shit, I'm sorry."

"It's fine. I came to terms with it long ago." Her shrug is casual and entirely inappropriate given the subject. "My father met another woman and moved to Canada."

"Mine moved away too," I muse, wondering if Lo has anyone at all. Anyone apart from me. "What about siblings?"

She shakes her head into my arm. "None."

"Friends?"

"I lost touch with them long ago. Life just got too . . ." She thinks before finishing. "Busy."

I hold my tongue. Busy? Or did they give up trying to pull her out of an unhealthy relationship? Did they get too upset watching Lo putting herself through that shit? That thought leads to another: will *I* ever try to remove her from an unhealthy relationship? And when she doesn't leave, will *I* walk away? Because I know I won't be able to sit back for much longer and see Lo like this. We're getting closer, easier, and with each day that passes, I care more about Lo and what the hell is going on in her life. "That's too bad," I say quietly. "Do I count?"

"As a friend?" she asks, peeking up at me.

"Yes." I look forward, making a silent promise to myself, and to Lo, that I will *never* give up on her, no matter what.

"Is it sad that you're my best friend?" Her eyes gaze into mine, and I see with perfect clarity how much I mean to her as a friend. I'm someone she knows she can call on when she needs to. It both paralyses me with helplessness and fills my cracking heart with happiness.

"No. It just means you're fussy and have great taste."

She laughs, nudging me as we walk. "You're cute, Luke Williamson."

"So are you, Lo Harper." I slow to a stop, leaving Lo looking up at me in question.

"Okay?"

"Yes." I turn into her and shove my hand into my pocket, pulling out my keys. She looks down at my hands as I separate my house keys from my car key. I pause when they're detached, looking down at my palm where they lay. I haven't given what I'm about to do much thought. Hardly any, in fact, but it just feels right for me to do it. I hold them out to her, and Lo steps back, her smooth forehead developing a few lines. "I want you to have these," I say, scanning her face. She's staring at me, quiet, maybe stunned. "Just in case you ever need somewhere to go." I cannot deal with Lo feeling as though there are no options if things are too much for her. The thought of her not having somewhere to escape to, a safe haven, makes my chest hurt. She trusts me, that's been proven each time she's reached out to me. She called me cute. And even though I don't know anything about her deeper, inner battles, the rest she wears on her sleeve. On her fucking beautiful face. I've never done anything like this before. I've only ever given my keys to my sister and my daughter, two women I love bone deep. And yet . . . here I am. Offering. Lo deserves more. More joy. More hope. More happiness. And if this gesture can provide that in some little way, I have to give it to her. Because she already has *me*.

Lo remains still and silent, looking at me in wonder. I've run out of words now, not knowing what else to say to her, so I slowly push my hand forward, hoping she'll accept. Selfishly, it'll ease me as much as I hope it eases her. Her eyes drop to my keys, and I see the internal battle she's struggling through. A few silent seconds pass, and I decide to make the decision for her. Reaching for her pocket, I slip the keys inside and take her hands, placing them back on my arm and getting us walking again. I can feel her gazing up at me, but I keep my focus forward, not prepared to make a huge deal of it. Because it isn't. "Let that be that," I say quietly, tugging Steve back when he wanders into a flower bed. *Again.* "Now, tell me how Boris has been."

She chuckles and replaces her head back on my arm, squeezing it in silent thanks. We continue to wander with no rush, silence falling between our chats, but each quiet time is comfortable, and it seems that neither of us wishes to fill it unnecessarily. It's cathartic. Peaceful.

When we reach the end of her street, I feel my heart sinking a little with each step I take, until she finally pulls us to a stop, not wanting to get any closer to her house. There's a brief moment of silence before she steps into my chest and curls an arm around my waist, resting the side of her face under my chin. I breathe in and tip my head back until I'm staring at the black sky, my spare arm slipping around her neck and holding her close. "You okay?" I ask, clenching my eyes shut. *Fucking hell, Luke. What's happening?*

She nods against me and breaks away. It's a good job, because I would never have released her otherwise. Reaching up on her tippy-toes, she moves in to kiss my cheek. I don't know what happens, but I can't stop it. I turn my face, just before her lips reach me, and her lips land on mine. I hear her sharp inhale, and I feel her body tighten, but she doesn't retreat. She just holds her lips there, her eyes glassy, staring into mine. I can see it takes everything in her to peel herself away, and though I'm suddenly desperate to grab her and haul her into me, I refrain. She swallows as she backs up, her fingers going to her lips.

"Good night." I smile sadly, fighting to stop myself from grabbing her and throwing her in my car, taking her home and keeping her safe.

"Good night, Luke," she whispers, turning and slowly walking away.

I don't get in my car, and Steve doesn't pester me to get moving. He just sits by my feet patiently while I mentally will Lo to look back before she disappears from view. I hold my breath, staring at her back as the distance grows, my hope dying with every meter she puts between us. And when my hope has just about diminished, she stops and looks over her shoulder, her eyes meeting mine. Her hand comes up slowly, and I follow suit, waving goodbye to her.

Chapter Nineteen

I couldn't shake the horrible ache in my chest for the whole of the next day. By the evening, I took a few paracetamol, wondering if I was coming down with something. An hour later, I still wasn't feeling right. Add to the fact that Lo hadn't contacted me, just made the horrible sickly feeling inside me all the worse. I held myself back from contacting her on Monday. On Tuesday, I literally had to sit on my hands all day at my desk. On Wednesday, I looked at Steve and convinced myself that all the barking he had going on was his way of telling me that I should call her. But I didn't. It killed me, but I didn't. Come Thursday, I was all out of restraint. I dropped her an email at lunchtime, suggesting —and hoping—that we could meet in the evening for a walk. Walking Steve isn't the same without Lo. Every night this week, it's felt wrong. Steve has been hopeless, barely walking in a straight line, weaving back and forth across the path and lunging for everything that floats by his little face.

She didn't reply. And I didn't sleep a wink all night while Steve was wrapped around my head snoring peacefully.

• • •

When Friday arrives, I decide to work from home. I look like shite, and I can't face the office. Todd's quietly observing me, and I know what he's thinking. He's right. I'm going out of my mind—worrying, imagining all kinds of scenarios. I listen in on three conference calls in the morning, not that I hear much. I swim fifty lengths of the pool, not that I remember. I dial her number twenty times and hang up before the call connects.

I go to meet her for lunch at one.

She doesn't show up.

By four o'clock, I'm back at my home office, pacing, trying to talk myself down, my mind constantly replaying the last time I saw her. The walk, our conversations, the laughs, the smiles.

The kiss I didn't mean to give her.

I grind to a stop, seeing Lo in my head as she walked away from me on the street. I see her turn around. I see her raise her hand in goodbye.

Goodbye.

I reach up and massage my pec. *Goodbye.* "No." I scan the floor at my bare feet. Goodbye. She was saying goodbye. Steve looks up from his bed in the corner and whimpers, as if agreeing. I rush to my desk and grab my phone, not thinking as I dial her office.

"Good afternoon, Red Well," a lady answers. It's not Lo.

"Lo Harper, please." I drop into my chair and pick up a pen, tapping it on my leather mouse mat.

"I'm sorry, Lo's off work."

I pull up, my tapping pen stopping. "Off?" She didn't mention being off work. "Is she on holiday?"

"I don't believe it was scheduled. Who's calling?"

I hang up before I'm forced to answer, staring at my mobile in my hand. It wasn't scheduled. My worry rockets, and all those scenarios I had playing havoc with my imagination recently are suddenly scarily more real. I breathe in and pull her mobile up, sending a text message to ask if she's okay. I get no answer.

"Fuck it." I dial her number, getting up from my chair and

pacing my office. It rings twice before going to an automated voice-mail, and I still on the spot, my heart quickening. It didn't go straight to voicemail, meaning her phone wasn't switched off. And it didn't ring long enough to automatically divert to voicemail. Which means she rejected my call.

I struggle for breath as my arse plummets to my chair, my breathing coming quick and fast.

She was saying goodbye.

She didn't pull away from my kiss, but that was because she knew in that moment she wasn't going to see me again. She was saying goodbye, and I didn't even realize it. I've fucked up. What was I thinking? I rest my elbow on the arm of my office chair and drop my forehead to my palm. I don't know what to do.

So I do what instinct is telling me to do. "Come on, Steve." I get up and throw on my Ralph Lauren gilet over my jumper, grabbing Steve and his lead and heading out. I drive to Lo's house in a haze of despair, constantly running over that goodbye, trying desperately to find another explanation for her elusiveness. There isn't one. I imagine her walking into her house that night. I imagine her husband waiting for her. I imagine him telling her that he saw her on the street kissing another man. Would he have gotten angry? Would he have taken his anger out on Lo? Jesus, I can't have her taking the blame for my stupidity. It was my fault. I've thrown away a friendship I value in a moment of foolishness. I smash my fist into the steering wheel, praying I'm wrong. Praying for that simple explanation that'll settle me. I'll explain to her husband. I'll tell him it meant nothing.

When I pull into Lo's street, I park at the end and pull out a dog treat from my pocket, giving it to Steve to keep him occupied, before I get out of the car. I remain on the opposite side of the road, walking slowly, my eyes trained on the front of her house. The subtle glow is coming from the front bedroom window again. I come to a stop opposite the door, my hands stuffed deeply in my jeans pockets. And I think, *what now?*

My pounding heart won't let up, and my whirling mind refuses to stop spinning. Pulling my phone from my pocket, I tap out a message.

> Just let me know you're okay.

I click send, and immediately regret it. She could reply, tell me she's fine to appease me. It doesn't mean I'll believe her. In fact, I *won't* believe her. I wait and wait, my worry growing with each minute that passes with no reply. Pushing my mobile into my forehead, I use all of my might to think clearly. It's too hard when my head is a fog of worry and questions.

> Let me know, or I'm coming to your house to find out myself.

I don't mean to threaten her, I truly don't, but I'm losing my mind, and I'm at a loss for what else to do. My phone lights up in my hand.

> I'm fine.

My lungs balloon with my intake of oxygen, but not in relief. Her short, simple reply, albeit what I asked for, only amplifies my concern.

> I need to see for myself. I'm outside.

The light in the hallway immediately comes on, shining through the window in the top section of the door. I stay where I am on the other side of the road and wait. The door doesn't open, but I catch the curtains at the downstairs window twitch. She's checking to see if I'm here. I step forward, putting myself under the glow of the streetlamp so she can see me, and only a couple of seconds later, the front door opens.

Lo walks out, tugging on a huge, knitted cardigan, pulling the door closed behind her. Taking a few steps that put her on the street, she stops, saying nothing, staring across the road at me. My eyes scan her willowy body, working up to her face. I try to zoom in on her, but the distance is too great, the darkness not in my favor. I need to go to her. Yet I don't move, mindful that through my own selfish need, I'm risking putting Lo in a very difficult situation just by being here, and that sudden comprehension fills me with guilt.

I need to go, leave, but before that, I just need to see her face one last time. I know this is it. I know I won't see her again.

And my fucking heart is breaking.

I don't get a chance to talk my legs into moving. Lo starts to cross the road toward me, and I can't explain how thankful I am when I get clear sight of her features, not a scratch or blemish in sight.

Coming to a stop, she lets me scan every inch of her, her body language telling me she knows what I'm doing and why. "What are you doing here, Luke?" she asks, the warmth of her voice gone completely. She sounds irritated, and I hate it.

"I was worried about you. You weren't answering my messages, you didn't meet me for lunch, and you've not been at work."

"You called my office?" Her irritation seems to grow.

"I didn't say who I was," I assure her, thinking maybe she's worried about office gossip. I look over her shoulder to her house, wondering why she doesn't seem as twitchy as I would expect. "I was told your leave wasn't planned."

"You have no right to pry like that."

I don't? I thought I was her best friend? "Then you should let me know you're okay," I retort, my voice raised. Yet Lo still doesn't become concerned by it, and I look back to her house again. "Aren't you worried your husband will come outside to find you?"

"No," she answers short and curtly, glancing away from me.

"He's out?"

"No."

I frown, confusion engulfing me. "You're not worried he'll see me?"

She levels a fixed stare on me, her neck lengthening, her shoulders straightening. I've never seen this resolute persona in Lo. She looks angry but calm. "He won't see you."

My eyebrows pinch. I'm totally lost. "How can you be so sure?"

"Because to see you, he needs to look out of the window. To look out of the window, he would need to walk to get there."

My frown deepens, my head trying to clue me in on what I'm hearing.

Her jaw tightens. "He's dying, Luke."

Something slams into my body, jolting it violently. Shock? "What?" I whisper, searching her face for more. Her declaration is so matter-of-fact, so full of acceptance.

"My husband is dying."

My stomach flips, every muscle in my body suddenly weighing me down, ensuring I can't move. I'm stunned, my body useless, but my brain is reeling off every second I've spent with Lo since we met. "Dying," I murmur, my eyes plummeting from her expressionless face to my boots. Her husband is dying? My insides twist and turn, nausea taking hold. "Why didn't you tell me?" I all but murmur, looking up at her. All this time we've spent together. I could have been helping her more than I know I have. *Should* have been.

"Because it felt too good having one person in this world who didn't look at me like they felt sorry for me. Because when we are together, you take my mind off the horrors of my life with your silliness. Because you talk to me like a normal person, not like a woman who is going through hell."

Panic claims me. "I can still do that," I tell her. I *want* to do that. Now more than ever.

"I can't see you anymore, Luke."

I look up, and I see it on her face. Guilt. For having me in her life. For smiling. For being distracted from her nightmares. God, she has nothing to feel guilty about. "Lo, I didn't mean to—"

"Don't." She looks away. "It's not your fault, it's mine. I shouldn't have encouraged our friendship."

"Why?"

Her eyes dart to mine. "Because it's inappropriate."

"Because I'm a man?" That's crazy.

"No, because my husband is dying, and my place is at home—"

"Dying with him," I say without thinking, making her head recoil sharply. She really did want me to run her down that night. She wanted out of this life. I feel so sick. "Lo"—I step forward, stopping when she steps back, wary— "I just want to be your friend."

Her bottom lip trembles, her arms holding her body tightly around her waist. "You can't be, Luke."

I go to argue, to tell her she's wrong, but she's already running back to her house, and when she gets inside, she shuts the door, not looking back. I stand motionless for an eternity, staring at her front door, shocked to my core. Her husband is dying. And I am a stupid, selfish idiot. What have I done? I've robbed myself of a friend, but worse of all, I've stolen one from Lo with my fucking idiocy. I just stand there, flummoxed, motionless on the street for an age, maybe hoping she'll run back out and tell me she does need me. That she wants me to ease her suffering. That she can't be without my silliness. That she still wants her best friend.

But she doesn't.

Guilt.

And I'm broken.

I blindly turn toward my car, my head ringing. How could I have got it so wrong? I drop into my seat, shut the door, and stare forward in the blackness, unable to process any of the last five minutes. Steve is jumping all over me, but I can barely register his excitement.

I'm absolutely stumped. Stumped for thoughts and stumped for words. I never in a million years imagined this is what I'd find when I came here tonight. I feel like I've had my guts ripped out.

He's dying. "Jesus," I breathe, absentmindedly starting my car.

I drive home, not remembering one second of the journey. I let myself in, take Steve out to the garden, throw my keys on the side, and head straight for my bar. The whiskey I pour is large, my first swig long, and my arse hits the leather of the bar stool with a thud. *Dying.* Amid the haze of tragic revelations, I manage to conclude only one thing. My secret wish to get Lo away from her misery is impossible. There is no escape. I can't help her. And now I've lost my best friend. My thought process seems selfish to an extent, but more tragic than the comprehension of my loss is the comprehension of Lo's situation. Her sadness makes sense. Her money struggles makes sense. Even my certainty that she wanted me to run her down that night makes sense. I've been more of a distraction than I ever imagined. The comfort she's taken from me, that I've willingly offered and given, has been a lifeline for her. And now she's giving that up, going back to being alone.

My glass hits the bar, my elbows following, and I stare into thin air.

It's not your fault, it's mine. I shouldn't have encouraged our friendship.

Why?

Because it's inappropriate.

She said I'm her best friend, and that has to mean that her husband no longer is. Our hugs have meant more to her too. Our conversation has just been so easy. So free. Honest . . . on my part. I've looked forward to seeing her, talking to her, being with her in any way. And she's giving that all up because she thinks it's inappropriate.

Because it felt too good having one person in this world who didn't look at me like they felt sorry for me. Because when we are together, you take my mind off the horrors of my life with your silli-

ness. Because you talk to me like a normal person, not like a woman who is going through hell."

And now she'll go back to hell . . . on her own.

And me?

I'm fucking heartbroken. Not only because I'm never going to see her again, but because there is nothing I can do to save her from her misery.

Not one thing.

And that is more painful, more difficult to accept, than admitting that I've fallen in love with her.

Part Six

Lo

Chapter Twenty

After I run away from Luke on the street, I don't know how long I sit on the floor behind my front door, my knees pulled close to my chest, sobbing. Maybe an hour. Could be two. I've lost all concept of time this week, every hour melting into the next, days passing painfully slowly. It's been slow and tough. Not only because Billy's condition has deteriorated drastically, leaving me no choice but to take emergency compassionate leave to care for him twenty-four/seven, but because I've lost my one and only form of comfort.

Luke.

I know deep down I can't see him anymore. That kiss, so simple, hardly even a kiss, said too much. That wasn't a kiss of a friend. Not for him. I thought I'd found acceptance of his presence in my life. Thought I could take it for what it was. Relief. Escapism. Friendship. But our relationship was inappropriate. It was wrong. No matter how much solace I took from it, it was wrong. That kiss told me so. I can't allow myself to depend on the mental relief Luke gives me any longer. I have to break away. It's for the best, because I've been so utterly stupid and selfish, and now I realize that in an attempt to make my life more bearable, I've actually made it a million times harder.

Because I gave myself something I can't keep. Something I should never have had. And right or wrong, it's tearing me apart that I have to walk away from it.

All the moments I've had with Luke, moments when I've forgotten myself, are now being trumped by the most wretched feeling. Guilt. More guilt than I'm sure I can shoulder. While I was smiling, laughing, having *fun*, my husband had been lying on his bed dying. There had been no solace for him. Nothing.

As the tears stream down my face, I fight to come to terms with the loss of the one thing that's brought me happiness in a long time. My heart is so . . . heavy.

Billy's only getting worse. My hope is fading along with his life, and I see his strength and spirit lessening by the day. He went to his appointment on his own in a taxi. It was hard to let him do that when all I wanted to do was hold his hand, but I had to put my feelings aside. He called me at work after he saw Dr. Smith. Told me the news with an infuriating acceptance. There is nothing more they can do.

He wants to go into a hospice and relieve me of my duties. I won't allow it. I've cried as much as one woman can cry. I have nothing left, only my strength to see this through to the end. The only two things I'm certain of in my life right now are that I will wake up in the morning, and I will go to sleep at night. What happens in between isn't something I can or *want* to think about.

Bringing my folded legs to the side of my body, I use the table in the hallway to pull myself up. And then I wander blindly to my single bed and crawl in fully dressed, pulling the duvet over my body and curling onto my side. Cruelly, my mind goes back to the beginning of my relationship with Billy. To the days when I felt full of hope. Full of unimaginable joy. When I was fun. Bubbly. To the night Billy woke me out of my daydreams, tapping on my window, desperate to simply see me. When we made love for the first time. And I remember being giddy, thinking two things for certain.

I'm going to marry Billy Harper.

And I'm going to live happily ever after with him.

But because the universe has other plans for me, I lie here in this bed, waiting for sleep to take me from my despair, even if only for a few hours.

Chapter Twenty-One

It's Saturday morning. As I sit in our silent kitchen sipping tea that's been made with the last teabag, I mentally write a list of things I need to buy when I go to the supermarket. I've forgotten it all by the time my unbearable mother-in-law knocks on the door. It takes me too long to answer, and her knocks have become impatient by the time I let her in. As is customary for Billy's mother, she pushes her way past me without a hello or inquiry about how I am, her focus set solely on checking her son. I guess it's understandable, and I'm also guessing she doesn't really need to ask how I am. I saw for myself in the mirror this morning.

I watch her disappear up the stairs as I shrug on my coat, not bothering to ask her how she is either. It'll only spike a conversation I can't be bothered to have. Collecting my bag and wrapping my woolen scarf around my neck, I pat Boris on the head and head out. I don't know why, but more frequently these days I find myself analyzing people I see on the streets, or wherever I am, quietly trying to figure out what's happening in their lives. I build all kinds of stories in my mind, some based on the happy faces, some the stern, and some the sad. But I never, not once, see someone who I think is as lost as I am. That's not to say that there aren't any, just maybe they're better at masking their wretchedness than I am. I'm not working at the moment, which means there's no need to make myself even remotely presentable each day. What's the point when all I'm doing is sitting around the house waiting to be needed?

The supermarket is rammed, every aisle chock-a-block with inpatient shoppers using their trollies as weapons to make it around the store alive. I tug a basket along behind me, not in any rush, throwing things in as I go. I stand in the queue to pay for ten minutes, and when it's my turn to unload my goods, I'm stopped by a man who pushes in front of me. He doesn't acknowledge me, doesn't apologize or give any excuses. And I don't argue. He obviously has somewhere he urgently needs to be. I don't.

I eventually pay for my shopping and trudge home, the handles of the bags cutting into my palms by the time I get there. I listen out for Billy's mother as I make my way up the hall, hoping she's still upstairs so I don't have to find the energy to engage with her. My hopes aren't answered. She's in the kitchen, but I don't look at her because something else is stealing my attention. A huge bouquet of flowers.

I blindly place my bags of shopping on the table, my eyes not straying from the blooms of vivid color. "These came while you were out," Linda says, pushing them toward me. "Who are they from?"

"Work, I expect," I answer without thought, reaching for the card nestled in the foliage. "How's he been?" I finger the little envelope open.

"Asleep." Taking her purse off the side, she passes me. "Make sure he has his tablets. I'll pop in tomorrow."

I hear the front door close behind her as I pull the card free.

I considered everything, but never that. I'm so sorry. For everything. xxx

The words are blurred by the time I get to the kisses, and I drop the card to the worktop to wipe them away as pain slices me. It's a pain I can't control, but a pain that I should. I didn't think my life could feel any emptier than it was. Then I met Luke, and a slither of myself allowed me to take comfort from his presence in my life.

I was still empty, but I wasn't empty *and* alone. I feel like my hollowness and grief have become suffocating since I lost him. Yet, the emptiness is easier to cope with than what I felt each time I looked at Billy.

Wandering over to the bin, I drop the card in. Where it belongs. Not because the words mean nothing to me, but because I should never have gotten close enough for him to need to send his apologies.

I unpack the shopping, open a new box of teabags, and make two cups of tea, taking them upstairs. When I enter Billy's room, he's awake, though still basked in the usual glow of the TV, the curtains pulled. He looks at me as I place his tea on his bedside stand, and I strain a smile, avoiding asking him how he's feeling. The question only irritates him. I also avoid asking him if he's hungry. That's irritates him, too. So I do all there is to do and sit in the chair by his bed and sip my tea, watching Formula One cars whizz around a track. I can feel him looking at me, but I don't let him know I'm aware, because I know what he's thinking. He's thinking I look as terrible as he does, and I'm not prepared to fight with him over the hospice again, the hospital appointments, food, drink, work, or whatever. I'm just not prepared to fight. I have nothing left inside me to contemplate fighting. It's as though I've been beaten down repeatedly and am simply conforming to be what he wants of me. *Nothing. Vacuous.*

"I want you to go back to work." Billy breaks the silence, and I close my eyes, bracing myself for the confrontation I was trying to avoid. "I'm fine. Last week was a bad week."

I sip my tea and look at him, forcing another smile. "You're fine?" I'm trying to make light of his ludicrous claim, but Billy doesn't give me even a trace of a smile. I find myself casting my mind back, looking hard in my memories for the times I remember him laughing. One springs to mind immediately. The morning we were due to fly out for our honeymoon when he found me in the bedroom trying to fasten my case. I was sitting on top of it, springing up and down in an attempt to close the gap on the sides. He'd laughed and ordered me to remove some of my clothes to stop it bulging. I refused, persevering, until Billy intervened and forced it shut. Then he heaved it from the cab at the airport. And then our lives changed beyond comprehension. I should have removed some clothes. I should have made it lighter. Then maybe his back wouldn't have given up. Maybe . . .

I sigh, knowing nothing could have stopped his back from failing that day. It would have happened eventually. Our worlds would have been turned upside down one way or another, one day or another.

Billy's voice breaks into my silent reflections. "Please go back to work, Lo." I watch as he struggles to sit up and edge himself to the side of the bed. He looks so frail and weak as he stands, literally half the man I met. I'm silent as he shuffles around the bed and heads for the en suite, shutting the door behind him. Sad as it seems, I'm happy to see him get himself there without my help, although I know he's only doing it to prove a point.

I return my attention to the television and finish my tea, and when fifteen minutes have passed and Billy still hasn't come out, I don't panic and rush to check on him. I get up and leave the room. Because he won't come out until I'm gone.

On Sunday, I spent the day making tea for visitors Billy didn't want. His mum, his dad, and an old work friend. I walked Boris three times and did the minimal amount of washing I had. I unwrapped the huge bunch of flowers and spent an hour slowly snipping the ends of each stem and meticulously positioning them in a glass vase. When I was done, I gathered up my pretty arrangement and threw it away. Not letting my mind wander to Luke and how much I missed him was impossible when I was reminded of him every time I caught sight of the colorful flowers that have no place in my dismal life, or the scent that was too sweet and filled my senses with something pleasant.

On Monday, I send Magda a message telling her of my intention to remain at home. I have no plans to go back to work, and nothing Billy can say will make me. His mum is right. I should be here looking after him. I make Billy a hot drink and deliver it to his room, getting no thank you or acknowledgment. I can't let it dampen my already low mood. Not when Billy's misery must trump mine tenfold. I take myself back downstairs and open the sideboard in the lounge, set on finding something to read to pass my day. I flick through the lines of books, finding nothing that takes my fancy. Not even Wuthering Heights. Because Billy can't read it to me.

I sit back on my arse, casting my eyes across to the piles of stock left from my store. I should upload them all onto the online shop Billy talked about. That might distract me for a short while. Or it won't. A box on the bottom shelf of the open cabinet catches my eye, and I pull it out, lifting the lid. Our wedding album looks up at me, daring me to open it and let myself reminisce on the happy times. Tentatively, I lift the cover of the leather-bound book and turn the first sheet of acid-proof paper. Staring down at the picture that greets me, a shot of Billy giving me a piggyback out of the church, both of us laughing, I wait for the tears to start flowing. They don't come. I feel completely detached from the memory, like I'm someone else looking in on a life had by others. Except the couple laughing in this picture haven't had a life beyond that day.

I turn the page and find a group shot with our guests. There's only maybe a couple dozen people, close family and friends. With the exception of Billy's parents, all of the people in this picture dip in and out of our lives now, swinging by sporadically to say hi, to drink tea, and to be miserable with us for a charitable hour before they resume their normal, healthy lives. Those visits have become less frequent. I'm pretty sure our home has a black X on the door, warning people away from the death that lingers beyond.

I don't look at any more pictures. Instead, I snap the album closed and stare at the wood of the cabinet. It's Billy's twenty-ninth birthday tomorrow. Maybe I'm stupid, I don't know. Maybe I'm naïve. Or perhaps there's still a teeny scrap of hope left inside me.

His birthday is tomorrow. And that means he's *lived* another year. But not lived at all, only suffered. I don't cry at that thought. Instead, I go to the kitchen and send out a group text to four of the people in the group picture at our wedding, inviting them to dinner tomorrow evening to celebrate. Our friends, Lewis and Helen, and Gareth and Penny. The six of us used to do everything together. Now, I'm lucky if I hear from them from one month to the next. I don't hold out much hope, it's short notice, so I'm surprised when I get two replies—one from Helen and one from Penny, both saying how good it is to hear from me and they'd love to see us, babysitters pending. I don't care if they are guilt-induced acceptances. They're coming.

For the first time in two years, Billy will have a proper birthday. I fiercely ignore the fact that I'm doing this because it'll be his last.

They managed to get babysitters, and my Tuesday is spent preparing a superb meal on my limited budget, as well as a huge chocolate cake. Billy loves chocolate cake. I don't tell him about the plans, keeping it a surprise, and I disregard the part of my brain that's yelling at me that he'll insist I cancel if he knows. He seemed brighter this morning, more with it, and definitely steadier on his feet as I watched him walk to the bathroom.

I manage to keep my plans for this evening from his parents

when they pop over to wish him happy birthday. I don't want Linda inviting herself, which I know she will. We've never been the best of friends, but it's particularly strained since our clash that resulted in her slapping my face. But for Billy, I'll tolerate her.

By six o'clock, I'm all done, and I quickly run upstairs to make myself look presentable, brushing my hair, throwing on a simple shirt dress, and applying a little makeup.

Everyone arrives at seven, and I hush them at the door when they pile into the hallway. It's so good to see them, and I embrace each of them before ushering them down the hall into the kitchen. They might all be guilty of avoiding Billy and me, but it's now I realize that a simple message from me would have remedied that.

"It's a surprise?" Penny asks, placing a bottle of red on the worktop as I nod and shoot over to the hob to stir the bolognaise. "How fabulous."

"How is he, Lo?" Lewis asks, taking Helen's coat from her shoulders and laying it over the back of a chair.

"Perkier today." I smile when he nods, happy, and everyone says how good that is to hear. Not that they can appreciate that *perkier than yesterday* doesn't really mean anything.

I set Penny the task of pouring drinks, chatting with her while I show her where to find the glasses. She looks as lovely as always, pristine in an oversized jumper dress and heeled boots. "How are the kids?" I ask, handing her the corkscrew.

She laughs. "Keeping me busy, you know."

I nod and get pulled away from Penny by her husband, Gareth. "I bought Billy this." He holds up a bottle of double malt Scotch whiskey, grinning. "You think he'll be up for a few after dinner?"

"I hope so. I better go fetch him." I usher Boris into his basket and shut the kitchen door behind me, jogging up the stairs to Billy's room. I poke my head around the door to find him making his way back to the bed. "Perfect," I declare, pushing my way into the room. "You're up."

"I've just been to the toilet."

"I have a surprise for you." I go to his wardrobe and pull out the first thing I set my hands on, which happens to be a striped shirt. I select some jeans too, and hand them to him.

Billy eyes me doubtfully, and I know why. My last surprise didn't go down too well. But this is different. The lasagna wasn't even really a surprise. This is definitely a surprise. "What are you up to?" he asks.

"Just put these on and come," I say, pleading with my eyes.

I can see the doubt on his face, and the urge to refuse, but he finally takes the clothes and heads back to the bathroom.

He won't get dressed in front of me.

He won't let me see his body anymore.

I've come to terms with that, but it still stings so much. He's withdrawn in so many ways. I guess I should simply be grateful he's not protesting and is humoring me.

I wait patiently until he appears again, and though I know he's lost so much weight, I fight to contain my shock at the sight of him in clothes he hasn't worn for so long. They're hanging from him. "You look handsome," I declare, taking his hand and leading on.

"You are a shocking liar, Lo Harper." Billy sighs, letting me gingerly guide him down the stairs. When we arrive at the kitchen door, I turn and brush down the front of Billy's shirt, ignoring the feel of his bony chest beneath.

"Ready?" I ask, looking up at his gaunt face. His sunken eyes. His sallow skin. It's all so hard to see. To accept. But his lips? I could literally burst into tears when they lift at one corner, his head shaking mildly, more through lack of strength than intention.

"Ready," he breathes, and I grin, swinging the door open.

"Surprise," everyone sings, but then silence falls abruptly, all of our guests faces dropping like lead when they catch sight of the friend they haven't seen for months. My nerves begin to fray, and I peek up at Billy, seeing he is, indeed, surprised. His deep-set eyes are wide as he scans the people in the kitchen.

Oh God, it's too quiet. I take Billy's hand and tug him on.

"Happy birthday," I sing, glancing at our friends and mentally willing them to snap out of their shocked states.

It's Lewis who does first, bounding forward with his bottle of Scotch and grinning wickedly. "Happy birthday, mate." He throws his arms around Billy, and I relish the sight of my husband's arms lifting to accept his friend's hug.

"Thanks," Billy replies, still seeming a little struck.

Everyone steps forward, each of them wishing Billy a happy birthday, embracing him, and never mentioning how terrible they think he looks. Neither do they ask how he is, because that much is obvious. But I'm grateful. Tonight isn't about Billy talking about his sickness. Tonight is about friends.

Billy moves across to a chair, and I see Lewis fight the compulsion to pull it out for him. *Please don't!* "I've got it, mate." Billy smiles his reassurance at Lewis, obviously catching his mental debate too. "Sit down." He motions to the other seats around the table. "Tell me about work."

Lewis visibly relaxes and starts talking, and Billy listens with apparent interest. Happy with the chatter at the table and my husband's willingness to interact, I go to the oven and pull out the bolognaise, serving everyone. I don't make a big deal of Billy's miniscule portion, nor do I encourage him to eat more when he barely touches what's on his plate. I do, however, pass him the wine Penny poured for him on a smile, and relish the small one I get in return. A smile from my husband has never made me so happy, and I battle to force back the sting in my eyes before it gives my emotions away. This is everything I wanted it to be, and so many memories steam forward of our group dinners together over the years, times when we'd take it in turns to host and sit around the table until the early hours, laughing and fighting to get a word in edgewise.

We talk for an hour, chat about old times, about work, and the whole time Billy remains alert and responsive to the conversation.

This is the best medicine he could have. Why haven't I done this before? It's been wonderful.

"Hey, Lo," Gareth says, leaning his elbows on the table. "I saw you last week walking Boris."

"I feel like I'm always walking Boris." I start to collect the plates, stacking them in front of me as everyone passes them over.

"You were with someone. A tall dude."

My hands falter, too much to go unnoticed, and I flick my eyes to Billy to find he's regarding me. I get back to stacking plates, trying not to look uncomfortable. There's only one person Gareth could mean. "I don't recall walking with anyone." I get up with the plates and take them to the sink, feeling Billy's eyes on my back. *Oh, God.*

"You don't recall?" Billy's voice is full of curiosity, and maybe a bit of suspicion.

I slap a smile on my face and turn to face the table. "Must have been a fellow dog walker. Maybe I was saying hi." I'm pleading on the inside that I wasn't latched on to Luke's arm when Gareth claims to have seen me. "The park can get busy in the evening. Let's do the cake." I grab the candles and start pushing all twenty-nine into the top of the chocolate icing, hoping that will be that.

I hear the chatter start again at the table while I'm busy and breathe out my relief. I was completely unprepared for that, and even if I was prepared, how on earth would I explain Luke?

Lighting the candles, I take a few moments to gather myself and settle my thumping heart rate. Then I flick off the lights. "Ta-dah," I chime, presenting Billy with the cake as the other break out in song.

"Please don't sing at me," he moans. "It's worse than death."

Everyone falls silent, their happy singing coming to an abrupt stop, all of them, including me, staring at Billy in horror.

"Jesus, lighten up. It was a joke."

A joke? *Then why the hell isn't anyone laughing?* I should be happy he's trying to be funny. I can't be. "Cake," I squeak over the lump in my throat, and Billy looks at me, his skinny shoulders dropping.

"I'm sorry."

"It's fine." I encourage him to blow the candles out, thrusting the cake toward him.

He inhales and puffs out a miniscule bit of air that barely makes them flicker.

"It's okay, try again," I say, smiling at his effort.

Again, Billy breathes in and blows, but only two of the candles go out. He tries again, putting another one out. I see his jaw clench, and I begin to worry, kicking myself for making him feel like he needs to do this. I pull the cake away. "Never mind about the candles."

"No." Billy slaps his hand over mine, stopping me from taking the cake. "I want to blow out my candles."

I stand back, nervous, flicking my eyes between our friends around the table. Everyone is still quiet, looking at each other cautiously. *What have I done?* Billy sucks in as much air as he can and pushes it out. The remaining candles remain lit. He tries again, and again, and with each failed attempt, the tension in the kitchen grows thicker and thicker until I can't bear it any longer. Keen to ease the atmosphere and ease Billy's struggle, I lean forward, set on blowing out the candles for him.

His hand moves fast, finding mine, and he looks at me. "Together," he says quietly, and I swallow, nodding, the lump back in my throat. Pushing out on his chair, he taps his lap, and I comply willingly and quickly, perching on his emaciated thighs but not releasing my full weight. We both lean forward and take in air, puffing it out across the cake. I know it's only my effort that extinguishes all the candles, as does everyone else in the room, but it doesn't matter. *Together.*

We get an applause, and I go to lift from his lap, but he somehow stops me. I look over my shoulder at him. His eyes speak a thousand words. "Stay," he says quietly, and the lump grows even bigger. So I remain on Billy's lap as I cut up the cake, passing it around the table, and when his arm snakes around my waist, I look down, seeing past the gray tone of his skin and focusing on the simple fact that he's holding me. Willingly. He wants me close, and I absolutely relish in it.

I don't move from his lap for the rest of the evening. It's uncomfortable, his thick thighs now bony, but I don't care. He wants me here. And it feels so incredible to be this close to him.

By ten thirty, he's exhausted, and as I go to remove myself from his lap, he strains again to keep me there. "No, I'm too heavy." I fight against his hold this time and get to my feet, starting to clear the dishes.

"I'll help." Billy stands, gathering up the pasta pot.

"No, you relax."

"Let me help, Lo," he insists, giving me the look he used to when he meant business. Just Billy looking at me like that makes me happy. Until I see him struggling to take only two paces before stopping. I take in air. "I've got it," he breathes, moving again. He loses his grip, and the cast iron pot hits the floor with a deafening crash. "Fuck's sake," he hisses, silencing the room.

"It's okay." I rush to gather up the mess. "No harm done."

Billy staggers back to his chair and plummets to the seat, his energy zapped, as Penny joins me to clear up the mess. I offer her a small smile that she returns, but it's meek and oozing that dreaded sympathy.

"It's okay," I repeat, the atmosphere in the kitchen unbearable again.

Gareth stands and declares he's beat, followed by Lewis. "It's been a lovely evening," he says, coming around the table to us, giving me a look of pity too.

"Yes," I hear Helen say. "Let me help you clear up before we head off."

"Honestly, I've got it." Having our friends clear away will only serve to enhance Billy's feeling of inadequacy. "Thank you for coming." I smile as brightly as I can.

Lewis comes to me, linking his arm around my neck and kissing my hair. But he doesn't say anything before breaking away and tapping Billy's shoulder as he passes. They all edge out to escape the crippling atmosphere, and every look back over their shoulders shows distraught disbelief. Yes. This is the reality they've all avoided. This is our daily heartbreak.

The door closes behind them, and the kitchen is its usual, excruciating silence again. Billy looks up at me, forcing a smile. "Thank you."

And what do I do? I burst into tears.

I'm so fucking stupid.

"Hey." He fights his way up from the table and hobbles his way over to me, and I feel nothing short of awful for forcing him into comforting me. His arms engulf me, and I hide in his scrawny chest.

"I'm sorry," I blubber.

He sighs, holding me as tightly as he can. Which isn't very tight at all. When Billy used to hold me, I'd struggle for air. Struggle to move. "I can't bear to see you like this, Lo. I can't bear seeing you so fraught and hopeless."

How can he say that? "I'm okay."

"You're not okay." Pulling back, he looks down at my tear-stained face. On a soft smile, he wipes my tears away. I close my eyes, unable to stare at his gray, ashen face. "I want more than anything for you to be happy."

Happy? In this moment, I can't imagine ever being happy again. Unless by some miracle Billy is cured. "The only thing in this world that can make me happy is you."

"I'm dying, Lo." He kisses the corner of my mouth. "I refuse to allow your spirit to die with me."

It's too late.

I'm a skeletal version of myself now too.

Chapter Twenty-Two

The distance between Billy and me is growing by the day. After I cleared up the kitchen, I went to bed and sobbed myself to sleep, cuddling up to Boris so tightly I probably restricted his breathing. I left my phone downstairs to limit my temptation to do something stupid. Like call Luke. Like succumb to my desperation to see him and have him make me forget.

I made it through the night and walked Boris at the crack of dawn. Then I showered and absentmindedly readied myself for work, applying foundation on top of foundation to mask my puffy eyes.

I left the house without checking on Billy, determined not to let him see the state of my face. I'm going to work today, and I text Magda on my way to let her know. I need to find the strength to be strong again. I need to leave the fucking pity party.

I pull my gloves off as I enter the glass door of Sharman House, stuffing them in my bag and retrieving my heels at the same time. When I notice the crowds of people at the elevators, I take a seat on one of the couches in the foyer to change out of my trainers and wait for the crowds to die down. Slipping my feet into my heels, I look up as I take my bag from the floor, freezing halfway between sitting and standing.

Our eyes meet. I fight to rip them away and instinctively hurry over to the elevators before he even thinks to approach me. I can't let Luke see me like this either. I concentrate on getting to my office before I give in to the overwhelming need to run into his arms. I just need a hug. Someone familiar to hold me and comfort me. I need my friend. But it's wrong. I shouldn't want that. What is he doing here?

I rush into the lift as soon as it opens and hit the button for the second floor, pushing myself to the back of the cart and watching as the doors slowly close until they meet in the middle. I use the time it takes for the lift to climb to my floor to check myself in the mirror. My eyes are glassy, brimming with tears. I roughly brush at my cheeks to rid my face of my emotional state.

"Hello, Lo." Scarlett is standing at my desk when I make it there, rootling through one of my trays. Her greeting isn't happy. It isn't friendly. It's drenched in that fucking sympathy. I smile— forced—and drop my bag by my desk, ignoring Scarlett's forehead that fails to wrinkle when she tries to frown. "You didn't need to come in today."

"I need to, Scarlett," I reply, and her lips press together as she thinks of what to say next. So I quickly change the subject. "You looking for something?"

She stands reluctantly, her eyes never leaving me, and points at my out-tray. "The month-end figures. I'm sure I put them back in here after you gave me them a few weeks ago, and obviously because you've been off work, and that's *totally* fine, you haven't updated the spreadsheet online. I just need to check something."

I bend and pull out the pile of papers from my in-tray, thumbing through them. "Here," I say, pulling out a spreadsheet.

"Oh, you saint." She takes the sheet and clicks away on her

Manolo Blahniks but stops just shy of her office. She inhales and turns. "I understand you need distraction. Just know, if you want to talk, I'm here."

What can I say, other than I *never* want to talk? "Thank you." But she understands, and that's good, I suppose.

"It's good to have you back, Lo." She smiles and disappears into her office as I remove my coat and hang it on the nearby coat stand.

I spend the first hour of my morning filtering through the paperwork that's landed on my desk in my absence, stacking it in piles of priority. I know anything deemed urgent would have made its way onto Rachel's desk, so there's nothing pressing to deal with.

When Scarlett presents herself at my desk again sometime later, I look up at her in question. "Everything okay?" I ask.

"Do you have my business card statement for last month?"

I cock my head. "Why'd you not call me for it?" She never comes to my desk.

She shrugs and looks down at her shoes. "Trying to break them in."

"Really?" I dip my head and look up through my lashes with all the suspicion I feel. She's checking up on me. What happened to understanding? *I don't want to talk! I want to forget!*

She huffs and stamps her foot a little. "You just look so drained. I don't want to expect too much of you when . . ." She trails off, and I fall back in my seat.

I look drained? What, more drained than usual? Because that must mean I look pretty much dead. "Scarlett, I wouldn't be here if I couldn't do my job."

"I know that." She pulls up a chair to my desk and sits down, taking my hand. I'm a bit taken aback. I've never known her to be so attentive. Quietly concerned, yes, but I thought she knew I'm better off being left to get on with my job rather than having unwanted pity poured all over me. She smiles cheekily. "You wouldn't be here, because I'd fire your arse if you couldn't do your job."

"Good to know," I quip, laughing under my breath. "Listen, Scarlett, I'm sorry about my unexpected time off, but—"

"This isn't about that, Lo. It's about your personal health. Good God, woman, you're wasting away before my eyes."

My lips straighten. "I'm fine."

"You're always fine. It's infuriating." She squeezes my hand in hers and stands. "I just want you to know your job isn't going anywhere. If you need time, take time."

"Thank you, Scarlett." I hope I sound as grateful as I feel. "But, really, all I want to do is distract myself as best I can and work helps with that."

"I understand."

"You already said that. And here you are *talking*."

She rolls her eyes and returns to her office. "Fine. No more talking."

I smile, continuing to power through the work I have to catch up on, and the day passes by in the blink of an eye.

As I'm packing up ready to head home, my phone rings, and I look blankly at the screen as Penny's name presents itself to me. I consider ignoring her call, but I imagine the four of them have been ringing each other off the hook for most of the day discussing the events of last night. I should put their minds to rest. "Penny," I say as I get up and wave through to Scarlett, signaling I'm leaving. She waves a flippant hand at me, and I start toward the elevators.

"Lo, I don't know what to say," she breathes, clearly struggling. Now I'm imagining them all tossing coins to determine who will be the lucky one who calls me.

"You don't have to say anything, Penny. It is what it is." I swallow down the lump before it has a chance to grow. "He's deteriorating by the day and there's nothing more the doctors can do."

"God, Lo, how are you coping?"

I press my lips together to stop myself from spilling my confession, from telling Penny that it was so much easier when I had a friend to lean on. Not just any friend. I know I wouldn't get the same comfort from any of the four of them, because they know. They're all aware of the mess Billy and I are in, and they would all drown me in that wretched sympathy I don't want. I just wanted someone to treat me like I'm me, and Luke did that. He struggled, I know, but he fought his curiosity to know the deal, because he knew I needed that. But now? Now he knows. He'll never look at me the same again. My respite has gone. "You just . . . cope," I say, hearing her sigh. I haven't coped at all. Not really.

"Lo, I know what your answer will be, but just know that we'll fight you on it all the way."

"What?" I ask, reaching the lift. I press the call button.

"Helen and I are going for cocktails tonight. We want you to come. Lord knows, you need some time for yourself, and I'm just so sorry we've been so absent."

"Honestly, I'm f—"

"We won't accept no for an answer. The boys are going to see Billy. He'll be fine."

I cringe. "He's not very visitor friendly, Penny."

"Then he can throw them out if he wants. But you are coming with us. There will be no talk of . . ." She pauses. "We'll gossip. Drink. Discuss butt implants."

I smile at her persistence, but I really can't afford to be drinking cocktails at London prices. Not that I would dream of sharing that.

"It's my treat," Penny says, as if hearing my dilemma. "What do you say? Come on, Lo."

I bite my lip, caught in a state of conflict. "I shouldn't be having fun," I say out loud, only meaning to think it.

"We won't. We're boring as shit. Didn't you know?"

I laugh lightly and slowly nod. "Just for a few."

"We're meeting at the Radio Rooftop at seven. See you there." She hangs up promptly, narrowing the chances of me changing my mind, and I breathe in as I step into the elevator. *Time out. Just look at it as time out.* Maybe it's the kind of time out I've needed all along, with appropriate people. Part of me is a tad resentful of my absent friends. If they'd been here all along, maybe I wouldn't be so crippled by this guilt I just can't shake.

I find Penny and Helen in the bar, and I get a squeeze from both of them. "How's Billy?" Penny asks, sitting down and pushing an elaborate strawberry daiquiri toward me.

"Yes, how is he?" Helen chimes in, her face a masterpiece of empathy. I look back to Penny, and hers is just as sorrowful.

"He's fine," I answer, lying. He's not gotten out of bed all day and he hasn't eaten a thing. I slide onto the stool and truly savor the first slurp of my cocktail.

"It's so tragic." Helen shakes her head slowly, looking thoughtfully past me.

"It is," Penny agrees. "I just don't know what I'd do."

I swallow and look down at my drink, stirring it slowly with my straw. Is this how it's going to be all night? Another pity party?

"I mean, the stress and the worry." Helen sighs. "Life can be so cruel."

"It can." Penny reaches over and squeezes my hand. "Poor Billy. He's so brave."

I strain a smile. I can't bear this. It was a battle to get myself ready to come here. I wouldn't have bothered had I known the mood would be so dire. What happened to the times we used to talk about . . . well, anything? "Did you go on holiday this year?" I ask chirpily, trying to move the conversation along.

"Yes," Penny chimes, indicating to Helen. "We all went to Cancun. It was wonderful."

I see Helen jolt on her stool, and then Penny winces. She just booted her under the table.

"I mean . . ." Penny's smile dies. "It wasn't that much fun."

I take refuge in another slurp of my drink before I slip down from my stool. "I'm just going to the ladies'." I walk away, hearing the hushed whispers of my friends as I go, no doubt Helen chastising Penny for being so inconsiderate. It's not inconsiderate at all. That's their life, happy and fulfilled. Fun. Just because mine isn't doesn't mean I don't want to hear their stories. Watching them looking and sounding so awkward isn't how I planned on spending my evening. This isn't helping. *I was promised no sympathy, for crying out loud.*

I use the toilet and wash my hands, leaning into the mirror to inspect my face. My eye sockets are so dark. Applying a little more concealer, I stand back, tilting my head to get all angles. It's no good. No amount of makeup will hide my exhaustion. I give up and head back to the table.

Penny and Helen quickly halt their conversation and both smile at me. I swear, if they offload anymore morbid comments, I'll scream. So to avoid that, I decide to tell them not to be so careful with their words. "Guys"—I look at each of them in turn— "I don't want you to—" My intended fix-it speech fades when I catch sight of someone across the bar amid the crowds. My heart starts to gallop, and I have no idea why. Nerves? Stress?

"Lo?" Penny reaches over and takes my hand, and I look at her blankly. "Are you okay?"

"Yeah." I scan the gatherings of people, but after searching every nook and cranny of the space, I don't see him. "I thought I saw someone I knew." I return my attention to Penny and Helen, certain that I'm seeing things. Picking up my drink, I try to remember where I was, but I fail to recall, so I toast the air and sip. I don't know what the hell I'm toasting.

Penny's phone chimes from the table, and I look down with Helen, seeing a message from Gareth. She picks it up, reads, fails to hide her anxious expression, and places it calmly down before taking a casual sip of her drink.

"They left, didn't they?" I ask, watching for her reaction to my question.

Helen waits pensively, reaching over to take my hand in a show of support when Penny delivers the answer I know she will. It's awkward again, so fucking awkward, her eyes refusing to meet mine.

"Penny, just say. It's totally fine."

She relents, letting her shoulders drop. "He told them he wanted to be alone."

I nod, smiling mildly, as if I can convince them I'm okay with that. And, of course, I'm far from surprised. Last night, Billy went along with my surprise because he knew it would be the last time he'd have to. He did it for me. And it exhausted him. I drop down from my stool. "I should go home."

"No, Lo. Please, stay," Penny begs.

"I can't but thank you for trying."

"Then we'll see you to a cab," Helen says, getting up from her stool.

I rest my hand on her arm, making her pause mid lift. "Please," I beg, and she slowly lowers back to her seat, glancing across to Penny. "I'm really not in the mood anyway. Stay and enjoy. You've managed to get sitters two nights in a row. I'm sure that's a miracle too good to pass up." I leave them both with a kiss before heading for the exit, damning myself for being so stupid, for being hopeful. Tonight has been everything I hoped it *wouldn't* be.

As I break into the freezing cold air, I pull my coat in tight and look left and right for a cab. There are no cabs, but . . . "Luke?" He walks forward, his face straight. I've missed that face so much; I hardly want to admit it to myself. "Are you following me?"

"You just got here. Are you leaving?" he asks, ignoring my question.

So I ignore his. "Are you following me?"

"You're not walking home alone."

"What are you, my guardian angel?" I look away from him

when his eyes flash with annoyance, finding it too difficult to maintain eye contact. I don't like that look, but I can't expect anything less when I'm being so defensive. And, worse, I really don't mean it. "I'm sorry." I sigh deeply, hearing his shoes hitting the pavement as he walks toward me, until he comes to a stop a few paces away. "I've missed you," I blurt, the words and emotion in them coming unstoppably. And then the tears. The tears fall down my cheeks like rivers, the whole miserable night catching up with me and releasing.

"Oh, Lo," he whispers, pacing forward and throwing his arms around me. "I've missed you too."

Powerful sobs rack my body, the kind of crying you can't control. I'm done for the day. The week. The year. Forever.

"Come have a drink with me."

I shake my head into him. "I shouldn't," I croak, ripping myself from his warm embrace. I glance over my shoulder, struggling with my desperation to scream *yes!* Yes, I want to get a drink with him. I want to listen to him talk, I want to lose myself in one of his hugs again, let him make me laugh. But I can't.

"I didn't ask if you should or shouldn't. I asked if you would *like* to."

His question is simple, yet so hard to answer. So I don't, looking away from him.

Penny and Helen emerge from the bar. "Oh God."

"What?"

I jump back into an unused doorway, panicked. What will they think, seeing me standing here with another man? *Shit.* Luke frowns, glancing between me and the bar entrance. I see realization fall, and he joins me in the recess, but he doesn't say a word.

"I can't see her," I hear Penny say, and I close my eyes, praying they don't walk this way.

"She can't have gotten far. Shit, Penny, we shouldn't have let her leave."

"I'll text her."

I inhale, rootling through my bag as Luke watches, turning my mobile to silent just in time for Penny's text to land. I quickly tap out a reply, telling her I'm fine and in a cab on my way home. Then I clutch my phone to my chest and look up at the dank ceiling of the doorway.

"She's in a cab," Penny says. "The poor woman. She looked utterly exhausted."

More tears, and I feel Luke's hand rest on my forearm. I peel my eyes open and find his solemn expression. *Yes, exhausted. Yes, a mess. Yes, poor Lo.*

Luke sighs. "Let's go somewhere warm," he says quietly. "We'll talk."

I swallow and look around the edge of the doorway, seeing Penny and Helen have gone.

"Please, Lo," he begs. "I feel like my right arm has been cut off. You've come to mean so much to me, and I'm so worried about you."

"You mean so much to me too," I murmur, admitting it, looking up at him. "You were the only thing holding me up, Luke." I lose control of my vocal chords, my voice cracking. "I just feel so guilty." I drop my head, my strength, if there was any left, beaten.

"Oh, fucking hell," he breathes, gathering me into his arms and squeezing the life out of me. I relax straight into his hug again, feeling so safe and warm, hearing his heart thrum under my ear. "I don't want to make your life any harder than it already is."

"You're not." I sniff. "You make it easier to bear. That's what's screwing with my head." I sniffle back my emotion, trying to clear my throat. "The guilt is because I feel like I need you, and it's so wrong. I should never have depended on you so much. It wasn't fair for you *or* Billy."

Luke's chest expands, his arms constricting around me. "Do you need to go home right now? Can we go somewhere quiet? Just to talk?"

"I don't want to talk about any of it," I admit.

"I think we need to." He says what needs to be said, so softly. Shifting me into his side, he cuddles me close to him. And, God, how I have missed being held. Cuddled. *Cared for.* "Come on."

We walk in comfortable silence to a small lounge bar nearby, and Luke chooses a little table at the back where it's quiet. He helps me out of my coat and pulls a chair out for me. I note the low lighting, pointlessly hoping it hides my blotchy skin and welling eyes. *And I'd thought I had no tears left.* How wrong I was.

He goes to the bar and orders two drinks, both Scotch, and brings them over, sitting down opposite me and handing me my glass. He lets me take a quiet sip before pulling his chair around to sit closer to me, taking my drink from my grip and holding my hand. "Why didn't you tell me what was going on in your life? I feel fucking awful, Lo."

"That's just it. If you knew, you would have joined everyone else and killed me with sympathy. You're the only person who didn't look at me like they felt sorry for me. I know you suspected something wasn't right, but you told me you wouldn't ask, and you didn't. You treated me like a normal person. You made me forget my reality. I know it was wrong, but . . ." I pause, not knowing how else to explain it. "You were just there, and I liked you there. And yet, that made me feel so guilty."

Luke breathes out, sliding his hand onto the back of his neck and massaging. "I thought you were in an abusive marriage." His eyes clench shut. "How miserable and withdrawn you were when I met you, it was the only explanation I could think of. I never imagined this." Luke takes what looks like a much-needed swig of Scotch, and I watch him as he seems to slip into thought, staring out of the window into the darkness. Quiet. And now it's uncomfortable, my head spinning all kinds of conclusions on his thoughts.

"I'll understand if you don't want to be my friend anymore." The words eat me up inside. This past week has been so wretched without him. But I'll understand if he doesn't want anything to do with me and my misery anymore. Why would he? He's not a care in the world. And given he was at Radio Rooftop tonight, he was probably trying to find another early-twenties one-night stand to have fun with. Getting on with his carefree life. A pain shoots through my stomach at that thought, but I don't completely understand why.

Luke's glass hits the table, and he turns to me, taking both of my hands and holding them on his knees. "Nothing's changed for me," he tells me through gritted teeth. "Now I understand. I care about you so much. It's nonsensical, I get that, but there was a reason I was driving the car that nearly ran you down." His speech is so sincere; it brings on another wave of emotion that collects at the backs of my eyes. "That night, you didn't want to be here, did you?"

The tears fall, and I confess, confirming his conclusion with a jerky shake of my head. "For a split second, it seemed like the easiest option."

My admission makes his lips twist with agony, and he pulls me onto his lap and swaths me in his body, burying his face into my neck. "Promise me you'll never think like that again," he orders roughly. "Promise me now."

"I promise." It's the easiest promise I've ever made. And that in itself is strange. Two years ago, I made a promise to another man to love and cherish him for the rest of our lives. That, too, was an easy promise because I knew I'd love Billy forever. And yet with Luke, whose friendship I treasure beyond words, my promise was instant as well. I couldn't ignore the plea in his words. I *can't* ignore how deeply thankful I am for him, and for fate once again bringing him onto my path.

I stare across his chest, taking the most incredible amount of comfort from our closeness, from the feel of him caging me in his arms. It's as if all the background noise is silenced, if only for a few moments, and the same peace I've found before in Billy's arms replaces the agony and pain. I love this man, but not how I love Billy. It's not a romantic love. Even though his presence in my life might only be temporary, like a guardian angel helping me through the darkest time of my life, I'll always love and appreciate his intrusion into my sorrow. His sacrifices for me.

"Cancer?" Luke says out of the blue, and I nod into him.

"It's a rare form. Radiotherapy was unsuccessful, and they can't operate because of the position of the tumor on his spine. Neither the doctor nor Billy were willing to take the risks."

Luke lifts me from his lap and places me on my chair, pulling my drink close. "Drink your Scotch."

I follow his gentle order and take a small sip, while Luke polishes off his glass and holds up the empty to the waiter for another. His mind is clearly racing. "Do you need the bottle?" I ask.

He huffs a quiet, disbelieving shot of laughter, then quickly reins it in. "Surely there's something that can be done. This is the twenty-first century, for crying out loud."

"They've explored every avenue. The only option isn't really an option."

"Which is what?"

"An expert in America. He would operate. He thinks he could remove part of the tumor successfully. But he's a private doctor. The cost of the surgery is tens of thousands."

"They put a price on saving someone's life?"

I shrug, the whole situation not maddening me anymore.

"It's not right." Luke accepts his fresh drink and downs it immediately. "So you just have to wait for the inevitable?"

"Billy refuses to see the doctors anymore. He's had enough. He's worn out, lost all hope." I stare down into my drink, striving to keep my voice strong. "And I'm tired of fighting with him over it. He's told me to leave him, Luke. More than once. He wants me to move on like he never existed." I look up at him and see agony in his eyes. "How could he ask me to do that?" I fold, gripping my glass like it can save me from my anguish. "I love him. It wasn't supposed to be like this."

Luke curses and shifts forward on his chair, cuddling me close. "I can't make this go away, but I can be here for you. And I will. No matter what happens, do you hear me? If you need me, you call me. If you want to be left alone, tell me, and I'll completely ignore you."

I smile over my body-racking sobs, nodding, because I don't want him to leave me alone. Not ever. Luke was right. We really did need to have this conversation, because now I feel like we're on the same page. He understands, and he still wants to be in my life. The gratitude I feel is immeasurable. So is my admiration for him. "I promise not to ask ever again," he whispers. "If you promise you won't push me away."

He's not running away. I take a deep breath. Well, neither will I.

I take a long swig of my drink and look him straight it the eye. "How's Steve?" I ask, telling him everything he needs to know.

He smiles, understanding. "Much better since I got a nanny."

"You have a nanny for your dog?" Is he for real?

"Yeah, I do. I also need eyes in my arse. That dog is the most mischievous creature I've ever met. He had my steak right off my plate last night. I only blinked, and *poof*, it was gone." He flicks his finger in the air. "And the little fucker runs like a whippet."

I laugh as I imagine Luke chasing Steve around his house with a big juicy steak hanging out of his mouth. "He's a beagle. What do you expect? You should have done your research."

"He was a bit of an impulse buy," he admits, smiling shyly. "Speaking of which, Steve misses Boris."

"He's only met him once."

"Yeah, well, sometimes once is all it takes to realize you can't live without someone." Luke frowns, looking off into the distance.

"Are you okay?"

"This is going to be harder than I thought," he says under his breath. To himself, I think, but I heard.

"What is?" I ask. "Has this got something to do with the kiss?" I pray to God he says what I want him to say.

Luke's palm meets his forehead, rubbing from side to side with his eyes closed. "Lo." He exhales my name, looking at me, and I wait, pensive, as he stares into my eyes. He eventually blinks, dropping his head, laughing under his breath. "The kiss," he breathes. "I have no idea what came over me." He lifts his eyes to mine again, looking at me with a determination I've never seen in him before. "I'm so sorry, it totally didn't mean anything, and I really need you to know that."

I exhale, so bloody relieved. "I know that."

"Good." He stands, my gaze lifting to keep his face in my sights, and he offers me his hand. "Let me get you home." He smiles, but it goes nowhere near his eyes.

"You're doing it already," I tell him. "Being weird. All awkward and sympathetic. I don't want that, Luke. I want us to be us."

He shakes his head, looking at his feet briefly. "I'm sorry."

"Who's flavor of the week?"

His eyes flip up, and he laughs. "No one you'll approve of."

"That's my phone," I say, hearing it from my coat pocket. I pull it out and read a rather unpleasant text message from my mother-in-law. She wants to know where I am. She wants to know why I'm not at home. "Can't we get another drink?" I ask, unwilling to face her wrath.

Luke looks down at his watch, wincing. "I'm already late."

"Oh!" I'm such a killjoy. "I'm sorry, I won't keep you." I turn to head off, feeling like an inconvenience, which I am. "I hope she's more your age," I quip teasingly as I go, anything to lessen any guilt Luke might be feeling.

"Lo, wait." He catches up with me and pulls me to a stop. "Do you want to come with me?"

I laugh. "I'm not sure your date will appreciate me tagging along."

He rolls his eyes. "I'm not going on a date."

"Oh? Run out of offers?"

Snorting, he starts walking us out of the bar. "Never." Grinning down at me, he winks, and it brings us that much closer to the usual us.

Chapter Twenty-Three

"Where are we going?" I ask as Luke drives us across town.

"It's a surprise," he replies, looking past me through the window. "And, we're here."

"Where exactly is *here*?"

"There." He points into the darkness.

I roll my eyes. "I can't see a thing."

"Just wait for us to get through this forest and all will be revealed." Just as he finishes talking, we break free of the trees . . . and my mouth falls open.

What the hell? I gawk at the sprawling pile of bricks. "Where are we?"

"My grandfather's place."

I swing an incredulous look at Luke. "You're taking me to see your grandfather?"

"He's a legend." The car rolls to a stop by a few pillars. "You'll love him."

I blindly reach for the handle of the door, my eyes rooted on the mansion, and let myself out as Luke reaches past me and pushes the door shut. He takes my hand and leads me on, unfazed by my awe.

I trail behind, our arms at full length between us, his hand tight around mine. We get to the door, and Luke presses an intercom buzzer. He leans in when a lady's voice comes over the speaker. "It's Luke."

"Oh, Luke," she shrieks. "Ladies, it's Luke."

I look up at him, just as he peeks down at me on a playful roll of his eyes. "I'm quite popular around here."

"Evidently," I say as he opens the door, revealing a huge foyer that's dressed luxuriously, a sumptuous claret carpet, super polished wooden furniture, and velvet couches. Three women appear, all elderly, and all looking like they could burst with excitement.

"Luke," one says as she claps.

"Luke," another sings.

"Oh, Luke," a third swoons. Then five more elderly ladies appear, all singing and chanting Luke's name, clapping, smiling, and descending on him until he's forced to drop my hand. I move to the side and watch as he's ambushed by a gaggle of elderly, excitable ladies, being pushed and pulled about, his cheeks being squeezed, his hair being ruffled, and his suit being tugged. And he just laughs, dividing his attention between them all in turn, satisfying their need for his attention.

"May I say how beautiful you all look?" Luke says, driving up the swooning to epic levels. Once they've piped down, he reaches for my hand and pulls me toward him, putting me in front of the crowd of old ladies. "This is my friend, Lo, everyone," he declares. I know he's smiling down at me, but my wary eyes are on all the old eyes regarding me, all with interest. A few *oohs and aahs* sound out, whispers too.

"I'm still lost," I admit, feeling slightly exposed and vulnerable as I stand and accept their scrutinizing assessments.

A loud cough has the gang of women freeing me of their

inquisitiveness, and they part, looking to the back of the foyer. I follow their stares until I see an elderly man, with silver hair and vivid green eyes—eyes I have seen before. But even without that massive clue, there would be no questioning who this old man is. It's Luke, just a lot older. He looks rather dapper in a brown tweed suit, and when he clocks Luke, he smiles so wide I'm sure there's a chance the brightness of it could short-circuit the power supply in the mansion.

"My boy," he murmurs, opening his arms.

Luke is gone from my side, heading for his grandfather, and I watch as they embrace, the old man smacking at Luke's back firmly but affectionately. I melt. "How are you, Pops?" Luke asks.

"Marvelous." He laughs, breaking away and taking Luke's face in his old hands. "Bloody marvelous."

"Good." Luke lets his grandfather kiss his cheeks one at a time. "I'd like you to meet someone, Pops." He turns toward me, as well as everyone else. Dozens of eyes all on me. My face slowly heats up. "This is Lo. Lo, meet my grandfather, Bert." Sliding his hands into his pockets, Bert joins everyone else in staring at me.

I raise a hand and wave. "Nice to meet you, sir."

The old man grins a devilish grin as he hobbles through the crowd of women, Luke by his side. "The pleasure is all mine, Lo." When he reaches me, he literally hauls me into his chest and squeezes me stupid. I'm a bit taken aback, my arms coming up reluctantly and tapping at his back on a nervous laugh.

"Put her down, Pops," Luke moans, prying us apart. "You'll scare her off."

"Nonsense." The old man laughs. "We're all about warm welcomes around here, ain't that right, ladies?" He turns to the peanut gallery of old women, who all nod their agreement enthusiastically.

"Not too friendly, eh?" Luke warns, slipping his hand around mine. I look down and once again marvel at the warmth engulfing me. I'm lost in a trance for a moment, forgetting where I am and how I came to be here. I look up and come eye to eye with Luke. He has this inexplicable ability to extinguish all my sorrows, even in short bursts of time. However short, though, they help. So much. "Okay?" he asks.

Swallowing, I flex my fingers in his hold. "Yeah."

Something passes between us, something significant. I have no idea what to make of it. I close my eyes tightly and drop my head, wondering if any of this guilt would be plaguing me if Luke were a woman. Would I keep swaying between shame and resoluteness if it were a female offering to distract me from real life for a short time? I don't know. All I know in life right now is that I feel like me again. Normal. Carefree. It feels good to let go, even if only temporarily. My mind is a crazy mess, but one thought is crystal clear: it seems like madness that I'm always thinking I should force pleasantness from my life in exchange for grimness. These feelings and thoughts I have where Luke is concerned should be a far better option that my usual hollowness. Luke's a blessing in my life. Is it wrong to accept that? Or is this something Billy would want for me? Not the angry, reclusive Billy of today, but the man I married. Wouldn't he want me to *not* be alone throughout this godforsaken time? It's probably why he urges me to go to work each day. *Interaction. Living.*

I'm brought back into the foyer of the mansion when Luke's pops claps his old hands. "Welcome to my home, Lo."

"Thank you." My arms take on a mind of their own and wrap around Luke's middle, and I feel the light pressure of something meeting the top of my head. His lips. Luke's affectionate move doesn't prompt me to free myself from his closeness.

In fact, his kiss reminds me of my dad, because that's exactly how he used to kiss me, and I always felt safer and lighter when he did. Moments like these, I wish my dad was more involved in my life. He seems so far away in more ways than simply geography. But he has his new life now. Apart from an occasional text or call, there's no connection anymore. It's almost like in order to forget the tragedy of losing my mother, he had to disconnect from me too.

"Pops is quite the star here, right, Pops?" Luke says.

"Right," he chimes, all happy with himself. "But not as big as my grandboy." His bushy gray eyebrows hitch slightly as he nods to the gaggle of old ladies still surrounding us. "You come in here and steal all the attention away from me, Grandboy." Turning on his heels, he wanders off into a room to the right.

I laugh now, too, letting Luke guide me after him. "Nice to see you, ladies," he says on a smile that sends their old knees visibly weak. We enter an impressive lounge space, with many high-seated armchairs that are positioned in small clusters here and there, providing plenty of separate seating areas. There are more elderly people scattered around, some men and some women. I note a few of the residents in here are dozing in their chairs, some looking a lot less mobile than others. "Your grandfather doesn't look like he needs caring for."

"He doesn't." Luke motions toward a collection of chairs in the far corner where his grandfather is heading. "Most of the time. This place encourages independent living for some residents. There are apartments both in the main house and in complexes around the grounds. He likes the company." Luke gives me a small smile. "And the attention. Take a seat."

I lower to the chair opposite the old man, smiling when he winks at me cheekily. "I'm as strong as an ox." He flexes his biceps at me, and Luke laughs, tugging his trousers up at the knee before sitting. "Has my grandboy told you yet that he has an unreasonable fear of spicy food?"

"He does?" I throw Luke an interested look, and he rolls his eyes dramatically, resting back in his chair.

"He does," Bert confirms, nodding, his lips straight and serious.

"It's not unreasonable," Luke sighs.

"I'd say it's pretty unreasonable to have a fear of spicy food." I back up Bert, who claps his hands in joy.

"See," he sings. "A big strapping man like you, scared of a few chilies."

"I'm allergic," Luke mutters.

"Allergic?" I ask, getting comfy in my chair.

Luke clears his throat and glances at his grandfather, which, in turn, has me peeking across to him too. The old man has a corker of a grin on his face. "Luke's not allergic." He links his fingers and rests them on his stomach. "Are you, Grandboy?"

I see the hollows of Luke's cheeks dip from the bite of his teeth, and then he mutters something under his breath. I lean forward to try and catch it, but I can't make out a word. Bert starts chuckling, though I know the old man couldn't have heard Luke either. He's sitting farther away from his grandson than I am, and not to be presumptuous, but I'm guessing his hearing isn't as good as mine. "Pardon?" I move forward some more, eliminating the risk of missing it again.

Luke coughs and rushes his words, this time loud, but disguised by his fake splutter. Then he shifts in his chair awkwardly, and his grandfather bursts into rip-roaring laughter. I'm super intrigued now, smiling at Bert's humor, despite not having a clue what's so funny. But I need to know. "I didn't catch that."

On an over-the-top sigh, Luke looks straight at me and scowls. "I've never liked spicy food."

"I thought you're allergic."

"He's scared," Pops pipes up.

"I'm not scared, I just don't get it."

"Not getting something is different than being scared of it," I point out. Fair enough, I'm not a fan myself, but I wouldn't run out screaming if I was presented with a hot curry. Sounds like Luke would.

"I picked a green chili out of my dinner once." Luke looks

away from me, and I smile, seeing how uncomfortable he is, telling me the reason behind his phobia. "And neglected to wash my hands afterward."

"Oh no." I slap a hand over my mouth. "You didn't touch your eyes, did you?" I've never made the faux pas myself, but I know people who have and, apparently, it's a hideous experience.

"No," Luke grunts. "Worse."

"Worse?" I question, while Bert continues to fall apart in his chair. What could be worse?

"I used the men's room, and . . ." Luke pouts, flicking his eyes down to his crotch, and without thought, mine drop there too.

Realization dawns quickly. "No."

"Yes." Bert chortles. "Yes, he bloody did. The silly sod touched his todger after handling a chili, seeds and all. Had to cut his date short and rush to the emergency room when the tip broke out in blisters."

"Oh my God." I'm horrified, but more than that, I'm amused beyond amused. "You got blisters?" I fall apart with Bert, while poor Luke's scowl deepens, and he fidgets in his chair.

"Yes, I got blisters. I'm allergic."

"Poor boy didn't get any action for months."

"Pops," Luke groans, disturbed.

"Well you didn't, and for a man who got it as frequently as you, I'm surprised it didn't kill ya off." Bert wipes under his eyes. "And you couldn't even polish the pearl yourself."

I choke on thin air, my sides splitting with laughter as Luke shrinks in his seat in dismay. "It was very traumatic," he grumbles.

"I bet." I'm wheezing, struggling to grab air through my hysterics.

"And you ask me why I never bring my friends to meet you." Luke laughs sarcastically, giving us both disapproving looks.

"Hey, boy, I'm doing you a favor. At least now Lo knows not to take you for spicy food on any of your dates."

"Oh, we're not dating," I pipe up, getting my laughter under control and wanting to make *that* crystal clear. "We're just—"

"Friends," Luke finishes for me. "We're just friends."

"Pull the other one." Bert shakes his head, completely exasperated.

"Friends," Luke repeats, stern and sure, cocking his head to the side in warning.

Bert relents quickly on a frown. "Right. Friends."

"Anyway," Luke rushes on, going to his inside pocket and pulling out a hipflask, glancing around warily, "I bought you this."

Bert's face lights up and he rubs his hands together. "Good boy."

"I'll get some mugs." Luke rises to his feet. "Coming?" he asks his grandfather.

"No. I'll wait here with Lo."

"I'm not leaving her with you so you can interrogate her."

"What's there to interrogate her about if you're not dating?" Bert cocks his head cheekily. "What would you like, Lo? Tea, coffee, or the good, hard stuff with me?"

I look around the room, fleetingly observing some of the other residents who are snoozing in their chairs or occupying themselves with knitting or the odd crossword puzzle. "Tea, I guess."

"I was beginning to like you, Lo." Bert tsks his disapproval at my choice. "She'll have the strong stuff with me, Grandboy."

Luke moves away cautiously, dividing his eyes between me and his grandfather. "Be nice," he warns.

"Yeah, yeah, yeah." Bert flicks him away, and I spend a few moments watching Luke soak up the attention from the female residents before I turn back to face his grandfather. He grins wickedly. "No need to blush," he says around his smile.

I reach up to my cheeks on a frown. "Why would I be blushing?" And then it occurs to me. "Oh, no." He thinks I was admiring Luke. "I was just finding the attention he's getting amusing."

"Well, my grandboy is a tremendous hunk of a male." He puffs his chest out. "He gets it from his granddaddy."

I press my lips together to stop my smile. "I agree, but I don't see him like that."

"Then how do you see him?"

"As a friend. A really good friend."

"And how did you get to become friends?"

Luke hasn't told him? "Well . . ." I frown, thinking this is going to sound as ridiculous as it is. "He kind of nearly ran me over."

For the first time since I've set eyes on Luke's grandfather, I see surprise on his face. "You became friends because he nearly killed you?"

"Well, yeah." I laugh under my breath. "I was walking my dog and managed to wander onto the road without realizing it. Luke stopped just in time."

Bert's eyes widen in shock, and he hums, thoughtful, crossing one leg over the over. "He nearly ran you over," he muses, studying me closely.

I look away, feeling he's reading between the lines. "I was daydreaming. And then my dog collapsed, and Luke kindly drove us to an emergency vet." I leave out that he kindly paid the bills too. He might think I'm taking advantage, and I wouldn't blame him.

"And you're just friends?"

"Just friends." I smile. "You find it odd, don't you?"

"My grandson isn't the kind of man who has female friends."

"But he has lots of female . . ." I pause, thinking how to word it politely. "Company."

"That's a way to put it. Though none of them seem to hold his attention."

"That's because they're all wrong for him. Luke needs to date women more his own age."

Bert smiles, and it's knowing. He agrees. "I think Luke should listen to you, Lo."

"Agreed," I counter, turning his smile into a devilish grin.

"Have you been anywhere nice this evening?"

I look down at my dress. "Just for a drink with friends. I bumped into Luke and he invited me here. I hope you don't mind."

"Of course not. Did you bring me a gift?"

"What?"

A loud clap rings out through the room when Bert smacks his hands together. "It's my birthday."

"Oh my God, happy birthday!" Damn it, why didn't Luke tell me? I feel so rude turning up with not so much as a card.

"Why, thank you." He brushes down his tie. "Ninety today. The staff have put on a small party for me next door." He thumbs over his shoulder to the double doors where all the women have disappeared. "They think I have no idea."

"It's supposed to be a surprise?"

"It is. I might be decrepit, but my senses haven't failed me just yet. I've been banned from that room all day, people are playing hush-hush, and my grandboy has just shown up with a date."

"I'm not his date," I say, smiling.

"Of course. You're Just-a-Friend Lo."

"That's me. So, are you expecting any more family?" I ask.

"The chance would be a fine thing. My son, that's Luke's father, and my daughter-in-law, Luke's mother, live in Croatia." There's definitely an edge of resentment somewhere there, though I don't pry, no matter how curious I am. "And Arabella, my granddaughter, that's Luke's sister, is a globetrotter." I listen, remembering Luke mentioning his sister. "She's back in London for a few days. Came to see me this morning, she did." He leans forward and scans the vicinity. "Stocked up my secret stash."

I lean in too, my head tilted in intrigue. "Secret stash?"

He takes a finger to his lips and motions to keep quiet. No problem, since I have no idea what I'm keeping quiet about. "But Luke is here every other day without fail." He's all smiles again at the thought of his grandson. "I know you shouldn't have favorites, but, well, Luke is my favorite. Hands down."

"Because he visits you frequently?"

"No. Because he's—"

"You when you were younger," I finish, sensing the connection between them. They don't only look alike, they also have many similar mannerisms, like their eye rolls, and their cheeky smiles and playfulness. Bert only confirms my conclusion on a proud smile, and then drops his eyes down to my left hand. I follow his stare until I find my wedding ring, my hand instinctively covering it.

"He's a good man, Lo," he says quietly. "Honorable too."

I look up, forcing my hand away. Because why would I hide the fact I'm married? I have nothing to feel ashamed of. "I know."

"Follow your heart, dear girl. I wish I did," he breathes out wistfully, looking off into the distance. "Oh, Milly. What a woman."

My teeth bite down on my lip as I stare at the old man, searching his eyes for more than that cryptic statement. Milly? Luke's grandmother? Bert gives me nothing, not answering my silent question, and Luke appears with drinks before I can press him. Or maybe just assure him that my heart will always lead me to my husband.

"Still alive?" Luke asks, flicking his attention between me and his granddad.

I nod and accept the mug being handed to me, frowning at it. "Thank you." I look inside and see a few inches of amber liquid in the bottom. "I think."

"House rules," Luke says. "We have to sneak it in." He passes a mug to Bert, who takes it in both hands before raising it and taking a small sip.

"So, then," Bert says, nodding in my direction, "you must be taking your new friend somewhere special since she's all dressed up."

"Yeah." Luke looks across the room when the door swings open and one of the old women appear, waving her arms excitedly. "Shall we give Lo a tour of the house?" Luke asks, offering me his hand.

"No." Bert's answer is abrupt and final, and I smile, seeing the devilish twinkle in his old eyes. "I'm fine where I am, thank you very much."

Accepting Luke's hand, I let him pull me to my feet. "Come on, Bert," I push lightly. "I want a tour."

We both stand over Bert while he sniffs his drink and swirls the liquid casually. I narrow a playful eye on him when he peeks up at me.

"Oh, all right," he sighs and wrestles himself up from the chair. Luke shoots over to help him, ignoring the grunts of displeasure from Bert. They lead the way, me following, until we break the threshold of the double doors, the room coming into view.

"Surprise!" a crowd of people, mostly women, sing, as party poppers start bursting everywhere, and a rapturous round of applause follows.

"Well, would you believe it." Bert looks across at me on an epic roll of his eyes. "I had no idea."

I grin like a fool as I stand to the side, watching everyone in the room descend on the old man, whooping and cheering his arrival. But mostly I watch Luke and his way with his grandad. They're close, it's clear, and their similarities, despite the decades between them, are uncanny.

At that moment, Luke looks up and finds me, and the smile that spreads across his face is striking. "Okay?" he mouths, and I nod, happy to remain where I am and take it all in.

But I'm not where I am for long. I glance to my side when my arm is taken, and I'm pulled off across the room. "This way, dear," an old woman declares, and I look in the direction in which I'm being pulled, seeing a table full of elderly ladies grinning at me. Glancing over my shoulder, I see Luke shaking his head in dismay. "Be afraid," he calls. "Be very afraid."

I laugh as I land in the chair that one lady has pushed me into, coming face to face with eight very interested-looking old ladies. Smiling nervously, I wait for who is going to hit me with my first question.

"How long have you been dating?" one asks.

"We're n—"

"You look younger than our Luke."

"I'm twe—"

"How did you snag him?"

"I didn't sn—"

"Do we need to buy hats?"

"Oh, goodness." I laugh. "Like I said—"

"Have you moved in yet?"

My eyes widen. "We're just fr—"

"Children," one sings, clapping her hands. "How many?"

"I'm sorry," I swallow, looking over my shoulder for Luke. He needs to rescue me, but I can't see him through the scatterings of old people that arc shuffling around the dance floor in pairs to some Frank Sinatra. I return my attention to the clan of inquisitive women. I smile nervously. "I don't think—"

"What's that on your finger?" My hand is grabbed, and suddenly all eyes are on my wedding ring.

"She's married?" another gasps, spiking a chorus of further gasps from the rest of the table. I snatch my hand back and hide it under the table, and they proceed to narrow eyes on me suspiciously. Oh God, this is horrible. I start to prepare my excuse to leave the table when Luke appears. He must read the relief on my face because he cocks a head in question.

"Would you like to dance?" he asks.

"Yes." I'm up from my chair in a split second, putting my hand in his. I'll do anything to get away, and if that means making a tit of myself on the dance floor, I'm there. I drag Luke through the small crowd until we're in the center of the floor, and when I turn to face him, I find his face looking stunned. "Sorry." I shrug one shoulder.

"Given how keen you are to get to the dance floor, I'm guessing you must be an amazing dancer."

"Oh no." I laugh, stepping back. "Quite the opposite, in fact. I'm terrible." Crap, this was a bad idea.

Luke steps forward and opens his arms. "Well, I'm not bad, so it won't be a complete train crash."

I scoff. "You've not danced with *me* yet." My ears prick up when I hear the next track kick in, and I look around when it sets off a whirl of excitement with the residents, including Bert, who tap-dances his way onto the dance floor. I laugh out loud. "I assume your grandad likes this song."

Luke's eyes burst with joy. "Who doesn't like Mack the Knife?" he asks, seizing me and yanking me into his chest. "Oh, darling, get ready to bust some moves."

"Woah," I cry as I'm flung back and spun in a messy pirouette before being hauled back into him. Our fronts bump, the force of the collision taking my breath away. His arm creeps around my back and pushes my waist into him some more, and his spare hand holding mine crushes gently. "I can't dance," I whisper, the track filling the room, drowning out my words, but he doesn't miss them.

Bringing his face down to mine, he puts his lips at my ear. "With me, you can do anything."

I close my eyes, feeling him break away, and when I open them again, he's smiling, the scale of it dazzling. That infectious beam is mirrored with my own as he secures his hold and starts moving us around the floor expertly, my steps following his naturally. "Not bad," I say, more than pleasantly surprised.

"I've learned from the best." Luke nods over my shoulder, and I glance back, spotting Bert holding court with the ladies, taking each of them in turn and giving them a spin here and a twirl there. "He'll put his hip out if he isn't careful."

I throw my head back on a laugh, my hair fanning the air as Luke flings and spins us around the dance floor, singing along with gusto to Bobby Darin. His smile is constant, keeping mine in place too, and his energy unstoppable. He weaves us in and out of our fellow dancing companions, all the while keeping me as close as possible. I'm not contributing, just following his lead, my attention rooted to his face. I'm in a world of my own, lost and happy. All I can hear is the music, all I can see is Luke, and all I can feel is contentment. Pure and complete contentment.

"You ready for the grand finale?" Luke asks, working us into the middle of the floor.

"I'm ready," I confirm, smiling like crazy.

"Sure?"

"Positive." I nod my affirmation and brace myself, flexing my hand on his shoulder as the orchestra reaches a crescendo toward the end of the song.

"Here we go." Luke pushes me away and grabs my hand, manipulating my body into a spin that I have no control over. Not that it matters. Luke knows what he's doing. I hardly get a hold of my bearings before I'm being spun again, this time into his body and back out.

"Luke," I cry through my laughter. "I'm getting dizzy."

"Me too," he declares, increasing my laughter tenfold. I'm utterly useless as I'm flipped, twisted, and pulled back and forth. I yelp as I hit his chest, and then I'm reclined back across his arm. My static position gives me a few seconds to focus on his face, which is a picture of pure delight. "You're worse than I anticipated," he says around his epic smile.

"I did warn you."

Laughing, he hauls me up to standing before grabbing me under the arms and literally throwing me into the air.

I'm a total slave to his strength, my body going exactly where he puts it, and I'm caught with ease, though he doesn't lower me to the ground, leaving my chin resting on top of his head. Until he eases up his hold slightly, making me slide down his body.

"What a finale," he murmurs, withdrawing and placing me on my feet. And he bows, over the top and on a dashing smile. "An honor, madam."

"Thank you, kind sir."

We both laugh as we make our way off the floor, me tucked neatly under Luke's arm. "Are you having a nice time?" he asks.

With him, always.

Chapter Twenty-Four

The following evening after a particularly long, draining day in the office, I stand in the kitchen listening to the kettle bubbling up to boiling point. I make Billy a cup of tea and take it up to him. He didn't eat much of his dinner, no surprise there, but if I can at least keep his fluids up, it helps. *I think.*

"You look lovely today," he says as I place his drink on his nightstand.

"Pardon?" I look at him, dazed, and he smiles mildly. It's a rare sight, and though I don't know what he's smiling about, I savor the sight.

Reaching for my hand, he holds it with his frail one. "I said, you look lovely."

"I do?" I look down my body, to my black boyish trousers and sheer black blouse. I haven't worn this outfit for years, nor the black ballet flats that have been hidden at the back of my wardrobe forever. I didn't register what exactly I put on this morning, not until Billy pointed it out now. I look in the mirror next to Billy's bed. I haven't seen the woman before me in too many years. I reach up to my long blonde hair that has been straightened, returning it to its former shiny self, even if my roots are still more than obvious. My silvery eyes are framed with lashes thick with mascara, my lids painted with my usual thick line of eyeliner, a little flick at the corner of my eyes. And what's strangest is that I honestly do not recall applying any of it. This morning was a blur.

"Lovely," Billy confirms, and I look down at him, indulging some more in his smile.

"Want to take me out for dinner?" I ask lightly, a complete joke that I hope he appreciates. When his weak smile widens slightly, I know he has. He and I both know he's going nowhere.

"How was your day?" He changes the subject while I tuck his sheets in around him.

"Long. Are you comfortable?"

"Dead," Billy mutters, and I throw him a horrified look. "Dead comfy."

"That's not funny."

It takes too much effort for him to smile again. "Sorry."

I roll my eyes and faff some more with the blankets on his bed, and he lets me. "You want some help having a shower before bed?" He hasn't had one since yesterday morning, and I know it's because he feels too crap to get himself out of bed. He can't deny my help forever. He has to let his pride go.

"I can shower myself."

He can't, but I refuse to argue with him. "Can I get you anything before I get ready for bed?"

"Get ready for bed?" His lined forehead frowns. "But it's only six thirty."

Yes, it is, but what else is he expecting me to do with my evening? "I'm tired," I tell him, wishing I could take it back the second it slips free, because Billy's face twists in displeasure as a result.

I'm saved from our potential confrontation when my phone rings, and I reach into my pocket to answer. "Scarlett?" I say to myself, taking her call.

"Lo, I'm so sorry to do this to you, and if it's not possible, please just tell me so." She sounds out of breath, like she's racing to get somewhere.

"Are you okay?"

"My mother-in-law has been rushed into hospital with breathing difficulties."

"Oh, Scarlett, I'm so sorry. Is there anything I can do?"

"Yes, that's why I'm calling. I have the annual fundraising gala this evening, and we obviously can't go now. Will you go in our place?"

"Oh," I breathe.

"I wouldn't ask, but we need someone there representing the company. It won't look good if no one shows up. The invitation is for two, so you can take a guest."

I laugh to myself. Yeah, because I have options lining up outside my door ready for me to invite them.

"Maybe a friend?" she adds, knowing what I'm thinking, as per usual.

"What about Rachel?"

"She's out of town, and Belle has a family function she can't get out of. There's no one else I'd entrust this to, Lo. I wouldn't ask. I know things for you are hard at the moment."

Hard? "Scarlett . . . I . . ." I look over to Billy and see him watching me.

"Go," he mouths, and I shake my head. He nods his in return, reinforcing his order.

"Would you, Lo?" Scarlett pleads. "Free champagne and free entertainment."

"I don't know, Scarlett. I'm not much of a socializer. I'd hate to let you down."

"Let me down? Never, Lo. You'll be perfect. I'm going to email the invitation to you now. Just show it on the door. Our donation for the auction should have arrived this morning. Try to have fun, okay?" She hangs up, clearly a ploy to prohibit my attempts to argue with her.

"You should go," Billy says as I stare at my phone.

"You heard all that, huh?"

"Scarlett's always been loud." Billy smiles, rests his head back on the pillow and closes his eyes, reaching for my hand blindly. I give it to him, and he squeezes. "Go and enjoy yourself, please. It sounds like Scarlett really needs you."

And you don't.

I bring my phone to my mouth and nibble on the corner, assessing his condition. He looks content, almost happy at the thought of me going out and enjoying myself. Not that I will. How could I?

"I won't be late," I assure him, kissing the back of his hand before resting it gently back on the bed. He doesn't answer that, and I back out of the room, opening an email when it pings, finding the invitation. It's at the Royal Opera House. Doors open at eight and the dress code states formal. What does formal mean these days? In a panic, I run to my wardrobe and scan the rails. Goodness, I have limited options. I pull out a little black dress that hasn't seen the light of day for years.

It's my only choice. Laying it on my bed, I take care of problem number two. My plus-one. Luke flits through my mind fleetingly—how I'd love to ask him to come. Why can't I? After all, he's kind of my only option. I pull his number up and dial, and he answers immediately.

"Hey, you."

"Hi," I chirp, wandering to the bathroom to flip on the shower. "Are you busy tonight?"

I hear him sigh, and that in itself gives me my answer. Of course he's busy. "Lo, I have a business thing that I really can't get out of."

"Oh, don't worry," I rush to ease him.

"Tomorrow? We'll walk the mutts."

"Deal." I smile and say my goodbye, hanging up and thinking. I don't want to go alone. I'll be standing around like a plum all night. Scrolling through my contacts, I stop on the only other person that's a possibility, and dial.

"Hello?"

"It's Lo." There's a long pause, and I know it's because he's wondering what on earth I'd be calling for. "I need a favor."

"You do?" Matthew asks, sounding as intrigued as I would expect him to.

"Want to be my date?"

"Huh?"

I drop to my arse on the bed. "Scarlett's asked me to fill her place at the charity gala tonight. The invite is for two."

"So you called me?" Understandably, the tech guy from work, a complete hermit, is stunned.

"Yes. What do you say?" I mentally beg for Matthew to accept, dreading the prospect of going alone. "Please?"

"Oh, all right, then," he mutters. "But only because it's you and I don't want to be the cause for further misery in your life."

I recoil, completely stunned. "Wow."

"Did I say that out loud?"

"Yeah, you did."

"Oh, sorry. What's the dress code?"

"Formal. Pick you up in a cab in an hour." I hang up and get myself ready.

Glancing at Matthew as we approach a waitress, I shake my head again, totally dismayed. "What?" he asks, taking two drinks from the tray and handing one over.

"I'm just wondering where you got that suit from." I gesture to his velvet-clad body, all the way down to his black patent, super pointy shoes.

"You said formal."

"Yes, formal in 2017, not formal in 1970. When was the last time you wore it?"

"1978."

I laugh and take a sip of my champagne as we wander through the crowds, greeting people as we go, shaking the odd hand and introducing ourselves. "This is a classic suit," Matthew argues.

"Classically dreadful." I quip. "You look like Austin Powers gone wrong."

"Well, I'm here. Just be thankful."

"I am. Thank you." I clink my glass with his. "Scarlett donated a prize to the auction. I need to find one of the organizers to make sure it arrived."

"How'd we know who the organizers are?"

"They're wearing huge sashes with Piper Foundation sprawled across it. Shouldn't be hard." I lift on my tippy-toes and scan the crowds. "Oh, I see one." I grab Matthew's hand and pull him through the crowd to a table at the back where a group of sash-clad women are gathered. "Hello, my name is Lo Harper from Red Well."

"Oh, hello," a red-haired lady in a garish green and red gown coos. "I'm Hilda, events coordinator. Where's Scarlett?"

"She told me to apologize profusely for her absence. There was a family emergency, and I've come in her place. Did her donation for the auction arrive?"

Hilda scans a spreadsheet on the table before her. "Oh yes, there it is. One of those iPhone thingamajigs, how lovely!" She looks to Matthew with a big grin. "And you must be the other prize." Her eyes drop down his velvet-clad body. "For the more mature ladies, perhaps."

I frown and look back at Matthew. He looks as equally confused as me. "I'm sorry, I don't understand."

"We're selling off men in the auction."

"What?" I balk.

"Yes, what?" Matthew asks.

"For the charity, dear. We'll be auctioning you off." She takes a clipboard to the side and ticks something off, before shouting some instructions to a nearby lady.

"Auctioning me off?" Matthew asks, slighted. "To who?"

"Well, dear, to whoever stumps up the most cash." She flounces away, and I start chuckling to myself.

"Well, great." Matthew swaps his empty for a fresh glass, obviously deciding that getting plastered is the only way forward. "Who's going to want to buy me? There's a reason I'm in my fifties and single."

"Oh, I don't know," I muse, turning him toward the table, where a gaggle of, let's say, *mature* women are faffing around. "I think they'll love your suit."

"I didn't bargain for this." Matthew stomps off, and I giggle, sipping my champagne.

"Wow, I love that dress," a lady says as she approaches me, pointing at the vintage material encasing my body.

"Oh, it's not . . ." I pull back my confession before I can tell this perfect stranger, who is perfect in every way, that my dress is probably older than her. That I could never afford anything so glamourous as what she's wearing. Her dark hair is swept up, her face is flawless, and her lips are painted to perfection. She's another Scarlett, but probably more extreme. Perfect, and the envy of every woman who encounters her. I feel inferior. "Thank you." I smile graciously, as does she.

"Can I ask where you purchased it?"

Oh, shit. "France," I blurt. "Paris, to be exact."

She nods slowly, taking a sip of her champagne as she smiles over the rim at me. "Well, it's beautiful on you."

"That's very kind of you to say."

"You're welcome, Lo."

My glass stops on its journey to my mouth. "Pardon?"

Her hand extends toward me, and she beams, her eyes

sparkling madly. Green eyes. "I'm Arabella Williamson. I believe you know my brother."

Oh . . . my . . . God. Ground, swallow me whole right now. I remember Luke telling me that his sister is in the fashion industry. She knows fine well this dress isn't out of Paris. I grab her hand and proceed to die a thousand deaths. "I'm Lo," I squeak. "But you know that."

"I do." She winks cheekily, and I die a bit more, glancing at my vintage number.

"Wait." I look up at Arabella when something comes to me. "How'd you know who I am?"

Arabella grins devilishly. "Luke pointed you out."

"He's here?"

She looks past me, pointing her champagne glass, and I turn, finding him immediately. "Hello, you," Luke says, sinking his hands into his black trousers as he approaches. Oh, he has a tux on.

Arabella slinks off on a fond smile, leaving us alone. "Nice to meet you, Lo."

"And you," I call, returning my attention to Luke. "I just made a total tit of myself in front of your sister."

"How?"

"I told her my dress was out of Paris."

Luke's laugh, deep and rich, sinks past my skin and fills me with warmth. "Paris or not, you look gorgeous. What are you doing here?"

"Scarlett had a family emergency." I extend my arms out to my sides. "So here I am."

"Here you are," he muses quietly.

"You look very handsome." I motion up and down his body while he reins in his laughs, rolling back on his heels.

"Good, then you'll dance with me."

"What?" I ask as he grabs my wrist and pulls me through the crowds. "Luke, we already established that I can't dance."

"And we already established that I'm not bad, so we'll be okay."

"But there's no one dancing yet," I cry, landing on the empty dance floor, being hauled into his chest.

"Someone has to get the party started." He twirls me out and back into his embrace, grinning at me in that devilish way that he does. "Ready?"

"No," I say, looking over his shoulder to see Arabella leaning against a pillar, smiling at us.

Nina Simone's *Feeling Good* starts, and Luke gasps, looking down at me mischievously. "My favorite."

I'm spun around on a laugh, powerless to stop him as he whirls me around the floor, a smile in his face. I have absolutely no control of our steps; I'm simply following Luke, our fronts compressed, his forearm snaked around my lower back, my palms resting on his wide shoulders. I can see other couples have joined us on the floor, yet like everything when I'm with Luke, they disappear.

"You're getting good at this dancing lark," he says casually, just as I trip over his foot and we stagger slightly. "Or maybe not."

"You did that on purpose." I smack his shoulder playfully, trying to find my rhythm again.

"Your accusation is wounding." He feigns a hurt expression that makes me tut my dismay.

As I trip over again.

"Luke." I chuckle, grabbing the sleeves of his jacket as I'm lifted from my feet.

"Maybe this will work better." He holds me to his front, my face now level with his, and ups the ante, spinning and whirling off again. Right now, I'm glad he's carrying me, because there's no way I could keep up with his current pace without face-planting.

I drop my head back, looking up at the gorgeously decorated ceiling, and laugh, the patterns above me blending together, the music blurring. I breathe in, close my eyes, and let Luke spin me into an oblivion as I link my arms around his neck and hold on.

And drift off to another world, a world far better than this one.

Peace.

Carefree.

No pain.

I'm brought back into my body by the sensation of us slowing, and I peel my eyes open and drop my head as Luke lowers me to my feet. The brightness of his smile momentarily makes me dizzy. "Your lesson for today is done," he says quietly, holding me while I regain my balance. "You'll be Ginger Rogers in no time."

I snort, fixing my dress. "Your expectations are way too high."

Luke offers his arm, and I slip mine through, and then he starts to walk us off the floor as a lady on stage announces the auction will be starting soon. Matthew appears through the crowds looking very disgruntled. "Oh, here's my work friend," I tell Luke, accepting the glass of champagne he hands me. "He's for sale."

"In that suit?" Luke laughs, and I nudge him in the side as Matthew joins us. "Hello," Luke coughs.

"Luke, this is Matthew. Matthew, meet Luke." I motion between them and take a sip of my third glass of champagne. It's the most I've had to drink in a long while.

"Nice to meet you." Matthew gives Luke a firm handshake. "Nice tux."

"Thanks," Luke replies graciously, gesturing down Matthew's front with his glass. "Nice . . . what is that?"

I glare at Luke, and Matthew rolls his eyes behind his glasses. "This, my friend, is a classic C&A piece."

"C&A? So it's vintage?"

"Vintage," Matthew muses, nodding his head agreeably. "Yes, it's vintage."

"Vintage is all the rage these days," I pipe up, peeking up at

Luke on a small smile. "You're trendy and you didn't even know it, Matthew."

"That suit just doubled your price." Luke points to the stage where Hilda is waving a gavel, shouting for all men offered in the auction to step on stage. "Time for us studs to raise a few quid." Luke smacks Matthew on the shoulder. "Ready?"

"What?" Matthew baulks at Luke in horror.

"Yes, what?" I parrot, unable to prevent my shock from revealing itself in my tone. "You're being auctioned too?"

"Yep." Luke wanders off toward the stage.

"Oh, great," Matthew mutters, trudging along behind him. "I'm up against Mr. Perfect."

I laugh and watch as they're welcomed on stage with a few other daunted-looking men, who I know haven't volunteered for this. Which makes me wonder if Luke has. He did mention that he had some business thing that he couldn't get out of. At least I know he declined my invite for a good cause. The crowd pipes down as Hilda introduces each of the men and explains how the auction will work. Basically, if you like what you see and want a man slave for the rest of the evening, as well as a dinner date on a mutually agreeable date in the coming weeks, then you bid. I watch on with the rest of the guests as three men are sold off to rapturous women in the crowd, and I laugh as each guy is show-cased, being ordered to walk up and down the stage to show themselves at all angles for the bidders. The space is buzzing, people clapping, cheering, and wolf-whistling.

When Matthew is called forward, he's asked to remind the crowd who he is, where he's from, and what he does for a living. He clears his throat, leaning into the microphone, looking every bit as uncomfortable as I know he is. "My name is Matthew, I'm fifty-two, I live in West London, and I like computers."

I snigger under my breath as Hilda asks him about his "jazzy" suit. "It's vintage," he declares proudly, making Luke cough behind him.

"We'll start the bids at five hundred pounds," Hilda shouts, gliding her gavel through the air across the heads of the crowds. "Who will give me five hundred for this fine specimen of a man?"

Poor Matthew looks like he wants the ground to swallow him whole as he waits with bated breath for someone, *anyone*, to bid on his geeky arse. I'm dying for him, the room's silent, and I wish more than anything that I had that kind of money so I could buy him and save him from this public humiliation. I scan the crowd, willing someone to bid.

"Five hundred!"

Everyone's head turns toward the back section of the room, hushed whispers starting. I look with them and spot a lady smiling at Matthew on the stage. I grin from ear to ear and return my attention to Matthew, finding him craning his head to try and get his bidder in his sights. I know the moment he spots her, because his shoulders straighten and push back, and a little glimmer brightens his eyes.

"Do I hear six hundred?" Hilda asks the crowd.

Matthew sags, rolling his eyes in exasperation. I see his lips move, and Hilda moves in to hear what he's saying. "Sold," she declares on a screech.

The crowd erupts into enthusiastic applause, and Mathew makes a speedy exit from the stage, meeting his buyer as he descends the steps. I watch on, satisfied, as they greet each other formally with a handshake.

"Luke is up next," Arabella whispers in my ear, smiling knowingly. I down the rest of my champagne and grab another as the waitress passes.

"I'm sure he'll fetch a healthy sum for charity," I say, wondering who might win him. Who will get Luke as their man slave for the rest of the evening? Who will get a dinner date with him? I don't know, but I hope it's a woman closer to his age, then maybe he might stand a chance of a long-term relationship. I cast my eyes around the room. There are dozens of preened, gorgeous women here, and they're all staring up at the stage in awe. I can't help but think that they've all been waiting for this one. I also can't help but think that the organizers have saved the best till last, because there's no denying that Luke knocks socks off the rest of the men. I feel an odd sense of pride as I watch him step forward and introduce himself. His eyes constantly fall to mine, and each time, he smiles the smile that lights up his face. And my heart.

"We'll start the bidding at five hundred," Hilda chants, not even getting the chance to point her gavel at the crowd before a woman behind me shouts her bid. I turn and see what I expected I would. A perfect woman, with perfect hair, perfect makeup, and perfect attire. "Do I hear six hundred?"

"Here," another woman sings. Another perfect woman. My head bats every which way with each bid that's made, Luke's price tag getting higher and higher by the minute. It's competitive, with looks passing between the bidders—challenging looks. Looks from determined women who really want to win Luke. I shake my head in wonder, hearing Arabella laughing next to me, and focus on Luke. He catches my eye, shrugs, lifts his trousers at the knees, and sits on the edge of the stage, getting comfortable. When the bidding reaches an incredible, record-breaking four-thousand-pounds for the charity, a few of the ladies drop out of the bidding war, clearly pissed off that they've failed to snag the prize. The front runner at the moment is a black-haired beauty, Spanish, I expect, adorned in a red gown with matching nails. She looks smug as she watches her opponents surrender before she sets her eyes firmly on her prize. And I note she's older than Luke's type. Good. I nod to myself, satisfied.

"Going once at four thousand." Hilda cranes her neck, scanning the crowd. "Going twice."

"Five thousand," a low, sultry voice announces, and I look around, discovering yet another perfect woman. I don't mean to roll my eyes, but I do. I feel like I'm on the set of *Britain's Next Top Model*. She's in her early twenties, easy. She's no good for my Luke.

Grimacing to myself, willing the Spanish beauty to take her down, I leave the sight of Miss Stunning behind me and find Luke again. He looks worried, his body no longer relaxed where he's sitting on the edge of the stage.

I frown, looking across to the Spanish woman. She's backed up, putting herself out of the race. *Damn it, no!*

"You have to bid," Arabella whisper-hisses in my ear, grabbing my arm and launching it into the air. "Six thousand," she shouts, and everyone looks at me.

I stand like a statue, the soul focus of pretty much everyone in the room, including Luke. His wide, anxious eyes soften when he spots me, a small smile on his face. I yank my arm down and swing toward Arabella. "I can't afford that kind of money."

"Seven thousand," the voice behind me purrs.

I glance to my left and find a pair of heavily lined eyes narrowed on me. I immediately want to jump to my defense, tell her that I have no intention of outbidding her, but Arabella tugs me away. "You can't let her win," she says, snarling at the woman.

"I can." I laugh. "I don't have that kind of cash."

"Don't worry about the money. I'll pay." She takes my arm and thrusts it into the air again. "Eight thousand here."

"Arabella," I gasp, ignoring the claps. "What are you doing?"

"Luke was seeing her," she spits. "Amanda."

"No."

"Yes." Arabella looks over her shoulder with a curled lip that could rival Luke's ex flame.

"Wait, was she the one who left—"

"The Tiffany catalogue on Luke's bed stand? Yes. Luke's told me all about her." Pulling me forward, she points at Luke. "Please, do not let her win him."

I look at Luke's face. It's straight. But he's definitely worried. "Nine thousand," Amanda calls from behind. I can literally feel the proverbial daggers hitting my back.

"She doesn't have that kind of money. She just doesn't want to lose."

"Neither do I," I breathe, and Arabella looks at me. "Have that kind of money." I neglect to point out the fact that I don't want to lose either, not now, especially to his ex-lover who shamelessly hinted to an engagement after a few dates. She's not right for Luke. Definitely not right.

"Ten thousand!" Arabella once again throws my arm in the air. "I'm paying. Stop worrying."

"You can't pay thousands for your own brother."

"I'm not. I'm buying you a gift."

I'm utterly speechless, and one thing that seems to be very apparent is that Arabella is determined. And clearly loyal, looking out for her brother. So I let her get on with it—my limp arm being hoisted into the air with each bid she makes on my behalf—until she hits a whopping fifteen thousand and the crowds are gasping. Amanda doesn't go any higher. Instead, she shouts her frustration, and Arabella turns a sly, satisfied look her way as she pushes me toward the stage.

I walk, a bit bewildered, toward the front on the room, crowds moving from my path to let me through. When I reach the front, Luke has his smile firmly back in place. I laugh, dropping my eyes to the floor. I actually can't believe what just happened.

"Do I call you Madam, or would you prefer Master?" He slips off the stage and takes my hand, bowing and kissing the back. "How can I serve you?"

"Stop it," I scold, letting him wrap an arm around my shoulder and hug me to his side.

"Phew, that was close," Luke whispers as he walks us back toward Arabella. I'm pleased to note Amanda is nowhere in sight.

"I didn't know who she was," I admit. "If she'd have been holding a Tiffany catalogue, on the other hand."

Luke laughs, a deep, rumbling laugh. "Here, drink."

I thank him for the fizz and chink glasses with him and

Arabella. "I can't believe you did that," I say to Arabella. "Fifteen thousand pounds for your own brother."

"Then you better make sure you get my money's worth." She puts her tongue in her cheek before she downs her drink, and I nearly spit mine out, feeling my face burning up.

"Yes, what will you do with me?" Luke asks, his face serious and straight.

My eyes bounce between the two of them, and not knowing what to say, I finish another drink instead. I'm beginning to feel a little tipsy, and I can't lie, it's a feeling I'm quite enjoying. "You two are terrible people," I mutter, making them both laugh.

Arabella sets her empty on a tray and reaches up to her brother, kissing his cheek. "I've endured this place for long enough. I have friends to catch up with."

"Yes, you go. Thanks for tagging along."

"It was really lovely to meet you, Lo." Arabella sounds so sincere as she embraces my startled body.

"I've cost you thousands, and I only met you an hour ago. Thank you."

She laughs. "Don't mention it. Just keep that witch away from my brother."

"I'll try," I promise. It seems we're both in agreement that Amanda is no good for Luke. "Hope to meet you again."

"Oh, I'm sure we will." She flounces off, just as Matthew dances toward us, looking significantly happier than the last time I saw him.

"Fifteen thousand pounds!" He punches Luke's bicep and gently taps mine. "Where'd you find that kind of cash to blow so frivolously?"

I feel myself withdraw slightly, the magnitude of it hitting me. Fifteen thousand pounds. That's a ridiculous chunk of money that would go a long way toward the surgery Billy needs to save his life. And Arabella just threw it away like it was nothing.

"She didn't," Luke says, sensing my sudden despondency. "My sister paid."

"Oh. Well, that's weird." Matthew thumbs over his shoulder, and Luke and I both look to find his buyer hovering nearby. "So, I was going to head off. Freda knows a nice place around the corner that serves the best pasta in town. Mind?"

"No, you go." It's nice to see Matthew focused on something other than computer programs and glitches. "Enjoy."

"Thanks." He backs away, rubbing his proverbial hands together.

"And remember to do what you're told," Luke calls.

Matthew's eyes sparkle. "Oh, I will."

I lean up and get my mouth close to Luke's ear. "I don't think Freda looks like the kind of woman to tell a man what to do."

"I think you might be right." Luke chuckles, turning into me. I don't realize that I'm leaning on him until I lose my footing slightly and stagger. "Oopsie, clumsy." He swoops in and grabs me, stabilizing me.

"Sorry." I gather myself and look around, embarrassed. Did I just drunken stagger?

"How many champagnes have you had?" he asks, looking at my empty.

"I don't know." I swap my empty for another full one and toast the air. "I'm enjoying it, though."

"I can see that."

I giggle and hiccup at the same time, my head suddenly feeling very fuzzy. "What now?" I ask, looking around the giant room.

"Well, we could have a little gamble." Luke points through to a casino, where people are gathered around tables, cheering. "Or you could take me on the dinner date my sister has paid for."

"I can't afford either," I say without thinking, looking down into my glass. "Perhaps it's time I go home." I shouldn't leave Billy for too long, no matter how much he pleaded with me to have fun. I *have* had fun. Now it's time to go home. And through my drunkenness, I also manage to consider the fact that Scarlett might not be best pleased if I start staggering around the place. It won't look good. And on that thought, I stumble once again, bumping into Luke's side.

He hums, running scrutinizing eyes down my tipsy form. "Maybe home is wise."

"But I don't want to go home," I mumble without thought, the drink allowing the truth to speak. It's been a lovely evening. I don't want it to end yet. I look up at Luke hopefully. "Can we go somewhere else?"

"Like where?"

"I don't know. Anywhere." I shrug and finish the fizz that I probably shouldn't finish.

"Come on." Luke confiscates the glass as it's at my lips, leaving a drop dribbling down my chin. "Messy pup."

I grin and wipe myself up, linking arms with him for support as we walk through the milling guests. My vision is a little strained, my steps purposely measured and slow. I can feel Luke gazing down at me, probably with a disapproving look on his face. I don't care. My head might be full of fuzz, but it feels empty of everything else usually filling it. "Oh no," I breathe, catching sight of a familiar, disgruntled face as we approach the exit. "It's Amanda."

Luke looks up and sighs, quickly diverting us in another direction. I could see she was miffed. I could also see she had every intention of intercepting our escape. "Where are we going?" I ask, my steps no longer measured, but now clumsy as I struggle to keep up with Luke's urgent pace.

"We're hiding."

I look over my shoulder and see Amanda clearly in a hurry to catch up with us. What's she planning on saying? Or doing? Will she kidnap Luke and wrestle him to a church?

"This way." Luke pulls me down a corridor, trying a few doors that fail to open on his way. "Shit."

"Just say a polite hello and we'll be on our way," I suggest. It's pretty simple.

Luke scoffs at my suggestion. "I'm not subjecting you to her viper tongue."

"I've already been subjected to her viper looks." I shrug. I can handle it.

"Trust me, Lo, she's scathing. My ears have bled every time I've listen to the voicemails she's left me." Luke finds an unlocked door and makes a grab for me, hauling me inside. "She's scorned. Trust me, we need to avoid her." He shuts the door and brings his finger to his mouth. "Shhhh."

I mimic him and shush too, breaking out in a fit of giggles when he rolls his eyes at me. "Sorry." I snort, earning Luke's palm over my mouth to shut me up. I grin behind his hand, hearing the clicking of heels from behind the door. He looks pensive as he keeps one eye trained on the door. Is she that bad?

I reach up and pull his hand down. This is utterly ridiculous, but I keep my mouth shut and rein in my chuckles, looking around the room. "A store cupboard?" I whisper, seeing mops, buckets, and a whole heap of other cleaning equipment and cleaners stacked on the metal shelves.

Luke doesn't answer, heading for the door and pushing his ear up against the wood. I wander over to a corner and reach for a broom, swinging one leg over the handle and holding it between my legs. "Hey, Luke," I whisper, probably too loudly.

He looks back on a frown, dropping his eyes to the broomstick I'm riding. "What are you doing?"

"I've found Amanda's ride home."

He bursts out laughing, folding over at the waist and bracing his palms on his knees. "Lo, you kill me."

I match his amusement, trying to get off my broomstick, but I lose my footing and tumble into a nearby shelving unit. "Oh, shit!" The clatters and bangs that engulf the small cupboard are deafening, and my arse hits the floor, various things falling off the shelf above me. "Ouch! Damn! Shit!" I cradle my head with my arms to protect me from the various bottles raining down on me, still laughing through the mild stabs of pain that keep hitting me. "Oh my God, how much stuff is up there?" I wail, not daring to look up for fear of something smacking me square in the face.

Finally, the tumbling bottles of cleaner cease, and I sheepishly look up, finding Luke in a heap by the door, holding his stomach, tears falling from his eyes.

"Ouch," I grumble, trying to push myself up, but once again losing my footing, my arse hitting the floor. I'm well and truly pissed. "You'll have to help me."

He sighs, and laughs, sighs and laughs, as he sluggishly drags himself up and makes his way over to me, reaching for my hand. And in an act of pure rebellion, I take it and use all my strength to yank him forward. He gasps and tumbles down, landing in a pile of laughter next to me. And there we lie, sprawled like two crazy fools surrounded by enough cleaning detergents to keep the whole of London gleaming for a century. I sigh and drop my head to the side, finding Luke gazing at me. "Bet you've never had such a fun date." I rest my hand on my belly and wipe my tears of laughter away. For the first time in years, I'm not crying tears of despair.

"I actually haven't," he admits, rolling into me a little. "You have a duster on your shoulder." Reaching forward, he peels the cloth away from my dress as I chuckle and giggle some more. My chin is taken and lifted to meet his gaze. "I believe you are plastered, Mrs. Harper." Before I can refute his claim, the door swings open, hitting various buckets and bottles in its path. Luke keeps hold of my chin as I turn my head and Amanda falls into the store room. Her startled eyes flit between Luke and me, back and forth, her face growing increasingly indignant.

"Well, you really are taking this auction seriously, aren't you, Luke?" She looks me up and down. "Though I'm sure most men would want the money themselves to venture there."

My mouth falls open in utter shock, and Luke's hold of my

chin tightens to the point he forces it closed. It's not intentional. He's angry. "Ouch," I hiss, wincing as I knock his grip away. Oblivious to hurting me, Luke stands, squares his shoulders, and turns to face the woman in the doorway. I follow him, scrambling up from the floor, kicking various cleaning products around my feet.

"Bite me, Amanda, you vindictive bitch," Luke mutters, pulling me out of the room. As I pass her, her lip curls, and I literally shrink on the spot.

"Nice to meet you," I sing while staggering along behind Luke. "Oh, wait." I drag him to a stop and take a few steps back to collect something. Amanda glares at me. I smile. "I believe this is yours." I hand her the broomstick, and her eyes fall to it, confused, as Luke sniggers, hauling me away before she can cast a spell on us.

"Bite me?" I ask mindlessly. "Did you actually say that?"

"I was lost for words." Luke gets us out of the building to the pavement and makes a fuss of me, pushing my hair back and scanning my face. He doesn't look happy at all and having experienced the delightful Amanda for only a few moments, I'd say he seriously dodged a bullet. "Don't let what she says bother you."

"Well, she's kind of right." I laugh, not so much bothered, but more shocked that a woman could be so malicious towards another. But then, given my husband hasn't touched me for two years . . .

I flinch. Am I unsightly to him now? And compared to all those perfect women inside, who are what Luke's used to, I'm absolutely and utterly shabby. Unpolished. "Next to her, I'm kind of plain."

"Next to her, you are a natural beauty."

"Really, Luke?" I give him a tired look, pointing at my roots. "I haven't had my hair colored for months."

"I like the rooty look."

"I hardly wear makeup."

"Like I said, natural beauty."

I narrow my eyes on him, and he narrows his on me, daring me to go on. My pursed lips crack, revealing a hint of a grin. "I'm *really* drunk."

Luke rolls his eyes, getting me in a headlock, and starts walking us down the street. "Where to next, master?"

"Anywhere you take me," I offer easily, craning my head to get him in my sights. "You smell of bleach."

"So do you." He grins, his eyes sparkling, and ruffles my hair. And I smile, clinging on around his waist for extra support.

Chapter Twenty-Five

Anywhere is a worn-out chip shop on the edge of Soho. "They do the best fish and chips in town," Luke claims, observing my dubious expression. "We'll order takeout and wander."

I shrug my agreement, even though I'm not sure wandering is the best idea. My feet are screaming at me, and my brain refuses to allow me to walk in a straight line. The fresh air has hit me hard, or more like smacked me in the face.

After Luke has paid and handed me a tray loaded with fat chips and a monster piece of cod, we start a leisurely stroll away from the hustle and bustle. "I'll never eat all of this," I tell him, poking at the pile of chips.

"You don't have to. Just something to soak up all the alcohol you've guzzled."

I grin as I pop a chip in my mouth. "My tipsiness is obviously evidence of the lack of alcohol I've indulged in recently."

He chuckles. "I like drunken Lo. How are your chips?"

"Really good," I answer as another couple wander past, looking at us and smiling. It makes me wonder, not for the first time, if everyone who see us together thinks we're more than we are. My mind is way too drunk to be thinking those things right now. All I know is that I can't eliminate someone from my life who makes me feel so alive amid the ruins of my existence. I realize Billy —or anyone else—probably wouldn't rationalize like I am, but at this point in my life, I must accept Luke for what he is to me. A friend. One of only two best friends I've ever had. The other is my husband. My husband who is dying. My husband who is disconnecting. Like he doesn't want to be my husband anymore. Doesn't want to be my friend. Doesn't want to comfort me and hug me, and his absence is screaming louder each day. Our friendship, the comfort I got from him in *every* way, was one of the most beautiful parts of our relationship. And it's fading faster than I can learn to accept.

Dumping the remnants of my meal in a bin on the edge of a square, I brush off my hands and look up at Luke. "I want you to know how important you are to me." I speak clearly and evenly, hoping he doesn't think it's the drink talking. It's not. I'm perfectly lucid, if a little wobbly.

He slowly extends his hand to the bin and drops his empty tray into it. "Okay," he says slowly. "Where did that come from?"

My shoulders lift on a shrug. "I just wanted you to know." *Because I'm not brave enough to say it when I'm stone-cold sober*, I add in my head.

"I already do." Luke slides his arm around the tops of my shoulders and hugs me into his side, starting to walk us through the square. "You might not say it"—he peeks down at me— "when you're sober, but I realize how much you appreciate me."

I smile and relax into his side. "I'm glad."

He squeezes me in response and kisses the top of my head. "I should get you home."

I reluctantly agree and let Luke direct our journey toward the main road, happy that I spoke up and told him how I feel. He's a good man. One of the best. And I feel like my spoken appreciation is the only thing I can actually give him.

Luke leaves me down the street after a hug, and I know he watches me until I've gotten into my house. I drop my keys on the table and kick off my shoes before wandering down the hall to the kitchen. Boris looks up from his basket, and I'm sure he frowns at me. "What?" I ask defensively, feeling under pressure to explain. He snorts and rests his snout back on his front paws. "I only had a few drinks," I tell him, grabbing a glass of water and drinking it as I zigzag my way up the stairs.

Tiptoeing along the landing, I creep toward Billy's bedroom door, pushing it open a fraction to check up on him. The usual glow from the TV is present, but I learned a long time ago that it doesn't necessarily mean he's awake. His body is still, his head dropped to the side. "Goodnight," I whisper-slur, pulling the door closed.

"Hey." His sleepy voice pulls me back into the room.

"You're awake," I say, surprised and, evidently by his flinch, a bit too screechy. "Sorry." I push my way into his room but keep hold of the handle to hold myself steady.

"And you're drunk." He smiles faintly, his eyebrows lifting.

"I'm not drunk," I protest, releasing the door handle. I immediately start to sway, and Billy chuckles. Why's he laughing at me?

"Sure thing, gorgeous. Did you have a nice evening?"

I fake nonchalance within an inch of my life, the guilt that's been lingering on the edge of my mind all evening creeping closer to the forefront. I can't tell him that I had a wonderful time. Neither can I tell him I had a wonderful time with Luke. He won't understand. No one would understand. And I have no intention of emasculating Billy any more than his wretched illness. "It was all right."

"You look lovely." His earnest words amplify that guilt by a million. And so does his sincere expression. Both make me bite into my lip to stop myself from drunkenly spilling my confession about my savior. Billy won't see Luke as anything less than a man trying to move in on his wife. He'll feel helpless, and I positively hate that thought.

"Thank you." I swallow, diverting my eyes from his. "Can I get you anything?"

"I think you should get yourself to bed, Missus," he quips lightly, but his use of my legal title takes the edge off his playfulness. Is he reminding me of my status? Well, of course he should.

"I think you're right," I agree, backing out of his room.

"Lo?"

I pause, looking across at him. "Yes?"

"Come here."

I cock my head in question at him, and he limply pats the mattress next to him. This is all very strange. "On the bed?"

"Yes, on the bed. Come on."

The frown I'm sporting as I make my way over to my husband can't be wiped away, no matter how hard I try. Gingerly sitting on the edge of the bed, I place my hands in my lap and start nervously twiddling my fingers. "Are you okay?" I ask, trying not to sound anxious. Does he know about Luke? I feel shame envelop me.

"I'm fine. Lie down."

I glance at him, surprised, and he nods, encouraging me. So I follow his order and lie on my back next to him, mirroring his position. I'm stiff as a board, nervous as hell. Can he smell Luke's scent on me? After dancing with him, walking arm in arm for an hour with him, surely I might smell like him. But Billy simply takes my hand and holds it between our bodies on the bed. "I know you love me," he says to the ceiling. "And I'm glad you had a lovely evening."

I drop my head to the side and stare at him, but he keeps his eyes upward. Why? Why can't he tell me *he* loves *me*? What does that actually mean? Has he stopped loving me? Just then, he didn't kiss me, he didn't cuddle into me. He didn't even look at me. He just held my hand and acknowledged that *I* love *him*. *Why?*

I feel no guilt now, but that's no consolation. Because in its place, all I have is incredible sadness.

Chapter Twenty-Six

I want to put my head in my top drawer and slam it shut repeatedly, because I'm sure it would hurt a lot less than my pounding headache. I'm slumped over my desk, one hand holding a pint of water, my other resting on the mouse as I squint at my computer screen. I feel so ill. Waking up this morning next to Billy should have put a smile on my face, but I felt too rotten, and it wasn't just my overindulgence of alcohol making me feel that way. He stirred as I slipped off the bed, but he didn't open his eyes. I was relieved—relieved because I'm certain I must have looked so shame-ridden. He was peculiar last night. Said things that baffled me.

"Morning." Matthew's delighted greeting cuts through my brain and thoughts, and I abandon my water and mouse to cover my ears.

"Not so loud," I whine, trying to get him into focus. He looks like the cat that got the cream. The memories flood back into me, straightening my back as they do. "Fiona."

"Freda," he says, perching on the side of my desk. "My, my, dearest Lo. You look . . . terrible."

"Don't sugarcoat it, will you?" I slump back in my chair as he laughs. "I think I've got two years' worth of hangovers all in one go. How was the rest of your night?"

His grin could split his face. "Well, I'm wearing the same boxers as yesterday."

I grimace. "Too much information, Matthew."

He shrugs nonchalantly. "What about you and your friend? What was his name?"

"Luke."

"Luke, yes. Nice chap. Did you hang around much longer?"

"A while." I go back to my computer so I don't have to face Matthew and risk him seeing my sudden uncomfortable face. "So, are you seeing Fiona again?"

"Freda. And, yes. She's delightful."

"It's always the quiet ones," I say without thinking, frowning at the curser on my screen. I know I'm considered a quiet one around here.

"Hey, what have you done to your arm?" Matthew prods my forearm, and I hiss, bending it to see.

"I don't know." I stare at the hefty purple bruise on my elbow as a mental repeat performance of myself going arse over tit in the cleaning cupboard gives me my answer. Matthew is prevented from pushing when Scarlett swans into the office, looking as pristine as usual. "How's your mother-in-law?" I ask, shooing Matthew off my desk.

Scarlett rolls her eyes. "It was a panic attack." She dumps a pile of papers on my desk. "How was last night?"

"Great." I muster a bright smile. It actually hurts my face. "Matthew came with me."

"Oh, he did?"

"Yes, and no one mentioned the man-sale I'd be dragged into."

"Oh, be quiet and find some clean boxers," I tease, making Matthew suck in a feigned hurt expression. Scarlett's perfectly plucked eyebrows hitch, so I explain. "Matthew sold for five hundred quid and it seems his buyer got her money's worth."

Scarlett laughs, looking Matthew's form up and down. "Well, well, Matthew." She rests all her weight on one hip, giving him a coy look. "Care to share?"

"No." He begins to head back to the IT department. "But Lo might want to share her purchase."

My jaw goes lax as Matthew's back disappears around the corner.

"Your purchase?" Scarlett questions immediately, not missing a beat.

Damn it. "Oh, it was nothing." I dive on my computer and start hammering at random keys. "A friend of mine was up for auction, and he didn't want his ex-lover to win him." I peek up at Scarlett and see all interest vanish from her face, but I wait until she's in her office before I sag in relief. It's only nine o'clock. I have a whole day to fight through.

When my phone rings, I slide it from my desk and slump back in my chair. "I feel awful," I say in greeting to Luke, immediately making him chuckle.

"I'm not surprised. I'm just going into a meeting. Want to walk the dogs tonight?"

"Seven?"

"See you then."

Come five o'clock, I'm ready to collapse. I spent the day convincing Scarlett that my lack of being on the ball was due to tiredness and not a raging hangover. The long walk home in the whipping wind was actually a relief. The biting cold allowed me to focus on something other than my lingering pounding head.

When I walk into the warmth of my kitchen, my phone starts ringing, and I answer, seeing a casserole resting on the hob and a note from Magda telling me Billy was asleep both times she stopped by. "Hello?" I lift the lid of the pot and inhale the hearty meat and vegetable aroma that billows up toward my nose.

"Lo Harper?"

"Yes, who's speaking?"

"My name is Derma Pierce. I'm an agent for DWS calling on behalf of MBNA. Your account has been passed over to us to contact you regarding the arrears."

I drop the lid of the casserole dish, causing a clatter to echo around the kitchen. "Hi," I squeak.

"I just need to ask a few security questions before we proceed."

I don't know what comes over me, but I disconnect the call and throw the handset on the worktop. It immediately starts ringing again, but I ignore it, staying well clear of the phone and focusing on feeding Boris instead. I can't deal with that right now; my head is pounding too much already. Tomorrow. I'll deal with it tomorrow.

I pour some biscuits into Boris's bowl and place it on the floor for him, blanking out the continuous ringing of the house phone until I'm forced to disconnect it. Billy will be wondering who's calling.

I make two cups of tea and head upstairs to him. I fully expect to be hit with questions when I enter, but he's asleep. Placing his mug on the side, I dip and kiss his forehead, noting how warm he his. He stirs, opening his eyes. "Hey." He shifts, flinching as he does.

"Hey. Are you okay? In pain?" He looks uncomfortable.

"I'm fine."

"You don't look fine. And you're hot." I feel his forehead again, highly expecting him to shoo me off, but he doesn't, and I know it's because he doesn't have the energy. If it's at all possible, he looks even more gray than usual. "I should call the doctor."

"Lo, please. I'm fine. Just feeling a bit rough today." He closes his eyes again, technically shutting me out, and I back off, assessing his face. He's sweating.

Glancing at the clock on his bedside, I see it's nearly seven o'clock. I'm meeting Luke soon, but I'm really not comfortable leaving Billy. He's never good, but tonight he seems particularly bad. I reach for the thermometer on the bedside table and take it into the bathroom to wash. When I get back to his bedside, his eyes are still closed. And I know for sure I should be worried when he doesn't protest me slipping the thermometer into his ear. He's only had fevers on rare occasions, and the doctor has always said that any spike could cause problems. It beeps and I remove it. Thirty-eight point two. He's burning up.

Heading downstairs, I text Luke telling him that Billy's not good and I won't make our walk, feeling a little bad as I know he's probably already in the park waiting for me. But as is the way with Luke, he doesn't make a big deal of it, replying with an order to call him if I need him. Then I call the doctor, settling on the couch. It's out of hours, but, thankfully, I soon reach Dr. Smith and he takes my call. "He's terribly hot," I tell him, making my way back upstairs. "His temperature is thirty-eight point two. Should I call the out-of-hours line?"

"Thirty-eight point two isn't too bad considering, but I'd like you to check it every thirty minutes. If it gets to thirty-nine point five—"

"Yeah, I know. Call the ambulance."

"Yes, and let me know. My shift finishes soon, Lo. I'll stop by on the way home. Shouldn't be more than an hour or so."

I thank him and cut the call, making my way to our room to sit with Billy until Dr. Smith arrives. I get halfway up the stairs when I hear the letterbox rattle. I turn and see an envelope on the doormat. Hurrying back down, I collect it up and turn it over, opening it up and pulling out a card. It's a gift voucher for a beauty salon. "What?" I ask myself, turning the card over. There's a note.

The salon appointment is optional. For the record, I like your hair rooty. Luke x

I smile down at the card and place it on the table before opening the front door. I see him halfway down the street. "Luke," I call, taking a few steps onto the pavement.

He turns, his face frowning. "Go inside, Lo, it's freezing out here."

His order reminds me that I'm standing here in a short-sleeved dress and bare feet. I wrap my arms around my torso, hugging myself. "Thank you."

"You're welcome." He waves a hand at me. "Now get inside."

I ignore his follow-up command and jog toward him, ignoring the icy concrete penetrating the soles of my feet. When I make it to him, I throw my arms around his shoulders and hug him tightly.

"It's nothing."

"It's everything. Thank you." I break away from his warmth and resist putting myself back in his hold.

"You're shivering, Lo." He takes his coat off and swings it around my shoulders, looking past me when a loud clatter comes from my house. "What was that?" he asks, as I, too, look back at the house.

My veins run cold, my feet beginning to move without instruction. I run back to the house, a nasty feeling increasing my speed. I approach the stairs, listening carefully. Nothing. Dread engulfing me, I charge up the steps two at a time and push my way into Billy's room, my eyes homing in on his bed. He's not there. "Billy?" My heart beats its way up to my throat as I race to the bathroom across the room. "Billy?" I fall into the small space. *Empty*. I swing around, panic gripping me. It's then I see him. "Oh my God." I rush over to his motionless body lying on the floor by the window. "Billy!" My voice breaks, my hands padding over his body. "Billy, can you hear me?" He doesn't move, doesn't make a sound. Water clouds my vision as I fight to locate the calm I need to act. *Ambulance*. I need an ambulance. But I don't want to leave him to fetch the phone. I look up through my fog of tears and find

JODI ELLEN MALPAS

Luke in the doorway of the bedroom, his face grave as he looks on. "Please," I sob. "Please call an ambulance."

His haunted eyes travel from Billy's body to me. He looks like he's gone into shock.

"Luke," I yell, snapping him out of his trance. "Call an ambulance!"

He goes to his pocket and pulls out his mobile, but his voice is fuzzy as he speaks into it. I can't hear a word, except for the pleas I'm screaming in my head.

This can't be it. No. This can't be the end.

Part Seven

Luke

Chapter Twenty-Seven

I t all seems so real now. Standing in their bedroom watching Lo hysterical, falling apart, cradled over her husband's lifeless body. She's begging him to wake up. It's all so surreal but real. I'm useless. There's nothing I can do as I look on, feeling like an intruder.

The ambulance arrives within minutes. Lo's husband is quickly assessed, his body lifted onto a gurney, and as they push him past me on the landing, I see his face for the first time. And I flinch. He looks like a shell of a man—weak, gray, and hollow. Old. So old. It's fucking cruel. I brush my palm down my bristle, blinking back my shock.

The paramedics are talking urgently, throwing orders back and forth between each other. Lo doesn't look at me once, her focus set firmly on her husband. As it should be. I'm desperate to go to her, to hold her and comfort her, but something stops me, and I remain a static, useless form in the hallway of their home as they wheel Billy out. I hear the doors of the ambulance slam, followed by the sound of it driving away, the sirens sounding soon after.

And then it's just me alone in their home.

I swallow, dipping and collecting my jacket from the floor

where Lo dropped it. I look around at my surroundings, seeing pictures hanging on the walls, photo frames set on a side cabinet. I wander over and pick one up, gazing at the man in the picture who looks nothing like the guy who was just carried out on a stretcher. The Billy I just saw looked elderly. Pale and hollow. The man staring back at me looks young, healthy, and delighted. It's not surprising. I cast my eyes across the picture to the young, beautiful woman cuddled into his side. Her silver eyes are alive and happy. Her smile wide. So damn wide. I've had the pleasure of a few smiles like that. But each one was clouded with guilt.

The picture starts to tremble in my hands, and I puff my cheeks out, setting it down carefully in its place. Jesus. They're so young. Their whole life together in front of them.

Coughing my throat clear, I turn away from the collection of photographs, struggling to see Lo and Billy looking like completely different people. It's gut-wrenching, for no other reason than their story is so fucking sad. I wander aimlessly down the corridor until I find myself in a kitchen. It's there I find Boris looking a little perplexed. "Hey, boy." I drop to my haunches and give him a little fuss. "Mum will be home soon." I check his water bowl is full and head out, but the sound of a phone ringing stops me. I look across the kitchen and see Lo's mobile on the countertop next to a set of keys. She'll need them. I collect them up, seeing a London number flashing up on the screen. It could be a friend of theirs, and I'm sure Lo would want whoever it is to know what's happened.

"Hello?" I answer as I make my way to the door.

"Mr. Harper?"

"No, he's unavailable at the moment. Can I ask who's calling?"

"My name is Derma Pierce. I'm an agent for DWS. I was speaking with Mrs. Harper earlier on her landline but we seem to have been cut off."

My pace falters as I near my car. DWS. "As in the debt collecting company?"

"I'm sorry, who am I speaking with?"

"A friend of Mrs. Harper's."

"Is Mrs. Harper available, please?"

"No, she's not."

"Then I would be grateful if you could get her to return my call at her earliest convenience."

I slide into my car and start it. Steve launches himself onto my lap, and I fight to get him back on the passenger seat. "I'm afraid Mrs. Harper won't be available for a while," I tell him firmly. "But, if you let me know the outstanding debt on her account, I will make a direct transfer on her behalf."

"I'm afraid I can't discuss the account without verbal or written confirmation from Mrs. Harper."

"Then you'll be waiting a while for your money." I hang up and race across town to drop Steve home before heading to the hospital. I knew she had money problems, but debt collectors are bad news. They're also relentless, as is proven when her phone starts ringing again. This time, I ignore it. Right now, Lo is all that matters.

It takes three nurses to finally tell me where I can find Billy Harper. I jog down the corridor of the hospital, my need to get to Lo urgent. I round corner after corner, scanning the dozens of signs on the walls for where I need to be. "It's a fucking maze," I curse, heading back the way I came.

I eventually locate the ward I need and push my way through the double doors. A huge bottle of clear liquid hangs by the entrance with a prominent red sign telling me to sanitize my hands. I squirt some into my palm and start massaging it in as I stride toward the nurses' station. "I'm looking for Billy Harper," I breathe, out of breath after my run around the hospital.

"Are you a relative, sir?"

"A friend."

"I'm afraid only close family are permitted outside of visiting hours."

I feel irritation start to bubble. "I'm not leaving until you tell his wife that I'm here," I say lowly, leaning over the desk.

The nurse coughs and looks over her shoulder, where a sign states that abuse toward staff is a criminal offence. Abuse? "I'm merely stating a fact," I point out, trying to calm myself down. "I would be grateful if—" My planned, more diplomatic request diminishes when I see Lo exit a door at the end of the ward. "Lo," I whisper, not possibly loud enough for her to hear me, but she glances straight up at me nevertheless. She looks utterly exhausted, ready to collapse. Her bottom lip starts shaking, along with the rest of her body. My legs are running toward her before I can even think to hold back, her body visibly folding before my eyes, and I just catch her before she crumbles to the floor. She collapses into my arms on a wretched sob, and I squeeze her frail body close, sinking my face into her neck. "I'm here," I assure her, absorbing the jerks from her crying. "I'm here now."

She breaks down on me, clinging to me with what little strength she has left, as I gently hush her, whispering comforting words in her ear. "I'm not going anywhere, darling."

"Please don't." Her plea slices me in two. "Please don't leave me."

I let her cry for as long as she needs to, looking through the window into the room where Billy is unconscious on the bed, a drip pumping him with meds.

"He has an infection." Lo sniffles and breaks away from me, wiping at her eyes. "His immune system is so weak, he can't fight it off. I need to call his mother."

"I brought your phone." I drag it from my pocket and hand it over. "Do you want a drink? Water? Coffee?"

She shakes her head and lifts her phone to her ear. I don't want to, but I force myself to give her space to make the call, heading for the nurses' station again. The scowl I get landed with would bother me . . . if I was at all bothered. "Where can I get drinks?" I ask.

"The cafeteria is closed. There's a coffee machine and vending machine at the nearest entrance." She turns away and gives her attention to the computer.

"Thank you."

Lo joins me, cutting the call. "I said I'd keep her updated. There's no point her coming down. He's as comfortable as he can be."

"Can I do anything?" I feel so fucking helpless.

"No," she says, looking past me. "There's nothing you can do."

"What about Boris?" I ask.

"Oh God, Boris." Lo comes over all panicky, and I rush to assure her.

"He's fine. I made sure he had plenty of water. Would you like me to pick him up and take him back to mine? I'm sure Steve won't mind a sleepover." I force a smile, wishing I could pick Lo up, too, and take her home to hold her all night.

"You'd do that?"

"Of course. I have your keys."

We're interrupted when a doctor approaches, smiling at Lo. "Mrs. Harper."

"Dr. Smith," she greets in return.

"Shall we?" He indicates to a private room to the left.

"Yes." She looks at me. "Would you come in with me?"

I'm taken aback, but I don't hesitate. She wants me with her. I swallow hard and nod, following them into the small, clinical room, with a few high-backed chairs pushed against the walls. I take a seat next to Lo and look down when she reaches for my hand and squeezes it.

"I'm sorry, sir, we haven't met," the doctor says, pulling my attention away from our held hands.

"I'm . . ." I stall, not sure how to introduce myself.

"This is Luke," Lo answers, looking at my dazed face. "He's my

313

best friend." Her eyes linger on me, her lips smiling a small smile. I'm her best friend. I'm caught somewhere between elation and devastation, and I'm utterly perplexed by it. A friend. Shit, my chest starts to ache. *What the hell?*

The doctor's light cough brings me back into the small room, where Lo is clinging on to my hand and my heart is thumping painfully. "We all knew it would take this to get him into hospital, Lo. Like I've explained, his immune system is weak. He has a urinary tract infection that his body is struggling to fight, so we're giving him antibiotics intravenously. Hopefully by morning we'll see an improvement. We can then think about an MRI to see what our options are."

"You told Billy when he came for his appointment last week that there's nothing more you can do."

The doctor frowns. "I haven't seen Billy for months, Lo."

Her mouth falls open. "He said . . ." She looks at the floor and takes a deep, shaky breath. "Never mind."

The doctor smiles. It's a sympathetic smile. "I'll have an update in the morning, but for now he's comfortable. I suggest you go home and get some rest."

"Can't I stay?" Lo asks, sitting forward in her chair.

"There's nothing to be done until morning. Come back then. You need some rest, Lo. I'll be on the ward around ten. We'll talk more." He gets up and rubs her shoulder affectionately. "Billy's in the best place he can be. We'll look after him."

Lo nods, the doctor leaves, and silence descends, a horrible, uncomfortable silence. She stares at the wall on the opposite side of the room for an eternity. "He told me he'd seen Dr. Smith," she says to herself. "He lied to me."

"You mentioned a specialist in America."

Her gaze dropping to the floor, she breathes in. "It's impossible."

Impossible. Because of the cost. But the doctor mentioned options. They have options. "I'll take you home," I say, standing and pulling her to her feet. She's fit to drop. She needs rest. Eat. Drink.

Lo looks up at me blankly, her beautiful gray eyes overflowing with a sadness that cripples me. "I don't want to be alone," she murmurs raggedly.

I clench my eyes shut, tormented by her grief and fear. Because after those few days where I thought I'd lost her forever, I know there is no way I could leave her right now, whether she asked me to stay or not. I'd felt lost. Bereft. That I'd been missing my soul. *But she isn't yours.* She. Isn't. Mine. "I won't leave you alone." *Not ever.* I hook my arm around her neck and pull her into me, letting her tears soak my shirt. "We'll get Boris, and you can come to mine, okay?"

She nods, her palms warming my chest where they lay. "Thank you."

I exhale, maneuvering her, and start to walk us out of the hospital, my mind an absolute blur. I just want to make her pain go away, protect her from this fucking nightmare she's trapped in. And I can't. All I can do is watch as her world falls apart, and mine falls apart with it.

Because I'm watching the woman I've fallen in love with suffer.

Her pain is my pain.

I'm in fucking agony.

And all I can do is hold her, because the man lying in that hospital bed owns her heart.

Chapter Twenty-Eight

After collecting Boris and a few of Lo's personal things, I drive her to my house. She's quiet the entire way home, while my head is screaming, feeling like it's set to explode with thoughts wrestling for pole position. How can I make this better? How can I ease her pain and comfort her? She doesn't want to be alone, and I'm here, but I feel so fucking helpless.

I open the front door, and Boris scurries on past, his nose hitting the marble floor and exploring his new playground. Steve welcomes him with a wagging tail and a few yaps. "Can I get you a drink?" I ask, placing her bags at the bottom of the stairs. "Tea, water . . . alcohol?"

Lo shakes he head. "Do you mind if I take a shower?" She pulls at the front of her dress on a wrinkled nose. "I feel grubby."

"Sure." I gather her bags back up. "Let me show you to a room." We climb the stairs in silence, the dogs scampering up past us, chasing each other. I smile at their obliviousness. How simple their lives are.

I divert past the room where Arabella stays, and past the next one too, where Todd's currently lodging, bringing us to the guest rooms by the master suite. My house has never been so full. "Here." I push the door of one open and place her bags on the chair in the corner, watching as she gazes around the fresh space. "The bathroom's through there."

She looks where my arm is extended and smiles. "Thank you."

Stuffing my hands in my pockets, I leave the room. "I'll let the dogs out. I'll be in the kitchen when you're done."

I close the door and head downstairs, Boris and Steve chasing behind. After letting them out in the garden, I head for the bar and pour myself a generous Scotch, dropping to a stool and scrubbing my hands down my rough cheeks. "Fuck," I curse quietly, slugging down half my drink. I put her in the room next to mine. The urge to continue down the landing and put her in my room was nearly overwhelming. I have to lie in bed tonight knowing she's mere meters away, probably weeping. I just want to wrap her in my arms and ease her pain. My desires aren't even sexual. They're instinctual. I've never felt this before, and I doubt it will ever go away.

Grabbing my phone, I call Pops, needing to hear a friendly voice. By the time one of the staff has found him and he's on the line, I'm on my second Scotch.

"Grandboy?" he says, gruff with tiredness.

"Did I wake you?"

"Goodness, no. I was just getting my groove on. We're raving tonight."

I smile, taking my seat back up at the bar. "I'm fucked, Pops," I sigh, getting straight to the point.

"Figuratively speaking, or actually?"

"Figuratively," I confirm.

He hums, thoughtful, leaving no words coming down the line at me. What's he thinking?

"Pops?"

"Does she know how you feel?"

"God, no." I slump over the bar. "I could never put that on her. She's married to a man who's on death's door. She's here right now, while her husband is fighting off an infection in hospital. You should have seen him, Pops. So fucking young."

"He works in mysterious ways, Luke. Very mysterious ways."

"No, Pops, right now I'm inclined to think that He's just plain cruel." How could He do this? To Billy. *To Lo.*

"How is she?" Pops asks.

"Destroyed." It hurts me to even say it, let alone see it.

"You came into her life for a reason. *Everything* happens for a reason, Grandboy."

"And what was the reason for you walking away from the love of your life?"

"You. I wouldn't have *you* had my life taken a different direction. That's my comfort. That's a good enough reason for me."

"Jesus, Pops." I feel my throat clog up, and I take another swig of Scotch to try and wash it down.

"Tell me what you want to do," he orders gently.

"I want to make her pain go away," I admit. "Above everything, I don't want her to suffer anymore."

"Then focus on that. You're caught in limbo, Grandboy. But sometimes you have to accept that doing the right thing hurts. Do the right thing."

I nod, knowing he's right, and slowly accept my fate. It's agony. But nothing compared to what Lo's going through. "Thanks, P—" A loud, high-pitched scream cuts me off, and I swing around on my stool. "Pops, I have to go." I hang up and run out of the bar, up the stairs toward the sound, my adrenalin pumping. "Lo?" I shout, rounding the corner at the top and staggering to an abrupt stop. I find Lo backed up against a wall, her palm resting on her heaving chest. And Todd on the opposite wall, eyes wide and . . . naked. I look down and see a towel puddled at his feet.

"Fucking hell," he breathes, reaching down and fumbling with the material to cover himself.

"You startled me." Lo looks toward me, her cheeks red with

embarrassment. Wet tresses fan her shoulders, her face fresh and clean. She's changed into shorts and an oversized sweater. "I didn't realize anyone else was here."

"Neither did I." I flick a scowl to Todd.

"I was in the shower," he grumbles, offering Lo his hand. "You must be Lo. Nice to finally meet you. I'm Todd."

"Oh, Todd?" She looks at me, and I nod as she accepts Todd's hand and they have an awkward exchange, Todd holding his towel up with one hand.

"Oh, Todd?" he questions, raising his eyebrows at Lo questioningly. "What's he told you about me?"

She shrugs awkwardly. "Not much."

"I'm sure." Todd gives me a filthy look and goes back to his room. "I have a date."

"Surprise, surprise," I mutter, making Lo chuckle.

"With your sister," he adds.

"What?" I shoot him a shocked look, catching him grinning. "Fuck off."

He chuckles and shuts the door behind him, and I divert my attention back to Lo. "Okay?"

She nods, puffing her cheeks out as she approaches me. "I'd love that drink now, if you don't mind." Reaching up on her tippy-toes, she sniffs. "Though you've beaten me to the hard stuff, it seems."

Hard stuff? No alcohol is hard enough for me at the moment. I smile and lead the way down to the bar. "What would you like?"

"Hard stuff." She wanders around the bar, reacquainting herself with the space as I pour us both a drink. "Should I be worried that Todd's going to come and eject me from the premises?"

I smile as I gather the glasses and join her on the sofa. "I've issued you with a VIP pass for this evening."

"I'm honored." Lo smiles weakly and takes the Scotch, circling the tumbler with both palms as I get comfy on the other end of the couch. "Could you sit any farther away?"

I look down at the leather, frowning, trying not to look as self-conscious as I'm feeling. *I need to do the right thing,* I tell myself. When I hear Boris and Steve both yapping relentlessly, I'm thankful. "Oh, I better let them in." I'm up fast, hurrying to the kitchen. The pair rush past me, and when I make it back to the bar, I find they've both dived on the couch. In the middle. I'm grateful. They serve as a barrier between Lo and me, stopping me from getting too close, therefore, lessening the chances of folding under the pressure of not gathering her into my arms. It'll only make me want her more, and I seriously don't need to be doing anything that's going to make this any harder for either of us.

"Luke?" Lo's soft calling of my name pulls me from my mental quarrel.

I look up at her, and her lovely face is riddled with questions. I smile, my attempt to convince her I'm here in mind as well as body. With no words coming to me, I lower to the couch and lift my Scotch, toasting the air before swigging the entire contents. I wince, not just because it burns its way down to my stomach, but because I just made a silent fucking toast. We're hardly celebrating. *What the fuck am I doing?*

Lo's face hasn't lost her inquisitiveness by the time I've swallowed and gasped. If anything, her probing look is more probing.

"Are you okay?" She slowly lifts her glass to her lips as she watches me fiddle with Steve's ear.

"All good."

"You sure?"

I nod far too enthusiastically. "Want to watch TV? A film or something?" I'm nervous, mentally figuring out how I'm going to say what I need to say.

"Sure," Lo replies quietly. "After you've told me why you're behaving all funny."

I look up through my lashes, and Lo tilts her head in question.

"Do you want me to leave?" she asks.

"God, no. No, I don't want you to leave." I place my empty on the table before me, thinking it's perhaps wise that I don't have any more alcohol. "Lo," I sigh, wedging my elbows into my knees and pushing my fingertips into my temples, willing the ensuing headache to clear off. "I feel so helpless."

My wrists are seized, and I look up, finding she's kneeling before me. "I don't expect a miracle from you. I'm not expecting you to make this all better," she tells me, her expression clearly trying to make *me* feel better. I should punch myself in the face. It should be me making *her* feel better, if that's at all possible. "I know you can't do that. No one can." Her gray eyes scan my face, and the words I should say get swallowed down on a gulp of strength. If I say those words, that'll be it. Game over. And although I know it's selfish, I can't bring myself to say goodbye to her yet. "Having you with me is enough," she whispers, moving her hold of my wrists to my hands and lacing her fingers through mine.

"I just want you to be happy again," I admit. "To smile with everything you have, nothing tarnishing it."

"That's never going to happen." Water fills her eyes, and she smiles through her sadness. And it breaks my fucking heart. *It's never going to happen.*

Completely lost, I stand up, pulling Lo up too. She tilts her head in question. I have no more words. Words won't make her feel better.

It's never going to happen.

I turn and walk out of the bar, leading her. She doesn't argue. She doesn't try to stop me. We move in silence up the stairs, and I bypass her room, taking us into mine. Still no objection. Pulling the covers back on the bed, I kick my shoes off and help her in. Then I crawl in behind her fully dressed and snuggle up to her back, squeezing her body to mine. It's peaceful. Quiet. No words needed. The mattress dips when the dogs jump up, curling themselves around our feet.

"Luke?" Lo says quietly, and I hold her tighter, my way of telling her that she has my attention. She breathes in and exhales. "I love you," she says quietly, reaching back and feeling at my hair.

Sadness creeps into every one of my veins. Because she doesn't love me like that. She would never allow herself to.

And even if she did, it wouldn't be enough to make her happy again.

And it's her lost happiness alone that makes me feel as broken as Lo.

Chapter Twenty-Nine

During the night, our bodies have moved, and I wake up with Lo's head on my chest. I make a point of keeping still, not wanting to disturb her. I don't want to take her from her dreams and bring her back to her stark reality. Her hair, which has dried naturally while we've slept, is wild and wavy, fanning my T-shirt-covered torso in every direction around her head. My hand rests on her back and caresses her over her sweater as I look up at the ceiling and come to terms with my loss. This is the last time I'll have her in the safety of my arms.

Dropping my head to the side, I look out of the window. The sun marking a new day is lost behind dense gray clouds and a light mist of drizzly rain. Gray. Gloomy. It feels like the standard is being set.

Lo stirs, rubbing her sleepy face into my chest, and I wonder what might be running through her waking mind at this very second. Slowly, her head lifts, and I wait for her to search me out. When she finds me, looking up at me through glassy eyes, she smiles mildly and shuffles up the bed, placing herself in my side and snuggling into me. I don't know if I should be welcoming her easiness or breaking away from it. But once again, the naturalness of it decides for me. I pull her closer and start to stroke her hair. Her body is so warm, and even though we've never done this before, it feels so right. I never thought this, waking up with the woman I love in my arms, would ever happen. She's not mine. Yet, right now, she feels as though she is. And then I think about Pops's words and wonder if he's right. He told me I'd know when I found my Milly Rose. Yes. But he didn't explain that the feelings would be so fucking confusing. "Morning," I say quietly.

"Morning." Her finger trails my stomach lightly as I watch its journey, and silence falls between us. I don't know what Lo's thinking during the prolonged quiet, and I haven't got space in my own head to try and consider it. What I'm doing instead is building myself up to what I need to say. "Lo—"

"Luke." Her traces of my stomach pause, and she looks up at me, smiling a little. "You go first."

I draw strength through my deep breath and encourage her to sit up, so I can too, telling myself that ripping the plaster off will be less painful than slowly peeling it away. I make sure there's no contact between us, putting myself on the other side of the bed. Lo's forehead crinkles, and she pulls the sheets over her dressed body protectively. I push forward. "I'm giving you the money you need for Billy's surgery in America." I gage her expression, unable to read it. Her face is straight, her eyes burning through mine. "Lo, did you hear me?"

She continues to stare at me, unmoving and unspeaking.

"I said I'm giving you the money for your husband's surgery."

"I heard you," she confirms clearly, getting up off the bed quickly. I watch her walk to the other side of the room, stop, breathe in, and turn around. "Why?"

I don't know what kind of reaction I was expecting. I hadn't thought about it, if I'm honest. It was too hard to get past the internal ache my intention was spiking. I look down at the bed, struggling to compose a legitimate response to her simple question. My heart and my head are having a full-on fight. I can't land my feelings on her now. Not with everything she's going through. "Because I'm your friend," I say, not too convincingly.

"Oh no," Lo breathes, pulling my face up. Her wide eyes, her tense body. She's clicked. "Don't do this, Luke," she begs, stepping back. "Please don't ruin what we have."

I look away, ashamed. "What do we have?" I ask quietly.

"An amazing friendship." Her voice shakes as she fights to hold herself together. I feel nothing short of awful.

I approach her slowly, anxiously, my mouth a straight line of frustration. Frustration with myself. She eyes me all the way until I come to a stop before her. "I'm falling in love with you, Lo." I say it so calmly, like it's something I've accepted. Because I have. Took me long enough to realize, though. I'm a prat.

"Then stop falling," she blurts, moving away from me, tears forming in her eyes. "Right this minute, you must stop."

"It's too late." I look away, my shame increasing. "I know I can't have you," I whisper, the pain caused by saying that out loud excruciating.

"Of course you can't. I'm married. My husband is dying, Luke. How could you do this to me?" She pivots and walks away, but my arm shoots out before I can think better of it, pulling her to a stop. Just the fact that she's so angry with me kills me. I don't want her to be angry with me. I know I can't expect her to understand, but I can't bear the thought of her hating me.

"I've never felt like this about anyone," I say sincerely. "You're so brave. So loyal and determined. You've made me see life differently."

"What do you even want me to do with this?" she asks through a hopeless sob.

"I don't want you to do anything with it." My hands cup her cheeks, my lips pressing into her forehead as I breathe in. It's all I can do not to break down in front of her when she takes my wrists and squeezes, her body jerking with her sobs. "I'm sorry. I'm so sorry." I release her and move back, putting distance between us.

"You can't control love. You can only feel it," I say quietly, shrugging when she glances up at me. "That's just the way it is."

"I'm angry with you," she whispers.

"I'm kind of pissed off with myself too," I admit, unable to stop myself from taking her hand and threading my fingers through hers. "This is all my fault, so please, please don't feel bad." I force my hand from hers and take myself to the bed, sitting on the edge. "This is on my conscience, not yours." She told me she loved me last night, and I knew it was platonic. But she was in my arms all night and it felt right. Yet I know I'll never get that again. It was a double-edged sword bringing her into my bed, but I couldn't have stayed away. Couldn't have left her to face her desolation alone. She'll never love me. She'll never allow herself to love me. Not now. Not ever.

This is my reality, and it hits me hard.

I will never be the love of her life. Whether he's alive or dead, her husband will always be her first. Maybe her only. "Falling in love with you has been the easiest thing I've ever done." I look up at her and smile a small smile, seeing her whole body shrink in response. It's for that reason I hold back from telling her that this, right now, is the hardest thing I've ever done. "I'm sorry if that's wrong."

Lifting my hand, I silently call for her to come to me, and she does, but then stands hesitantly before me. This is killing me.

"I'm sorry too," she whispers.

"Please don't be sorry, Lo."

"But, I shouldn't have stayed . . . shouldn't have slept—" She swallows a sob, and I pull her onto my lap, where she then hugs me with a force that could crush me. The pain inside of me intensifies, my eyes closing before my emotion starts to leak from them. "No. I wanted to hold you, Lo. Wanted to be the one you needed. Please don't feel guilty about that."

"I hate that I'm hurting you."

No more than I hate myself for doing what I said I wouldn't

do: leave her. But I can give her what she truly wants—what she needs. Her husband's health. And what I want more than anything: Lo's happiness. And to do that, I must leave her. Because I can't look at this woman a moment longer knowing I can never make her mine.

With strength I had no idea I possessed, I force her away from my body so I can see her face. Gently, I wipe under her eyes and push her hair away from her cheeks. Her hand clasps mine on her face and squeezes, and I let my gaze drift back onto hers. "I'd rather not have you at all than have you heartbroken." I'm honest. She's barely together now. If Billy dies, she'll be completely shattered. I can't compete with a dead man's memory. I couldn't live with myself knowing I could have done something to prevent her agony, even if it causes mine. I can't win here, and I need to stop trying. This is the right thing to do. Giving her the money to save Billy is the right thing to do.

"I'm heartbroken either way." Her voice cracks, and the tears spill from her eyes again. Our foreheads meet, green glass staring into gray. "Either way, I lose one of you."

I yank her into my chest and let her overwrought body vibrate against me, breathing her into me. "You're the best thing that's ever happened to me." I barely get the words past the colossal lump in my throat. Ironically, she's also the worst thing that's ever happened to me. I don't know how I'm going to get over Lo Harper, but I must move on and take comfort from the fact that I loved her enough to let her go.

Her sobs are low and suppressed, and though I'd love nothing more than to keep her here with me, I can't. Breaking away, I get up off the bed. I can't look at her. "You should call the hospital," I say, hating myself more for stalling her in doing what she should have done before I offloaded my shit on her. "I'll be in the kitchen when you're ready to go." I walk out in a haze of ruin, my heart shattered, my eyes brimming with tears. I sniff and roughly wipe them away. Destroyed. But at least Lo will heal.

Once I have a coffee in my hand, I look down into the still, dark liquid and wonder where it came from. I recall none of the motions of making it. Not loading the machine, fetching a mug, nothing. I look across the kitchen, vacant, and see Steve and Boris tucking into a bowl of biscuits. I don't recall feeding them. Should Boris be eating puppy food? Then I shiver and see the French doors into the garden open. I don't remember letting them out to go toilet. I'm losing my mind.

I drag my feet to my home office, glancing up the stairs as I pass. I call a cab and then find my check book in the top drawer. I sign it blank, slowly ripping it free and folding it in half.

This is Lo's ticket to happiness.

It's my ticket to despair.

I call Dr. Smith and wait ages for his secretary to find him. I explain Lo's change in financial circumstances. I hear hope in his voice. I hang up and slump back in my chair. And I stare at thin air for what feels like a lifetime.

"I couldn't find you in the kitchen."

I look up and find Lo in the doorway, though I refute my mind's desire to drink her in, to make notes on what she's wearing and how lovely she is. "There's a cab on the way." A car horn sounds from outside, and Lo looks over her shoulder.

"For me?" she asks, definite hurt tinging her voice.

"To take you to the hospital after you've taken Boris home. Is there someone to look after him while you're at the hospital?"

She slowly pivots back toward me and runs assessing eyes all over my face. "I could ask my mother-in-law."

I nod and get up, closing the distance between us, handing her the small piece of paper. "It's blank. I wasn't sure how much exactly you needed."

She stares at the paper hovering between us. I can feel her sudden hesitance.

"Take it, Lo," I order calmly, reaching for her hand and placing it in her palm. "Now go. The taxi's paid for."

Lifting her chin, she faces me, and though her eyes are clouded, I see hope beyond her current, temporary turmoil. And that's the whole fucking point, isn't it? I am just a temporary ache that will be eased with time and the recovery of her husband. Any other way than this, the pain will linger forever.

"The cost of his surgery runs into tens of thousands, Luke."

"There's more than enough in that account. Use what you need."

She shakes her head, thrusting the check back into my chest. "I can't do it."

"You can and you will."

Her hand drops, her glassy eyes staring into mine. Her lip wobbles. *Shit, please don't cry. I can't promise I'll keep myself together.* "Why can't I have both? Billy better, and my friend too?"

I can only smile at her naivety. "If you were mine, I wouldn't let you be friends with a man who's in love with you." I swallow, fighting to keep my emotions in check, and Lo's lip goes from wobbling to vibrating. "I can't do it to your husband," I whisper. "I can't do it to you." I reach up and stroke down her wet cheek, relishing this one last touch. "And I can't do it to myself, either, Lo." I inhale, drop my hand, and walk past her quickly, back to the kitchen to find my coffee. Only because it's too early for alcohol. Standing with my back to the door, I roughly brush at my eyes again, shouting at myself repeatedly. I feel her behind me.

"Luke?"

I don't turn around. Can't look at her. I finally understand how Pops felt letting go of his Milly Rose.

"Luke, please look at me."

But her pleading like that will always win. I turn and find her, unable to hide the tears in my eyes.

She blinks and swallows. "I'll never forget you," she says jaggedly, quickly turning and collecting Boris.

Leaving to find her happiness.

While I watch mine walk away from me.

Chapter Thirty

They say life's a bitch and then you die. I believe them. This past week has been a constant bitch. Work's been a bitch, Amanda has been a bitch, even Pops has been a bitch. If I was to get mowed down by a car right now, it would be about right. My last thought makes me physically flinch. It's only been seven days since I watched Lo walk out of my house. It feels like seven years. It doesn't bode well for my future. I feel like some callous bastard has cut my heart from my chest and is brandishing it before my eyes, taunting me, laughing, telling me I'll never get it back in one piece.

I've been drunk. A lot. It was only eight a.m. when Lo walked out of my house and my life. But I got drunk, nevertheless. The time didn't matter. Hours and days have melted into nothing. My life feels like it's melted into nothing. I miss her so terribly, the ache constant. The pain relentless. And when I saw a few days later that the check had been cashed, all that pain twisted into a conflicting mixture of anger and guilt. I should be feeling fulfilled, happy that I've done the right thing. Saved him. Instead, I feel like I've sacrificed my life for another man. And it sucks to high heaven.

And yet I know I mustn't think like that. This isn't about me.

For you, Lo.

Arabella jetted off to New York, but Todd remains an unwelcome house guest. I just want to be alone, but there's no chance of that happening. He's using Amanda as a perfect excuse to hover on the periphery of my life. I should be thankful. It would be easy to do something incredibly stupid, like relent to her incessant attempts to get me back in bed. Lord knows, I've been drunk often enough to let my control slip. And despite the fact I hate her, hate her for the things she said to Lo, she's a means of escape. A way to forget. And, actually, she wants me.

But, thankfully, Todd's made sure I've not given in to my unbearable sense of loneliness, confiscating my mobile every time he's seen me with a tumbler of Scotch in my hand before trying his hardest to distract me with something or other. He knows I'm not thinking straight.

The only constructive thing I've done these past few days is research. It's been a great way to pass the painfully dragging hours and stay off the drink. It's also taken me on a journey through time. If I can't have my Milly Rose, then Pops should have his. I feel like I'm clutching at straws again. Milly Rose must be in her late eighties. There's no guarantee she'll still be alive, but I have to find out. Hence the reason Pops is being a bitch. I've picked his old brain to pieces, spinning him some story about building our family tree. I'm being sly, but if Milly *isn't* still alive, I don't want him to know. I'll let their story die with her, and let Pops keep his memories fond and blissful.

My research has taken me to the library, the news office, and through an arena of websites and online records. Nothing has cropped up. Not one damn tiny thing. It's not surprising. She would have married, changed her name, and I have no way of knowing when that happened. I've searched through every marriage record over a fifty-year period, from 1945 to 1995, and come up blank. My eyes are crossed and my brain aching. But, like I've said, it's a great distraction.

After a bitch of a day at work, I pull up outside my house and sit in the driver's seat for an age. This place is too big for me. Me, on my own. On a sigh, I peel myself from the leather seat of my BMW and pull my briefcase out with me. It's Friday. What am I going to do with myself all weekend?

Get drunk.

Get drunk.

And get drunk.

"Honey, I'm home," I call sarcastically, trudging toward the kitchen.

Todd's head pops out from around the door, a mischievous gleam in his eye. It stops me in my tracks. "Evening, dear." He strides toward me and pulls my suit jacket from my shoulders, draping it over an occasional chair in the corner of the entrance hall.

"What are you doing?" I ask, following his every move with narrowed eyes as Steve comes bolting out of the kitchen with a sock in his gob, his tail whipping madly. I reach down and give him all the fuss he wants. And deserves. He's been my shadow, following me around the house non-stop, looking at me with those droopy eyes. He knows I'm not right.

"I have a surprise for you." Todd tugs me up and links arms with me, starting to walk us onward.

I immediately break free. "No, I don't like your surprises." They usually involve women, mostly naked, and lots of alcohol. Alcohol is okay right now. Naked women, however, won't be okay, if only because I can't have the woman I actually want.

He pouts, over the top, and bats his eyelashes at me.

I throw him a filthy look. "I'm taking Steve to the park." *And me to another pity party.* I head for the stairs.

"I bet you're not," Todd counters, confident and cocky.

I laugh. "I bet I really am." I make it halfway up the stairs before a sound from the kitchen stops me. I look over my shoulder, finding Todd grinning. "What was that?"

He shrugs, all nonchalant. "Off you go for your walk."

I turn, intrigued, hearing another sound, this time clearer. "Is that . . .?" I take the steps back down and jog toward the kitchen, feeling life in my bones for the first time in a week. Skidding to a stop at the threshold, I see her immediately.

"Daddy." Tia dives off the bar stool and flies across the kitchen towards me, crashing into me with force.

"Oh, God, it's so good to see you." I gather her up and make up for the cuddles I've missed since she went traveling. "What are you doing here? I thought you weren't due back until April."

"Change of plan." She takes a step back and inspects me, pulling at my rumpled suit. "You look awful."

"Thanks." I follow Tia's lead and drink in my girl. What's happened to her? She's wearing clothes that are a hundred times too big. "What's all this?" I ask, pulling at the cotton things hanging from her tiny waist. "Are these trousers?"

"Yes." She widens her stance to demonstrate, revealing the crotch of the trousers hanging past her knees.

"And your hair looks . . . grubby." My nose wrinkles, wondering where her perfectly glossy chocolate waves have gone.

She smooths over it, rolling her eyes. "Shampoo is about the worst thing for your hair."

"It is?"

"Yes. Anyway, I want you to meet someone." Moving to the side, she opens up my line of sight to the breakfast bar. I groan under my breath, hearing Todd chuckling from behind me. "Dad, meet Trent. Trent, this is my dad."

Stig of the Dump struts on forward, smiling broadly. His nose ring is the first thing I note, followed by his masses of blond dreadlocks and the pink bandana holding them back from his face. He has some of those stupid trousers on too, the crotch even lower than Tia's, and his arms are weighed down by millions of wrist bands in various shades of leather. "Mr. Williamson, it's so nice to meet you." He speaks with a thick American accent, reminding me that he's from the opposite side of the fucking world.

"Trent the River," I say under my breath, my elation that my girl is home dying fast.

"Tia doesn't shut up about you." He gives me a firm, manly shake, which is ridiculous when he's standing here wearing this shit. His eyes twinkle when he looks at my girl, and Tia's virtually explode with happiness. She doesn't shut up about me? Pride muscles in on my slighted state.

"We're close," I say for the sake of it, or perhaps to remind The River that any attempts to abduct her and ship her off to his homeland will be fought with violence.

"Oh, I know." He drops my hand in favor of Tia's shoulders, pulling her into his side and kissing her grubby hair. "We weren't allowed to go anywhere until she'd come to see you."

I smile, unable to stop myself, and resist stealing her back from his embrace. She's looking up at him dreamily, her eyes glittery, her face alive. I step back and observe them for a few moments, allow myself to take them in. I hate and love my conclusion all at once. Love. It's so strong, I can feel the intensity of it myself. I hate to admit it, but I think my baby girl has found her soul mate. God damn her. God damn *him*.

"So what happened to the travel plans?" Todd joins us and hands me a much-needed beer. I nod my thanks, and we all take a seat at the breakfast bar.

Tia's stool is so close to The River's, she's virtually sitting on his lap. "We did Cambodia, and then flew on to New Zealand. Trent's last stop was New Zealand, then he was due to go home." She sighs, and The River takes her hand. "I didn't want to continue without him."

"So you abandoned your trip of a lifetime," I finish for her.

"I couldn't leave him." Planting a kiss on his cheek, she gives me her full attention, an expression I can't read traveling across her face. "How are you?" she asks tentatively.

Looks pass between her and Todd, and even Steve pipes down at my feet. I look at my mate, who refuses to acknowledge me, his head shaking mildly at Tia. "I'm good," I breathe, glaring at him. He's told her. Great. Now is the perfect time for a change of subject. "Have you spoken to your mother?"

"Not yet." Tia thumbs the bottom of her glass of water, unbothered.

"Does she know you're home?"

She shakes her head, looking up at me. "Can we get dinner before I contend with her drama?"

I smile, knowing exactly where she's coming from. Granted, Tia's change of image and choice of man is a shock to me, but I can see she's happy. Probably the happiest I've ever known her to be. Who am I to take someone's happiness away from them, especially from someone I love? Tia's mother, with her ladies who lunch in two-piece suits and pearls, will be having a meltdown of epic proportions. I might go along for the show. "Sure. You want to go out?"

"Chinese takeaway?" she suggests, eyes bright. That's our thing. Chinese food, slumped on the couch watching trash. It's been too long.

"I'll get the menu." I wander over to the drawer that houses the endless takeaway menus. So it won't be totally the same, what with Tia's new shadow and Todd tucking in as well, but she's home, and that's all I care about right now. I have questions. Lots of questions. Most importantly, where will my daughter and The River reside? Specifically, what country? What's his trade? Will he be getting job? Can he support her? But it can all wait. For now, I'm just going to enjoy her. And the distraction she's providing me with.

"Hey, Dad, can't you go fetch Pops?" Tia calls from behind. "I'd love Trent to meet him."

"Yeah, go get the old boy out of jail for a few hours." Todd backs her up.

I toss the menu on the worktop. "You lot order." Grabbing my keys, I head for the door. "And no hot shit."

I leave behind a pair of amused people, and one baffled one. The River won't be baffled for long. I'm sure Tia and Todd will fill him in on my dick's encounter with a chili.

The dining table is loaded with various dishes, and everyone tucks in. It's a casual affair, everyone muscling each other out of the way to access the food. "So, Trent," Pops says, his face and tone telling me that he's about to land Tia's new boyfriend with some sarcastic enquiry. "You not take a razor with you on your travels?"

Trent laughs, and Tia grins. "Actually, sir, it got tiresome shaving all the time. With the world at my feet, I didn't want to waste any time on trivial stuff. It's why I went traveling in the first place, you know, to escape the mundane routine of everyday life."

"Not so trivial now, is it?" Pops motions to the masses of facial hair suspending from Trent's face. "You're getting your noodles stuck in it."

Smiling, he returns to his food as Tia fondles with his facial hair. "I like it," she declares.

I peek at Todd, who rolls his eyes with me. I'm guessing Tia would like any outlandish style The River chose to sport.

I slide my fork onto my plate and reach for Todd's empty. "You done?"

He falls back in his chair and holds his stomach. "Stuffed."

"Here, I'll help you, Mr. Williamson." The River rises from his chair and starts gathering up all the empty plates.

"Cheers." I silently praise him for his effort and manners. "You can call me Luke."

He follows me over to the dishwasher and starts helping me load, scraping the plates as he does. "So, Luke," he says with an edge of hesitation.

I peek up at him, slightly hesitant myself. "What?"

"Well, I wanted to do this properly." He looks past me to the table, and I follow his line of sight, finding Pops, Tia, and Todd all engrossed in conversation.

"Do what properly?"

"Ask you for permission to marry your daughter."

The plate I'm holding slips from my grasp and crashes to the tiles. I look at him in horror. "Come again?"

"What's going on over there?" Tia calls.

"Nothing," I call, finding the dustpan and sweeping up the scattered porcelain, fighting Steve back constantly as he tries to lick the broken crockery. "I'm sure I didn't hear you right."

The River smiles, a little awkward, a little amused, and a lot nervous. "I want to marry Tia. I'm asking for your permission."

I'm hot and bothered as I stamp on the pedal of the bin and drop the contents of the dustpan in. "You've known each other a matter of minutes," I splutter incredulously as my eyes drop to his flip-flopped feet. It's fucking freezing outside. *The idiot.*

"Over a month, actually." He smiles at my skeptical face. "And I knew the first day I met her that I was going to spend the rest of my life with her."

The flat of my fist rests on my chest and massages. Ouch, that hurts.

"Are you alright, Luke?"

"It's Mr. Williamson to you," I snap, facing this . . . this . . . interloper. Stig of the Dump wisely backs off, hands up in surrender.

"Sir, with all due respect, I love her. I'd never be able to put into words how much but, and it might sound soppy, she's literally my world. I know how much she adores you. I'd love for you to give me your blessing."

"Does she know?"

"I wanted to ask you first, since you're so close. It felt only right."

I stare at the man in front of me, and though I thoroughly hate myself for it, I want to shake his hand. I want to congratulate him on a speech well made. But I don't. "Can I think about it?"

The River laughs deeply. "Sure you can, Mr. Williamson." He's humoring me. Good. I need it. "When can I expect an answer?"

"Let me sleep on it." I return to the dishwasher and mindlessly stack the plates. Fucking hell. Here's me, forty-two years old, single, no potential takers, and now I'm faced with giving my daughter away to that fucking thing called love.

Life fucking sucks.

Once I've cleared up, we all move to the bar, Todd giving Tia an evening pass to our male-only joint. I watch as Pops settles in his favorite seat, right at the end so he can see the whole room, and point to his favorite Scotch on the optics behind. I put the jukebox on, getting a loud hoot of glee from the old fella when The Rat Pack launch into song. "This is the best bar in town," Pop announces. "Get me my tipple, Grandboy."

"You'll have to stay here tonight, Pops. I plan on indulging." After The River's bombshell, I'm officially back on the drink.

"A sleepover?" he asks. "Marvelous!"

I fetch everyone drinks and watch while The River mindlessly throws Steve's ball for him to fetch. "What possessed you to get a dog, Dad?" Tia asks.

Lo. Lo possessed me. "Company." I shrug off her question.

"You need a woman, not a—" She flicks Todd a *shit!* look. "Sorry."

"We talking about Lo?" Pops asks.

"No," I answer flatly. "We're talking about Steve."

"Stupid name for a dog," Pops grumbles.

"Yeah, where did that come from, anyway?" Tia asks, reaching down to lift him onto her lap. "He looks nothing like a Steve."

"Oh, I don't know," The River pipes up. "It's a solid, manly name. Steve looks like he's going to be solid and manly to me." He gives my pooch a scratch, and I narrow suspicious eyes, deliberating over whether he's licking my arse or being genuine.

I settle on a stool, silently observing Tia and her man-thing as they coo over my dog, often throwing each other gazes. If it wasn't so endearing, I might throw up in my Scotch. And that would be a waste of damn good Scotch. *Sacrilege.*

"How are you getting on with that family tree of yours?" Pops asks, presenting his empty for me to fill.

I top him up on demand. "Good," is all I say, because there's nothing I can tell him, since I've not been researching our family tree.

Pops knocks back his fresh drink, savoring the flavor before swallowing. "Mildred wanted to dabble in all that ancestry nonsense. Mind you, she was an orphan, so it's understandable. You, Grandboy, know exactly where you come from. I don't know why you feel the need to explore it."

My brows come together in a deep frown. "Mildred? Who's Mildred?"

His thick busy brows match mine, pinching, as he looks into the bottom of his empty glass. "I've never called her Mildred before."

"Who?" Tia asks.

"Milly," Pops confirms. "Her name was Mildred, though no one ever called her that."

I sit up straight. "Her real name's Mildred?"

He smiles, going off to that place he goes when he's thinking of the woman who stole his heart all those years ago. "She always thought it was too old-fashioned."

Well, damn. I laugh under my breath. That would explain why I've drawn no results while searching for her. I have to hold my feet back from taking me to my home office to bash her *full* name into all the websites I've become a member of over the past week. Tomorrow. I'll resume my search tomorrow. Mildred Rose. The love of his life. I was beginning to think he'd made her up with the endless brick walls I was meeting.

The night goes on, full of happy chatter and alcohol, and when Pops starts swaying on his stool, I wisely decide that it's time to get him in bed. "Come on, you old soak." I help him down and present him to everyone to say their goodnights. "Will you make sure Steve goes out for a pee?" I say to Todd.

"Sure." He slides off his stool. "Come on, Steve. Let's go piss."

"We should be going up too." Tia stifles a yawn. "Jet lag is kicking in."

"Take the third bedroom." I walk Pops toward the stairs. "The River can room with Todd."

"The River?" Tia asks. "Who's The River?"

"He can?" Todd blurts, looking back from the doorway.

"Sorry." I cringe. "Trent."

"Seriously, Dad."

"What?"

My girl shakes her head and takes The River's hand, following me and Pops to the stairs. "He'll be rooming with me."

"Actually, Tia, I think your dad's right." Trent drops my girl's hand and moves away, leaving her with a rather indignant expression. "I wouldn't want to disrespect his rules under his roof."

Todd sniggers, obviously missing the fact that The River's chivalrous declaration means he'll be snuggled up with him tonight.

I nod to myself in silent agreement, and Pops starts jerking from laughter as I negotiate his inebriated body up the stairs. "What are you laughing at?"

"The fact that you were a father at Tia's age."

I scowl at him. "And?"

"And stop being so prudish. This was the twenty-first century last time I checked."

"Your input isn't welcome."

"Tough, because you've got it. Let the lovebirds sleep together."

I look over my shoulder and find Trent and Tia climbing the stairs. They're both smiling at my wayward grandfather. "Fine," I mutter. "But no hanky-panky."

My order only serves to encourage more laughter. I've no idea why. I'm being deadly serious. My head's a total mind-fuck at the moment, and that's only going to bend it more.

After directing Pops to the bed and stripping him down to his huge stripy underpants, I tuck him in and smile when he sleepily mumbles Milly's name. The sound stirs a big melting pot of conflicting feelings: joy, because his sleepy smile is something to behold, and concern, because seventy years after he met the infamous Milly Rose, he still dreams of her.

Fuck, I'm doomed.

Shutting the door behind me, I scrub my hands down my face. "All right?" Todd asks, his hand resting on the handle of the door to his room.

"Tired," I answer, but I'm not physically weary. I'm mentally drained. "See you in the morning." I head for my room, ready to collapse into bed and drive myself insane with a mind that will refuse to sleep, despite being exhausted. But I pause as I'm pushing my way into my room, a noise coming from downstairs. "What was that?"

Todd must have heard it, because he's looking down the landing too. "Everyone came up, didn't they?"

"Where's Steve?" I ask. "Did he come in from the garden?" Just as I say that, he appears at my feet.

I tread the carpet carefully, glancing at my watch. It's gone midnight. I look over the banister into the blackness below, Todd looming behind me. "Where'd you keep your baseball bat?" he whispers in my ear.

"I don't have a baseball bat."

"You fool. Everyone has a baseball bat."

I ignore him, hearing the pitter-patter of . . . paws?

"Oh." Todd's hand rests on my shoulder. "It's just Steve."

"It's not Steve." I nod to my feet and Todd looks down.

Then his round eyes fly up to me. "Steve's here."

"God, you're clever," I sigh, creeping to the top of the stairs, feeling the wall for the switch, squinting into the darkness. My fingers brush the chrome plate, and I flick on the lights, bracing myself.

"Holy shit." Todd jumps back, his hands grabbing my arms to take me with him, but my feet are cemented to the carpet, my ears turning the silhouette of a person into . . . "Lo?"

She holds up something in her hand. "I tried knocking," she says quietly, removing Boris's lead when he tugs, and he and Steve meet and greet each other halfway up the stairs, while I stand like a statue taking her in. She looks like she's been crying for a year, her face red and blotchy. "I still had your key."

"Jesus," Todd breathes, relaxing his hold of me. "Well, I guess I'll leave you two to it." He massages my shoulder in a move that I suppose should rub some reassurance into me. It won't work. "I'll be in my room." He leaves me standing at the top of the stairs staring down at Lo, who's staring up at me. My head's in chaos. What is she doing here? I can't say she's brought back all my memories of her to the surface by being here because the memories didn't even begin to recede. But what she has done is intensify each and every one of them, as well as my feelings. It took everything out of me to let her walk out of my life. She knows that. Making me go through that again isn't fair. Am I being selfish?

I hear her gulp, her lips straightening through her trembles, her head shaking so very faintly. "It's too late," she whispers. "It's too late to save him." She slowly folds to her knees at the foot of the stairs, her whole body starting to rack and convulse.

It's too late? The consistently aching muscle in my chest fractures. "Oh, God, Lo." I race down the stairs like a speed demon and pick her up from the floor. The strength of her arms clinging to me is indicative of her desperation. Her relentless tears are evidence of her pain. My squeezing heart is a sign of my sorrow. Sorrow for her. Sorrow for Billy. I sit on the third step and cradle her in my arms, holding her to me and comforting her as best I know how while she sobs her heart out. It's too late. It can't be too late. There must be a way. I want to ask her questions, find out what's happened to change things, but for now I concentrate on soothing her, keeping her tear-stained face tucked under my chin. I won't allow myself to enjoy the feel of her in my arms. I won't relish in her warmth. Not when she's so distraught. She can't seem to control her juddering movements, so I know talking through her emotion isn't going to happen for a while.

"Dad?"

I look up the stairs to find Tia sanding in a T-shirt, her face a map of questions. "I'm fine. Go back to bed, darling."

"You sure?" She looks to her left when Todd comes out of his room, gently coaxing her away as she looks down at me.

I offer a smile that takes too much effort and goes nowhere near my eyes. But it's as much as I can muster to reassure her. "I'll talk to you in the morning."

She nods and lets Todd escort her back to her room, and I breathe in deeply, waiting patiently for Lo to get a handle on her sobs. I've never heard so much pain before. "I'm sorry," she finally sniffs, pushing herself from my chest. "I wouldn't have come had I known you had company."

"Don't be silly." I slowly pick away the strands of hair that are sticking to her wet cheeks. "What's happened, Lo?"

She looks me directly in the eye, her grays dull and blanketed by grief. "It's spread into his bones, his blood, everywhere. It's over."

"Oh, Jesus." I pull her into me and squeeze her. "I'm so sorry."

"He's refused to attend his appointments at the hospital, and now he's riddled. Now there really is nothing that can save him."

I close my eyes and sink my face into her hair.

"I shouldn't have come. I know that. But . . . I didn't know where else to go."

Fuck that. "You come to me. You always come to me." I grind the order out, hating myself for cutting the contact, for making her believe she's an unwelcome burden. Like she couldn't depend on me when she needed me most. What was I thinking? "Do you understand me?"

She nods into my chest. "I've missed you so much."

My fractured heart cracks. "I've missed you too," I admit. "More than you could ever know." I reluctantly let her free herself from my viselike grip, and she takes a few long inhales, wiping at her face. She looks so tired, so completely empty. I just want to put her in my bed and let her sleep for as long as she needs to. And she looks like she needs to sleep forever.

Standing with her in my arms, I carry her up the stairs to my room. She doesn't object, doesn't breathe a word. I lay her on my bed and remove her boots, letting them hit the carpet with two thuds. Then I quietly help her out of her coat and unfasten the fly of her jeans. There's nothing sexual about my moves. I'm taking care of her.

Lo watches me slowly undress her until she's left in her T-shirt. Then her eyes follow me around the bed. I pull off my jeans, leave my T-shirt in place, and crawl into bed beside her. I don't touch her. She rolls onto her side to face me, and I mirror her position, our heads resting on separate pillows. The mattress dips twice, Boris and Steve joining us and curling up at the end of the bed, and we lie in the dim light in silence until Lo's eyes become heavy and I watch her lose her battle to sleep. Only when I know she's in a deep slumber do I reach for her face and gently trace the contours of her cheek. "I love you," I whisper, kissing the tips of my fingers and resting them on her forehead. "It was all for you." My voice breaks. "I promise never to abandon you again."

Even if it tortures me.

Because isn't that what sacrificial love is?

Chapter Thirty-One

When I blink my eyes open, I spend a few sleepy minutes piecing together the evening before, wondering whether I've been dreaming. Then I feel the heat of her body pressed into my side and reality hits me. A reality where her world is falling apart and there is fuck all I can do about it. The notion kills me. No man wants to see the woman he loves so distraught, no matter what the reason may be.

I need to get out of the house and try to clear my head, so I leave Lo sleeping and quietly coax the dogs from the room. I walk for miles with Steve and Boris, through parks and down streets. The morning fog is low, the air damp, and my thoughts are as bleak as the weather. I let Steve rummage through the undergrowth while I stroll behind, Boris at my heels, inhaling the refreshing, clean cold air.

By the time I've made it home, I'm no clearer on what happens next.

I walk into the kitchen to find everyone, except Lo, drinking coffee at the breakfast bar. The quiet and pensive looks on all their faces tells me what the topic over caffeine has been. I drop the leads on the side, feed the dogs, and make sure the water bowl is full.

"Her husband can't have the lifesaving surgery he needs," I say as I take two mugs down from the cupboard, killing the silence with my brutal announcement. No one responds, leaving me to push on. "The cancer's spread too far. It's too late. I should have tried to help sooner." I pour the coffee and add milk.

"Daddy." Tia comes up behind me and wraps her arms around my waist, resting her cheek on my back. The display of comfort forces me to blink back the sting that's threatening to turn into tears. "What you did was an incredibly selfless thing. You can't blame yourself."

I swallow and collect the coffees, turning so she's forced to relinquish her squeeze.

"God has other plans, Grandboy." Pops nods, as if he truly believes that. "No one can manipulate His plan."

While I understand that my grandfather is trying to ease me, I can't help but feel resentful. God's plan sucks. "I'm going to take this up to Lo." I look to Todd, who's silent, thoughtful. "Would you mind taking Pops home?"

"Sure, not at all." He stands, looking to Pops. "Fancy a breakfast date before I take you back to jail?"

"We'll come too." Tia rushes to invite herself and Trent, and everyone swings into action, gathering bags, coats, and the boyfriend. "I'll call you later." She reaches up and kisses my cheek before leaving with everyone else, so it's only me and the dogs left in the kitchen. Not that they're aware of the quick evacuation, their snouts buried in a bowl full of with biscuits. Poor Boris is probably wondering what kind of hotel this is, serving him puppy food.

On a heavy inhale, I make my way up the stairs and shoulder the door of my bedroom open. She's still asleep, one thigh kicked over the duvet, her hands buried under the pillow. The sight of her, so consumed by sleep, brings a welcome smile to my face. Placing my coffee on the bedside, I sit on the edge of the bed, taking in her peaceful face. I feel cruel for waking her, for dragging her from the only respite to be found, but it's nearly 9 a.m. She'll want to call the hospital and check on Billy. I extend my hand to her face and sweep her hair from one eye. "Lo?"

She sighs, rolling onto her back, and languidly stretches out. Then she settles, drifting back off again.

"Lo, wake up."

Her eyes flutter open, a frown immediately wriggling its way onto her forehead. She's caught in limbo between sleep and consciousness, her eyes jumping around the room, her mind whirling. Propping herself up on her elbows, she finds me, opens her mouth, shuts it again, three times, before realization dawns on her.

"Morning," I say, offering her coffee.

She breathes out, taking the cup. "Morning."

"How're you feeling?"

"Like I've had a taste of sleep and I want more." Sitting up and crossing her legs, she wraps both palms around the mug and sips. "I'm sorry for showing up here last—"

I cut her off by resting a hand on her knee. "Don't apologize."

She nods mildly into her mug, falling into thought. Real life is seeping back into her waking brain, and I hate the gradual fall of her face that comes with it. "What time is it?"

"Nine. I didn't want to wake you but thought you'd want to call the hospital."

Her alarm is instant, so I reach down for her handbag and pass it to her. "Thank you." She dives right in and retrieves her phone, and rather than sit and listen in on the conversation, I head for the bathroom, giving her privacy, and finish my morning coffee while I rest against the vanity unit. Who the fuck knows what today might bring? More heartbreak, probably.

I shower, brush my teeth, and ignore the too-long scruff I'm sporting at the moment. Wrapping a towel around my waist, I go back to the bedroom, finding Lo deep in thought, still sitting on the bed. "Did you get through to the hospital?"

She shoots her eyes my way, startled from her daydream. "He's drifting in and out. No change." She takes my offered hand and lets me pull her up from the bed. "I'd better be going."

"I'll take you," I declare, not bothering to ask her if she'd like me to. I'm taking her, and that's it. I head for my wardrobe, hearing Lo's accepting *okay* as I go. "Boris can stay here with Steve." It'll be one less thing for her to worry about. "And we'll stop off at yours on the way through so you can change." I throw on a sweater and drag some jeans up my legs, fastening them as I walk back into the room.

"Okay," she agrees easily again.

I nod and sit on the end of the bed to pull on some socks. "Anything else you need to do while we're out?"

"I don't think so." She looks off into the distance, maybe trying to think about that.

"Well, if you think of something, tell me." I shove my feet into my Timberlands. "I'm at your disposal." I'm also taking charge.

Lo smiles as I stand. "Thank you."

"Stop thanking me," I order, uncomfortable with her constant gratitude. "Why don't you take a shower and finish your coffee while I sort the dogs out?"

She nods, her eyes following me as I leave the room. "Luke," she calls, stopping me at the door.

I look over my shoulder.

"You're a good man," she says, almost hesitantly. Hesitant, because she knows deep down that it's not what I want to hear. Being a good man, doing the right thing, will never give me her heart.

On the journey to her house, Lo explains everything with a surprisingly steady voice. I listen to her tell me how she contacted the specialist in America, how they tentatively agreed on a date, how she paid an instalment of the medical bill . . . and then it all went pear-shaped. Billy's infection wouldn't budge, and every test the doctors did came back with dire news. Lo went from soaring to drowning in the space of a week. From hopeful to hopeless. The lifeline I offered has been cruelly snatched away by nature. And I wasn't there for her. I hate myself in this moment. I should have been there. How I feel about Lo doesn't matter anymore.

I reach over and take her hand, squeezing when I sense her voice breaking. "Stop now," I say quietly. She doesn't need to go over this again. I've heard enough.

"They've said he could have days, weeks, or a month. He's just gone downhill so rapidly."

I wince at the brutality of her situation as I come to a stop at some lights. "I'm so sorry."

"Stop apologizing," she says seriously, gazing out of the window. "You sound like you're blaming yourself."

"I should have given you that money sooner."

Lo swings toward me violently. "Don't," she shouts, fuming mad. I recoil and stare at her in stunned silence. "Don't ever say that to me again. What you did for me was a beautiful thing. You put your feelings aside and gave me that money to save my husband's life. It spread over time, Luke. Way before I knew you."

Maybe, but she's wrong about one thing. I didn't put my feelings aside. I couldn't. They were very much at the forefront of this mess, hurting more and more with every second that passed after she walked away.

I stare at her, seeing rage in her broken-hearted gaze that's new to me. She's angry. I guess she needs to be angry, and if that means she takes it out on me, then so be it. I'd give her a bat if I could, let her pound me while she shouts and screams to get it out of her system. But I realize, she might never get it out of her system. There are seven stages of grief. I truly believe in all of them, except the last. Acceptance. No one should be expected to accept losing a loved one so tragically. No one.

A honk from behind me pulls my eyes to the lights, and I pull off slowly. My car is bathed in silence for the rest of the journey to Lo's. Silence really is the most powerful scream. My head is fucking ringing. I make an excuse to wait in my car, telling her I have calls to make. I'm not up to facing their family home again.

While I sit, twiddling my phone, I get a message from Tia.

> Loving someone can screw you up as much as losing someone. X

I laugh under my breath, thinking she's not far wrong. I feel thoroughly screwed up. The ultimate love is loving someone who can't love you back. Unrequited love. With or without Lo, I'm in pain. But, again, my feelings are at the bottom of my pile of priorities right now. Lo is losing the future she'd believed was hers. Losing the man she chose to be by her side long before I met her. She comes first.

Chapter Thirty-Two

Rolling to a stop in the drop-off zone, Lo turns to face me. "Will you come in with me?"

Her request knocks me back. "Into the hospital? I'm not sure—"

She grabs my hand. "Please," she begs.

What can I say? I promised I'd be here for her. *Here* means anywhere. That includes the hospital. I discreetly breathe in, put the car back into drive and park up in the carpark opposite. As we walk together to the area of the hospital we need, I quietly observe Lo. Her gaze is focused straight ahead, her small body walking taller with every step as feigned strength lifts her. She's bracing herself for what news she'll be met with today.

All the nurses we pass through the ward offer sympathetic smiles to Lo, all of which she acknowledges with her own. I wish they wouldn't. I know she hates that. And yet she's just too fucking nice to yell her frustration.

I can smell death, the scent drifting up my nose and practically suffocating me. Billy's room is at the far end of the ward, the blinds closed, the door closed. Closed off from this world. Lo takes the handle and pauses, her shoulders rising as she inhales one last dose of fortitude before she faces her reality.

Hovering a few paces behind, I study her attempts to calm herself. I have to resist telling her to stop trying to be strong. "I'll be here if you need me," I say quietly. She looks back to me as I point aimlessly over my shoulder. "Or I could go get us coffee? Something to eat?" The latter is far more appealing to me. I need to keep moving, focus on something, even if it's the mundane task of fetching food and drinks.

"That would be nice, thank you." She takes a deep breath and disappears through the door, closing it quietly behind her. I don't hang around outside the room. I make my way back to the entrance where I saw a café and order two coffees and a muffin, taking my time about it. I take a seat and empty two sachets of sugar into my cup and slowly stir it in. When my phone rings, I'm grateful for the excuse to remain where I am for a while longer.

"Hey, bud," Todd says, his tone unusually soft. "How's it going?"

"Horribly," I admit. "Fucking hell, Todd, the guy isn't even thirty. How the fuck does this shit happen?"

"It's tough, man. Really tough. How's Lo?"

"Pretending to be strong." I reach up to my temple and try to massage the stress away, then immediately feel shame for it. I know nothing of stress. I know nothing of suffering. "She shouldn't have to deal with this."

"Kind of puts things into perspective, doesn't it? There's me going into meltdown over a trashed apartment. At least I still have my health. I'm seriously revaluating my life."

Hearing my best mate—the mate who could be labelled shallow and selfish—talk so deeply is alien. But I get it. "In what way?"

"I don't know. I'm forty-two years old. If I ever got ill, the only person I have to worry about me is you. How fucking sad is that? I guess being on the outside looking in has just made me realize how empty my life is."

"Your life if full," I point out. "Of women."

"Plural. Maybe I need just one."

I laugh under my breath, turning my coffee cup on the spot. "Just don't fall in love with someone who you can't have, yeah?"

His silence speaks volumes. "Be strong, bud. She needs that."

I smile through my mental exhaustion. "Pops okay?"

"I just delivered him back to jail. Tia and The River have gone to see her mother."

"Oh dear."

"Yeah, expect a call."

My memory is quickly jogged, the bombshell I was dealt last night coming forward through all of the shit currently polluting my head. "He asked me for Tia's hand in marriage."

Todd coughs down the line. "Shit. Your life right now, though."

"Tell me about it."

"Hey, I don't know if you want my input—"

"I don't."

"I like him."

Fuck. I hate to admit it, but I like him too. He's not conventional, but what's conventional about love? It's something I've fast learned in recent months. "He's a good kid."

"So what did you say?"

"I told him I'd think about it."

Todd laughs loudly, and I have to laugh with him. Because I'm fucking hilarious. Truth is, I couldn't stop them if I tried. Trent asked me. Respect to him. "And have you thought about it?"

I get to my feet, ready to drag myself back to Billy's room. "I can't think of much past Lo right now."

"Call me if you need anything, bud."

"I'm not sure how I feel about this new, kind, sensitive Todd."

"Fuck you," he mumbles, as if to make a point, and hangs up.

I collect the coffees, heading back to the ward, and as I approach Billy's room, I see the door ajar. At first, I assume a nurse or doctor must have entered, but after ten minutes sitting on the chair outside waiting, not wanting to disturb them, I hear not a peep, and no one leaves. I look toward the entrance of the ward and back to the door, pondering what to do. Is Lo even in there? Rising to my feet, I take a few steps and peek inside the room. It's dim, the TV glowing, and Billy is asleep on the bed. But there's no Lo, or medical staff. I purposely keep my eyes from lingering on the frail man lying deathly still and back up.

"Come in," a low, rattily voice virtually gasps.

I freeze where I stand, watching as his head strains to turn toward me. Sunken eyes find me, and I physically withdraw at the full-on sight of his skeletal face. So ashen. So hollow. Cowardly, I look away, shocked to my core. "I'm sorry, I have the wrong room."

"No, you don't."

What? Cautiously, I lift my stare, preparing myself to face the dying man once again. He smiles at me, and I have no fucking clue what to do with it.

"Sit down," he rasps, his arm lifting from the mattress before dropping straight back down heavily.

"No, I should leave you to rest."

"You going to argue with a dying man?" There's a lightness to his tone that defies the heaviness surrounding him.

"I have the wrong room. My apologies."

"You're as bad a liar as my Lo. You're clearly made for each other."

His words stop me in my retreating tracks, my eyes wide and now fixed on his serious face. *Does that mean what I think it means?* The thin cardboard coffee cups in my hands are burning my palms, but I'm in no position to remedy it. I can't move. Can't think.

"Please, sit down."

My eyes fall to the chair by his bed, and I stare at it for way too long. *Sit down.* I force my feet to move across the room, taking me closer to Lo's husband. Uncomfortably close. His appearance was brutally disturbing from across the room. Here, this close, it's death personified.

Looking down at the coffees in my hand, I will my hands to stop shaking. I can't. I place them on the cabinet next to his bed and lower to the chair. Fidgeting in my seat, I try to get comfortable. I could try for a year. I'll never relax. My body refuses to settle, and I'm pretty sure he can hear my heart thumping. That in itself is cruel. He's barely able to draw breath.

"Nice to finally meet you." He coughs over his words, flinching at the pain it causes him. I can do nothing more than wait for him to overcome his coughing fit. I have no idea where this conversation is going. All I know is that Lo's husband knows about me. How? I would've put my life on the fact that Lo would never tell him. I'm clueless on every level in this moment. "What's your name?"

"Luke," I answer quietly on a swallow.

"You're the one who gave Lo the money for my operation." He states it as the fact it is, and I nod in response, my throat increasingly clogging up with unease. I don't want to make a difficult situation for Lo.

I look back to the door, contemplating leaving quickly before I engage any more with him.

"I knew there was someone else," he rasps, with an odd sense of acceptance that I can't quite fathom. I return my eyes to him as he drags his head back to the center, looking up at the ceiling.

"There isn't someone else," I say quietly. I am not the *someone else.* "I'm a friend of your wife's. It's never been anything more than that." I should be ashamed of myself, lying to a dying man. For me, it's been so much more. I realize that now. When Lo's text messages made my day. When I had no desire to go looking for a hookup. When I felt more . . . fulfilled. Content. Pop saw it, and he called me out on it.

Trust me, boy, when she comes along, you'll be ready for anything.

That old man is wiser than I ever gave him credit for. But I'm really not ready for this.

A strained smile passes over Billy's lips. "I saw something change in her." He ignores my lie, undoubtedly knowing that it is a lie. I just hope he knows that it's a lie only on my part. I hope he knows his wife well enough to know that she would never betray him. "There was a lightness in her that she tried to hide from me," he goes on, coughing a few times before composing himself. "She's never been any good at lying. How did you meet her?"

My fidgeting becomes more profound. "Would you like some water?"

"No, I want to know how you met my wife."

Wife. His *wife*. "She was walking Boris."

"You have a dog?"

I nod when he looks at me, not feeling it necessary to divulge that I obtained Steve after meeting Lo. I also don't feel it's necessary to enlighten him on the circumstances of our first encounter. Without knowing him on a personal level, I know that the knowledge of his wife's intentions that night will destroy him. It would any decent man, and I know Billy is a decent man. "A beagle."

"I like beagles. Crafty characters."

I hold back my frown, feeling like I'm floating somewhere in the twilight zone. "Steve is definitely crafty."

"Steve?" He almost laughs, but a coughing fit turns his amusement into more discomfort.

"You sure you don't want that water? Can I get you anything at all?"

"A new body?"

I smile at his humor, and silence falls, though it's not uncomfortable. It's peaceful. I'm sitting in a room with the husband of the woman I'm in love with. A few weeks ago, before I knew of the tragedy surrounding their relationship, I would have told you that if I was ever put in a room alone with him, I probably would have punched him repeatedly for making Lo so miserable. Now, ironically, I'd do anything to rid him of the agony he's in. It's etched on his gaunt face. This young man who had his whole life ahead of him. A young man who married the woman of his dreams. Do we have an invisible date stamped on our forehead? When we enter his world, is it already determined when we will leave? I reach up to my forehead and rub there, stupidly wondering what my date is. How long have I got? How much time to waste? Or, rather, how much *more* time to waste.

Billy turns his head and regards me closely, and I wait for where he might lead our unexpected conversation next. You could give me a lifetime to ponder that, but I would never have anticipated the question he asks me next. "Are you in love with my wife?"

I suck in air and go rigid, staring into eyes that are full of death. I know I don't need to answer. He's looking so deeply into my eyes, I'm certain he must see all of my sins. And, make no mistake, loving Lo is a sin. "Deeply," I whisper, my short, if powerful confession, rolling off my tongue naturally. I can't hold back my truth. "And I'm so very sorry."

"Sorry for me?"

"No. I'm sorry for me, because I know Lo inside out, and I know you will always own her heart."

He blinks rapidly, looking surprised. "I just need her to live again," he says, so quietly I hardly hear him. But the plea in his tone? It screamed. He closes his eyes, his wheezing terrible.

"Should I get the doctor?" I ask, getting to my feet. "Do you need some pain relief?"

"I'm done with it." He inhales deeply, shakily. "When I'm unconscious, they can put whatever they like . . . in . . . me." Another breath. "But for now, I need my mind . . . c-clear." He swallows. It looks painful, just that small movement. Then he drags his heavy eyes open. I find myself lowering slowly to my chair, pensive and edgy. "I wish you'd have come along sooner." His words are so honest and filled with sincerity. Part of me wishes the same thing, but the other part wonders if I'd have survived this for longer. "You'll look after her for me when I'm gone." He's not asking me. "Help her live . . . again."

Fucking hell, I'm struggling to keep it together. The man before me is dying, but he's lucid and strong. Not in body, but in mind. It's a lot more than can be said for me. I don't want to give him the impression that he's entrusting his wife's wellbeing to a fucking pussy. "You have my word," I whisper on a swallow. I'm utterly struck.

"Good," he says simply, his eyes becoming heavy again. "I'll haunt you for eternity if you hurt her."

My smile isn't strained. It's natural. And it's really fucking sad. "I'd never hurt her."

Turning his head, he gasps for air, fighting to fill his lungs with the air he needs to keep breathing. Seeing a man so unwell is frighteningly sobering.

"You're a good man, Billy." I only just manage to push out my words, but I feel I need to tell him.

"No, I'm . . . a dead . . . man, Luke." He looks at me, straight into my eyes. "I came to . . . terms with it some time ago. I think I was just waiting for you . . . to come along before I go."

Jesus Christ.

I sit where I am for a few minutes, bewildered, until I can finally find the will to slowly stand. My legs are slightly shaky. I feel a bit disorientated, in another world, in a haze of shock, as I walk away from Lo's husband.

I need fresh air. Maybe a drink. I'll even take a cigarette.

When I reach a bench outside the hospital entrance, I drop to the wood and slump back, staring ahead at nothing. I'm trying to unravel what just happened, but my head is one big jumbled fucked-up mess right now.

I don't know how long I sit in the cold going over and over the time I spent in Billy's hospital room. The words he said to me. The strength through his weakness, his resolution. *Look after her*. I just told him I love his wife. He didn't even flinch. If anything, he took comfort from it.

That's all good and well, but if Lo won't let me love her . . . then what?

Looking up at the heavens, I take in the thick clouds moving with pace across the sky. And I wonder, what's God's game? How does He justify His choices to Himself? I've never bought into the proverb *God moves in mysterious ways*. In recent months, I feel like I've had an onslaught of things happen that are forcing me to rethink things. From the very beginning, from the second I laid eyes on Lo Harper, I feel like I've been part of a greater plan. If this was wrong, if Lo and I were not destined to be together, then why would the Mighty One put me at the wheel of the car?

My phone rings and pulls me from my silent surmising of what makes the world go around. I think I could spend the rest of my days trying to figure it out and still not know. I sit up straight when I see Lo's number. I've been gone for . . . I look at my watch. An hour? "Hello."

I'm greeted with silence.

"Lo?"

She speaks with such calmness. "He's gone."

I shoot to my feet on a sharp inhale of air. "I'm coming." I don't build up to a sprint. I break out into one, tearing through the hospital to get to Lo. *He's gone*. But he was talking to me an hour ago. My legs are working without instruction, my head ringing with his words. *You'll look after her for me.*

I steam through the ward, panicked that she's alone, and when I see her, I break down my run to a jog until I finally come to a stop. I try to read her disposition, try to fathom her state of mind.

My answer comes when I watch her start to slowly fold to the floor, her strength becoming too much to uphold. Instinct throws by body forward, catching her before she collapses to the hard tiles. "I've got you," I murmur, carrying her to the nearest empty room and kicking the door closed behind me, settling us on a high-backed chair. She cries. She cries so hard, my whole body shakes with her. She cries with an intensity that cuts me to my soul. She cries with such devastation, I can't help myself from letting my own emotion roll down my cheeks into her hair. She's hurting, which means I'm hurting too. More than I've ever hurt in my forty-two years of existence. The constant sobs are likely to imprint themselves on my brain for the rest of my days. I can't fix this. I can't make everything better for her, and it's breaking me.

"I went to call his parents." Each word is spoken on a ragged breath. "I knew it wasn't going to be long."

I close my eyes and pull her closer to my chest, remaining quiet.

"He said something to me." She wriggles free of me, and I quickly use my available hands to brush away the sadness staining my cheeks. She doesn't need to see me crying. She needs me to be strong.

Lo looks into my eyes, reaching up to my forehead and pushing a loose strand back.

"What did he say?" I ask, not because I feel the need to know, but because I can tell she wants me to ask.

"He told me . . ." She sniffs and swallows, working hard to gain some control of her vocal chords. "He told me he loved me. I've waited forever for those words to come again."

"Oh, Lo," I whisper.

"He also told me to let *you* love me."

My heart convulses in my chest, my fight to stop myself from crumbling under the weight of everything becoming harder. I have nothing to say in response. I'm blank.

"He said that to me, Luke." Her bottom lip starts to vibrate again, fresh tears building. I'm questioning whether I should tell her what Billy said to *me*. Part of me wants to, but the other part is worried she won't want to hear it. Or won't be able to face it. "He told me I should let Luke love me. He knew your name. He knew about you," she says, in some kind of wonder. "He knew you were in my life, and now I feel wretched." Her head drops, and unnecessary shame takes hold.

It propels me to confess. "I spoke to Billy." Her gaze catapults upward, and I go on quickly before she draws the wrong conclusion. "I didn't intend to. You'd been gone for a while, and I wondered if you were in the room. The door was open."

"I was trying to get hold of his parents. I then . . . spoke to Dr. Smith. He'll . . . organize for Billy's body—"

"Shh. You don't need to explain, darling." I graze her cheek with my fingertip. "I peered through the door. I was silent as a mouse, but he knew someone was there. I told him I had the wrong room." I pause for a second, letting what I'm telling her sink in. "He told me I was as bad at lying as you."

A choke of laughter spills over her sobs, and I can see she instantly chastises herself for it.

"He asked me if I was in love with you," I tell her quietly, regaining her eyes. "I didn't lie to him."

A small hitch of breath is barely disguised by another sob. "He asked you that?"

I nod. "He also told me that he'll haunt me forever if I ever hurt you."

Lo's eyes well to bursting point again, her teeth biting harshly down on her bottom lip.

"I'll never hurt you, Lo," I say ardently. "Never. I'll be here for you, but you need to help me navigate this, because I'm truly lost." I feel so stupid telling her this. She's lost her husband, and I'm asking her to help me? But I have to be honest with her if I'm going to come out the other side a sane man, *and* if I'm truly going to avoid hurting her. "I won't break my promise to Billy. I'll look after you for him, in whatever way you need me to. If I'm suffocating you, tell me to fuck off. If you need to talk, speak to me. If you want me to hold you, say the words. I can't bring him back, but I can try my hardest to help you through this." Reaching up to her cheek, I circle the pad of my thumb over her cheekbone, smiling a sad smile when she takes my hand and holds it in place. "This isn't conventional. I can only *try* to comprehend your pain and anguish. But I won't give up on you, Lo. No matter how long it takes. No matter where it takes us. I'll be here no matter what." Rivers of tears stream down her red face, and she collapses against me heavily. "He's not in pain anymore, Lo. He's not suffering."

She sniffles and nods against me, huddled into my body, and I gently comb my fingers through her hair, patiently waiting for her to sob her way through it. It's peaceful, but that peace is broken when a distressed cry rings out from beyond the door. Lo's out of my arms quickly, scrambling to her feet.

"Billy's mum." She stares at the door, like she's dreading seeing her.

Slowly getting to my feet, I join Lo's side. "This is one of those times when I need you to tell me what to do." I rest my hand on her shoulder and gently massage, feeling the tightness there. She's worried.

Her gaze bounces from me to the door a few times, her uncertainty obvious. "You should stay here," she breathes, giving me apologetic eyes. "Billy's mother can be . . . difficult."

I nod my acceptance, though Lo's summary for her mother-in-law doesn't fill me with ease. Difficult? "Okay. I'll be here if you need me."

Lo tries to smile, but her lips are too straight and her jaw too tight. Taking a deep breath, one I know is an attempt to drink down some calming air, she leaves the room. I sit myself on the chair by the door, and my arse has barely met the hard plastic before I hear shouting.

"You selfish little bitch," a woman yells. "How could you?"

I look at the door that's forming a barrier between Lo and me, astounded by the venom in the voice. *Stay where you are, Luke.*

"How could I what?" Lo asks, her return question quiet and calm.

"You know what. Seeing another man while my son was fighting to stay alive."

My eyes close, dread for Lo taking hold. My feet itch where they are on the floor, screaming at me to get up and go to her. To explain. It's an effort to talk myself down. I tell myself that she's his mother, that her emotions are running high. *Stay out of it.* So I push myself farther into the back of the chair, fighting to regulate my increasingly agitated breathing.

"Luke is a friend."

"A friend?" she shrieks incredulously. "You liar. Billy knew. How does that make you feel? Your husband knew that you were off gallivanting around town with another man while he was dying."

"He told you?" Lo's astonished voice must match my current expression, my eyes swinging to the door.

"Yes, he told me. Last night he told me. You make me sick."

Then I hear the sound of what can only be a stinger of a slap. I'm out of my chair like lightning. Nothing will keep me back. I heard what Billy said to me. I listened to Lo tell me what he said to her. This woman is his mother. She might have listened to her son, but she didn't hear him.

I fly out of the door and find a nurse fighting to hold back a middle-aged woman, and Lo with her palm covering her cheek. Rage consumes me, my teeth grinding. *What the fuck?*

"You've never looked after him properly." The woman struggles and strains against the nurse, who is demanding she calms down. "You didn't care about him."

"I did a better job than you," Lo retorts, dropping her hand from her face. The handprint there adds fire to the white-hot blood racing through my veins.

The woman calms. She's still snarling, but when she looks past Lo and finds me, I know that calm will be lost again very soon. "I suppose this is him, is it?"

Lo looks over her shoulder, unaware that I'm behind her. She sighs, and I step forward, not wanting to poke the rattlesnake, but definitely wanting to demonstrate my presence. "Are you okay?" I ask.

"Oh, she's fine." Billy's mother laughs coldly. "My son is dead so now you can continue your affair without him in the way."

My nostrils flare. "There was no affair," I grate. "Lo's done everything a wife should." Lo reaches for my forearm and squeezes, a silent signal to keep my cool. I will keep my cool. But I refuse to have this woman rip Lo apart any more than I know she's ripping herself apart already.

She tugs her bag onto her shoulder and looks at me like I'm something stuck to the bottom of her shoe. "You should be ashamed of yourself. What kind of man are you?"

"I'm a man who was there for your daughter-in-law when no one else was." I take Lo's arm and turn her, set to get her away from this poisonous woman, but she resists, keeping herself facing Billy's mother.

"I'll let you know about the funeral arrangements, Linda." Lo turns and walks away, and I follow, itching to escape the bad feeling lingering in the air. It shouldn't be like this. Family should come together during tragic times, not tear one another apart. "Difficult?" I say as we reach my car, opening the door for Lo.

"She's never liked me." Lo drops into the seat and pulls her belt on, staring forward out of the windscreen. "After the funeral, she'll never have to see me again."

The funeral. Something else Lo will need to guide me on. And what about now? I know I said I'd take charge, but I'm being cautious too. "What do you want to do now, Lo?"

She thinks for a short while before craning her neck to look at me. "I don't want to be alone."

"I don't want you to be alone, either," I assure her. But I don't think I can stay at her house. A man's house is his castle and all. That's Billy's castle. I have no place there.

"Can I come to your house?"

I don't think I do a very good job of hiding my relief. "You can stay with me for as long as you want." I know she didn't ask if she could *stay* with me per se, but I want her to know that she's welcome.

"Thank you."

I raise my finger to my lips and shush her silently.

Chapter Thirty-Three

I showed Lo to the guest room next to mine. It was the right thing to do, and she didn't argue. I suggested a walk in the afternoon that she gladly accepted, so we hooked the dogs up and ambled through the nearby park for nearly two hours while the dogs romped around, oblivious to the heaviness hanging in the air surrounding their owners. She didn't speak once, and I didn't try to force her, my main objective to just be there with her. To let her try and process her loss. But I fear there's not enough time in the world.

When we got back to my place, I forced her to eat a sandwich —tuna, no cucumber—and drink some tea, and I let her go up to her room when she silently slipped out of the kitchen. She needs space. I'm willing to let her have as much space as she needs.

I spend the rest of the afternoon catching up on emails in my home office, and checking in with Tia, Todd, and Pops. Their compassionate tones were nearly too much to bear, and it made me appreciate all the more what Lo's had to contend with these past few years. It also made me wonder where her friends were. Where were the two women she'd gone out for drinks with? Where is the group of friends from their wedding photos? Why weren't they the ones Lo called at the hospital? *Why is she so alone?*

My family and friends are offering me comfort, and yet it's not I who has lost someone. Technically, I've found someone. I should be delighted, my friends and family should be delighted, but the circumstances surrounding my journey to finding my one true love can't allow me to celebrate it. How can I when I've watched Lo's world fall apart? I can only pray that I can put it back together for her. I want to be the man who helps her find happiness again.

Staring at the Google search bar on my screen, I tap in *"Mildred Rose"* and begin to scroll through the results. There aren't many, and most of them are obituaries. My heart sinks as I click my way through all the articles, looking for key information that'll tell me if any of these Mildred Roses are Pops's Milly. None were born in 1927 or 1928. Not one. Biting my lip, I click on one final result, a page from the BT Phonebook. I'm not optimistic as I read the address in Brighton, but it's my only shot. I call the landline number given, and it rings and rings. I'm about to hang up when a female voice answers. A sweet, *old* female voice.

I sit up straight in my chair, wishing I'd prepared better for this. "Hello, I'm hoping you can help me."

A tut comes down the line. "I have double glazing, I have a new boiler, and I don't want cavity wall insulation," she declares.

I smile a little. "I'm not a salesman."

"Then what are you?"

"I'm looking for a lady called Mildred Rose."

"Who's asking?"

I clear my throat on a hesitant laugh. "My name is Luke Williamson. I'm the grandson of Bert Williamson." There's a shocked inhale of breath down the line. It makes me sit up in my chair, alert. "Is that name familiar to you?"

"Yes," she barely whispers. "Yes, it is."

"Milly?"

There's a long, long silence, and for a moment I panic that she might hang up. "Yes."

I breathe out, a million questions charging forward. "You met my grandfather in 1946."

"I did. He nearly ran me down on a flaming pushbike."

My grin is face-splitting. "It's his favorite story. He tells me it all the time."

"All the time? Oh my gosh, he's still alive?"

"Oh, yes. He's alive and kicking all right." I chuckle, hearing her gasp, before silence falls again. "Are you okay?"

"I just need to sit down, dear. Oh my goodness. How is he?"

"He's very well, thank you. Frequently causing havoc in the independent retirement home where he lives."

She chuckles too, and it's the sweetest sound. "He was always a comedian."

"Nothing's changed, Milly. Can I call you Milly?"

"Of course you can, my dear. You must get your chivalrousness from your grandfather. Are you close?"

"Very. At the risk of sounding mushy, he's my hero."

"He was my hero too." She pauses for a beat, and then sighs. "But it wasn't meant to be. You must be the son of Bert's son, yes?"

"Yes," I confirm, knowing she'll be remembering the reason Pops walked away from her.

"And why on earth are you calling me?"

I go in for the kill. She can only say no, and Pops will never have to know. "How would feel about seeing Pops again?"

She inhales sharply. "See Bert? Does he want to see me?"

"He doesn't know I've been trying to find you," I confess sheepishly. "I want it to be a surprise. He's been in love with you all these years, Milly. He's never forgotten you, and my own life has been impacted so much by your story. It would mean the world to me if you would agree." I scold myself for resorting to begging and tugging on her heartstrings, which is basically what

I'm doing. What if she's happily married and doesn't want to see—

"Okay," she says simply, shocking me.

I shoot up from my chair. "Really?"

She laughs lightly. "I'm too old to live with regrets."

"Thank you. Thank you so much. When? I'll pick you up. I'll take you home. You don't need to worry about transport."

"That's good, because I'm not as mobile as I was in 1946."

I look to the office door, thinking of Lo upstairs sleeping. About the funeral. I don't know when it'll be just yet, and I'd much rather do this after Lo lays Billy to rest. "Can I call you in the next few days? You see, my friend just lost her husband and I need to help with the funeral arrangements. Be here for her."

"Oh, that is a pity. Yes, of course. You just call me when you're ready. I'll be waiting."

I smile brightly for the first time in days. "Speak soon, Milly."

"Goodbye, Luke, dear."

I hang up and stand over my desk, somewhere between excitement and apprehension. I've found her.

"You okay?" Lo's voice creeps into my office, and I pivot to find her looking sleepy in the doorway. My excitement would be totally inappropriate right now, so I dampen it down. I have to tell her, though.

"I found Milly Rose."

Her sleepy eyes squint. "Who's Milly Rose?"

For a second, I stall. *Who's Milly Rose?* Then my shoulders drop. I've heard the story so many times, have been thinking about it so much recently, that I forgot Lo doesn't know. "Sit down," I order gently, taking her hand and leading her to the couch. A bit bewildered, she waits for me to explain. "Something happened to Pops years ago and he's got this bee in his bonnet about it." I pause a beat. "And us."

"Us?"

"I mean how we came to be friends."

"Right . . ." she says slowly, encouraging me to go on.

"In 1946 Pops nearly ran a woman over."

"Wow." Lo bites her lip, thinking for a second. "Milly Rose?" she questions, and I nod. "Your pops mentioned her. I thought it might be your grandmother."

I shake my head. "Milly was the love of his life," I explain. "But he couldn't be with her." I feel my cheeks heat slightly with embarrassment when Lo's eyes widen.

"Why couldn't they be together?"

"Well, Pops had been sewing his seed." I give her a cheeky smirk. "He'd been to war and got back with a set of blues balls."

She chuckles. "Sounds painful."

"Trust me, it is." I laugh, but immediately stop when Lo recoils. Shit. I didn't mean to say that. *Onwards, Luke.* "So he was sewing his seed, in particular with my grandmother, but they soon realized there wasn't much spark and that ended," I go on. "Then he nearly ran down Milly on his pushbike. They spent the summer together, fell in love. Then my grandmother showed up pregnant."

"Oh . . ."

"Back then, you definitely married a woman who you got pregnant. Pops had no choice but to walk away from Milly Rose and marry my grandmother."

I see realization dawn on her tired face. "That's why Pops told you not to marry Tia's mother," she says, and I nod. "Did he ever see Milly again?"

"No, but he says there's not a day goes by when he doesn't think about her. My grandmother was a wonderful woman and Pops was a devoted husband and father, but he never forgot Milly. He said she was his soul mate."

"That's so sad, but a happy story too."

"Sad because he lost Milly, but happy because he lived a long, rich life with my grandmother?"

"Hmmm," she hums, briefly looking past me. Happy and sad. *Can you be both?* "And you've found her?"

I nod, elated to see a glimmer of happiness in her expression. It sure is a sight for sore eyes. The best. "She's agreed to see Pops. He doesn't know. I'm going to surprise him."

Lo's shining expression fills me with hope. "I think he'll love that."

"Me too." I try to imagine his face when he sees her. I can't. He'll think he's died and gone to heaven. "I'm going to pick her up. She lives in Brighton."

"When?"

"I don't know. I didn't want to be too hasty, what with . . ."

"What with Billy's funeral. You can say it, Luke."

My lips press together, showing my discomfort. "How are you feeling?"

"Okay." She shrugs and looks at her phone, rejecting the call immediately.

Her hasty move brings something back to me. The call I took from someone chasing Lo for unpaid bills. Now isn't the best time, but I need to lessen her worry as much as possible. "Lo, when I brought your phone to you at the hospital, I took a call from someone."

She looks up through her lashes at me. "You did?" She knows where this is leading, her discomfort obvious. The last thing I want to do is make her feel uncomfortable. I take her hand and kneel in front of her on the couch. "How much do you owe?"

She pulls her hand out of mine and looks away. "Nothing. I owe nothing."

"Lo . . ."

"Luke, please don't. I already feel like a failure. Please don't highlight my shortcomings."

If there were any words that could stir the anger within me, she just said them. I snatch her hands back and lock down so she can't escape. "Use the money I gave you for Billy's operation to pay them off." She shakes her head, and I nod mine. "This isn't up for discussion. You *will* do it. Is there enough?"

"More than enough," she splutters. "But that's not the point, Luke. I've been a burden on you since the day I met you. I'm not your responsibility. I was going to transfer it all back to you, but . . . what with . . ." She swallows, breathing in deeply, her beautiful silver eyes glazing again. "I just hadn't got around to asking for your bank details."

My anger increasing, I lift on my knees and grab her cheeks, getting my face close to hers so she can see just how serious I am. "You have never been a burden. Don't ever say that to me again."

"What are you still doing here with me?" she asks over a sob. "Why are you voluntarily putting yourself through my hell?"

"Because I'm hoping your journey through hell will be a lot less painful with me by your side," I say quietly. "I'm not looking for anything else but your happiness, Lo. For your peace. Whether that is with me in your life or not isn't at the forefront of my mind. I just need your peace."

"You're mad."

"Probably," I say. "But love makes you mad, right?"

Her palms wrap around my wrists where I'm holding her face, pulling them down. And she tries so hard to smile at me, but she doesn't say anything. I wouldn't want or expect her to. Besides, I just . . . know. I run a thumb under each of her eyes, wishing the brightness back. The glimmer I saw when she laughed at me. The moments of fleeting happiness.

The front door closing in the distance attracts both of our attention, and I sigh, pulling Lo up from the couch. "It's probably Todd or Tia. I'll understand if you want to escape upstairs."

"No, I can't hide forever. And I'd like to meet your daughter. I mean, if she wants to."

I see a wealth of doubt pass over her. "I'm sure she'd love to," I say to ease her. "You'll get to meet her new boyfriend too."

"Oh?"

The displeasure that I feel, and that no doubt Lo can see, isn't stoppable. "He's asked me for her hand in marriage."

Lo's face lights up. It's comparable only to a long-lost sun breaking through the dense, bleak clouds. "That's wonderful."

"Is it? They've known each other a few weeks and . . ." I trail off when I notice the sarcastic look Lo's quickly sporting. "Point taken," I mutter indignantly. She's right. I'm a hypocritical idiot.

We head for the kitchen, which is alive with happy chit-chat. "Hey," I say, cutting that conversation dead in its tracks. Tia and The River are obviously awkward. I try to give a look to suggest they should act normal. They don't catch it.

"We'll leave you alone." Tia knocks The River's elbow.

"No." I direct Lo to a stool and sit her down. "I'd like you to meet Lo. Lo, this is my long-lost daughter, Tia, and her friend, Trent."

"Boyfriend," Tia corrects, ignoring the roll of my eyes as she approaches Lo. My daughter's smile is sympathetic, and I mentally yell at her to rein it in. "I'm so sorry for your loss."

I slump where I stand, throwing Lo an apologetic smile. I can't chastise Tia for it, though. That's what people do when someone loses a loved one. They offer their condolences.

"Yes, me too." Trent raises a hand in awkward acknowledgment. "That's rough, man."

Oh, Jesus. "Drink, anyone?"

Lo slips down from the stool and backs away. My heart sinks. "Actually, I think I might lie down, if you don't mind. It was lovely to meet you both."

"Of course." Tia's face takes on another level of sympathy. "I understand."

Lo smiles, so forced, and disappears out of the kitchen. "Tia," I hiss, so bloody annoyed.

"What?" She shows the ceiling her palms. "What am I supposed to say to her?"

I start snatching down mugs from the cupboard, not bothering to answer. Because, truth is, I don't know what she should have said.

"Dad?" I don't like the slow way she says that.

I continue making coffee. "What?"

"I know you're thinking about Lo right now, but what about you?"

"What about me?" I fetch the milk from the fridge, silently willing her not to go there. I can't think beyond this moment. Now. How I can be here for Lo. I pour and stir, and then I have nothing left to do except try and face my daughter. I haven't seen her for months. You'd think I'd want to stare at her for as long as I could, but I don't. Not with that empathy riddling her pretty face.

"Everything about you, Dad."

I languidly turn around, hoping she sees the effort it takes me and notes my reluctance to have this conversation. "I'm forty-two years old, Tia. I've never met a woman who has consumed me like that woman up there." I point to the kitchen door, though Tia doesn't look. She just gazes at me with a mixture of sadness and that dreaded sympathy. "I love her, darling. As much as I love you, and you know how much that is." I expect a peeved face, but it doesn't come. "I just have to hope she'll eventually see me here, waiting for her."

"What if she doesn't?"

I retreat and think really hard about her question—the question I have silently asked myself a thousand times. "Then I'll still be here for her."

Quite unexpectedly, Tia's eyes well with tears and she runs to me and cuddles me like I need to be cuddled. It offers me a moment's solace, a place to hide, and as I look up and see The River soundlessly watching my daughter comfort me, I give him a mild nod, silently giving him my blessing.

No man should be kept from the woman he loves.

Chapter Thirty-Four

Sleep isn't easy to find. I'm shattered, yet the damn land of nod is clearly playing an unfair game of hide and seek, and I can't fucking seek. I toss, I turn, I slam my head down on the pillow a million times in frustration, and I count two hundred woolly fucking sheep.

No sleep.

I'm pondering the benefits of downing a bottle of Scotch when I hear a shuffle of movement outside my door. Steve stirs on the end of the bed as the door opens quietly and bathes my room in a soft blanket of light. Lo's silhouette appears, and she starts padding over toward my bed, Boris on her heels. She's getting into bed with me? I still, hardly breathing and, quite childishly, I slam my eyes shut and pretend to be in that illusive place of slumber. If I'm asleep, I can't technically object when she gets into bed with me. I can't consider the consequences of the guilt that will possibly bury her tomorrow. The fact that I'm actually wide awake and capable of pointing out the disadvantages of her intentions will be a secret I'll keep forever. I'm here for her. No matter what. No matter how much it kills me. And I will not fault Lo for this either. Yes, she knows that I love her and that this could be hard for me, but as I told her earlier, she is not and has never been a burden to me. I'm glad she's allowing me to comfort her, and the fact that she's survived the last two years without affection still astounds me. Especially from the man she'd planned to live the rest of her days with. And I truly understand the need to be touched by someone. Even if it's only a cuddle.

She crawls in, snuggling into my side and, shame on me, I sleepily lift my arm to give her space. She sighs and settles while Boris joins Steve, and with her held close to me, I settle too, sleep now finding me quickly.

When I wake the next morning, I feel refreshed and sated after a good night's sleep. But I'm alone in bed. I lie quietly in the dim light, thinking hard about whether I was dreaming last night, or whether she really did crawl into bed and snuggle with me all night. I stroke up the mattress beside me to the pillow, feeling a lingering warmth there. Then I roll over, my movement wafting the pillows and blankets. The faint scent of Lo hits my senses, waking me fully. *Where is she?*

I drag myself out of bed and make my way downstairs, groaning as I stretch my arms up, feeling every muscle in my back pull satisfyingly. The sound of chatter hits me as I approach the kitchen, and I enter to find Lo and Tia sitting at the breakfast bar, both with their hands wrapped around steaming mugs of coffee. Lo is showered and dressed in some worn skinny jeans and an over-sized shirt, her hair pulled into a scruffy knot at the nape of her neck, and Tia is still in her pajamas. Both look up when they hear my bare feet hit the cold tiles.

"Morning." Tia smiles, wide awake and chipper. Her greeting directs my eyes down to her ring finger. It's bare. No proposal yet?

"Morning." I join them, seeing the dogs dashing around garden out the window. I help myself to the pot of coffee, returning Lo's smile. "Where's Trent?"

"Still sleeping. His body clock is all over the place." Tia slurps her coffee, looking over her mug at me with high brows.

The coffee pot pauses in midair as I go to set it down. "What?"

"You forgot to put some clothes on."

I look down my torso to my boxers and my bare thighs and shrug, hearing Lo laugh under her breath.

"It's fine, Tia. I've seen it all before." Lo suddenly sits up straight. "His chest, I mean." Her cheeks flame.

I mentally try to assess her disposition. Aside from her embarrassment, her face is fresh and free of makeup, and her cheeks aren't red and blotchy with tears. She looks well-rested. "You okay?"

Lo nods as Tia slips down off the stool and excuses herself. "I need to get ready." She beats a hasty retreat, leaving me and Lo alone.

"Did you sleep well?" I ask, and she nods again, taking the small jug of milk and pouring some into my mug. "Thank you." I smile and take a seat beside her.

"I hope you don't mind that I helped myself." Lo raises her mug before taking a small sip.

"Don't be daft." I brush her concern aside, starting to nibble on my bottom lip. "Did I imagine you in bed with me last night?"

Her mug falters on its way back to the table, and I detect her discomfort. "I couldn't sleep." She smiles awkwardly. "I'm sorry if I overstepped the mark."

Placing my hand over hers, I squeeze gently. "Did you sleep after hijacking my bed?"

She presses her lips together, hiding her small smile. "Yes."

"Then I served my purpose well." I wink cheekily, trying to relax her, and go back to my coffee casually. "Have you eaten?"

"I'm not very hungry." As she says that, her tummy growls, and her hand starts to circle it over her shirt.

I raise a questioning eyebrow. "I don't think your stomach agrees."

"It's churning too much. I wouldn't keep anything down if I ate."

"You need to eat, Lo." I try to keep my voice soft, yet I hear the annoyance I've not concealed too well. "Just some toast or something." Without waiting for her agreement, I get up and load some bread in the toaster before letting the dogs in. Once the toast has popped up, I spread it lightly with butter, not too much, and slide the plate before her. She looks down at the toast like it's the biggest challenge she could face.

"I have to go to the funeral directors soon," she says to the plate.

"Would you like me to come?"

"I'm not sure." She looks up at me as I take a slice of toast and put it in her hand.

"Just tell me if you do. Or I can drop you off and pick you up. Whatever you want." I nudge her hand toward her mouth. "Eat."

She takes the smallest bite and spends ages chewing her way through it before swallowing on a wrinkle of her nose. "I think I'll go on my own. Billy's mother might be there, and I can't handle another confrontation."

It pains me, but I nod in understanding. "Do you want me to take you?"

"Do you mind?"

"Of course I don't mind. I'll get ready." Heading for the shower, I turn back at the door and point at the plate. "You don't leave the table until that's all gone." I'm deadly serious, though she smiles and takes a sarcastic bite. "Good girl." I carry on my way but get pulled to a stop when she speaks.

"Luke?"

I turn to face her. "Yes, darling?"

Her eyes drop to the table and she shakes her head. "Nothing."

I don't push her. The poor woman must feel like she's in a vortex of emotions. She's lost her husband, who told her to let me, a stranger to him, love her. My head is still unable to wrap itself around Billy's dying words. How he looked at me. The resolution in his unstable voice. I can only imagine the state of Lo's mind.

I can only love her if she lets me.

And I'm petrified that no matter what Billy said, guilt won't allow her to do that.

Ever.

Part Eight

Lo

Chapter Thirty-Five

My life feels like a split between a thunderstorm and the calm and peace that can be found in the eye of a hurricane. I feel empty and lost, at the mercy of the destruction tainting my life, but calm and serene too. Almost accepting. The calm comes when I think of Luke. The hopelessness comes when I think of Billy. My mind is constantly split. Loss and hope.

I can't believe he's gone. I can't believe the things he said to me before he slipped away from this world. My head could explode with questions—questions I wish I could ask him.

As I stand before his lifeless body in the funeral home, I realize I *can* ask him. Yet I know I won't get any answers. My eyes journey down his body. He's in a suit. Billy never wore suits. His hair is combed to the side. He never wore his hair like that. They've attempted to inject color into his gaunt face with thick makeup, trying to make him look as close to the Billy that I married. He looks nothing like the man I married. He hasn't looked like the man I married for years. Now, lying here, he looks like a poorly made-up mannequin. I wish I'd never come. This isn't an improvement on the dying man I loved. This isn't my Billy.

I pull out a picture from my bag. This is the man I married. Fresh, fit, healthy, and full of zest for life. I stare at the image of us on our wedding day, all laughter and smiles, and a single tear tumbles down my cheek. This was the last time Billy was seen smiling properly. It was the last time he picked me up and swirled me around. It was the last time he held my hand with strength and ownership. A teardrop hits the picture, and I frantically brush it away before it can soak into the paper.

"Do you know how much it hurt me every time you told me to leave you?" I ask his smiling face. "It hurt terribly. I would never have abandoned you. Never. You were a stubborn, cantankerous sod, but I would never have left you." Keeping my voice steady is easier than it should be. Perhaps because I need him to hear each word clearly. "I love you, Billy. More than my own life, I love you. Asking me to leave you was cruel. And I don't think I'll ever understand why you distanced yourself from me. How you pushed me away. I'll never understand why you kept your walls up and didn't allow me to have that extra time with you, when I needed it. I needed it so much. And, honestly, I'm not sure I'll ever forgive you for that." I feel my voice starting to break and find some tissues, wiping my face and blowing my nose.

This. Hurts. God, it hurts so much.

I'll never stop loving him, but I hope and pray that one day I'll be less angry with him. I needed more time. I *wanted* more days.

I lower myself to a nearby chair, keeping my eyes on his picture, feeling like I have a connection far deeper than any time since Billy was diagnosed. "I never slept with Luke," I say. "But he's cuddled me a lot. I needed those cuddles, Billy. I needed them so much." My voice finally fails me, and I spend a few minutes breathing steadily, trying to keep myself together. "Luke isn't a bad man. He just tried to be there for me. When he told me that he'd fallen in love with me, I was stunned. I mean, who could possibly love me other than my husband? And now you're gone, and I don't know what to do." I lose my battle and tears begin to pour from my eyes unstoppably, my words now cracked and broken, and I'm furious about that. I want them to be steady. Together. Billy would want me to be together. "I don't want you to feel inadequate. I don't want to feel this guilt that's chewing away at my insides. I feel guilty because I'm relieved you're no longer suffering. I'm relieved you're now at rest. And I feel guilty for looking at Luke and being glad he's here for me." I grit my teeth. "I don't want you to haunt him forever if I can't let him look after me. Promise you won't do that," I demand, shaking his picture lightly. "Promise me, Billy." More tears form and start to gush, my stability leaving me completely. "Promise me," I shout at him. I drop the picture when I get no answer, burying my face in my hands and sobbing my heart out. My stomach's aching from the force of my crying, my eyesight as blurred as my world feels. There's no definition. No clear direction for me to head in. I feel trapped between worlds, more helpless now than I've ever felt before.

Hiding seems like the only way. Hiding with the hope that when I'm found, everything will be much better. That I won't hurt so much. That I won't feel as though my heart has shattered into a million pieces. That I won't feel so hopeless.

After numbly being walked through the arrangement with the funeral directors, I step outside into the rain, not bothering to find my umbrella in my bag. The rain feels good pelting at my scalp. I feel like I'm in limbo, caught between life and death. Between turmoil and peace.

I'll bury Billy on Friday. I'll give up his broken body to the ground where it'll decompose and rot to nothing. But, really, Billy started to decay two years ago.

"Lo, what are you doing?" Luke rushes across the road toward me, his arm bent over his head in a poor attempt to shield himself from the pounding rain. "I've been honking my horn at you."

"I didn't hear you." I catch sight of his car across the street. It's in exactly the same place as it was when he dropped me here over an hour ago. "Have you been waiting this whole time?"

He drops his arm, his green eyes framed with lashes that are weighed down with raindrops. "Always," he murmurs. There's more meaning to his words than just simply waiting for me today. I know that. And yet, I have no room in my mind to process it.

I quickly look away from him. "The funeral is on Friday. Leaving from my house at eleven." I go to my phone and start texting Linda. "I need to let Billy's mum know. And our friends."

"Okay, darling, but shall we do that in the car?"

I look up blankly, now not feeling the rain at all. Luke, however, must be, because his shoulders are high, his face soaking and twisted. I let him guide me across the road and help me into his BMW. The warmth sinks into my wet clothes, condensation spreading across the windows. "I want you to come to the funeral," I say to my phone as I click *Send* on the message to Linda before composing a generic one for our friends. *Did I even message them and tell them he was gone?*

I look at Luke when he doesn't respond, finding an expressionless face. "I want you to come," I repeat. I don't care what Linda says. I don't care what people think. The thought of facing it alone is enough to make me not want to go to my own husband's funeral.

"Then I will." His words are strong and resolute.

I nod and return forward. "Good."

I don't know how I get to Friday. I don't recall much of the past few days. I've slept for most of it, ate little, and privately agonized over my decision to ask Luke to be here. I'm standing on the grave's edge, staring into the black hole at Billy's coffin. It's a perfect day for a funeral—bleak, gray, and cold. The priest's words are distant and undistinguishable through the fog of my mind. I slowly cast my eyes around me, to all the people with their heads bowed. I haven't seen many of them for years. It's sickening how death encourages people out from wherever they've been hiding, their need to be here more selfish than supportive. They'll go home and resume their lives like nothing ever happened. They'll get back on the merry-go-round of life, and I'll be floundering on the side, wondering why their lives haven't been ripped apart like mine.

Billy's mother catches my eye opposite, her glassy stare nailed to me. She's not happy. I drop my gaze back to the black hole, unable to face her disapproval. We stood quietly in my house, waiting for the funeral cars to arrive this morning. She didn't speak to me, and I didn't speak to her. The journey to the church was deathly quiet. It was only when she saw Luke in one of the aisles that she spoke to me. "Have you no shame?" she asked. I didn't answer. Shame was definitely lingering somewhere inside of me, somewhere deep—has been since I met Luke—but, as always, his mere presence blanketed that shame with comfort that I'm too desperate for. He's kept a respectful distance. Until now.

As I step forward to drop some earth onto Billy's coffin, I stagger. I'm not sure if it's the uneven ground that causes my stumble, or my weak legs. Regardless, Luke's by my side in a heartbeat, his arm wrapped around my waist to steady me. I look up at him, but he doesn't acknowledge me. He simply walks me toward the edge of Billy's grave and holds me steady while I release the pile of dirt in my hand. And then he constricts his hold minutely.

"Earth to Earth, ashes to ashes, dust to dust," the priest solemnly mumbles.

I remain by the graveside with Luke long after everyone has filtered away to make their way to the wake. I'm dreading the wake. At the wake, I'll be forced to interact. I don't want to stand in a room of people I barely know anymore and listen to them tell me what a good man Billy was. I already know that. I don't want to force smiles and let them embrace me. I don't want to do it. My throat clogs up with anxiety. I think it might finish me off. I've said my goodbye. I've prayed for him. Socializing with all the previously absent mourners isn't appealing to me at all. In fact, it's making me panic.

"I think it would be wise for me to skip the wake," Luke says out of the blue.

I swing my stare up to him in horror. "What?"

He's clearly agonized over this, his face pained. "I've paid my respects, Lo. You can't stop people from being curious about me, and I honestly feel if I turn up at the wake, that curiosity will be fueled. I'll just be giving Linda more ammunition. I'm not prepared to put you in that position." He looks across the cemetery to check we're now alone before he wraps an arm around my neck and pulls me into his chest, cuddling me with a strength I'm envious of. "I've wanted to do this since I saw you walk into the church."

I relax into him, grateful for his hug. For the first time today, I feel calm and stable. I know he's right. I know asking Luke to accompany me would be deemed inappropriate. But he's my best friend.

"I'll have my phone on hand. The second you need me to come get you, call, okay?"

I nod into his chest, bracing myself to face the wake alone.

I've always wondered what it must feel like to be the center of attention. To reduce a room to silence when you enter it. Now I know. Horrendous would be the word. The large room at Billy's old football club is packed with people, all holding drinks, all staring at me as I enter. It's all I can do not to turn and run away. Breathing in deeply, I head straight for the bar. Within seconds, I'm surrounded by six people who want to buy me a drink. I say yes to them all. Wine, wine, wine, wine, and two more wines. My first goes down in one go. I'll drink my way through the rest of the day. It's the only way I'll survive it.

"Lo, I'm so sorry," says Stu, Billy's ex work colleague.

"He was a blinding bloke," Lee, an old school friend, tells me.

"How are you coping?" someone else asks. *I don't know who.*

"Such a waste of life," Billy's ex college tutor muses sadly. I'm hugged and showered with commiserations while I keep my faithful wine in my hand, gulping it down as I listen to them all. Gareth, Penny, Lewis, and Helen all hug me, but they don't say anything other than asking me if I want another drink. Yes, I want another drink. More drinks. Line them up.

"Take as much time off as you need to," Scarlett says, clucking my cheek like a child.

"I'm so sorry for your loss," Matthew adds.

I've been here only an hour and I've had as much as I can take. *Sorry. My condolences. My deepest sympathy. He was a good man. Such a waste of life.* I might scream if I hear any more. I feel like I'm drowning, and no matter how hard I kick my legs, I can't get to the surface. I pour another glass of wine down my throat as I listen to Billy's mother's neighbor tell me what a delightful child Billy was. How he radiated happiness. Then Linda catches my eye and I know immediately that she's had a few drinks herself. Understandably, of course. She's lost her son. But Linda, alcohol, and her grief means I'm undoubtedly in for an earful. I breathe in as she stomps her way over to me and use the time it takes to drink yet more wine in an attempt to numb myself.

"Didn't bring your lover to your husband's funeral then?" she seethes, drawing attention from every corner of the room. I deflate and grit my teeth, not prepared to get pulled into her showdown.

"He's a friend."

She scoffs, looking me up and down like I'm filth. "You're disgusting."

Breathe, breathe, breathe.

"He's a friend who supported me." I speak resolutely, clearly, and concisely. "Billy thanked Luke for that face to face, and you know it."

"Billy didn't know what he was talking about. He was dying."

The whole room is watching now, ears twitching to know the juicy details. "He knew exactly what he was talking about," I counter, realizing in this exact moment that he really did. He was lucid and calm. Accepting and relieved. He took comfort in the fact that he could pass over to the other world, knowing I wouldn't be alone. Because, let's face it, I had no one except Billy. His mum never really liked me. His father is indifferent. My own mother died, and my father is living in ignorant bliss on the other side of the world. Our friends have their own lives, and . . .

There *was* no one else.

I had no one.

Then I had someone.

I had Luke.

I *have* Luke.

"I don't need to justify myself to you. The only person I care about is Billy, and he understood Luke's and my friendship. He accepted it. I won't let you tarnish your son's good intentions. I won't let you make something beautiful seem sordid and wrong." I finish my wine and face the peanut gallery, wondering where all those words came from. All true words. Words I've struggled to find and accept for days. "Thank you so much for coming, it means more than you'll know." I grab my purse and skirt past Linda, hearing her gasped disgust as I escape.

Pushing my way out of the door, I reach for my phone to call Luke, but I don't get to dial him. He's sitting in the carpark in his BMW waiting for me. Waiting to hold me together. He's been here the whole time. He knew I'd need him. Always there for me.

I exhale, the last of my anxiety leaving me, and hurry over. There's a definite stagger to my steps, the wine reaching my head with the help of fresh air. "Please get me out of here," I beg as I fall into the passenger seat.

"You smell like a wine cellar."

"It was the only way I could get through it." I hiccup and press my lips together. "I'm a little bit drunk."

"You're entitled to be drunk." Luke starts the car and pulls away. "Am I taking you home?"

His question gives me pause. *Home.* My house hasn't been my home since Billy died. It's empty, soulless, and silent. "I think I should move. Get a smaller flat somewhere."

"Okay," Luke agrees easily. "But what now?"

"Just drive. Anywhere. I don't care where."

"I know just the place." Luke hardly even thinks about it, taking a left at the roundabout and putting his foot down when he hits the M25. I rest back in the seat and breathe in deeply, content for him to take me away from here.

Chapter Thirty-Six

Brighton? My neck cranes as we pass the sign welcoming us to the eclectic British seaside town. I've never been here before, despite it being within easy driving distance of the city. After navigating the streets with ease, Luke pulls up on the seafront. It's cold, there's hardly anyone around, and the waves are bashing the shoreline in loud, foamy surges. It's still dull, still drizzly, and the horizon can barely be seen in the distance.

I get out, keeping my eyes on the sea. It might be a dreary day, but it's still beautiful. Oh, how I'd love to see it in the height of summer. I imagine hordes of people, tourists and locals, wandering the promenade, bumming on the beach, paddling at the shore. I breathe in the thick, salty air and sigh. My lingering thudding headache clears for the first time in weeks.

Bunching my hands in my pockets and huddling my shoulders up to my ears, I turn to find Luke. He doesn't have a coat; his only protection from the bitter cold is his suit jacket. "Brrrrrrr," I shudder, the whipping wind made more biting by the sea, working its way into my bones. "Don't you have a coat?"

"No." Luke blows into his hands and rubs them together. "I didn't think this through, did I?"

I look down at my gray trench coat. "I don't think we'll both fit in here."

He smiles and wanders over, his green eyes seeming greener, like they could be reflecting the sea. "I'm a brave man. I'll power through."

"Your lips are turning blue." I surrender the warmth of one of my pockets to reach up to his lips, padding them lightly with my fingertip. "They're freezing."

He moves suddenly, playfully snapping at my fingers. I jump back, startled, and then smack his bicep. The sound of his chuckle takes the edge off my cold skin. "I'm fine." He takes my hand and pushes it back into my pocket before wrapping his arm around my shoulders and tucking me neatly into his side. We start to walk down the promenade, and though I'm wondering why he chose here of all the places he could have driven me, I don't ask. The crisp, briny air, the sound of the sea, it's just what I need. Escape, out of London, away from the relentless sympathy and, now that Linda has spouted her mouth off, the judgments too.

"Do you think I'm a bad person?" I ask. I don't look at him, choosing to keep my eyes on the sea.

"Do you think *I'm* a bad person?" he asks in reply.

"No. You're one of the kindest people I've ever met."

"And so are you."

"Can a person be kind *and* bad?"

"We're not bad, just to be clear." He bumps his hip above mine, and I smile. "I think sometimes people do things that others might frown upon. But it's the right thing for them to do. You can't control how outsiders view your choices, and you shouldn't have to. It was the right thing for me to put myself in your life. It was the right thing to give you the money you needed, and it was right to walk away when I did. At the time, I thought I was making all the right decisions. Hindsight can sometimes be a brutal thing."

"What do you mean?"

"I shouldn't have walked away from you after I'd given you

that money." He looks at me, his lips too straight to smile. "I'm sorry I did that."

"You have nothing to be sorry about."

"And I'm sorry I didn't give you that money sooner." Luke looks ahead, and I see with perfect clarity the tangle his mind is still in over it. By saving Billy, he lost me. But nothing could save Billy. It's not Luke's fault. Though something tells me that no matter how many times I tell him so, he won't believe it.

"They say God has a plan, right?" I realign my focus on the sea, feeling my nose going numb.

"You sound like Pops. He said that."

"I have to have faith in something. Anything to try and make sense of all this." I feel his nod of agreement. "Why did you bring me here?" I ask, letting Luke slow us to a stop at the end of the promenade.

"Take off your shoes." Luke kicks his boots off, and then pulls his socks from his feet, leaving him barefooted on the freezing cold concrete.

"Are you mad?" I ask seriously.

"Take them off."

I frown and dip to rid my feet of my shoes. "I notice you didn't deny it." Wriggling my toes, I shudder, the cold traveling up my legs to my torso. "Oh!" I yelp as Luke scoops me up and starts to carry me down to the shore. "Oh my God, don't you dare take me in there." I cling to his neck tightly, making it as difficult as possible for him to put me down. "Luke!" The sea is getting closer, the salt stronger, the cold colder.

When he reaches the shore, he drops me to my feet and crouches in front of me, rolling the bottoms of my trousers up to my knees. Then he does his own and takes my hand. I look at him in question as he starts to walk forward, tugging me on. He says nothing, just gives me a look of encouragement. I don't know his game, but I fill my lungs, bracing myself for the killer cold, and walk forward with him. The moment the water touches my toes, I crush his hand. "Jesus."

"Keep going," he whispers, hardly heard over the crashing waves.

I shake my head in dismay and keep going until the water is nipping at my ankles. It's still not enough, Luke pulling me onward. Every time a wave crashes in front of us, the spray hits, splashes of icy, salty water hitting our faces and making me flinch. Luke only stops us when the water is midway up my calves.

"It's not safe any farther," he says, showing no signs that he's freezing to bloody death.

"That's a relief," I retort, looking down at the foamy swells of water lapping around my legs. "Why have you brought me into the freezing cold water, Luke?"

"Because I want you to remember something," he says, taking both of my hands and turning into me.

My eyes jump up to his. "What?"

"I want you to remember that you're still alive, Lo."

My throat dries up on me in an instant, my tongue swelling in my mouth, stopping any words passing my lips. I look away from him, staring out across the sea again. I know he's right. I know many people have lost someone they love and have somehow gotten on with their life. But I feel so raw, and the pain is so intense. It's hard to see past that right now. I have someone here, someone devoted and patient, to help me walk the path of grief. I wouldn't want it to be anyone else. He made a promise to Billy. A promise I shouldn't let him break, but I need time to get past the anguish before I can even think about trying to love Luke. Because he doesn't deserve some half-baked love. He deserves everything my heart can offer. I just have to find the strength to build myself up again. And, most significantly, I know he's prepared to wait, tolerant and willing, for me to accept what I have with him and embrace it for what it is. A lifeline. A chance to be happy again. A chance to love with all my might and have that love returned.

I want you to remember that you're still alive, Lo.

Isn't that what Billy wanted too? And if I follow Billy's instructions, that will also mean I'll remember that I can still *love* too. When I can find the peace to do that. I do love Luke, but it's a different love at the moment. And right now, I don't know how to love two men at once.

I sniff back my tears and look back to Luke, who, God love him, is doing what he does best. Being patient. I smile, not forced, but actually very easy. "I can't feel my legs," I tell him, fearing my toes could break off as I wriggle them on the seabed.

His smile is small but blazing. "There's somewhere we need to be."

"There is?" I look over my shoulder.

"Somewhere here in Brighton." He picks me up and walks us back to our pile of socks and shoes.

"Where?" I collect them up, my feet too wet to even entertain putting my shoes back on, and we start to walk barefoot back to Luke's car.

"Remember I said I found Milly Rose?"

I falter in my pace. "Yes." There's excitement in my voice that *nothing* could extinguish. We're in Brighton. Of course.

Luke smiles and nods. "She lives a mile up the road."

"And we're taking her to Pops?" Another nod. "Does he know?" A shake of his head. I squeal. I can't help it. And then without thought, I launch myself at Luke, nearly smacking him around the head with my swinging shoe. He catches me with ease, laughing. "He's going to pee his old pants."

His laughter increases as he carries me back to his car. "He may well do," he agrees. "He may well do."

As soon as we get in the car, Luke cranks the heating up and my feet begin to thaw out. We wrestle in the small space to get our shoes back on before Luke pulls off. The drive to Milly's takes only a few minutes, and Luke slows down to a crawl when we hit the right street, looking around between keeping an eye on the road. "It's around here somewhere. Look out for number four."

"There's number ten," I point out as we roll past. "It must only be a couple of houses up."

"There." Luke pulls into a parking space and points across the road to a small bungalow with a pretty, well-kept front garden and curtains in a busy floral material hanging at the front window. "I feel a bit nervous." He looks at me, somewhat blank. "This woman feels like a legend to me, and now I'm going to meet her."

His nerves are endearing, and I reach over to his knee and squeeze. "Is she expecting us?"

"No, this was a bit spontaneous. I said I'd call."

"What if she's not home?"

"Then we drove an hour to freeze our toes off." Luke gets out of the car, his eyes rooted to the quaint bungalow across the road. I walk around to join him and knock him from his daydream by placing my hand in his.

"Ready?" I ask.

His line of sight doesn't waiver. "Ready."

We wander across the road and up the narrow, paved pathway to a bright red front door. A sign on the letterbox states *"No Doorstep Sales."* Luke laughs and points at it. "She thought I was a salesman when I called." He raps the door and stands back, wriggling his tie into place. Both of us are silent while we wait, listening for any signs that someone is coming to the door.

"I don't think she's home," I say, looking at Luke. The disappointment on his face is rife. "Maybe you should call?"

His shoulders drop, his knuckles tapping the wood of the door again before he reaches to his inside pocket to get his phone. He starts to dial when we hear something come from beyond the wood. I hold my breath, as does Luke, as a catch sounds, followed by another, and another, before the door finally pulls open, revealing a dear old lady with a walking stick. Her bobbed hair is shiny silver, her body round, her bosom beneath her floral blouse ample. The wrinkles on her face are deep, but her skin so smooth. One look at Luke sends her old hand to the edge of the door to hold on, her thin lips parting. "Goodness me," she breathes, old, clear eyes full of wonder. "Well, I needn't ask who you are, dear."

I look at Luke and see a stretched smile. "Hello, Milly."

"I feel like I've been transported back to 1946. Look at you." She wobbles forward on her stick, reaching for Luke's cheek, feeling, smoothing, looking at him in disbelief.

"I'm a bit older than Pops was when you met him."

"So handsome." Her hand pulls back, going to her mouth, her fingertips resting on her lips. "Oh dear, this is all a bit too much." She wobbles, and Luke shoots forward to steady her.

"Are you okay, Milly?"

"Yes. Yes, dear. It's been a long time since my knees have gone weak." She can't take her eyes off Luke, her whole being truly astonished. "Come in, come in."

My heart swells at the scene playing out before me—Luke's tenderness, the endearing shock of Milly. I watch on a small smile as he helps her down the tiny hallway, his big body nearly filling the space. She points her walking stick to a charming room on the right, and I follow them in, gazing around at the chintzy space cluttered with furniture that's too big for the tiny bungalow, every surface loaded with bric-a-brac, trinkets, ornaments, and figurines.

"You can sit there." She indicates to an old brown velvet couch, and Milly lowers gingerly to a high-seated armchair, resting her stick to her side. Then she stares at Luke while he tries to get comfy on the couch. The seat is so low, his body is zig-zagged. I smile and join him.

"This is my friend," Luke says as I take a seat beside him. "Lo. Lo, this is Milly Rose."

"It's so lovely to meet you, Milly."

Her old eyes reluctantly give up Luke to find me. "My dear, are you Luke's friend who lost her husband?"

Luke reaches over to me and rests his palm on my forearm, a

sign of comfort. It occurs to me in that moment that I haven't thought about what a dreadful day it's been for a good twenty minutes. I'm not sure if that's a good thing or a terribly bad thing, don't know whether to feel guilty or not. I strain a smile and nod. "I laid him to rest this morning."

"Oh, my dear girl." Her old face, so woeful for me, doesn't bother me as much as everyone else's compassion, and I have no idea why. "I'm so very sorry. You must be near the same age as I was when I lost my Phillip."

"You lost your husband?" I ask, shuffling forward on my chair. The potential that there is someone sitting before me who has experienced this wretchedness and can maybe offer me some understanding on what lies ahead is almost too overwhelming.

"I did, dear. To that wretched C-word."

"Cancer," I all but breathe.

She nods solemnly, and Luke's hold of my arm shifts to my hand. "It was a dark time."

"Does it get any easier?"

"Time is a wonderful healer, my dear."

I fall into thought, feeling as sorry for Milly as I know she is for me. She lost Pops, and then fate took her husband away too? I look up at Luke next to me. What would I do if I lost him as well? "Did you meet anyone else?" I ask, unable to hold back my probably inappropriate question. Why am I asking? Validation, maybe. To ease my conscience?

When her head shakes, I feel my heart sink, and Luke's grip of my hand constricts. "There was only one other man for me, and he wasn't available."

My sinking heart bottoms out, and Milly's eyes drop to her lap. "You've been on your own ever since?" I ask. That's over fifty years. Fifty years of being alone?

"On my own," she confirms, looking up at me and smiling, though there's no happiness beyond her feigned gesture. I look around the room, seeing only a couple of framed photographs, both black and white. I get up and wander over to the sideboard and pick up the first, being sure not to knock any of the surrounding brass wear and trinkets. The picture is of Milly and a man, standing arm in arm on a pier. She looks trimmer, but the beauty hidden beneath age across the room is obvious in the shot. She was a stunning woman, curvy in all the right places, lips plump and pouting, her curls set and pinned to perfection. I imagine many men fell at her feet. "That's Phillip and me in 1956."

"You're so beautiful," I say, making her chuckle lightly. There's a powerful allure in her eyes, something that would draw men in and hold them rapt. Even as a woman, I can see the magnetism. She was a siren.

Luke joins me and looks at the picture, the pad of his finger running the length of the glass protecting the photo. Glancing at him, I smile, and he returns it on an endearing tilt of his head. He turns to return to the sofa, but pulls to a stop, his stare falling to the other picture among the clutter. Following his hand as he retrieves it, I see Milly again, younger, but just as captivating, and there beside her, standing tall and proud, as handsome as the man standing next to me now, is Pops.

"Oh, wow," I whisper, studying the picture. They're on Trafalgar Square, standing on the edge of the fountain, both laughing, both absolutely beautiful.

"Handsome devil, your grandfather," Milly says from beyond.

"You've kept this all these years?" Luke asks, flashing the photograph at Milly.

"Why wouldn't I?" She sounds almost defensive. "He was my first love."

"I can't believe it," Luke whispers. "You've been on your own all these years. Why didn't you look him up?"

"I wouldn't know where to start, dear. Besides, he married your grandmother. I wasn't about to intrude."

"She's been gone for thirty years." Luke sighs and places the picture of Pops and Milly back in place.

"If things will be, then they will be." She places her hands in her lap, and I find my fingers worrying my wedding band around my finger. She's been alone all this time. No children. It seems like a frightful waste, and it pulls painfully on my heartstrings to hear she found love and lost it again. How cruel can life be? The only man she wanted after losing her husband wasn't available, so she went on alone. Thirty years of them both alone have been wasted. I look at Luke, seeing a man who loves *me*. Milly found someone who loved her twice . . .

And then it hits me. I'm blessed. It seems like a ludicrous thing to conclude, but I am. Beyond my helplessness, beyond my loss, I'm blessed.

"Oh my, how rude of me." Milly pushes her old hands into the arms of her chair to struggle her way up. "I've not even offered my guests a cup of tea."

"No, please, there's no need." Luke crosses the small room in a few strides, encouraging Milly to sit again. He kneels in front of her, taking a hand in both of his. "Do you have many visitors, Milly?"

"Oh yes, dear. Mr. Sands visits on Friday to deliver my groceries, and my late sister's granddaughter pops in from time to time when she's in town."

"She lives out of town?"

"Yes, up north somewhere. Newcastle, maybe. Or is it Hull? I forget."

"That's quite a way," Luke says. "Is she in town often?"

"Once or twice a year, dear. But it's always so lovely to see her."

Luke visibly deflates before my eyes, and my heart clenches for the old lady. She gets one visitor a week? And I can't imagine she gets out much; she's not very mobile at all. The comprehension of her loneliness hits me hard.

"How would you like to go on a little road trip?" Luke asks. "To see Pops."

Her old hand covers her chest, her eyes brimming. "I'm not the young, vivacious blonde I was all those years ago, Luke."

"You're perfect."

"Oh behave, you scoundrel." She smacks his arm on a chuckle. "Are you going to take me now?"

"Yes." Luke stands and turns to me, his face pained. "Will you help Milly pack some things?"

"Pack? Am I staying away for long?" Milly glances around the room, like she could be checking to see if there's anything that needs taking care of while she's gone. There's a plant that will maybe need watering before we leave. That's all.

"It's evening now," Luke says. "It may be too late to bring you home tonight. I thought you could stay at my home? Maybe even for a few days?"

"Oh, a holiday. How exciting."

Luke helps her to her feet and passes her the walking stick. "Lo will help you pack your pajamas."

She chuckles as Luke passes her over to me, and we walk through to the only bedroom. "All these years," she says quietly, turning her old eyes onto me. "All these years we've both been alone. Such a dreadful waste." Her words strike a nerve and I smile, thoughtful, as I prepare her for her reunion. *Such a waste.* I've heard that too many times today. There are many things in life that seem to be *such a waste.* Lost friends. Lost lovers. Poor health. The death of a twenty-nine-year-old man.

But, like Milly, I think I need to embrace what's within reach and cling to it earnestly. The alternative is being alone for the rest of my life. Or until it's deemed acceptable to love again.

402

Chapter Thirty-Seven

God love her, she didn't stop talking the entire way back to London. You would think she never gets the chance to speak to people, and then I remember . . . she really doesn't. Luke and I peek at each other out the corner of our eyes constantly, smiling at her non-stop chitter-chatter, about anything and everything, the trees, the birds, the fields, the barren M25. She has something to say about everything, and Luke and I indulge her enthusiasm for the outside world, even stopping for a Starbucks at a service station. Milly called it *"fashionable coffee like she's seen on the TV"* as we walked her back to the car. I was stunned she'd never even tried a cup before.

When we're half an hour away from the city, Luke makes a call to Todd, asking him to pick up Pops and take him to Luke's house. Obviously, he's curious, but Luke refuses to tell.

Milly is full of oohs and aahs as we roll to a stop outside Luke's impressive home, her neck craned to look. It's a million miles away from the poky bungalow she's just come from, and her wonder is evidence of that.

"I have butterflies in my tummy. I haven't had butterflies since 1946." She's unsteady on her feet, more unsteady than usual, and she's relying on Luke to help her up the steps. "Do I look okay?" Milly asks, forcing Luke to stop. She looks at him, clinging to his arm for support. Her dusky-pink floor-length skirt and matching blouse are lovely on her, the pearls around her neck finishing it perfectly. She's even boofed up her hair a little, and I definitely detect a hint of stain on her lips. There's no need for blush. Her cheeks are tinged pink with excitement and nerves.

"You look beautiful, Milly," Luke says softly, stroking her cheek. "You'll make his old knees weak, I just know it."

"Oh, you rascal," she scolds on a shy giggle, letting Luke tuck her arm into his.

I join her other side, taking her walking stick and bag so she can link arms with me, too. "Are you ready, Milly?"

"I'm ready." She looks up at the door on an assertive nod, which is followed by some not-so-sure words. "What if he isn't happy to see me?"

Luke scoffs at the mere suggestion. "That's not going to happen, I assure you." He leads us on at a slow pace that Milly can cope with, and the door opens as we approach, Tia appearing. Her instant, gaping mouth tells me she knows who this is.

Milly looks around the grand entrance hall in awe, her fingers clawing into my forearm the farther we get inside.

"This is a bit posh, isn't it?"

I smile as Todd appears, followed by two very excitable dogs. "Boris," I coo, handing Milly's things to Todd to free up a hand and give Boris some fuss. God, I've missed him. "Has he been okay?" I ask, and Todd nods.

"Yeah, I've got a right good doggy day care thing going on. I'm thinking of a career change. They're quite therapeutic, aren't they?"

Luke laughs as Milly chuckles at the dogs doing laps around her feet.

"He's reading his paper in the lounge," Todd says with a smile.

"Thanks, mate. Ready, Milly?"

"Just hold me up, dear," she replies as we help her along. Luke turns as we near the door, his deep green eyes packed with excited sparkles as he smiles at me across Milly's head. I feel my own stomach flutter madly, my lungs straining to collect air. When I look up, I see Pops at the far end of the room sitting in the window, his nose buried in a paper. He looks dapper, one fine, handsome man.

Milly's slow shuffles falter, her intake of breath sharp, and we're forced to stop in the middle of the room for her to collect herself. Her eyes are instantly watery, her chin trembling.

"Pops?" Luke calls.

The old man looks up from his paper, an instant smile on his face at the sound of his grandson's voice. But his delight plummets from his face when he spots the woman standing between us, his paper falling from his grasp into his lap.

I feel the weight of Milly become heavier on my arm.

"I found someone who wanted to see you," Luke says quietly.

Pops looks lost in shock, his green eyes blinking repeatedly as he stares at Milly. "Hello, Bert," Milly says softly. Her voice seems to flick Pops out of his stupor, and he slowly rises from his chair.

"Mildred?" he says, staring hard. "Is that really you?"

"Yes, Bert." Milly pries herself from our holds and steps forward without the aid of her stick. Like Pops has given her life. Stability. "Yes, it's really me."

"My God." He loses his ability to stand and collapses back to the chair, but his eyes never stray from the dear lady before him. "You're as beautiful as I remember."

She shuffles forward some more, ignoring my attempts to pass her walking stick. "And you're as devilishly handsome as I remember."

Pops is out of his chair in a heartbeat, a new lease of life taking over. He paces forward to Milly and takes the tops of her arms, scanning her face, feeling her cheeks, running his hands over her gray hair. "Am I dreaming?"

"No, Bert." Her old hands find his and happy tears burst from her eyes on a gasp of disbelieving laughter. "It's really me."

Every muscle in my throat tightens and makes it impossible for me to swallow, the dying muscle in my chest being injected with life and hope. I watch, so emotional, as Pops's shock turns into tears, and he pulls his long-lost love into his tweed suit jacket and cuddles her tightly.

"Oh my goodness," I breathe, feeling my own knees go weak. I lean into Luke's side, my hand resting on his chest as I watch the reunion through clouded vision.

"Okay?" Luke drapes an arm over my shoulder.

"I don't know if I should be sad or happy," I admit. "All these years they've been apart."

"Be happy, Lo. Look at them. It's like they were never separated."

I do look at them, carefully, admiring the old couple who have to keep touching each other to make sure they've not died and gone to heaven.

Pops's old hands encases Milly's and he leads her to where he was sitting, helping her down to a chair before dragging his as close as he can to be near her. And they just look at each other, Milly giggling every now and then, Pops shaking his head in wonder.

"I never should have left you," Pops says solemnly.

"Now then, Bert. We'll be having none of that nonsense." She smacks his knee. "I didn't travel all this way to listen to your regrets. I came to see you."

Their hands hold between them, and they talk like they've never been apart, laughing, gasping, touching, feeling. They're in their own world, and it's one of the most beautiful things I've ever seen.

"I don't think we'll be missed if we leave them for a while." I glance at Luke, who isn't without emotion either. I swipe the pad of my thumb under his eye, but he reaches up and catches my hand, taking it to his mouth and kissing my knuckles.

"Come," he whispers, pulling me out of the room and leading me to his office. I know what he's going to say before he says it.

He gets me inside and closes the door. "I'll wait for you as long as I need to, Lo." Dropping my hand, he clasps my face, bringing his forehead to mine. "Ten years, twenty, one hundred. However long it takes. You'll never be alone, I promise."

I nod as best I can in his hold, telling him I get it. I understand. And we stare. For the longest time, we just stare at each other, our hands remaining in place. His green eyes spill sincerity all over me. I need him to know how much he means to me. Words just don't seem enough anymore.

My eyes drop to his lips and I slowly advance, until our flesh skims so delicately. He breathes out, starting to shake before me, as he pushes his mouth firmer to mine. "Lo, what are you doing?" he asks against my lips. I'm at war in my head, swaying back and forth between accepting and denying us.

My soft lips travel across his and down, reaching his jaw. My heart is pounding as I peck lightly and nuzzle into his scruff. "Loving you," I whisper.

Acceptance. It's a beautiful thing. A release.

Sliding my face out of his neck and my hands into his hair, I come nose to nose with him. My lips meet his again, kissing him gently, and his mouth naturally responds to it, opening up to me.

I can feel myself coming to life in his arms, possibly because it's been years since I've been kissed. *Desired*. It's been years since I've felt so cherished. *Treasured*. My tongue slips into his mouth, my body pushing against his chest. Our kiss is slow, measured, and careful. It's just about the most perfect kiss I've ever shared with someone, under the most imperfect circumstances.

My heartbeat is strong. So strong.

I search for the absent guilt and moral tangle I should be dealing with.

It's nowhere to be found.

I wait for the sea of remorse to crash through me.

It doesn't come.

I compress us tightly together, and Luke's thumping heart against me jump-starts mine.

And I accept, I can live again. I can be happy and love and *be* loved.

For us.

For all three of us.

THE END

Turn the page to discover more of Jodi's series and standalone novels or head to www.jodiellenmalpas.co.uk.

Also by
Jodi Ellen Malpas

The This Man Series

This Man

Beneath This Man

This Man Confessed

All I Am – Drew's Story (A This Man Novella)

With This Man

The One Night Series

One Night - Promised

One Night - Denied

One Night - Unveiled

Standalone Novels

The Protector

The Forbidden

Gentleman Sinner

Perfect Chaos

Leave Me Breathless

For You

The Smoke & Mirrors Duology

The Controversial Princess

His True Queen

The Hunt Legacy Duology

Artful Lies

Wicked Truths

The Unlawful Men Series

The Brit

The Enigma

The Resurrection

The Rising

Book 5 Coming Soon

The Belmore Square Series

One Night with the Duke

A Gentleman Never Tells

This Woman Series

(The This Man Series from Jesse's POV)

This Woman

With This Woman - Coming 2023

Book 3 - TBC

About Jodi Ellen Malpas

Jodi Ellen Malpas was born and raised in England, where she lives with her husband, boys and Theo the Doberman. She is a self-professed daydreamer, and has a terrible weak spot for alpha males. Writing powerful love stories with addictive characters has become her passion—a passion she now shares with her devoted readers. She's a proud #1 *New York Times* Bestselling Author, a *Sunday Times* Bestseller, and her work is published in over twenty-five languages across the world. You can learn more about Jodi & her words at: www.jodiellenmalpas.co.uk